SUDDENLY THE AIR SEEMED TO ERUPT WITH EXPLOSIONS AND FLAMES ... as a blast of autocannon fire scored huge hits on the 'Mech's chest. Duncan's head hit hard on the rear wall of the cockpit as the 'Mech jolted backward.

"I'll teach him," Trane said. The knight thumbed the trigger for the *Warhammer*'s two PPCs. Duncan, still dazed from the head-banging, saw the error and reached out, grabbing Trane's arm.

"Let go!" Trane shouted.

"You'll kill us," Duncan screamed back, as two laser beams from the opposing *Rifleman* stabbed through the smoke like deadly searchlights, just missing the *Warhammer* as Trane sidestepped the attack.

"Let me fire," Trane insisted, moving the weapon's joystick to a lock on the advancing *Rifleman*.

"You've got both PPC's on line, Trane! This old 'Hammer can't vent heat like the ones you're used to piloting! We'll fry in this cockpit."

BATTLETECH®

STAR LORD

Donald G. Phillips

A ROC BOOK

ROC
Published by the Penguin Group
Penguin Books USA Inc., 375 Hudson Street,
New York, New York 10014, U.S.A.
Penguin Books Ltd, 27 Wrights Lane,
London W8 5TZ, England
Penguin Books Australia Ltd, Ringwood,
Victoria, Australia
Penguin Books Canada Ltd, 10 Alcorn Avenue,
Toronto, Ontario, Canada M4V 3B2
Penguin Books (N.Z.) Ltd, 182–190 Wairau Road,
Auckland 10, New Zealand

Penguin Books Ltd, Registered Offices:
Harmondsworth, Middlesex, England

First published by Roc, an imprint of Dutton Signet,
a division of Penguin Books USA Inc.

First Printing, February, 1996
10 9 8 7 6 5 4 3 2 1

Series Editor: Donna Ippolito
Additional Writing: Blaine Lee Pardoe
Cover: Roger Loveless
Mechanical Drawings: Duane Loose and the FASA art department

RoC REGISTERED TRADEMARK—MARCA REGISTRADA

For Mort

You will fight to the last soldier, and when you die, I will call upon your damned souls to rise and speak horrible curses at the enemy.

—Stefan Amaris to his troops defending Terra, 15 January 2779

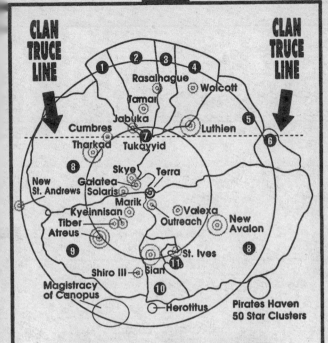

MAP OF THE
INNER SPHERE

1 • Jade Falcon/Steel Viper, 2 • Wolf Clan, 3 • Ghost Bear,
4 • Smoke Jaguars / Nova Cats, 5 • Draconis Combine,
6 • Outworlds Alliance, 7 • Free Rasalhague Republic,
8 • Federated Commonwealth, 9 • Free Worlds League,
10 • Capellan Confederation, 11 • St. Ives Compact

Map Compiled by COMSTAR.
From information provided by the COMSTAR EXPLORER SERVICE
and the STAR LEAGUE ARCHIVES on Terra.

Prologue

Court of the Star League
Unity City
Terra, Terran Hegemony
22 February 2774

Stefan Amaris, Emperor of his own grand Amaris Empire, self-proclaimed First Lord of the Star League, sat on the seat of the throne he'd had specially built and carved for his use. As one hand stroked the smooth, deep brown wood of the high-backed seat he reflected on how different his throne room was from the one used by the Star League's previous First Lords. That other chamber had been sealed for nearly eight years now, ever since the day he had assassinated young Richard Cameron, along with every living trace of his bloodline. They remained there, entombed where they had fallen around the throne.

Amaris knew that in time he would rewrite the history of that day. He would make the rest of humanity understand why he had been justified in seeking the power of this throne. Then they would know that his actions were righteous. And they would honor him and sing his praise and he would bask in glory.

Yes, this room was one of the few in the palace that contained no reminders of the Camerons or other long gone days in this palace. Amaris laughed at the thought, one hand brushing the massive medallion hanging from his neck as he idly scratched at his bulging belly. The huge platinum disk was engraved and painted with the image of a deep blue shark against a sea of red, the emblem of the Rim Worlds Republic, his Periphery kingdom and homeland far from Terra. Gone was the old eight-pointed emblem of the Star League, replaced by this one. In his other hand Amaris held the sceptre used for centuries by the Cameron First Lords. Wrapping his short thick fingers even tighter around it, he felt infused, as he always did, by its power.

Before him was a holographic map of the former Star League, his empire. The glowing colors now embraced a smaller area than on the cold wintry day he had swept into the palace to seize power from that spineless child Richard. But that did not worry him. He was the Star Lord, rightful ruler of the greatest interstellar alliance in the history of humanity. He had not slowly and carefully and craftily plotted his rise to this place for years to be defeated by a few military setbacks now.

The other House Lords of the star empires that formed the League had refused to help him fight off that old fool Kerensky. Of course those cursed despots were only looking out for themselves, and had not helped the General either. Their states had remained untouched by Kerensky's long assault, while Amaris had temporarily lost his Rim Worlds Republic. On the map it glowed red—the color he had assigned to Kerensky and his army, who were slowly attempting to surround him.

The crimson color encircled Terra and the worlds around it. Terra—birthplace of the human race and the eternal heart of the Star League. But Amaris was not at all worried about that red circle that was tightening like a noose around his holdings. He was, after all, Stefan Amaris. How many years had he spent setting in motion his plan, his vision? How many years had he waited, biding his time and cleverly winning the trust of the spoiled child who would one day inherit his father's throne as First Lord? And when the time was right, after he had watched and waited so patiently, so cun-

ningly, he had singlehandedly captured the greatest power
ever known in the history of man.

While he sat staring at the planets hanging in space before
him, he was joined by a man wearing the olive drab and red
sash of Amaris's own Republic Guards. It was General
Legos, the man who had helped plan the coup and who was
now the commanding officer of the Greenhaven Gestapo.
Amaris turned slightly to face his longtime advisor, reposi-
tioning the sceptre to better support him.

"I trust you bring me good news from the front?" he said,
though it had been a long time since any of his commanders
had brought him good news. Indeed, the predecessors of
Legos had all been dour old doomsayers, who saw nothing
but gloom and defeat. But as Amaris always told himself,
those who failed him did not do so for long. He hoped that
Legos would not have to be tortured to death like the others,
but even Legos would have to go if he could not properly
serve the Emperor's vision of the future.

"Operations on Saffel are proceeding well," Legos said,
but he looked fearful. Kerensky's army was paying a heavy
price, but he was slowly grinding the Republican forces
under.

Amaris saw that the man had more to say. "But . . . ?"

"The city of Millilo fell today, but our forces have re-
grouped and General Johnston sends word that he is preparing a counterattack to recapture the city within the week."

The First Lord sighed heavily at the news. "I am dis-
pleased," he said, his tone seeming to promise unspeakable
punishments.

"I am sorry, my lord." The general's voice cracked slightly,
and Amaris savored the fear he heard in it.

"The fault is not yours, this time. The fault is with
Johnston. His loss of Millilo is unacceptable. Order General
Johnston arrested and returned to Terra for trial. Have our
aerospace forces bomb the city. If I cannot have Millilo, no
one will."

"What charges do you wish to bring against him, lord?"

"Treason, of course," Amaris snapped. "I ordered Johnston to hold that city no matter what the cost. He failed me,
and now he will pay the price."

"It shall be done, lord," General Legos said, his will to resist broken by what Stefan Amaris had become in the passage of time.

"And on the matter of my wayward mistress?"

Legos stiffened at the mention of the task he'd been given. "Shera Moray has been making her way toward the worlds occupied by Kerensky and is currently on Slocum, which is under attack by the 159th Royal BattleMech Division. According to my agent, he will intercept her today and complete his mission. With luck, the targets will be eliminated within the day."

"You said 'targets'?"

"Yes, my lord. According to the operative pursuing her, she gave birth to a child four weeks ago on Altair."

"Male or female?" Amaris demanded.

"A boy child, lord. She named him Andrew."

Amaris rose to his feet and stepped down from the throne to come face to face with his general. "You will order them both destroyed, particularly the child," he screamed. In case there was any doubt about the order, he pounded the heel of the sceptre against the floor. The boom echoed throughout the vast chamber.

"It will be done as you command, sire."

"So it must. If that child lives, he or his heirs will be future pretenders to my throne. Rivals to my own rightful heirs. I want them destroyed, even if you must throw an entire division to the task. Do you hear me, Legos? The future of the Star League depends on it!"

Rolund City
Slocum
Terran Hegemony

Shera Moray looked around to see if anyone was watching, then quickly stuffed the money into the other woman's hand.

The woman adjusted the bundled child in her arms as she furtively accepted the wad of bills. "That's a hefty price just to exchange identification papers," she said. Shera also had to heft Andrew up in her arms as she drew close enough to exchange her small brown packet of travel papers for the other woman's.

"I cannot let the boy's father find us," she said, trying to hide her terror. Shera Moray had no doubt what Stefan Amaris would do to them if he could. On New Earth she'd only narrowly managed to escape his men by taking passage in the cargo section of a transport. What a stroke of fortune it had been encountering this woman traveling with a child Andrew's age, a woman who resembled Shera vaguely enough to buy her some time, even if it was only hours or minutes. There was so much confusion these days, with the net of Kerensky's force drawing tighter, so many new laws and regulations, so much priority being given to the movement of troops to and from the front, that Shera was counting on the fact that few would pay much heed to a shabbily dressed peasant and her infant.

The woman laughed roughly. "He's a drunk, is he? Or what, maybe he beats you? Well, never mind, I don't care who you're trying to hide from. It can't be any worse than starving to death." Then she stuffed the money and the travel documents into the bodice of her filthy dress, and turned and walked away. Shera also turned and crossed the street, moving in the opposite direction. Andrew stirred in his tightly wrapped blankets, squirming slightly in his mother's arms. Soldiers were everywhere and she knew that she must be very careful.

She'd hated Stefan Amaris, having become his mistress only under duress. Emperor he might be, but he was also some kind of madman who wandered through the palace shooting off his laser pistol at the paintings and statues of the Camerons and other high and mighty folk that filled the place. He had warned her to take precautions, that he would never allow her to bring any bastard of his into the world. But she had defied him and run away upon learning she was with child. Shera had seen the horrors that were now a daily occurrence in the once beautiful Unity City. She had seen what Amaris was, had touched his madness. He would stop at nothing to prevent her from giving life to a potential heir.

She looked over her shoulder and saw that a small group of soldiers had stopped the woman with whom she'd just exchanged identification papers. Her heart raced. More and more of them were gathering around, and it was obvious they'd been looking for her and had no intention of letting her go. The woman shouted something, but Shera couldn't make out the words over the bustle of people on the streets. No one even stopped. They knew that resistance to the Amaris troopers would either get them killed or sent to the "Re-Education Camps." She wanted to flee, but another part had to see what would happen next. She stopped only for a moment, pretending to examine some fruits at a sidewalk stall, but watching the encounter out the corner of her eye.

One of the soldiers held the woman's papers, another reached out for the child. She screamed and clutched the infant all the tighter, the baby also shrieking in fear by now. The circle of soldiers closed in even tighter. Suddenly, the woman bolted, pushing past the soldiers and breaking into a run. Two of the infantrymen leveled their laser rifles and, despite the crowded streets, opened fire.

The shots riddled the woman and the infant, cutting her down in mid-step with the child still in her arms. She spun slightly, then crumpled in a heap to the pavement. The child was still in her arms as she lay there, her blood already staining the walk around her head. The child was bleeding too, but would never move or cry again. Two passersby were struck as well, falling wounded near where Shera stood. The rest of the people on the street saw what happened, stopped for only a moment, and then continued quickly on their way. They had all seen enough friends and family taken away to be tortured and killed. They knew that resistance to the occupation forces was futile. They let the stranger and her baby lay dead in the middle of the street.

Shera Moray drew a long breath. It was her own death she was watching, for those shots had been intended for her and her son. But she had been spared, whether by luck or fate, she could not say. All that mattered was that she was alive, and her son still safe in her arms. And in that moment, she swore that her child or his kin would one day right the wrongs of his father.

1

Lieutenant Hermann Bovos checked his 'Mech's long-range sensors and saw the faint image of a DropShip nearly a dozen kilometers ahead of him. Damn! he thought. What was it with this planet? Were the only ships that came here ones with captains who couldn't pilot their way out of a paper bag? This wasn't the first time he and his lance had been sent to pick up the crew of a downed ship.

But that was life in the military. Two years ago they'd been chasing bandits, and then his unit had pulled every warrior's nightmare—garrison duty. Turning his joystick to the right to avoid the cluster of rocks in the path of his *Hermes II*, Bovos told no one in particular that protecting a desolate world like Shiro III wasn't the reason he'd joined up with the Second Oriente Hussars. He cursed silently again. He'd been raised on tales of the unit's daring exploits and the tactical brilliance of its commanders. How proud he'd been to be accepted into the same famous unit that had been his father's.

Flanked on either side by the other three members of his lance, Bovos saw from the map on his secondary monitor that they were closing on the target zone. It certainly wasn't something his eyes could have told him. One jagged rock formation and twisted tree looked no different than any other on this stretch of parched ground known as Shimgata Mesa.

"There it is," he announced into the chin mike of his

neurohelmet. But his thoughts were still on the eight generations of Bovos men and women who'd fought and served in the Free Worlds League military. In some cases their units had been on the wrong side of civil wars, like when the Hussars had supported Duncan Marik in his attempt to seize the throne that now belonged to his cousin Thomas. But all that was old news; the only thing that mattered was where they put their loyalties now. And both Bovos and his sister, an infantry trooper in the First Oriente Hussars, were fiercely dedicated to the Captain-General.

Bovos and his lance had been out on maneuvers when they got word that a commercial DropShip had crash-landed on the far side of the mesa. Being so close to the site, the lance was ordered to head over there, investigate, and if possible, rescue any survivors. Bovos had tried to tell his CO that they weren't equipped for medical operations, but he'd been overruled.

"Gramps, this is Ox," he signaled Sergeant Master Leo Striber.

"I copy," came back Striber's voice. The Sergeant was much older than most of his fellow Hussars. He'd fought on the side of the Anduriens when they'd tried to secede from the League back in 3037, and he'd been on Xanthe III during the ill-fated assault in which Duncan Marik lost his life. But like so many who'd fought in that war, Striber wouldn't talk about it. It had been a war of brother against brother, a tragic time for the League. Even Bovos's father was close-mouthed about those days.

"Target dead ahead. What do you get over the comm-line?"

"Not a peep," Gramps said. "Either there are no survivors or they can't communicate."

Bovos scanned the terrain and slowed his 'Mech slightly. The ground ahead was even more difficult and rough than what they'd already crossed, but it was the only approach to the area. They had no choice but to proceed as ordered.

"Ox to lance," Bovos said. "Take this slow and easy. There are a lot of tight areas between us and the DropShip, so keep a close eye on your scanners."

"Roger, Ox." That was Simon Dozer from his *Wasp* on the

far right flank. "Hell of a day for a stroll in the country, eh, Lieutenant?"

"Cut the chatter," Bovos returned.

"Hey, this is just a milk run, boss. We come in like the cavalry, rescue the stranded settlers, and ride out."

Bovos shook his head and smiled in spite of himself. Dozer never stopped joking, never seemed to take anything seriously. He'd been shuffled through three other units before being assigned to Bovos, who was apparently the only commander with the patience to deal with him. "The order stands, Dozer. Kill it."

"Roger, Ox, sir," Dozer said snappily, always determined to have the last word.

"Lieutenant." This time it was the heavily accented voice of Corporal Gustav Hoffman in his *Griffin*. "Request permission to open fire on Dozer if he keeps it up."

"Request denied . . . for now." Bovos glanced at his chronometer. Time to make contact with HQ in Timothy, the nearest town. He switched over to the regimental line and transmitted his lance's coordinates, as was standard procedure every hour. The tactical display immediately showed that the coordinates had been sent, but no echo came back from the Hussars command.

Either regimental communications were down or he was getting interference from these rock formations. Bovos transmitted again and still received no echo response from the base. *If we were at war, I'd be worried,* he thought. *Somebody back at base is asleep at his post.* He moved the *Hermes* along a rocky outcropping and began to punch in the direct communications link that would let him contact the base personally. Procedures had to be followed, even if it meant getting the comm officer busted for dozing off.

A signal from Striber interrupted him. "Ox, this is Gramps. Did you just pick up some signatures on your short-range sensors?"

Bovos checked his sensors and their settings. He saw nothing, but cut his speed slightly to maneuver through the rock outcroppings that surrounded him like an obstacle course. "Negative, Gramps. Did you?"

There was a pause. "I thought I saw reactor pulses— 'Mechs. Just for a minute, then they disappeared."

"Bearing?"

"Ahead and on the flanks." There was something in Striber's voice that Bovos had never heard before—it sounded like foreboding, maybe even fear.

"Ox to lance, all halt. Short-range scans. Anyone picking up readings out of the ordinary?" Bovos checked his own sensors again, but saw only the blips of his lance. They were spread out and blocked off from each other by a maze of rocks and pathetic clumps of dried-up trees.

"Hey, Lieutenant, this is a cakewalk—remember? Maybe Gramps has spent a decade too many in the cockpit, eh? I'm not picking up—wait a minute—what in the name of—"

Dozer's words were cut off by an explosion and a wave of static before the line went dead.

"Dozer, come in!" Bovos watched as a pair of red fusion-reactor signatures came to life on his screen right next to Dozer's *Wasp*. His battle computer raced through the readouts in its database and displayed the icons as BattleMechs. A medium *Centurion* and one of the most heavily armed and feared assault 'Mechs—an 80-ton *Awesome*. Dozer's 20-ton *Wasp* was no match for even one of them, especially in such tight quarters. *They've either been running silent or operating some ECM so we couldn't pick them up. This whole DropShip crash was just a trick to lure us in.*

"It's a frigging trap!" he shouted in rapid-fire. "Dozer, get out of there. Jump, damn it! Hoffman, give him cover. Gramps, form up on me." Suddenly a pair of short-range missiles streaked from behind a tortured cluster of rocks nearby, slamming into the torso of the *Hermes*. The 'Mech staggered back under the impact even as its torso armor fragmented and rained down over the rocks. Infantry with SRM launchers! So much for a simple rescue mission.

Bovos aimed his flamer at the cluster of trees, and opened up with a jet of fiery death. The dry trees and brush danced to life as the flames burned a swath through them, leaving only charred ground and black smoke. Though he'd probably missed, right now Bovos would settle just for keeping his attackers on the move and not shooting at him.

Dozer's panicked voice came on line for a brief second. "They've got me pinned, Lieutenant. It's them, it's the Kni—" Another blast echoed from the distance, shaking the ground. In the air, Bovos suddenly saw the outline of a 'Mech, Dozer's *Wasp,* aloft and in mid-jump. Then, just as suddenly, it plunged downward, engulfed in an inferno of fire and explosions, until it disappeared from view behind the rocks. Another explosion followed a moment later, the death knell of the young MechWarrior. Checking his sensors, Bovos saw that they no longer registered Dozer's 'Mech. Twenty tons of high-tech metal and electronics destroyed in an instant. Dozer had been outgunned and outmassed in that light 'Mech. *He never had a chance against those bastards.*

But Hermann Bovos had no more time to ponder fate, his own or anyone else's. "All fall back on my position. Watch for enemy infantry." The words were barely out of his mouth before the *Hermes* shuddered under the impact of a wave of missiles that came streaking at him from a 'Mech outside his field of vision. Several missiles slammed into his right arm and torso. Three others missed, but hit the rock formation behind him, bringing down a shower of debris on his thinner rear armor. The 'Mech reeled slightly and probably would have fallen if not for its gyro and some fancy piloting by Bovos. *I've got to get out of here,* he thought. *This is an ambush plain and simple and the worst thing we can do is dig in. We've got to break out—and now.*

Striber's voice over the commline didn't offer much comfort. "I've got a *Whitworth* moving in on me, and that blasted *Awesome*'s headed toward you, Lieutenant."

"We've got to get out of here, Gramps," Bovos said, his sensors painting a similar story. "You and Hoffman, head back, fall back toward the city."

Hoffman's *Griffin* came into view at the same time as the *Centurion.* Bringing his Imperator Ultra-5 autocannon online, Bovos targeted his cross hairs. The approaching *Centurion* ignored him, too busy trying to evade fire from the *Griffin.* The *Hermes*'s battle computer locked on target, the enemy 'Mech's red and silver paint scheme no more than a blur as Bovos fired his autocannon.

Everything happened in less than a heartbeat. A stream of autocannon shells peppered the *Centurion*'s right side, pitting armor and sending a spray of steel, smoke, and shrapnel out over the rocks and trees. Hoffman was still firing too, triggering a barrage of PPC fire at the *Centurion*. The blue lightning missed by less than a meter, striking a nearby rock with a mighty *crack!*

The *Centurion* was fighting back with its medium lasers and autocannon. The wave of the fire washed over Hoffman's 'Mech like an unstoppable tsunami of destruction and death. Several of the autocannon shells slammed into the *Griffin*'s cockpit, blasting away armor and shielding. The rest tore into the 'Mech's right torso and upper chest. Bovos ignored the rising heat in his cockpit, concentrating on trying to see the *Centurion* through the smoke. *Hoffman must be in some serious hurt after that round. He's got to break off the assault or he's toast.*

But the *Centurion* was charging straight toward Hoffman. Pulling back its giant left arm, the pilot swung and punched, with pile-driver precision, its armored fist striking squarely into the *Griffin*'s chest. Bovos heard Hoffman's scream over the commline as he fought to keep his 'Mech standing, but the scream didn't last long. The *Griffin* fell backward, leaving much of its internal structure and myomer bundling wrapped in the twisted and coolant-smeared fist of the *Centurion*.

Bovos stared in horror as the *Griffin*'s fusion reactor erupted in a ball of flame, Hoffman's screams echoing in his ears. Hoffman was dead, but there was no time to mourn now. In a cold rage he triggered another wave of autocannon shells at the attacker. Most of them missed, but those that hit slammed into the *Centurion*'s legs. The 'Mech turned and faced Bovos just as the red and silver *Awesome* entered the battle zone.

Bovos knew he would never survive a direct assault by this super-charged, mammoth 'Mech. The *Awesome* was well-armed, but it was also slow-moving. His only chance would be to outrun it, so he followed his own orders and broke the *Hermes* into a mad dash. Despite the twisting path he made, the *Awesome* very nearly scored with its extended-range PPCs. Scanning ahead, Bovos saw Striber's *Phoenix Hawk* and another enemy 'Mech. "Gramps, I'm closing on your position. Are you in trouble?"

"Get out of here," Striber fairly screamed over the commline. "Forget about me!" The thunderous racket in the background told Bovos that the Sergeant was under heavy attack. His heart began to race even faster with the fury of losing the last member of his lance. Just at the edge of his field of vision he saw the outline of the enemy—a *Battle-Master,* a 'Mech even more prodigious than the *Awesome.* Firing on the heavily armored assault machine was almost useless, for it could withstand severe punishment. But what else could he do? Bovos triggered his lasers, sending a pulse beam of burning energy out at the massive foe. From the smoke and debris he could tell that Striber wasn't giving up either, but trying to fight his way free. Stray blasts of laser light illuminated the smoke clouds and gave Bovos an idea of his lancemate's position.

"Fall back, Gramps. The cavalry's on its way."

"Much appreciated, Ox." Striber sounded grim and determined. "He's an older model, but still a killer."

Firing the *Phoenix Hawk*'s jump jets, Striber shot up and away from the *BattleMaster.* But the red and silver 'Mech replied with a salvo of SRMs from its left torso and PPC fire from its right arm. The stream of high-energy ion bolts hit the right leg of Striber's 'Mech, blasting away most of the armor and severing several large bundles of myomer muscle. Striber did not return the fire, probably intent on putting as much distance as possible between what was left of his *Hawk* and the *BattleMaster.*

Bovos didn't want to get too close to the monster 'Mech either, just enough to draw its fire away from Striber. As the *Phoenix Hawk* dropped toward the ground about 200 meters from the *BattleMaster,* Bovos triggered another volley of autocannon rounds. He wasn't really even trying to hit the bigger 'Mech, just trying to land them close enough to do damage and divert its attention.

It didn't work.

The *BattleMaster* hefted its right arm upward and fired again at Striber. The lightning burst of PPCs hit the *Phoe-*

nix Hawk's cockpit on the side, blowing away armor and sending arcs of excess energy dancing around the torso. The PPC attack was followed within seconds by several medium laser hits, one of them slicing upward like a knife across the chest of the *Phoenix Hawk.* Up, up, up until it tore open the front of the cockpit.

They were all gone now, but Bovos had to get to battalion headquarters and warn the rest of the Hussars—if any were still alive. Again breaking into a run, he noticed that he was not alone. Between him and the way back to Timothy was a *Whitworth*, with the *Awesome* moving up slowly on his right flank. While Bovos had been concentrating on the *Battle-Master,* these two had been maneuvering into position to encircle him. *The* Centurion *is out there somewhere too*, he thought. *These 'Mech pilots were savage and they'd staged a perfect ambush. Who the hell were they?*

Choosing the *Whitworth* as the weakest of his foes, Bovos turned the *Hermes* toward it and pulled his throttle back to maximum speed. As the targeting cross hairs locked on, he switched all the weapons over to his primary trigger circuit. Bovos knew he couldn't afford to hang around in a fight for long. He'd have to fire everything at once at optimum range. If he was lucky, that would be enough to break him out of this little trap and get back to the city.

Not waiting for Bovos to get closer in range, the *Whitworth* opened up with a literal wall of long-range missiles. Bovos didn't try to dodge them but charged straight through, the warheads exploding across the surface of his 'Mech, rocking the *Hermes II* with each gigantic *pop.* His tactical readout was more red than anything else, screaming for his attention. It showed him armor shredded almost everywhere, with the 'Mech's upper torso taking the most damage.

Looming in front of him was the *Whitworth*, its red and silver paint scheme shining in the sun. Bovos had seen the design before, several times, mostly on holocasts. Those were the colors of the Knights of the Inner Sphere! *What in the name of Kerensky are they doing attacking us? We're on the same side!*

The *Whitworth* cycled another full salvo of long-range missiles as Bovos opened up with autocannon, laser, and flamer simultaneously. His pulse laser stitched away the armor plating on the enemy 'Mech's right arm while the autocannon rounds ripped the limb off at the shoulder actuator. The flamer scorched the 'Mech, burning away the shield symbol of the Knights and leaving the torso a ball of fire. Bovos was feeling the heat too. The temperature of his cockpit soared as he fought for air inside the neurohelmet. Only his cooling vest was keeping him from roasting alive, but how long could it hold out against this heat?

What happened next took him totally by surprise. The *Hermes* shook violently as its left leg took a PPC shot that felt like a hit from a battering ram. Bovos never saw it coming. The blast shattered the knee joint from behind and he felt the 'Mech's gyro fight his every effort to remain standing. In the end the *Hermes* collapsed, falling forward as it went. Bovos was tossed around in the command couch, the body restraints digging deeply into his flesh and his head banging into the communications controls. As the battle computer and displays went completely dead, a wave of nausea swept over him and bile rose in his throat. *I'm dead. I didn't even take out one of them, and now I'm going to die.* The air had the metallic taste of ozone and he could smell burning myomer and coolant. He tried to raise his head to see, but the cockpit was dark. The only sight was the rocks and dirt of Shimgata Mesa breaking through what was left of his viewport.

Bovos waited what seemed like an eternity, waited for the final shot that would finish him off. But it never came. Shaking his head groggily, he reached down and released the restraint controls, which threw his body against one side of the cockpit. *We were ambushed plain and clear by Thomas Marik's own Knights of the Inner Sphere,* he thought. *They're supposed to be an honorable order, the best of the best and all that rot.* While Bovos and his lance were getting slaughtered, the Knights must have struck at the rest of the battalion as well, which would explain why he hadn't been able to raise them earlier. Why would Captain-General

Marik order the Knights to attack his own troops? Was h‍
making overt moves against the Duchy? Why now? Bovo‍
couldn't guess the answer, but surely it must be as mysteri‍
ous as the reason why he alone had been spared.

2

Hauptmann Garth Hawkes sat back lazily in his seat near the bar, tipping his glass and watching the foam atop the dark ale drift about. The tavern was in what was left of the village of Lucille, only a few kilometers from his unit's posting. Battered, almost a forgotten dot on the map, it was one of those towns that barely survived the three centuries of war since the fall of the Star League.

Looking around him at the other few patrons in the place, Hawkes thought about his unit's recent posting to the world of Valexa, a planet close enough to what was lately becoming a troubled Sarna March. It was no secret that Sun-Tzu Liao had been stirring up trouble on many of the Sarna worlds for the past two years. And it was no surprise that he was doing a good job of it because many of its people still considered themselves Capellans. His unit, the Sixth Crucis Lancers, had been sent to Valexa in the recent spate of troop movements to the area, but there wasn't much to do beyond endless patrols to every little village and hamlet. It was the kind of duty Hauptmann Garth Hawkes hated—pure busy work. Still, orders were orders and his duty was to carry them out no matter what his opinion of them.

Now he was being pulled away again. Not by a military matter but by family obligations. The man he was to meet was a close friend of his father, "The General," as he was affectionately known even to his children. Hawkes had wel-

comed the summons as a respite from the constant touring o
the countryside. Not often did a young officer trying t
make an impression and win a possible promotion find man
chances to rest.

He was startled from his reverie by the sound of a chai
scraping across the floor as the impressive form of Leftenant-General Mel Aleixandre took a seat at the table.

"Still wearing that pony-tail, eh, Garth?" Aleixandre said
while signaling the bartender to bring him the same as
Hawkes.

"It's within regulation, sir."

Aleixandre laughed and clapped Hawkes on the back. "So
it is. But tell me, Garth, how's it going? It's been a while
since we've had a chance to talk. Too damn long for the son
of one of my best friends. And how is the General anyway?
Have you spoken with him lately?"

"Not in a good two months. The mails are having a hard
time catching up with me."

"I guess that's partly my fault. I'm the one got the Sixth
Crucis Lancers posted to Valexa in the first place." Aleixandre took a long draw on his ale and smiled.

"Remind me to thank you some other time," Hawkes returned, then swallowed the last of his. The bartender was at
the table to refill the mug even before he was done.

"Listen, Garth, maybe you should consider yourself lucky.
Things are relatively quiet here on Valexa, but next door in
the Sarna March Sun-Tzu's guerrillas have some planets in
open revolt, not to mention all the home-grown local resistance movements. Count your blessings. Valexa isn't a hot
spot—not yet anyway."

"Politics," Hawkes muttered as though the word left a bad
taste in his mouth. "I'm a MechWarrior. What you're talking
about is just politics. Give me a foe and a good fight, a fight
where I can do what's just and right."

Aleixandre chuckled slightly. "Your father always said
you were an idealist. Head in the clouds. I guess I should be
thankful you've stayed with the AFFC instead of running off
to join Thomas Marik's Knights of the Inner Sphere."

Hawkes had heard of the Knights, everyone had. Thomas
Marik had only recently created them as a kind of private

force, with the express aim of encouraging a high moral tone among warriors. They were supposed to be the best of the best, and Marik had recruited them from all over known space. In answer to his call, more than a hundred and fifty MechWarriors had made their way to the capital of the Free Worlds League and sworn their allegiance to Thomas Marik as their liege lord.

"I appreciate the compliment, General, and also that you invited me to this meeting. It's not often a member of the command staff spends time with a junior officer like me." Hawkes felt almost guilty for his earlier comment, but did not retract it. He'd known Leftenant-General Mel Aleixandre as long as he could remember, and thought it might be good for this old friend of the family to hear how decisions from on high affected the troopers.

Aleixandre shook his head. "You're very welcome. I only had to place a call to your CO to get you off duty today."

"Well, like I said, I appreciate it, sir. I haven't had any liberty in a month, with all the moving around the Lancers have been doing." Garth Hawkes didn't give himself much slack. Though a young man, he was obsessed with working hard and performing well. A day's leave was a luxury many in his own company couldn't enjoy.

But these few minutes were all he was going to get, because the next thing Hawkes heard was an ominous rumble in the distance, a sound most civilians would have said was thunder rolling across the foothills of the mountains to the north of town. To someone whose profession was war, the noise was not any voice of nature but the unmistakable sound of destruction. Hawkes and Aleixandre looked at each other, then toward the door as the General's wrist-comp began to beep insistently. Hawkes felt a chill run up his spine. *That was an explosion. Maybe an accident . . .*

The General's wrist-comp beeped again, almost like an echo of Hawkes' thoughts. Aleixandre punched in his access code, then spoke into the device. "This is Iron Maiden. Status report." His voice was grim now, the banter and chitchat of moments before suddenly forgotten. It was the voice of command, confident and sure, reminding Hawkes of his father.

Coming over the wrist-comp, a tinny voice answered immediately. "Lancer command is under attack. Raiders are attacking at company strength. We've sent Bravo Company to intercept."

At those words Hawkes shot out of his chair, and the only reason he didn't dart out the door at a mad run was the desire to hear the rest of the report. That was his company, his unit. Here he was sitting in a tavern in town and they were out there being attacked. Damnation and hellfire!

Aleixandre's voice was terse. "Any ID on the attackers?"

"Unconfirmed, Iron Maiden. Visual contact shows them as Free Worlds League—Knights of the Inner Sphere." In the distance came another roar of explosion. The barkeep had gone to the door and opened it to look out. Glancing over, Hawkes saw people in the street stopping to stare off into the distance, finally realizing what he already knew, that it was not a thunderstorm but war coming to Valexa.

"General . . . my unit . . . I must join them," Hawkes said, his heart racing. His hover car was outside, but his 'Mech was a full five kilometers away. Aleixandre was also on his feet.

"Watch yourself," he called out to Hawkes, who was by now out the door. "Bravo is the only company in the area. I've got two others nearby, but it will be at least thirty minutes before they're close enough to help."

"By then it'll be too late," Hawkes shot back over his shoulder. "In thirty minutes this will be all over." *One way or another . . .*

Hawkes's *Caesar* seemed to throb with life and energy as the 'Mech sprinted across the hard-packed soil of the Aux-Huards Plain, throwing up a cloud of dust as he closed on the path Bravo Company had taken a mere fifteen minutes earlier. Though a fairly heavy 'Mech, the *Caesar* moved as if it were much lighter. He pushed its seventy tons of myomer and steel to near-maximum speed, but he was racing into the fight blind. Whoever had hit Bravo must be running electronic countermeasures, making communications and long-range scanning nearly impossible.

His sensors fanned out across the rolling plains, but the

smoke rising beyond a low hill easily told him the location of the battle. The short-range sensors showed several different readings, some of 'Mechs active and running, others hot from battle but shut down. *Kills.* The *Caesar*'s battle computer read in the sensor data and fed in the telemetry from the battle area, but Hawkes didn't wait for the readings. Instead, he switched over to his primary target interlock circuit and ran the pre-charge sequence on his Poland Gauss cannon.

The screen was activated in less than a heartbeat and he saw the story unfold. Seven enemy 'Mechs were operational nearby and Bravo Company only had two. Running on pure adrenaline, he switched his heads-up display to target mode and swept the nearest target, a *Banshee*. The *Banshee* was a gigantic assault 'Mech with twice the firepower of his *Caesar,* but for now Hawkes had the tactical advantage of surprise. He closed the distance, locked on and fired.

The Gauss rifle used a series of magnets to accelerate a nickel-ferrous metal slug ten centimeters in diameter. The payload burst almost silently from the barrel, but the violent kickback rocked the *Caesar* back slightly. Moving at incredible speed, the Gauss slug streaked like a line of silvery light at the *Banshee*'s right leg. Even from this distance Hawkes could see the dust rise as bits of the *Banshee*'s shattered kneecap fell to the ground.

The wave of static that had filled his communications channels suddenly cleared to the chatter of the combat zone. Lynn Martinson was on the line, obviously in a panic. "Where in the name of Gaffa's Ghost did that shot come from?" she gasped.

"Who cares as long as they're shooting at our guests and not us," came the voice of John Volks. "Give me some cover, Bravo Six. If I don't fall back I'm gonna get my metal ass blown to bits."

Hawkes activated his own channel. "This is Bravo One," he said as another Gauss round cycled and loaded. Once more he let fly at the *Banshee,* this time tearing a gash across its chest and arm. The hit mauled more armor, but enough still remained to protect it. "Give me a status report."

"They hit us bad," Volks said, the pulse lasers of his *Hatchetman* opening up with a torrent of fire at the *Banshee* and the *Grasshopper* closing in on him. Some of the shots went wild, but even those that found their mark didn't slow the attack. "First and Second Platoon took out one of the them before withdrawing. We've lost three 'Mechs and two tanks. Leftenant Marrow's dead, sir."

Hanna Marrow had been Hawkes' second in command, the officer who'd led the company into combat instead of him. The weight of her death was heavy. "Fall back on my position. We're outgunned. Help is on the way, but we've got to buy some time."

"Easier said than—" Martinson's words were cut off by a wave of fire from two enemy 'Mechs, a *Dervish* and a *Clint*. The *Clint*'s PPC sliced into the right leg of Martinson's *War Dog*.

With the distance closed, Hawkes switched to his medium pulse lasers and again fired on the *Banshee*. The heat in his cockpit rose as the bursts of laser light blasted away at the red-and-silver-painted 'Mech. There was a crackle of sparks as internal structure was hit, giving Hawkes some encouragement.

Martinson's *War Dog* pivoted to break away, but it was too late. Four Streak SRMs from the *Dervish* tore into her 'Mech, three of them mangling the *Dog*'s arm, tearing myomer and sending coolant flowing like green blood down its side. The last missile severed the already-damaged right leg, tumbling the 'Mech into a mangled heap of debris and certain death.

The *Banshee* broke off its pursuit of Volks' *Hatchetman* and turned toward Hawkes in his *Caesar*. It fired its own Gauss rifle at the same moment the *Caesar*'s battle computer squealed a warning of weapons lock. Hawkes tried to brace for the impact, but the silvery slug was already striking with such force that the impact tossed him hard against the restraints of his command couch. Recovering, Hawkes felt his head aching from the feedback of his neurohelmet, but he was still in control of the 'Mech.

Then, suddenly it was over.

The silver and red 'Mechs turned as if on cue, and began to pull back. They could still have pressed their attack and taken Hawkes and his people out without any trouble. Maybe they detected reinforcements approaching, or maybe it was something else.

Hawkes sped toward Martinson's *War Dog.* "Volks, cover me. I've got to get her out of there." He stopped the *Caesar* near the fallen 'Mech and checked his sensors one more time to be sure that the attackers were indeed fleeing.

Then he opened the cockpit hatch and half-fell, half-climbed down the footholds to the ground, his cooling vest snagging on one of the pegs and the medical pack digging into his thigh as he went. Passing where the Gauss rifle slug had hit, he tried not to notice how much damage had been done. Once on the ground, he leaped over some scrubby brush and came to where the *War Dog* lay, lifeless but for the occasional electrical pop and sizzle.

Martinson's 'Mech had crashed down onto a pile of jagged rocks that had driven straight into the cockpit. Hawkes could only stand and stare. Blood ran down the rocks before being quickly sucked up by the dry clay of the Mesa. Inside the cockpit were the disemboweled remains of Hammond Martinson, impaled on a jagged rock. It was a freak accident. A meter in any other direction and she would have walked away from the fall. Instead she hung there, hair matted with blood and torn lung tissue. Hawkes felt anger and guilt well up within him like a storm.

He should have been here, with them, with her. They trusted him. He was their commanding officer, but was out having a drink instead of here where they needed him. He was to blame for all that had happened. He looked at one of the fallen enemy machines nearby and strode over to it, only half-conscious of his actions and intention. His mind was awash with dread and guilt. He could not shake the image of Martinson in her *War Dog.*

He walked over to the other fallen 'Mech, its red and silver paint scheme charred and twisted from the damage his company had done. It was a *Stinger,* an older model that had not been refitted with improved weapons or armor. Viewing the damage, he fought the urge to spill his gut, hoping maybe he'd wake up suddenly and discover it was all just a terrible nightmare. But the smell of fried coolant and insulation told him it was no dream—the nightmare was real.

What the hell was going on? Thomas Marik had no reason to attack the Federated Commonwealth. Especially with his son Joshua in the hands of the doctors at the NAIS. It just didn't make sense. The *Stinger*'s cockpit was as blasted as the rest of the machine, but the tears in the armor had not come from any outside attack, but from an explosion within. The armored and polarized glass was pushed outward, as was the side hatch.

Blown up from within. The Knights of the Inner Sphere were elite, not barbaric. This MechWarrior had blown him or herself up rather than be taken prisoner, and not even the Clans were known to do that. *What are we facing here? These couldn't have been the Knights. But if not them, then who?*

Hawkes looked back at Martinson's mutilated *War Dog* and bit his lip at the memory of her mutilated body in the cockpit. He was shaking now, shaking with anger. Anger at whoever had done this and anger at himself. If he'd been here, perhaps none of this would have happened, perhaps they would still be alive. *This was my command and I failed them. Their blood is on my head. But I will see them avenged. In that,* Garth Hawkes promised himself, *I will not fail.*

Kalma Estate
Marik
Marik Commonwealth, Free Worlds League

General Harrison Kalma, Retired, stood waiting at the door to his study, and drew in a deep breath as he vowed to hold his anger in check. His temper had always been the problem in dealing with Duncan. Half the problem. The other half was that his son seemed to know exactly what it took to bring his father's temper to a boil. This time he would maintain his dignity, would not be the one to lose control.

There came a knock at the door and he opened it slowly. Standing there was a young man of about thirty, his hair as fair as Kalma's own had once been. The face, though, was not a mirror image, but more like a holo of his beloved Cynthia. How she'd hated seeing them argue, and Duncan's startling resemblance to her suddenly calmed the elder Kalma. The memory of his wife would give him the strength he'd need for the inevitable confrontation.

"Welcome home, Duncan." Harrison Kalma reached out to clasp his son's hand.

"The prodigal son returns," Duncan said dryly, as he stepped through the door. Kalma tried to fill in the awkward moment by busily taking his son's cape and hanging it on a silver-tipped hanger in a small coat nook.

Duncan stood in the middle of the room, hands clasped behind his back, legs spread combatively. "I understand you're the one who decided to 'rescue' me, Father."

"If you're referring to the fact that you were bankrupt and about to be tossed into a debtor's prison, then, yes, I did rescue you."

Unfazed, Duncan glared at his father. "And now you expect me to thank you?"

Kalma knew that tone all too well. Their many arguments of the past echoed in his mind like the tolling of a distant bell. Again he pulled himself up mentally, determined not to lose control. "A thank you is customary."

"Father, I appreciate your gesture, but it wasn't necessary. I incurred the debt all by myself. And I'm not ashamed to say I gambled the money away. But even if you hadn't transferred funds to my account, I had a plan." It wasn't his father bailing him out that irritated Duncan, but that he'd done it in such a meddling fashion, hadn't even asked if Duncan wanted his help.

Harrison Kalma didn't answer immediately, but merely gestured his son into the study.

"Well, Duncan, to set the record straight, let me say that I did this for me, not for you. Once upon a time I wouldn't have lifted a finger."

Duncan seemed startled. "I don't understand."

Kalma sat down in a comfortable old chair that seemed to wrap itself around his aged body like a warm blanket. His son sat across from him, his attention distracted briefly by the lively flickering of the fire. Kalma smiled, apparently pleased to have caught his son off guard. "As you know, I proudly served the Free Worlds League for years. Indeed, I still enjoy the Captain-General's confidence, and he often consults with me on a wide range of matters. But politics is politics, and anyone with power has enemies. Not just people whom I may have crossed in the past, but those who are jealous of the trust Thomas Marik places in me. Perhaps they would like to step into my shoes and have his ear. Tarnishing my reputation would serve their purposes only too well."

Duncan smiled thinly. "You're talking about General Milik, I presume?"

Harrison Kalma nodded, impressed that his son had kept up with political struggles going on halfway across the Inner Sphere even while roaming the distant Periphery as gambler or mercenary—or whatever he'd been doing these past years. "Who else? The old goat learned of your troubles and would have had a field day using the story to smear me personally at Court. So before you get angry at me for acting like an honorable father trying to rescue his loving son, the truth of the matter is that I was saving my own old skin."

Duncan burst out laughing, genuinely amused. "That's the most open you've been with me in years."

The General's expression was hard to read in the flicker of firelight. "And this is the first contact we've had in more than two years."

Duncan's smile faded and he nodded, acknowledging their rift. "Touché."

"No, Duncan. This isn't a verbal fencing match. Things are changing here in the Free Worlds League as well as in the rest of the Inner Sphere. The League is stronger than ever before, and that will attract us enemies. We need good MechWarriors like you, son. You graduated at the top of your class at Allison. And I can imagine that making your own way in the wilds of the Periphery has taught you some things you could never learn in school."

"Like my gambling skills . . . ?" Duncan said slyly.

It was the elder Kalma's turn to throw back his head and laugh. "I've followed you carefully, son—one of the advantages of close contact with the intelligence community, you might say."

Duncan Kalma knew that his father's passing mention of "the intelligence community" was no small understatement. Though recently retired, the General had been Director of Military Intelligence of the LCCC, the League Central Coordination and Command. Ranking even over SAFE, the state intelligence agency, the LCCC enjoyed wide-reaching influence and power in military circles. From the hint his father had just dropped Duncan guessed that he hadn't truly retired at all, but was still deeply involved in LCCC operations.

"Why can't Thomas Marik use his Knights of the Inner Sphere to make whatever special gestures he thinks necessary? People admire them, look up to them. Why should anyone want the help of a renegade like me?"

The gray-haired General leaned forward, his face taking on an almost stony appearance in the yellow glow of the fire. "A man like you is *exactly* what's needed, son. Somebody raided Shiro III a few days ago, and whoever it was, they were impersonating Knights of the Inner Sphere. The LCCC received a Class A Priority message a few hours before you arrived that indicates these impersonators have also been involved in the ambush of a commercial transport in the Capellan Confederation. The last thing the Free Worlds League needs is for our own military to think Thomas is sending the Knights against them or for Sun-Tzu Liao to think we're using the Knights to attack his ships.

"Someone apparently has a burr up his or her butt and is trying to make trouble for Thomas Marik by tarnishing the image of the Knights."

Duncan leaned forward and met his father's dark eyes. "You're serious, aren't you?"

"Dead serious, Duncan."

"Any idea who's behind it?"

Harrison Kalma shook his head. "Not yet. But I do have another idea, son. And it's one I need a renegade MechWarrior to help me carry out."

3

The warrior activated a wide-beam communication system tied into her DropShip as it lifted away. "Hail and tremble at my batchall, for you stand against the Fourth Viper Guards and your destiny awaits you. Twenty-fourth Lyran Guards, this is Star Captain Dawn of the Steel Viper Clan, upholders of the true heritage of the mighty Kerenskys, keepers of the honor of the Clans. With what forces do you defend?" Star Captain Dawn did not really expect an answer from these Inner Sphere barbarians, but issuing a formal challenge, or *batchall*, was the time-honored Clan way.

Indeed, even the landing had been executed with classic Steel Viper precision. It was a standard dusting, the *Broadsword* DropShip sweeping across the lowlands to release the Steel Viper force in a tight drop, then withdrawing to a pre-arranged pickup point.

Star Captain Dawn was the leader of the entire operation as well as personally in command of a Boa, the Steel Viper name for a Star of medium to heavy 'Mechs. The Boa was part of Trinary Bravo of the elite Fourth Viper Guards, known to the rest of their Clan as Deadly Venom. The Trinary's two other Stars, another Boa and a Mamba, were deployed in a triangular formation. Checking her tactical display to verify that her warriors were in proper formation, Dawn was pleased to see them positioned precisely as in their three practice runs on Jabuka.

The mission was a simple one. Star Colonel Brett Andrews, under orders from Khan Perigard Zalman, had ordered a raid on the planet Cumbres, a world about halfway between the Steel Viper Occupation Zone and the Lyran capital of Tharkad. The mission was simple: the three Battle Stars under Dawn's command were to cross the four kilometers separating their LZ from the Guards garrison, crush the defenders, and destroy the headquarters. Then the Trinary would rendezvous with their DropShip and depart the planet.

To Dawn it was almost a set-piece battle. Hit suddenly, catch their foe off guard, defeat them, and depart victorious. It was the Steel Viper way, strike fast and hard, finishing the kill with one deadly bite.

Moving her *Crossbow* forward, Dawn couldn't help but remember the last time she'd met Inner Sphere freebirths in combat. *Tukayyid.* The largest battle ever fought in the history of mankind, the might of the Clans squaring off against ComStar's Com Guards to determine the fate of the Clan invasion. Her memory of the furious fighting on that world was as vivid as if only a single day, and not six years, had passed. This time would be different, Dawn told herself. This time my honor will be restored.

Every one of the Clans had met humiliation and defeat at Tukayyid, but perhaps none so great as the Steel Vipers. When it was all over, Khan Natalie Breen had stepped down in shame, Perigard Zalman taking her place. The worst of the fighting had occurred at Devil's Bath, a living hell of boiling mud, steaming pits, and scalding geysers interspersed with towering granite columns. Even the forbidding homeworlds of the Clans had not prepared them for such a hellish place.

But that only made the challenge greater, and what else did a warrior live for? When their enemy turned tail and headed into Devil's Bath, Dawn and the rest of Gamma Galaxy had gone in after them, without fear, without hesitation. They struck at sunrise, within minutes engaging in some of the bloodiest fighting in the twenty-one days of battle for that planet. Most of it was at point-blank range, with whole Stars lost in erupting geyser fields or disappearing into bot-

tomless pits of boiling mud. Firing as they sank, those warriors fought to the end.

The Steel Vipers suffered losses of nearly twenty-five
percent on Tukayyid, but for Dawn the defeat was doubly
intolerable. She'd been the only member of her Binary to
survive the grueling combat among the steaming sinkholes,
hissing geysers, and fiery mud. Two months in the hospital
had healed her physical wounds, but some deeper, secret part
of her still festered. Dawn felt shame that she alone had survived while all her comrades had gone to glory dying for the
Clan. Had she failed in courage? Had she failed in ferocity?
How was it that only she had not fought to the death?

The only way she would ever answer those questions or
live down the shame of Tukayyid was to prove her worth on
another field of combat. And Cumbres was her chance. The
Twenty-fourth Lyran Guards were defending their regimental HQ with a heavily reinforced company of mixed compo-
sition. In the bidding for the right to lead the raid, Dawn had
neither overbid nor underbid the forces needed to win the
objective. Despite Tukayyid, Dawn was confident of her
prowess, confident she could still prove herself as a warrior.
She'd borne the shame of Tukayyid, the scorn it had earned
her among her mates. No mere battle could be more difficult
than that. Neither did Star Colonel Brett Andrews make any
secret of his disdain, treating Dawn like a blight, and refus-
ing to trust her with anything worthwhile. But he could not
hold her back forever. In the end, she had won the bid to
lead the raid on Cumbres. A victory here would restore her
honor and her place among the Vipers.

"Charlie and Bravo Stars, concentrate your scanning on
the flanks," Dawn said crisply while checking her sensors.
She and the rest of the Trinary were rapidly closing with
their target, and soon the fight would begin.

She caught the first of the Twenty-fourth Guard 'Mechs
on her secondary monitor at the same time as Bravo Star.
"Enemy BattleMechs at the outer marker, Star Captain,"
came the voice of Star Captain Bidgood. "Closing rapidly on
our left flank. Request permission to engage."

"Aff, Bravo. Engage. Execute primary battle plan." The
plan had been carefully laid out by her three weeks ago.

Whichever flank engaged the enemy first was to break off and lure away the opposing forces.

The tiny speakers in her *Crossbow* came to life with the sounds of Bravo Star charging into combat. One by one each Viper warrior issued his or her challenge of one-on-one combat. By the icons and their firing patterns she knew that the worthless Inner Sphere freebirths were ignoring the challenges. No matter. It was the way of the Clan to offer honorable combat to one's foe. And hers was not just a Clan, they were the Steel Vipers. They alone lay coiled in readiness to preserve the true intentions of Nicholas Kerensky. While the other Clans lost their way in pursuit of power or dreams of glory, the Steel Vipers remained true.

Dawn was closing to almost visual range of the headquarters when Captain Bidgood signaled her. "Reporting, Star Captain," he said.

"Proceed."

"There are at least two companies of 'Mechs here, as well as supporting infantry and ground armor. But that is not all. It looks like the Guards are already engaged with another raiding party. Unable to—"

Static cut off his voice for a second. Probably a PPC hit or near miss, Dawn thought, but she didn't need to hear anymore. It was time to change the plan. "Alpha and Charlie Stars, divert from primary targets and sweep to the flank to reinforce Bravo Star." As she spoke Dawn swung her *Crossbow* away from the Guards HQ. It was almost in range. She could have taken it out with one salvo. Remembering that Charlie Star had an *Ice Ferret,* one of the fastest OmniMechs of its class, she considered sending it on alone to destroy the objective, but then decided against it.

She wanted to win, but only through true victory. The way of the warrior, a Steel Viper warrior, was to accomplish her mission. First crush the defending forces, then destroy the HQ. Those were her orders. Anything else would not be worthy of the Viper she was.

Her orders hadn't included being suddenly outnumbered by the presence of some other unknown force, however. Who could it be? Troops of one of the other Clans? Perhaps a unit recently rotated in?

Captain Bidgood's voice came in again as she and the rest of the Trinary closed on the battle zone.

"—cut off. Do you read? Unknown force coming in on our rear flank."

A blast nearby rocked the ground under her *Crossbow.* Dawn switched to long-range scan and felt a cold shiver run through her body at what she saw. A full company of BattleMechs was closing rapidly on what was now her Trinary's left flank. In front of them was what was left of two companies of the Twenty-fourth Guards. Bravo Star was down to three 'Mechs and fighting a retreat back to where the rest of the Trinary was closing. *We must be vastly outgunned to have lost two of our 'Mechs so quickly,* Dawn thought. They'd been light 'Mechs, but that didn't make the loss any less significant.

"We are closing with you, Bravo One," she said, suddenly coming upon the battle site as she crested a small hill. All that was left of Bravo Star was a *Stormcrow,* a *Timber Wolf,* and an *Executioner,* the three 'Mechs steadily moving backward and firing at their targets in the distance. The smoldering remains of the two downed Steel Viper 'Mechs were belching black clouds into the air. Also visible were seven Lyran Guard 'Mechs, either destroyed or so close to it they were no longer viable targets. One of the fallen Vipers was tangled in a smoldering mass with what looked like a Guard *Battle Hawk*—a kind of mutual death grip. Though Dawn had not seen the fight that killed those two warriors, the struggle had obviously been fierce. The Viper warrior had met her fate with true honor.

Now the rest of the enemy Guards were charging forward, throwing up a literal wall of fire at the battered remains of Bravo Star. Lasers sliced the smoke-filled air, some hitting their mark, but many more going wildly off target. Missiles swarmed over Bidgood's *Executioner,* stinging and tearing at his ruined armor. On the far flank she saw Charlie Star deployed to their rear, engaging the unidentified force that was also closing in on them. The mysterious 'Mechs glimmered in the sun, a hint of red and silver against the deep green of the Cumbres grasses.

The Bravo Star *Timber Wolf* halted its flanking movement

and triggered a blast of its powerful lasers and LRMs at a Guard *Scarabus*. Dawn recognized the 'Mech as that of Vasha, the only other one of her sibmates to test out as a Clan warrior. Vasha was digging in to protect her Star, even if it meant sacrificing her own life. The missiles charged out of the launchers on her shoulders, hitting the *Scarabus* in the legs and lower torso. The damage slowed the 'Mech long enough for Vasha to fire the large lasers in each of her arms. One missed by nearly ten meters, but the other beam seared the *Scarabus* in mid-chest. The shot dug deep into the heart of the light 'Mech, rupturing its fusion reactor and gyro. As the *Scarabus* fell, an intense glow spread throughout its chest, then burst out like a new star. Its armor was pushed from the inside out as the 'Mech exploded.

Dawn was sweeping the area to determine which Vipers were engaging which enemy when an enemy *Grand Titan* locked onto Vasha's *Timber Wolf,* firing its LRMs and a deadly pair of large pulse lasers. The lasers hit first, ripping into the *Timber Wolf*'s left side. One beam bored into its elbow joint, which exploded in a ball of sparks that left Vasha's laser assembly hanging limp and lifeless. The LRMs also hit their mark, tearing into the beleaguered left side of the *Timber Wolf.* Vasha fought to maintain control of the wounded 'Mech, but could not.

The giant machine spun to the right and fell onto the soft grass, down but not dead. Vasha fought to bring it up, but within a heartbeat another salvo of LRMs ate into her raw left flank. Fires broke out inside the 'Mech, followed by an enormous blast as its remaining laser and missile ammunition exploded from within. The *Wolf*'s CASE panels, blocked because of the 'Mech's felled, contorted position, could not discharge the blast and save the 'Mech as they were designed to. Instead the full force and fury of a ton of long-range missile ammunition went off and gutted the *Timber Wolf.* Vasha never had a chance to punch out. Seeing that, Dawn felt a cold rage rush through her. Vasha was the last of her sibko, but she would not die unavenged.

The space between the two sides became a blur as her own Alpha Star leaped fearlessly into the fray, moving in alongside Bidgood and his surviving comrade. Missile trails, thunderous autocannon explosions, and the lightning flashes of PPC fire lit up the heavy smoke of battle. Lasers, some beam and some pulsing, cut through the thick air like overheated knives. It was a storm of death and fire, but Dawn's forces were holding their own—for now.

Through the thick smoke Dawn spotted the *Grand Titan* that had destroyed Vasha and her *Timber Wolf.* Locking onto it with the infrared beam of her Artemis IV targeting system, she prepared to fire her LRMs. *This one is for Vasha,* she thought. Because the *Titan* had fired at Bidgood and missed, Dawn considered the 'Mech an honorable target for her wrath. She overrode the Guards' communications channel so he could hear her challenge directly. "I am Star Captain Dawn of the Steel Vipers. Face me like a true warrior and prepare to meet your fate." Without waiting for a response, she triggered a salvo of long-range missiles from each of her 'Mech's arms.

The *Titan* paused, as if looking for who dared challenge it. In that instant the lasers hit. The 100-ton 'Mech was the largest of the Lyran Guard machines, but still it reeled under the attack. Bearing the brunt of the damage was its right arm, shedding armor like dry dead skin as the 'Mech rotated to return fire. Several missiles strayed into the right torso, devouring the armor there.

Dawn never saw the 'Mech fire, but the force of the impact told her the *Titan*'s large pulse laser had found its mark in her 'Mech's protruding center torso. Damage lights bled red in the dim half-light of the cockpit, and the *Crossbow* teetered backward as the multiple beams gouged through her armor. Dawn fought the controls and the whine of the gyro, somehow keeping her footing and preparing another salvo of missiles. The Artemis IV gave a shrill squeal as it achieved a lock onto the goliath Lyran 'Mech, and Dawn fired.

The *Grand Titan* pilot triggered another rapid pulse of laser beams. Dawn saw the hit coming and mentally braced for the impact. The laser fire tore into the *Crossbow*'s tubular arm, wrenching the 'Mech so hard that it froze, half-twisted to the right and permanently jammed. Again she struggled with the controls, once more managing to keep the 'Mech upright. The blast had knocked out her Artemis IV system, though she could still operate the launcher manually. Not, of course, with the accuracy of the target control system.

With grim determination she adjusted the launcher and tried to take aim while moving the *Crossbow* along the foot of the ridge line, turning slightly to the left to adjust for the wrenching damage to her torso. She carefully homed in as the *Grand Titan* opened up with its own LRMs, pitting her 'Mech's right leg with deep holes that spilled florescent green coolant and smoke from the internal mechanisms. Dawn triggered her missiles, aiming for the *Titan*'s heavily protected chest, but the worst she managed to do was blacken the giant war machine's paint. Correcting her targeting, she was sure now that it was adjusted as precisely as possible. Then she slowed her pace and fired again.

She had adjusted the weapons to lock onto the *Titan*'s giant head, and most of the shots did just that. Those that missed slammed solidly into the upper chest, burning and ripping away the armor plating. A blast of smoke obscured her view of the cockpit briefly, then she saw it again as the *Titan* fell sideways. It had been cored in several places, and a glimmer of light told her a fire raged within. The pilot ejected, blasting up through the inferno of weapons fire as his fearsome 'Mech toppled. It had been a lucky shot, Dawn knew that. But that did not make it any less satisfying.

Assessing the situation, she felt another cold surge of anger. What chance had her force now? An attack on the Lyran Guards had been a worthy challenge, but the presence of these other raiders made the odds virtually impossible. She watched as Charlie Star positioned itself on a low rise and began to engage the unforeseen enemy one 'Mech at a time. Their new foes responded in typical freebirth fashion, massing firepower against one lone Clansman at time. Their cowardliness drew from her a scream of rage as she ran along the slope of the hill, getting into position to fire from her diminishing supply of missiles.

No honor with these foes, she thought. *Just like Tukayyid, only death and loss. We can stay here and die, never achieving victory. But there will be no glory in those deaths, just the stain of failure. Just like Tukayyid.*

Then another voice inside her answered. *No, not this time.*

Studying the tactical display Dawn saw that the arrival of her Star had slowed the Guard advance, and it was turning into a pitched battle. The unknown force was pressing Charlie Star, but it too was being slowed. The unidentified raiders also seemed to be exchanging fire with the flank of the Twenty-fourth Lyran Guards. Regardless, her Trinary didn't have a chance. Whoever the unknown raiders were, they were no allies.

Looking out at the woods and the hills she mentally marked out a path for her forces. If they could punch through that unknown force, those who survived could make it to the DropShips.

"This is Star Captain Dawn to Viper Trinary Bravo. All forces form on me. Fall back by Star to the DropShips." The words were nearly drowned out when the *Stormcrow* next to Bidgood's *Executioner* suddenly exploded in a devastating fireball, shaking the ground as what was left of it rained down in small fragments on Dawn and several other remaining Steel Vipers.

Dawn cared little whether or not she made it out. Having failed on Tukayyid, a similar failure on Cumbres would spell her end in the Clans. She was just turning the contorted *Crossbow* when she took a missile hit from a *Stealth,* further weakening her 'Mech's chest and upper left leg. In reply Dawn charged along the length of the ridge where she had first entered the fray, firing her LRMs at the *Stealth* as she went. Most of the missiles missed, but those that hit made a spectacular series of impacts, ripping armor and showering the hillside with pieces of the 'Mech.

Now reduced to half their number, what was left of her command formed a tight wedge behind her as the Lyran Guards turned to pursue their Clan attackers and to face the unidentified raiders. Dawn had counted on them splitting their attack and thus unwittingly providing her with enough support fire to punch through the unknown force. She charged straight at two of the red and silver raiders, firing her LRMs at a *Shadow Hawk* that had moved to flank her.

The *Hawk*'s pilot opened up on Dawn as she passed, as did the other 'Mech, a *Vulcan*. The *Vulcan*'s shots narrowly missed, but the *Shadow Hawk*'s autocannon found its mark on her right side. The already-damaged LRM mount blew off under the exploding artillery shells that raked her side. A wave of dizziness hit her as the neurohelmet feedback sent her brain and stomach into seemingly different directions. The damage display was a blur to her watering eyes, but from what Dawn could see, for her the battle was nearly over. Her 'Mech's right leg had taken several laser and autocannon hits and lost its precious heat sinks. The *Crossbow*'s chest was more open space than protecting armor, and the loss of the weapons pod cut her remaining firepower neatly in half. But Dawn pressed on, her troops following through the hole she'd punched. Beyond were the DropShips and a chance for some of them to survive.

But not her.

As the rest of the Trinary passed, Dawn made a half circle to face the *Shadow Hawk* that had fired on her. "Make for the DropShips," she commanded. "I will cover your withdrawal." One warrior, Handly, swung his *Battle Cobra* next to her. Without a word, he opened up on the *Vulcan* that had turned to pursue, his six pulse lasers hitting the red and silver 'Mech almost everywhere, leaving armor plating and severed myomer strands flailing about. Dawn was about to order Handly to retreat when a pair of brilliant blue flashes engulfed his 'Mech. PPC fire, probably from a nearby enemy *Marauder,* had slammed into it. Handly's OmniMech toppled in front of her, rolling slightly as it dropped. It had been gutted, eaten alive by the charged particle beam. Handly never stood a chance.

Dawn fired her last salvo of missiles at the *Shadow Hawk* as it moved to engage her. She knew the *Marauder* was nearby and probably locking onto her. But until it actually fired, the Clan code of honor would not allow her to target it—even if that initial attack killed her. Some other Clans no longer held stringently to the code, but the Steel Vipers did. They remained true. It was the hallmark of her Clan and a bond Dawn would never betray, no matter what the risk.

Dawn's missiles met their mark. The *Shadow Hawk*'s lethal right arm was left mangled and smoking from her fire, but it fired back at her with its shoulder-mounted autocannon. Most of the shells missed by mere meters, but some hit her left foot, frying the ankle actuator. Dawn held her ground. *The survivors have to get away.* Again she experienced a surge of fury. *This is the ground where I will die.* Though the raid had failed, she might still win honor by giving her own life. Perhaps even enough to merit having her ashes mixed with the nutrient solution that would help nourish a new generation of warriors in the Clan genetics labs.

But that was not to be her fate, for the attackers inexplicably turned away from the retreating Steel Vipers and left the field, heading along the far flank of the approaching Lyran Guards. Seeing them go, Dawn's anger died suddenly, replaced by an almost unbearable dread. She had failed in her mission. More than half her Trinary was dead, perhaps even more. It was as if the ghost of Tukayyid had risen from its grave to wrap its cold arms around her in the stifling cockpit of the *Crossbow.*

When they returned to Jabuka, Star Colonel Brett Andrews would neither ask for nor accept any explanations. An explanation was just words. No words could raise the warriors that had fallen under her command. No words could wipe away this stain.

Dawn had been given her orders and she had failed. Now all that was left was to return to face her commander and her comrades and this new shame.

4

Cavern of the Skull
New St. Andrews, The Periphery
Rimward of the Circinus Federation
13 April 3057

As Captain Kemper Varas entered the small alcove, the balding man looked up quickly from the desk where he was working. Varas eyed him carefully. He knew the man was prone to fits of rage when provoked—and even sometimes when not. Seeing him sitting here in this old Star League base hidden centuries ago was an irony not lost on him.

"Greetings, lord," Varas said, bowing slightly. The man nodded and motioned to the chair facing him. Varas sat down, still watching carefully. The man he'd come to see was dressed, as always, in a suit of body armor. Varas waited for him to speak, more out of cunning than caution. He knew that one day all this would be his if he was patient and could bide his time.

"What is the status of our units?" the man asked, sitting back in his chair and steepling his fingers.

"The force that struck Shiro III has signaled arrival at the pre-arranged coordinates, and reports being in good condition with minimal losses. Repairs estimated at one week. Our raid on Valexa also caught the Sixth Crucis Lancers totally unaware and unprepared. The Lancers have been bloodied, and word is beginning to leak that the Knights of the Inner Sphere were involved. We lost three 'Mechs and MechWarriors, but none were recovered or captured alive."

The round-face man barely reacted to the news of these deaths. If anything, he looked satisfied. "They died for a cause," he said. "One of such grand scale that their deaths will immortalize them in the new empire we shall forge. But what of Cumbres, Captain? Did the Twenty-fourth Lyran Guards feel my wrath?" His voice seemed to tingle with excitement, as though this was some game and not a question of life and death.

Varas lowered his eyes, pausing deliberately to emphasize his next words. "The Cumbres operation went off with losses equal to one full lance and damage to both other lances. Apparently, just as our people were about to spring the ambush, a company of Steel Vipers turned up with the same idea of raiding the Twenty-fourth Lyran Guards. Our troops held back, not attacking until the other two sides were already engaged."

"We have struck at the Clans then?"

"Yes, my lord."

"Sooner than I had planned, but so much the better. And were we successful?"

"Indeed we were." Varas knew that success was hard to define in such an operation. These were not like the missions he'd planned and executed so many times before, but rather were aimed at provoking a political action rather than military conquest.

"Excellent," the man said, smiling to himself. "And now the Steel Vipers have also felt my sting." He gave a short laugh at his own little joke. "And the 'Mech pilots downed during the operation?"

Captain Kemper Varas drew his breath. "Per your orders, sire, all were destroyed. All the 'Mechs were equipped with the hidden explosives our DropShip commanders detonate when the machines become disabled. None fell into the hands of the Guard troops."

"Excellent." The man rose from his chair and began to pace back and forth, hands clasped behind his back. "Fortunately, we have replacements for those that were lost."

Kemper Varas nodded. "Some, my lord. Our raids on those Capellan shipments have helped us refit many of the 'Mechs brought in by our new recruits. In all honesty, sire, the 'Mechs are no match for the best Inner Sphere or Clan models, but our unique variants may provide some rude surprises. Still, in a straight battle, 'Mech against 'Mech, we would be hard pressed to win."

"How can you say that, Captain Varas? We have won three victories—four, if you count the Steel Vipers. And the rest of the Inner Sphere will blame Thomas Marik and his Knights for my deeds."

Varas felt bound to speak the truth. "We have not won based on skill or technology, but because the raids were carefully planned ambushes, sire."

The man shook his head and waved his hand in the air as if to brush away the Captain's words. "Regardless, they are victories. It has begun."

"It will not be long before people realize it was not the Knights of the Inner Sphere carrying out these raids. And then the leaders of the Inner Sphere will set their dogs to tracking us down." Varas knew they might all die when that day came, but the other man's name would make him the prime target. And that would give Varas the time he would need.

"A wasted effort. Our operatives will plant counterintelligence pointing the finger at each one of the House Lords. Have not our teams on New Avalon, Luthien, Atreus, and Sian already signaled that they are ready to strike? They only await the word."

Varas knew the plan all too well, having been one of its chief architects. When he had first been recruited by the balding man who now stood before him as lord, he'd never dreamed how far the scheming would go. Now he did. First, it had brought them here to New St. Andrews, this forgotten Periphery world on the far side of the Free Worlds League. The next stage would take them to the capitals of the Great Houses of the Inner Sphere, into the palaces of those who ruled the star empires that had once formed the grand alliance known as the Star League. And their teams of assassins were poised and ready to go off like carefully planted explosives. In the chaos following the collapse of leadership in the Inner Sphere, his lord planned to step in and take over.

This man was cunning, Varas knew. One of the first things he did for every unit they brought here was to memorize the profiles of both unit and commander. Varas served him now, because it suited his plan. One day, that would no longer be true. Plans had been made to ensure that one day, sometime in the future, he would take care of the man who lorded over him. One day, Varas himself would rule where a madman now claimed succession.

Yet Varas was not immune to the force of the man's personality. His voice was compelling, and he spoke with a fierce conviction that at times fired the Captain to his very soul. It was the same charisma that had drawn others to their cause. "The House Lords are as suspicious and fearful of one another as they were three hundred years ago when their infighting destroyed the Star League," the man said. "But this time we will use those suspicions and fears to play them off against one another. While they plot and plan each other's demise, we will prepare here, in the Periphery. It was here that it all began so long ago, and it is here that the climax will unfold. Remember, Varas, history repeats itself." The man moved past his Captain and toward the door. "Come now, let us go meet our newest followers."

The Cavern of the Skull was not a natural cave, but one that had been carved out by the engineers of the Star League Defense Force as a base from which 'Mechs could operate. During the two decades of the Reunification Wars, the cavern had housed nearly a regiment of 'Mechs and support personnel. The walls had also been dug out to create various rooms and quarters. But more than three centuries had taken their toll. The meeting would be held in the massive open area in the center of the cavern.

Unmatched chairs had been set up throughout the area, with two placed on the dais for Varas and his lord. Milling about were dozens of MechWarriors, infantrymen, tankers, and technicians. Standing guard at the entrance and along the walls of the vast cavern were uniformed men wearing red berets and sashes across their chests. Each one was armed with a rifle.

The man entered the room and passed regally through the crowd to reach the podium. His appearance had created a buzz of interest that now gradually became an expectant hush as all those gathered turned their gaze upon him. The man held the podium with both hands and stood surveying the assembly. At the back stood the Clave Lords, leaders of the highlanders who eked out their existence among the lonely mountains of St. Andrews. Varas had defeated them in combat when he and his lord had first arrived, and then the man had won them over by offering protection as well as desperately needed food and supplies. Now, many of the Claves had come over to him, were under his dominion. Finally, the man smiled, if only for a moment. It was a cruel smile, one that Varas had seen before and dreaded.

"I welcome you to your new home," he said, spreading his hands wide as though to embrace the assembly. "It is temporary, I assure you, but your 'Mechs and equipment are safe here. Uniforms will be issued to you all in the coming weeks."

"My men don't want to wear uniforms," a voice called out belligerently from the crowd. Varas recognized the man immediately as Captain Parker Don Hua. He and his unit, the Red Hell, were some of the worst of the new recruits. The Mercenary Review Board had banned them from employment by any House in their Inner Sphere for acts of savagery during a raid on a Word of Blake compound—their choice of target only adding it to the list of problems. They'd turned to the Periphery for employment, but had torn up one too many towns to win many contracts or a decent pay rate. Varas and his lord were the last hope for Hua, as they were for most of the mercenaries in the room.

"You are Captain Hua, are you not?" the lord asked coolly.

"Damn right!"

"Well, my dear Captain, I regret to tell you that I do not intend to fail in the great work for which I have brought you here. You will abide by the stipulation of the contract. *All* the stipulations. None are insignificant. I do not offer you the luxury of choosing which parts to honor and which to ignore. No stipulation is unimportant, because this contract is the first step in binding and uniting us in our will to succeed. I will not compromise on this issue, Captain." The man's voice was deep, made even more commanding by its echo off the walls of the enormous cave.

"Contract or not, we don't wear uniforms. You got a prob-

lem with that, you take it up with the Merc Board," Hua retorted, drawing a laugh from several of his comrades. They
knew that this contract was *not* binding, that they were beyond the law as far as the Mercenary Bonding and Review
Board was concerned.

The man at the podium shrugged. "Very well. You have
traveled far to sow the seeds of dissent among my loyal
men. Of all things I do not tolerate, insubordination is the
first." He pulled a small laser pistol from a fold in his body
armor and fired it at Hua, the laser bolt striking the mercenary squarely between the eyes. Hua's body collapsed like a
bag of wet meal, people around him jumping back as it fell
heavily in their midst.

Several Red Hellions pulled their weapons, but the red-
sashed guards around the room already had theirs leveled,
ready to mow down the dissenters if so ordered by their lord.
One by one, the mercenaries holstered their pistols. Other
Red Hell members bent over the body of their fallen commander, not certain what to do next.

"He was weak, and you will find that the weak are dis-
pensable. All of you are fine warriors, but for one reason or
another, the leaders of the Inner Sphere have turned their
backs on you. Most of you, like the Black Warriors
there"—he pointed to a small band in the corner of the
room—"have been wrongly accused of crimes. Others, perhaps the Red Hell among them, have simply lacked true
leaders, leaders with a vision.

"I am a man with such a vision. A vision of the future."

As his lord paused to let the words sink in, Varas saw that
the audience seemed mesmerized. *He tells them what they
want to hear and they swallow it like starving men.*

"How many of you are tired of being cannon fodder for
the House Lords? How many of you grow weary of fighting
battles in senseless wars for petty politics? Are you saddened by the loss of your comrades who have been sent to
their deaths by little lords sitting in their ivory castles?"

A chorus of affirmation swelled from the floor of the Cavern of the Skull, the sound reverberating off the ancient
stone walls.

"You need a leader who promises you not only a paycheck, but a future. I am that man." He took a staff from behind the podium and held it high so all might see. Then, as if to strike a blow through the winds of time he slammed the staff down hard on its heel. The cavern had gone totally silent, and the staff hit with a sharp, resounding *crack!*

"I am Stefan Amaris the Seventh, Star Lord of the Amaris Republic, ruler of the Rim Worlds Republic and rightful heir to the throne of the First Lord of the Star League!" Again he pounded the heel of the mighty staff against the cold stone floor.

There was a brief silence as the assembled men and women absorbed this astounding statement. Where they had been nearly mesmerized moments before, their faces now showed only shock and dismay. *Amaris,* a cursed name. The name of the Usurper, the Pillager, the destroyer of the Star League. If not for Stefan Amaris the golden age of mankind might still be unfolding. No Clans, no centuries of Succession Wars. The name Amaris was the embodiment of evil, even after all these centuries.

Varas remembered his initial reaction of disgust when the man had first showed him the irrefutable genetic proof. It had been pure chance that the document had fallen into the man's hands during the split in ComStar that created the rebellious Word of Blake. The man had been a ComStar adept back then, taking advantage of the organization's extensive archives to discover why his family could identify no ancestor beyond the start of the fall of the Star League.

Amaris again held up both hands, stilling any objection before it could be voiced. He'd expected their reaction. "Yes, I know what you must be thinking. I know that every history book teaches that Stefan Amaris was evil, power-hungry—a kind of devil. But, I ask you this, who wrote those histories? Lackeys of the same House Lords whose bickering and power struggles led to the collapse of the Star League, the worst disaster in the memory of mankind. And I have brought you here today to tell you those histories are false! When the great General Kerensky captured my grandsire, the true First Lord, and then killed him and every member of his line, this so-called great general covered up his crime by making the Amaris name cursed throughout the Inner Sphere.

"Heed my words. I am a direct descendant of the Amaris line and my genetic heritage has been confirmed. But even I did not know of it until recently. Like you I had been taught the stories, the lies. If not for my studies of history, I would have had no clue to my true lineage." He held up a parchment for all to see. Varas knew what it was—the Amaris seal.

"In searching through the history of my own ancestors, I discovered poof of my great inheritance. If Stefan Amaris the First committed an error, it was in failing to grasp the depth of the treachery of the House Lords. His dream was to hold the glory of the Star League together. That was the motive behind all his deeds. There was nothing—*nothing!*—he would not do to achieve his ends. He saw the petty greed and weakness of the Council Lords. He saw General Kerensky betray his trust. Had the General joined with Stefan Amaris instead of opposing him, the Amaris Empire would have been the crown jewel of the history of mankind. Instead Kerensky and the petty lords crushed the best and only hope for the future of mankind.

"Until now." Again the man paused, which had an electrifying effect on his listeners. A shout went up from them.

"I have re-formed the Republican Guards, and they have already struck at several Inner Sphere worlds, damaging some of the best House units in existence. What's more, we have the parts and supplies here to refit your BattleMechs to peak condition. You and your kin will enjoy all that has been denied you by the House Lords who turned their backs on you and your comrades."

One of the men called out from the floor. "What will we have to do?"

Amaris held up his hands as though to still a babble that did not exist. "My vision is one of grand scale. We will strike again soon, hitting the Periphery and turning its people against our foes in the Inner Sphere. The various House governments all suspect each other of conducting these raids, and that suits my purposes splendidly. Meanwhile, rest assured that I have a plan, I have the resources, and I have the will to take my fight to your enemies. One day, we will laugh in their faces as we take their power for ourselves.

"My plan is to so totally disrupt the governments of every one of the five Great Houses of the Inner Sphere that people will gladly turn to us for leadership and a bold vision of the future. And we will ride that wave of revolution straight to the cradle of mankind, to Terra, where we will storm the gates and once again raise high the banner of the Star League! Follow me and you will become my generals, my leaders, my templates to forge a brave new empire. Like no one else alive today, I alone possess the true heritage. I alone am the rightful heir to the Star League. I am the Star Lord. Stand in my ranks as Republican Guards. Join me, and let us forge a brave new future as the leaders of a great new empire!"

A bedlam of cheers rose up from the floor as many raised their fists in a gesture that was as much bravado as salute. Stefan Amaris nodded to one of his men, who tugged at a rope hanging down one wall. A giant banner unfurled, a blue shark swimming against a sea of red. It was a symbol that had been banned for centuries, as much from fear as from hatred. The symbol of the House of Amaris and the Amaris Empire. In unison the men and women, even the Red Hellions still surrounding the fallen form of their leader, began to chant aloud his title, over and over again.

"Star Lord, Star Lord, Star Lord . . ." Even the Clave Lords, normally so suspicious and aloof, seemed infected by what was going on around them. Varas himself almost joined in, except that a part of him understood too well that this rally was a masterpiece of orchestration and planning.

Stefan Amaris smiled thinly, basking in his victory. As Varas watched him, he understood that this man operated in that dangerous zone somewhere between madness and divinity. He would either build an empire or destroy anyone or anything who tried to stop him.

Kalma Estate
Marik
Marik Commonwealth, Free Worlds League

"Duncan," the elder Kalma said, motioning to the report he had spread out across the table. "Look at this."

Duncan walked over to the massive oak table and leafed through the sheaf of hardcopy. He began to scan them, almost casually, sipping from his drink as he did so. "You could get into some pretty hot water showing me this, Father. It's all very classified and I'm not even a member of the Free Worlds Militia."

For the first time in hours Harrison Kalma smiled, if only fleetingly. "What can they do, fire me? Technically, I'm retired. Besides, no one knows I've got these reports. They came to me through my own sources."

Duncan continued reading though the sheets. "So, the Knights of the Inner Sphere have struck again."

"It's not the Knights," his father said flatly.

Duncan put down his drink and threw up his hands in mock despair. "But that's just it, Father. You can't know for sure."

"I have station reports that the Knights are currently posted on Epsilon, Rochelle, and Nestor. This wasn't them."

Duncan shook his head. "What if those reports were faked to cover their raiding activities?"

Harrison Kalma sighed deeply as they picked up the thread of the same argument they'd been having since the night before. "All right, Duncan, let's assume it's not the Knights conducting these raids."

"So then the question is, who is?"

"To know that we must ask who has the most to gain."

Duncan didn't have to think long on that one. "Just about everybody who sits in power in the Inner Sphere. The Free Worlds League hasn't been hurt by the Clan invasion the way the FedCom and the Kuritas have been. In fact, the war effort only strengthened the economy and Thomas Marik's prestige and power. Plenty of people would like to discredit him, knock him down a peg or two to keep him in line.

What better way than to destroy his pet project, the Knights of the Inner Sphere?"

"That's right, son. Since these raids have begun, every House leader must be thinking that the Free Worlds League is a danger to what little peace any of us have known in recent years. It could be the start of another great war. But who would benefit? Not Sun-Tzu Liao. He's to marry Isis Marik soon enough, and can look forward to gaining the League's power via the bedchamber rather than the battlefield. Not Victor Steiner-Davion, either. He's having trouble enough just holding together his own realm, let alone trying to spawn a brand-new war. Not to mention the Clans poised all along his Lyran border. That leaves Theodore Kurita and the Combine. The Kuritas don't even share a border with the Free Worlds League. Besides Kurita's got his mind on other matters—the very grave threat of the Clans, for one."

Duncan stood looking at his father for a moment. "I'll give you this, your arguments are logical. So maybe it's one of the Clans . . . or one of the Periphery governments . . ."

Kalma shook his head. "Our intelligence about what goes on inside the Clan Occupation Zone is pretty weak, but my best guess is that the Clans are too distracted by their own internal problems to mount a concerted effort at this time."

"That leaves the Periphery, but I can't imagine any of those wild and woolly worlds able to organize such a devious campaign."

"None of the Periphery governments would be rash enough to try and start a war in the Inner Sphere, then risk retaliation once they were found out. And none of the Periphery governments has the motivation to try this kind of stunt, especially given the planning and resources needed to pull off such an operation."

"Well, Father, I'd say you've just ruled out everyone known."

The General raised his eyebrows knowingly. "Which means what?"

"Which means we're dealing with a new threat." It was only once the words were out that Duncan fully understood the implication. The last great threat the Inner Sphere had faced was the Clan invasion. Now, suddenly, here was a possibility of yet another danger emerging from the unknown. The Clan invasion had been a bloody one, costing millions of lives and carving up huge areas of known space. The Free Worlds League had been spared so far because the invasion had halted before the Clans could reach their space. Had they only been spared for something worse?

Duncan's train of thought was interrupted by a manservant opening the oaken door of the study to announce an unexpected visitor. The General had just enough time to gather up and stuff the hardcopy report into a briefcase.

"Please see him in," he said calmly.

The servant opened the door, ushering in a man who was obviously a MechWarrior, though very tall to be one. His eyes were an unsettling gray and his black hair severely slicked back. He wore a formal dress uniform of red adorned with a pair of crossing silver sashes clasped in the center of his chest with a brilliant silver starburst buckle. His high black boots were buffed to a spit-polish shine, and he clicked the heels smartly together as he snapped to attention for the General. The man was a MechWarrior—and more—Duncan knew. He was a Knight of the Inner Sphere.

Duncan stared at the Knight in his impressive uniform and felt what might have been a twinge of envy. That could have been him, he told himself. He was a damn fine MechWarrior, plenty good enough to join their ranks of the Knights. But Duncan also knew he didn't have the heart for it. What he'd always craved was adventure, the kind of excitement he'd found on the freewheeling, often lawless worlds of the Periphery. He didn't think he could survive a single day of what he imagined must be the stiff, honor-bound life of a Knight. Let him wear that uniform, Duncan thought. It suits him.

"General, I am Captain Rod Trane, Knight of the Inner Sphere and loyal servant of Captain-General Thomas Marik."

"Welcome to my home," the General replied, motioning to a chair. "To what do we owe the honor, Captain?"

Trane flicked a glance at Duncan, then turned back to Harrison Kalma as though the son were beneath his notice. "The Captain-General arrived on-world last night. He asks that you come to meet with him of an evening three days from now."

"I'd heard nothing of the Captain-General's arrival."

Captain Trane nodded. "He came unannounced. May I inform him that you agree to his request?"

"Of course," the General replied in his best court-tone. "Please convey to the Captain-General that I would be most honored."

Again Trane snapped his heels together as he saluted Harrison Kalma, then turned to leave.

"Oh Captain," the General called after him.

Trane turned. "Sir?"

"Will you also advise Thomas that I will be bringing my son?"

Second Oriente Hussars Field Headquarters
Shimgata Plains
Shiro III

"Bovos, are you sure you want to do this?" his senior officer asked, staring at the forms in front of him.

"Yes, sir," Hermann Bovos said. He had changed in the weeks since the raid that had destroyed his lance. His face was drawn and his eyes were sunken into dark circles. He'd obviously become a stranger to sleep and it was beginning to take its toll.

"I'll approve your discharge, but I think it's a mistake. It wasn't anyone's fault that the members of your lance didn't make it. It was a raid. Resigning your commission with the Hussars can't change that. It won't bring them back."

"I beg to differ, sir," Bovos said, remaining at attention and staring off into space instead of looking at his commander.

"They're dead, Hermann. Those bloody damn Knights killed them. It's over. Such things happen, even in times of peace. The sign of a true warrior is the ability to pick up the pieces and continue on. What you want to do is wrong. To take up arms on your own, to strike out blindly on a mission of revenge, with no direction or support, is madness."

Bovos wavered slightly as he stood. "Permission to speak freely, sir," he said.

"Granted."

"It wasn't the Knights that did this. I think it was impostors and so do you, regardless of what the Oriente government is saying. No, I wasn't responsible for my men's deaths—I'm not so wet behind the ears that I don't know that. I've seen men and women die before. And, yes, I know I can't bring them back. Still, if there's an answer, it's not here, but out there, somewhere." Bovos gestured toward the window and the sky and the vast space beyond. "But I also know this, the politicians won't bring whoever did it to justice. I can." And I will, he added silently.

The only reply was the sound of his commander slapping the thermo-stamp against the paperwork.

Hermann Bovos looked down and saw the word "Approved" lasered in red across the top sheet. From this day forward, he was no longer an Oriente Hussar. All that was done, finished, part of the past. He was no longer following in the footsteps of his famous father. And he was no longer just a loyal son of the Free Worlds League, sworn to protect and defend it. No, those days were over. But his own mission, his personal quest, had just begun.

5

Council Hall, Steel Viper Garrison
Jabuka
Steel Viper Occupation Zone
15 April 3057

Star Colonel Brett Andrews smiled proudly as he slipped the glittering snakeskin cape over his shoulders. Wearing it always seemed to lend him some of the power of the great viper of Arcadia. A truly fearsome beast, it possessed strength and tenacity unmatched by any other predator on that world. Today he would wear the cape and the rest of his ritual garments as a member of the Council presiding over the Judgment of Star Captain Dawn. Like the viper, they would coil around their prey, then finish it with deadly precision. Next he fastened the thick rolled collar that simulated the huge size and distinctive markings of Clan Steel Viper's fearsome namesake. As Leader of House Andrews, he was entitled to wear the full representation of the Viper, whereas others would not. Tradition, for the Steel Vipers, was sacred.

Brett Andrews could not remember the last time a Judgment, a trial of formal disgrace, had been called. He wondered if anyone alive among the Steel Vipers could. The hundreds of Bloodnamed warriors who would hear the evidence had come from near and far in the Occupation Zone, for they understood what was truly at stake. The charge of incompetence and conduct unbecoming a warrior would hold, he was sure of it. Had he not already met privately with various Council members who might have wavered on the vote, and persuaded them to side with him? Yes, Star

Captain Dawn would be judged guilty and she would be publicly disgraced, for that was what she deserved.

The Steel Vipers must purge their ranks, must shed the old skin in favor of the new. Ever since the shame and decimation of their numbers at Tukayyid, all acknowledged the pressing need to rebuild the Clan's strength. The grip of the Steel Viper was viselike, its deadly bite pitiless. The Clan must be no less. It was this steely resolve that had made Khan Perigard Zalman refuse to engage in Trials of Possession for nearby Jade Falcon worlds. The Steel Vipers could no more spare the loss of troops than they could harbor third-rate warriors or weakling Wardens in their midst.

And Brett Andrews considered that to be the greatest of Star Captain Dawn's failures—she was a Warden among a Clan that was more strongly Crusader than ever before.

First she had dishonored herself at Tukayyid, losing every member of her Binary. Then she had bid for the right to lead the raid on Cumbres and failed again. Instead of holding fast like a true warrior, she had called a retreat. And still the members of her unit had died almost to a man. Once more, other warriors fell while Star Captain Dawn survived. As commander of the raid, she should have given her own life to save the rest, *quiaff*?

Dawn stared straight ahead, her eyes fairly boring into the blank white wall of the waiting chamber. So deep and hard was her concentration that the wall and her mind became as one. Blank, calm, pure. It cleared her confusion and opened her thoughts. Even to things she would have preferred not to think about.

It was no surprise that the Clan wished to make her answer for her failures. What surprised her was the gravity and formality of the proceedings. It was not just her commanding officer who would decide the charge of incompetence, but all the Bloodnamed of Clan Steel Viper. They had been arriving, hundreds of them, on Jabuka from near and far for days.

With her thoughts stilled and her mind clear, Dawn saw that she had no chance to prevail. The Steel Vipers wished to make an example of her. No matter. She would hold her head high, remain staunch before any Judgment handed down. She was a proud Clanswoman, a product of the Clan's breeding program to produce a race of superior warriors. And, above all, she was a warrior of Clan Steel Viper, destined above all other Clans to fulfill the vision of Nicholas Kerensky.

Dawn understood that it was not for the raid on Cumbres that she would be publicly shamed, but for the fact that she was a Warden among a Clan of Crusaders. Indeed, Star Colonel Brett Andrews was one of the most fervent, rejoicing when the Steel Vipers had won the right to participate in the long-awaited invasion of the Inner Sphere. Against the still waters of her mind Dawn recalled how her beliefs had come to diverge from the way of her Clan.

Like all Steel Viper warriors, Dawn had survived a cadet training that was as grueling mentally as it was physically. While the combat masters had been honing her physical abilities, the loremasters had fortified her warrior's spirit with the visionary words of the two great Kerenskys. Aleksandr Kerensky, the general who had led their ancestors far from the Inner Sphere to a new home among the stars. And his son Nicholas Kerensky, founder of the Clan eugenics program to breed a race of warriors who might one day restore the Star League.

One of those loremasters had been especially strict in his interpretation of the Clan's destiny. He had taught the cadets to learn *The Remembrance* by heart as a touchstone for their lives, and often quoted one of its most famous passages:

> *Without a pure soul we cannot give sight*
> *To blind eyes, but will only blind ourselves.*

It was a passage that called for a crusade to cleanse the Inner Sphere of its dark ways, the very lines from which the Crusaders had taken their name. But that one loremaster had given sight to Dawn's blind eyes, reminding the cadets that Aleksandr Kerensky had prophesied that his people's destiny was to *protect* the Inner Sphere, not conquer it. Yes, Kerensky had predicted that his exiles would one day return, but when that day came they must come clear of eye and pure in heart. And thus had Dawn become a Warden.

That did not make her any less a warrior. Like every other member of her caste, she had been bred for war. When she fought, it was without fear or thought of anything but victory with honor. That was the way of the Clan. But by the time she and her battered command lifted off Cumbres, there were only three other survivors of the battle. One was still in the hospital. Most humiliating of all was the loss of her 'Mech, the *Crossbow* now little more than a shell, to be dismantled for parts rather than repaired.

It was true that Dawn had failed in her mission, but she had expected to meet only the Twenty-fourth Lyran Guard, not the Guard *and* another company of unknown attackers. She and her Trinary had been outnumbered. Only a miracle could have saved them, and no Clan warrior believed in miracles. And no Clan Council would accept excuses from a warrior.

Her Advocate today would be Star Colonel Ivan Sinclair, commander of the 94th Battle Cluster. Despite Ivan Sinclair's Crusader beliefs, Dawn was pleased to have him speak for her. The man was stubborn and uncompromising, as any warrior must be, but she also knew him to be honest and fair. His assessment of her chances had been typically blunt.

He had told her that the convocation of a Trial of Judgment, the Clan equivalent of a court martial, was so rare as to be almost unheard of. And it was no surprise to learn that not a single warrior brought up for Judgment had ever been acquitted of the charges. Most had been branded with the dread stain of *dezgra,* some had been banished, and a handful had been executed. Dawn saw with calm clarity what would be her fate.

The sound of the door opening disturbed the still pool of her mind. It was Star Colonel Ivan Sinclair come to fetch her. "The Council has assembled," he said. "It is time."

Her thoughts troubled again, Dawn rose to face her accusers.

* * *

As the door to the Council chamber opened before her, Dawn saw Khan Perigard Zalman standing motionless and proud on the podium before the High Council of Clan Steel Viper. The room was only dimly lit, but from the slight stirring sounds she knew that hundreds of Bloodnamed warriors were seated in circular tiered seats rising high above the floor. She could just make them out in their masks and capes and ritual dress, illuminated by the small terminal screens in front of them.

The Khan stood in a spotlight shining down on the podium. He wore a robe and cape of silvery gray, woven together from the gleaming skins of the Clan's namesake. It was ancient, as was his mask, which had been worn by every Khan of the Steel Vipers in the centuries since the Clan's founding. It was shaped like an enormous viper's head, the Khan's face showing through the massive jaws gaping as if to bite. Framing his brow were the two dagger-like teeth.

The Khan raised his arms, the palms pressed together, then brought them down in a sharp movement, his arms pointing straight ahead. All sound ceased except for an ominous and powerful hissing, the Khan calling the Trial of Judgment to order.

Then he spoke, arms still raised high. "Let all assembled know that the true followers of the great Nicholas Kerensky, the Steel Viper Clan, have gathered here in the tradition of our forefathers and of our people. As Khan of the Steel Vipers, I hereby convene this Judgment in this, the seventh year of the Truce of Tukayyid, in the 257th year of the Clans. Let all who speak only speak truth. Justice, above all, shall prevail."

"Seyla!" chanted the joined voices of the Bloodnamed warriors seated in tier upon tier of the near-dark chamber. The word was as old as the Clans, and what it meant no one knew except that it signified a unity of will. It was uttered only as part of the most formal ceremonies and rites, and always with reverence. Dawn too raised her voice in affirmation, realizing that this might be the last time she did so as a peer. Her chest tightened as the proceedings began.

The Loremaster spoke from the darkness. "We, the Bloodnamed of Clan Steel Viper, are gathered in Judgment of Star

Captain Dawn. The charge is incompetence unbecoming a warrior of our Clan. That, during a raid she planned and led against a Lyran Guard garrison on Cumbres, her unit was virtually destroyed at the hands of the enemy, costing the lives of twelve warriors. Furthermore she retreated from the field of combat without having engaged her primary target. These charges are so entered into the record. Star Captain Dawn, before the Bloodnamed of the Steel Vipers and upon your honor as a warrior, how do you plead?"

Dawn lifted her voice, loud and clear. "Loremaster and members of the Council, I plead innocent of these charges." If they thought to make her cower, they were wrong.

Loremaster Arthur Stoklas motioned from his station, and a man in a starched white lab coat stepped forward. The coat was adorned with badges and insignia that marked him as a member of the scientist caste. "Relinquish your codex for all to review and read, Viper warrior," the Loremaster said as the scientist came to stand before her.

Dawn removed the circlet from her forearm and handed it over. The act itself was ominous. She never removed her codex, it was like a part of her own body. Though the Clans did not prize individuality, every warrior wore this identification bracelet. It contained the names of the original Bloodnamed warriors from which a warrior was descended, her generation number, Blood House, and the alphanumeric code noting the unique aspects of her DNA. It also contained a recording of her career as a warrior, updated from battle ROMs and field reports, imprinted on the EPROMs. The scientist caste performed the work of maintaining the codices, and it was one of the few places where they interfaced with the warrior caste. But a codex was more than a record of battles and victories, it was the genetic imprint of the warrior who wore it.

The scientist placed the codex chip in a small device at one end of the room and activated the mechanism that would download the data to the displays of every member of the Council. The box then projected a rapid series of holographic images and reports before the gathered Steel Vipers. The same image in two-dimensional form was broadcast to each one's individual monitor. The images were a rapid-fire montage of Dawn's life. In sixty seconds she saw scenes of 'Mechs, reports, battle damage statistics, lasers and missiles, tactical readouts, and more. Dawn caught images of the battle on Tukayyid and it stirred, as always, the painful memories. Meanwhile each Council member was sorting through the images, concentrating on the parts of her life that had the most importance to him or her and the proceedings. The balding scientist bowed deeply to the Loremaster and vanished again into the darkness.

"This warrior's codex has been entered into the record. Let this Trial of Judgment begin," Loremaster Arthur Stoklas intoned, deepening his voice in the ritual manner.

The Inquisitor prosecuting Dawn was Star Colonel James Andrews of the Striking Serpent Galaxy, a rabid Crusader and a member of the same Bloodright as Brett Andrews. He moved into the middle of the chamber where another spotlight, only meters from Dawn, shone down on a slowly rotating podium. As he stood, the platform turned slowly so that all the gathered warriors could see him.

"My kindred, before you stands a warrior who is a blight on the honor of Clan Steel Viper. After winning the bid to lead a raid against Cumbres, she was given command of a Trinary. Her primary mission was to destroy the headquarters of the Twenty-fourth Lyran Guards. She bid far too low, then blatantly directed her forces against a superior force she could never hope to overpower."

"I object," Star Colonel Sinclair cut in. "This is a trial of fact, not of what the Inquisitor assumes were the hopes or fears of Star Captain Dawn. These speculations have no bearing on these proceedings."

"This is a trial of Judgment," Star Colonel James Andrews spat back. "Fear was her motivation, and as such must be entered into the record."

Dawn knew she was not allowed to speak, but the angry words were out before she could stop them. "I do not know fear. I am a Viper to the core."

The Loremaster turned to stare at her coldly. "Advocate, advise the Star Captain that silence is the order of the day in any Clan trial. Speaking out of turn and ignoring our rules and traditions does nothing to help her case."

The Inquisitor smiled thinly. "Overcome by fear, she panicked and withdrew from Cumbres. But not before her forces were nearly obliterated. Her battle report has already been submitted to the record and you have all had a chance to examine it. To excuse her incompetence, she has invented the existence of another raiding group, one that, in reality, was nothing more than other members of the Twenty-fourth Lyran Guard. You have all read her battle report, seen the blatant falsehoods she dares to present. She fabricates this other group of BattleMechs to cover her cowardice. Lies, unbecoming a true warrior, that is what she shamelessly offers in her own defense." There was a rumble of voices throughout the hall, the Bloodnamed whispering and muttering, a sinister sound.

The Loremaster spoke again. "Star Captain Dawn and Advocate Sinclair. Evidence has been presented to this solemn Council in support of the Inquisitor's charge. How do you respond to these allegations?"

Both Dawn and Ivan Sinclair stepped forward to join the Inquisitor on the rotating dais. The three of them turned slowly before the Steel Vipers' most honored Warriors.

"We submit to this honored Council that these charges are false in both nature and intent," Star Colonel Sinclair began. Judging by the angry sounds from the tiers, many of the Bloodnamed did not agree with Sinclair.

"The battle ROMs from the OmniMechs that survived the raid on Cumbres support the fact that another company of BattleMechs was present on the field. And you have all seen them in evidence. These tapes substantiate the truth of Star Captain Dawn's battle report. This unexpected force so tipped the balance of the battle that Star Captain Dawn was forced to withdraw or face total slaughter. It was not fear that motivated her retreat. Clan warriors have withdrawn from battles before, to fight on at another time. This evidence cannot be refuted."

"The so-called evidence from the battle ROMs is inconclusive at best," the Inquisitor said quickly. "All three of the recovered chips were damaged, and those that were even partially readable show only that opposing 'Mechs were engaged. No origins or even configurations were readable.

None of the telemetry data or visual images survived to refute the charge. Again I contend that this is a desperate lie, a cowardly excuse to explain Star Captain Dawn's own failings as a warrior. For a warrior there can be no excuses."

It was just as Dawn had expected, and she knew James Andrews was right. Her orders had been to crush the opposition, then destroy the Guards headquarters. It did not matter that her Trinary had met a stronger force than expected. War was no game. Dawn knew that. It was a contest from which the superior warrior emerged victor.

Ivan Sinclair pressed on. "We have submitted into the record the depositions of the warriors who survived the raid on Cumbres. They verify that the additional company of 'Mechs that struck on the south flank of the battle zone were painted in a different scheme and were actually fired upon by the Lyran Guards. That proves that these were raiders and not units associated with the Guards garrison on Cumbres. More important, it substantiates Star Captain Dawn's version of events." For the first time, Dawn heard murmurs that might have been in support of her. It lifted her spirits.

"You have all read those sworn statements, taken from brave warriors," Inquisitor Andrews said. "What Star Colonel Sinclair and his charge Dawn would have you believe is that those survivors support the lie of another raiding group. However, we know that all units, including the Twenty-fourth Lyran Guard, have individual paint schemes. These BattleMechs were simply another company of Guards, called in to shore up their defense.

"And, as for the allegations that several of the enemy 'Mechs fired on each other, you will note that the sworn statements of our warriors did not indicate any kills. Only weapons fire. I contend that these were merely friendly fire incidents, shots aimed at our own Steel Vipers that went awry. We all know that the warriors of the Inner Sphere lack our gunnery skill and prowess. In the heat of battle they accidentally fired on their own forces. None of this supports Star Captain Dawn's story in any way."

Star Colonel Sinclair stepped toward the Inquisitor. "Star Captain Dawn has an honorable history as a warrior in this Clan. Her codex supports that much. There is nothing in her past to show signs of the alleged cowardice or incompetence with which she is charged."

James Andrews spun to face the Advocate, narrowing his eyes and leaning back slightly on his heels. "Yes, we have all seen her codex. And we have seen that on Tukayyid she was just as cowardly and incompetent. There, she cannot even claim to have led three others to survival. No, on Tukayyid, only Dawn survived to tell the tale, for all the others perished, did they not?"

Advocate Sinclair's voice was even and cool. "Star Captain Dawn is not here to answer for Tukayyid. What happened there has no bearing on the events of Cumbres."

"Neg. I contend that her failure there is what led to her failure on Cumbres."

"Inquisitor," the Loremaster said finally, "you will refrain from any mention of Tukayyid," but it was too late. The damage was done. Mention of Tukayyid had stirred the embers among the Vipers, had touched on their mutual shame. The humiliation of that defeat was what now drove them so relentlessly to rebuild. This portrayal of Dawn as a failure who had risen in their ranks but who could now be purged would appeal to many of the Bloodnamed warriors. By eliminating her, they would also purge themselves of their own sense of shame and guilt. And by removing her, they also sent a message loud and clear to the few other Wardens in the Clan—their days were numbered. All around her Dawn heard the sound of angry muttering. Mention of Tukayyid had touched a deep chord among the Vipers.

Seeing Sinclair just about to launch another verbal attack, she reached up and placed one hand on his shoulder. Touching the ceremonial robe, woven from the skins of Arcadian vipers, lent her courage, despite the sense of impending doom.

"Thank you, Advocate," she said. "I release you from your charge." Her voice was calm, perfectly audible throughout the chamber. There was nothing more Ivan Sinclair could do. Nothing more to say. All she could offer to this Council was excuses, and Dawn knew that she herself would have scorned any warrior who hid behind such a petty and dishonorable defense.

"Star Captain—" Sinclair said, but Dawn shook her head

and forced a weak smile. Ivan Sinclair nodded and took a step back. Perhaps he understood.

She looked at Inquisitor Andrews, then peered around her at the faces barely visible in the darkness. "Loremaster, I speak for myself now. There is no more testimony to present. I stand ready for judgment and waive the right to speak in my own defense if the Inquisitor will also waive his right to any final remarks. I am a Steel Viper warrior, and I honor the ways of the Kerenskys that have brought us so far. Like all of you I was born and bred for war, it is all I know. My deeds speak for themselves, for I am a warrior bred and true. How you read those actions, I cannot dictate. But I offer no excuses." Her bold words stirred some in their seats to rise, ready to leap down onto the dais and fight her if necessary. She knew she had lost; now was the time to force them to end it all.

The Inquisitor smiled broadly and nodded. "I waive the closing comments, the evidence stands for itself. Let us bring this matter to a vote now."

The Loremaster spoke solemnly and with conviction. "Testimony in this matter is closed and sealed in accordance with our traditions. To the Council members gathered here and those far, I bid you cast your votes. May justice be served."

The voting took less than half a minute, electronically tallied in seconds. The Loremaster's voice echoed in the room, chilling Dawn to her bones. "Star Captain Dawn," he intoned, his voice deepened in the ritual manner. "you have been found guilty by a margin of nine to one."

The verdict was no shock. "I demand a Trial of Refusal," she said, speaking up loud and clear. "And let the time and place be now!"

She would be allowed to fight to reverse the verdict, but the opposing force could bid based on the margin of the vote. The murmurs from the gallery told her that many of the warriors were already beginning the process of bidding. Khan Perigard Zalman monitored his own video screen as the bids were made. Dawn stood on the rotating pedestal staring into the darkness.

After several minutes of intense activity all around him,

the Khan spoke again. "You will face odds of three to one. In the tradition of our people, the Inquisitor chooses the defenders of the verdict and has named Star Captain Stern Chapman and Star Captain Mitch Thibaudeau to represent the Council in this matter. We accept the time and place you name. Are you ready, Warrior Dawn?"

She noted that the Khan had already dropped her rank from his address. And she knew both of the warriors he named very well. *An Elemental and a MechWarrior.* Dawn did not expect to win the Trial, but that did not mean she would not try. She looked up at the Khan and nodded with all the calm and confidence she could muster. *They will see no fear in me because there is none, despite this verdict.*

As Dawn descended from the dais to meet Stern Chapman, the lighting came up slightly. Chapman was, beyond a doubt, the best Elemental warrior in the Steel Vipers, his genetic heritage and codex adorned with numerous victories. Even at Devil's Bath, he had managed to take out three ComStar BattleMechs before being knocked unconscious himself. He let fall his ceremonial robe and stood before her in knickers and tee shirt that emphasized his towering height and the powerful muscles of his body. At his height and weight, this Elemental was the equivalent of two warriors. Behind him, almost dwarfed by his comrade, was MechWarrior Thibaudeau. If Dawn survived the contest with Chapman, he would be up next to break her.

The Elemental warrior, a virtual mountain of muscle compared to her, wasted no time. With a speed almost shocking in a man of his size, he swept to Dawn's right, forcing her to twist to meet his attack. But Dawn was quick enough, her sharp chop hitting his right shoulder with a resounding crack. Though the blow would have felled any normal warrior, with Chapman there was more noise than damage. Himself a product of genetic engineering, the Elemental towered over her. And at twice her mass and pure strength, he merely took the hurt. Pivoting from her blow, he jammed backward at her with a powerful movement of his elbow. The pain was intense but the effect on her balance was the key.

She saw his left leg sweep out, but her move to evade

wasn't fast enough. The leg hit her right shin and sent her flying backward like a load of bricks. Reacting almost totally by reflex, she rolled away, just missing a pounding with both of his fists balled together. They struck the floor near her like a jackhammer, and Chapman winced in the pain from the impact but did not break off. Dawn swung her hand in a chop to the right eye, blinding him momentarily. As blood streamed from his eye, he lifted his cupped fists together again and jumped toward her, his whole massive body weight behind the assault.

Dawn kicked hard with both feet, hitting him in the chest and deflecting the attack, but at the same time rolling to one side and not seeing where he fell. When she turned to where she thought he should be, he wasn't there. At that moment his kick found its mark on the back of her head.

The impact lifted her body up and forward. Her eyes seemed to be looking down a long dark tunnel while in her ears was a deep buzzing. She felt the floor slap her face hard, but her arms and legs seemed helpless to block the fall. There was a salty taste in her mouth as she used the last reserve of her strength to roll over and stare up at the lights that glared down on her. Dizziness and pain wracked her head as she staggered drunkenly to her feet.

Chapman moved quickly around to face her and to deliver the final blow. She saw it coming and her only response was to leap at what seemed to her like a living wall of flesh and muscle tissue. She half-fell, half-punched as Chapman's furious fist slammed into her right cheekbone. Her blow did nothing, a mere bruise. His cut her cheek and she heard the sound of cracking. A tooth had shattered under the punch. She dropped to the floor like a rag doll, conscious, but no longer able to fight.

The buzzing in her ears seemed to drop slightly with each painful breath. Her mouth ached and the cool air on the exposed nerve of her tooth stabbed at her like a hot knife. She felt a hand grab her, lift her to a semi-standing position. Warm blood trickled down her face and she realized it was all over. Drawing a deep breath she tasted her blood and smelled the tang of sweat still in the air. She stood before

Khan Perigard, beaten and lost, yet forever unyielding. *I am innocent. This changes nothing.*

"This Trial of Refusal is over," Zalman said from inside the jaws of the Steel Viper mask. In Dawn's dazed state, he seemed to loom before her, more apparition than human. "You are judged guilty in the eyes of this Council, Dawn. I now pass sentence for all to hear.

"You are stripped of rank and caste from this day forward and banished from the ranks of Clan Steel Viper. Your name is not to be spoken, and your genetic material will be purged from the gene pool. No member of this Clan is to speak with you or acknowledge that you were ever spawned. I could offer you death, but that would be too quick an end. This banishment will forever remind you of those warriors who died by your hand. You will be taken by one of our merchant caste vessels to the nearest system from our territories and your name will never again be uttered by any member of this Clan. From this day forward you no longer exist in either our minds or our memory."

The Bloodnamed of the Steel Vipers rose to their feet and spoke in unison as Dawn scanned the near darkness. "Seyla," each one affirmed, one by one turning his or her face and body away from her. The sign of banishment. The eyes of the Bloodnamed would no longer acknowledge her. Only Star Colonel Ivan Sinclair did not immediately avert his eyes. Then, he too, slowly turned and would no longer see her.

Loremaster Stoklas stepped over to the codex reader and withdrew the circlet that stood for Dawn's Life as a Steel Viper warrior. He dropped it to the floor, pulled out his laser pistol, and shot the codex with a fiery bolt of red laser light. Dawn stared, too stunned and weak from the fight to respond. Her life as a Steel Viper was over. They had purged her as if she had never existed.

She fought to maintain her balance but a wave of dizziness overcame her. Dawn collapsed in pain.

Headquarters, Sixth Crucis Lancers RCT
Aux-Huards Plain
Valexa
Capellan March, Federated Commonwealth

"It's something we've got to take care of ourselves, Garth," Lieutenant-General Mel Aleixandre said. "You've seen the intelligence reports. The MIIO wants to put the blame on the Knights of the Inner Sphere simply because the raider 'Mechs were painted in their colors, but that's only because they want to wrap this whole thing up nice and tidy. Somebody just wants to file the matter away, get it off his desk, and out of sight because our intelligence people can barely keep their heads above water right now. They don't need something new sending them off on another merry chase." The General shook his head sadly. "Those very same reports also estimate only a twenty-five percent chance that those 'Mechs actually were Knights of the Inner Sphere."

Garth Hawkes nearly exploded. "Don't they want to do something about it? Don't they want to make whoever was responsible pay damn good and hard for killing our own people?"

"The intel boys have their hands full, Garth. They're scrambling trying to keep up with whatever little tricks Sun-Tzu has the Maskirovka and the Death Commandos playing in the Sarna March and the Tikonov region. They're also trying to keep tabs on the Skye region in case anyone else decides to try more funny business there. Not to mention—"

"You mean raiders from who knows where can just drop onto a Davion world, attack a Davion unit, and nothing will be done about it?" Hawkes couldn't believe what he was hearing.

"We're talking about politics here, Garth. Things are never black and white. Think about it—Joshua Maris is on New Avalon under the care of Victor Davion's top physicians. I'm not sure how the MIIO or anyone else could believe that Thomas Marik would raid the FedCom with the life of his heir in their hands. Maybe that's why there haven't been any formal concessions called for from the

Free Worlds League. The press and politicians call it a
Marik attack, but Prince Victor presents a calm, statesman-
like front. Things aren't always what they seem, Garth. And
they're not always simple."

The General crumpled up the sheaf of paper he'd been
holding. "No, Garth. If we want justice we're going to have
find a way on our own."

"What do you mean, sir?"

"The official reports put the blame on the Knights, but
you and I don't believe they were involved at all. It's just
not Thomas Marik's style. He hasn't come this far by pulling
off such hare-brained stunts. All right, so the MIIO doesn't
have the manpower to take this on right now. They're too
busy. Or maybe they just don't take it seriously enough. But
what if we sent one of our own to do some looking around?
And if that person could find something, then we could
come back and get some official action."

Aleixandre stared up at Hawkes for a moment before
speaking again. "I've been thinking about this a lot, Garth.
Not one of the House leaders has anything to gain by discrediting the Knights of the Inner Sphere. In the old days I
might have suspected ComStar, but Focht and the Primus are
totally focused on the Clan threat. No, I think it was someone from outside the inner circle, maybe somebody who
wants in so bad that he or she will try anything to make
trouble.

"What I propose is to send somebody undercover to Galatea, Outreach, Solaris VII—wherever mercenaries are hired.
I'd wager that whoever was behind the raid got his troops
from one of those places. Our man will go there looking for
work, keep his eyes and ears open, and try to turn up some
real leads."

Hawkes put both hands on the desk and leaned toward the
General. "I'm the only person for this mission, General.
Those were my men and women who died. I'm the only one
you can count on to go the distance, the only one who
wouldn't care about the risks. My comrades are gone, but at
least I could see them avenged. Maybe that would make up
for the fact that I wasn't out there with them when the end
came."

"You'll be on your own, Garth," the General cautioned. "I won't be able to toss you any support unless you can come up with some real, hard evidence. Then I'm going to need the Field Marshal to grant me authorization for a raid. We can cashier you for not being with your unit when it was attacked. For all intents and purposes, you will be alone. I can maintain your position in the unit on paper—for a while, at least."

Hawkes nodded. "I understand sir."

"Good. You leave in the morning." Aleixandre reached out and shook Hawkes's hand firmly. "Good luck, my boy. Your father would be proud of you."

Hawkes nodded, but he couldn't shake the feeling that he might never see General Mel Aleixandre again.

6

Standing in the elegant drawing room of the sprawling Winter Palace in the heart of Dormuth, Duncan Kalma suddenly felt the full import of where he was and who he was going to meet. Captain-General Thomas Marik. The man who had done what no one else ever had—create a semblance of unity in the Free Worlds League. For that he had won the respect of his people, including even men like Duncan, who had abandoned his homeland for a life of allegiance to no man.

Duncan looked around with real curiosity at the richly appointed room, with its gleaming dark walnut wainscoting and tiers of real hardcopy books. Lighting the huge chamber was a chandelier of several dozen candles as well as tapers flickering in ornate wall mounts all around the room. At the far end a roaring fire added its warm glow. Antiques were everywhere—Terran tables and chairs, ancient maps, real oil paintings, richly colored Andurien carpets and brilliant Shasta tapestries, curios in the shape of beasts no longer seen on any world, and more. Thomas was famous for his fascination and reverence for the past.

It was ironic, Duncan thought, that this man had risen to such heights, not only in the Free Worlds League, but even beyond, his prestige and power acknowledged across the Inner Sphere. It was not always so. As a Precentor of Com-Star, the quasi-religious order that once controlled all interstellar communications, his life must have been rather secluded. Then had come the bombing attack that took the life of his father, Captain-General Janos Marik. Thomas, too, was assumed dead when his body was not recovered after the explosion.

Eighteen months later he stunned Parliament by suddenly reappearing, healed and strong, claiming his right to the throne. He had been severely burned in the explosion, but the flames that had ruined his face seemed to have fired something powerful within his soul. Though untutored in either war or politics, Thomas Marik had assumed the mantle of the Captain-Generalcy, a precarious duty even in the best of times. Not only had he managed to hold his often turbulent realm together, but under his rule the Free Worlds League had prospered while the rest of the Inner Sphere only barely survived the Clan invasion.

Thomas would surely be remembered as one of the great Mariks, his popularity among the people even higher than what old Janos had enjoyed at the peak of his career.

Hearing the sound of footsteps Duncan turned to see the lanky form of Captain-General Thomas Marik enter the room. He was flanked on one side by an equally tall man with long, flowing white hair and on the other by the Knight who had visited the Kalma estate several days before. Harrison Kalma bowed. Duncan quickly mimicked his father's actions, trying to remember any shred of the court protocol he'd learned as a child. He'd never cared much for such things, never been good at them, and now he felt stiff and awkward.

"Such formality from an old friend is not expected," Marik said, placing his hand on Harrison Kalma's shoulder and prompting him to rise.

"It's good to see you again, Thomas," his father said. "I must admit it was a surprise hearing that you were back on Marik."

Thomas smiled, but he looked weary. "A matter of great importance has arisen and I wanted to be free of the many demands on Atreus in order to deal with it." He turned to face Duncan, who quickly bowed again.

"And you must be Duncan. I've heard a great deal about

you from General Milik," he said. "You certainly don't look like the rogue he's made you out to be."

Duncan smiled slightly, not sure what else to do. "It is an honor to meet you, sire," he returned firmly.

"I'm delighted you could come. Your special acquaintance with areas of the Periphery may be helpful this evening." Marik turned to the white-haired man. "Director Cherenkov, I believe you know everyone here except General Kalma's son."

Duncan stepped forward quickly and offered his hand while the Captain-General introduced him to Wilson Cherenkov, Director of SAFE, the League's intelligence arm. He also nodded to Rod Trane.

"Of course I thank you all for coming," Marik was saying, "but I must caution you—this meeting never took place."

All nodded their understanding, but Duncan noticed his father and Cherenkov staring suspiciously at each other like the longtime rivals they were. As the head of SAFE, Cherenkov had always resented Harrison Kalma's influence as Director of Military Intelligence of the LCCC.

"Let us sit," the Captain-General said, gesturing to a long table surrounded by high-backed chairs near the fireplace. He took a seat at the head, with his back to the roaring fire. Rod Trane and Duncan sat down to one side of him while General Kalma and Cherenkov took seats on the other. The flickering of the candles lit Marik's face strangely, but also softened the scarred ruin of his visage.

No one spoke as Director Cherenkov produced a small disk-like device, then held it out over the table as he activated it with a flick of his thumb. A light flashed green several times, and then he put the device away. "This room is clean, sire."

"Excellent," Thomas said, laying his hands palm down on the table top and leaning forward as he let his gaze travel around the group. "Gentlemen, I have brought you here to discuss a problem I would like to handle personally rather than delegating to advisors or to the military. As you have all heard by now, some mysterious raiders have made at least three separate strikes against the other Houses of the Inner Sphere, and these raiders came impersonating my

Knights. This cannot continue without irreparable damage to me personally and to the Free Worlds League politically, and that is why I intend to find out who is behind it and to stop them before more harm is done."

Duncan squirmed in his chair. This was obviously a high-level meeting, and he did not feel at all comfortable participating in such a discussion.

Harrison Kalma spoke first. "I agree with you about the seriousness of the situation, Thomas. Obviously, it couldn't have been the Knights because of the nature and timing of the raids. But others won't be so quick to realize that. What kind of reaction have you gotten outside Marik space?"

"All the other House leaders have filed formal protests and made the usual political gestures," Marik said. "They're doing exactly what I would do in their place, pointing an accusing finger and making veiled threats while their intelligence agencies scramble to learn whether or not my Knights really were involved."

"What has SAFE learned, Director Cherenkov?" Rod Trane asked, and Duncan noticed that his speech had become more clipped and enunciated, as though he had a special voice for speaking in the presence of his liege lord. "Have you come up with any intelligence on the identity of these mysterious raiders?"

The man next to Kalma shifted slightly as he leaned down to pull several thick stacks of paper from his briefcase on the floor. Watching him, Duncan remembered what he'd heard about Wilson Cherenkov. He and Thomas had been friends for many years, beginning when both were young acolytes of ComStar. The man was known for both his cunning and his total loyalty to the Captain-General.

Cherenkov took a pair of reading glasses from inside his jacket, and put them on as he spoke. "The strike on Shiro III did not yield any real clues except for one of the extensively damaged raider BattleMechs left behind after the strike on the Hussar headquarters. My men have crawled all over the 'Mech and were able to trace some of the repair parts to a shipment of refit kits stolen, apparently by pirates, in Liao space months ago."

Duncan spoke up for the first time. "What about the reactor core stamp? That should tell you who the 'Mech belonged to in the first place." The stamp was a specially coded optical-read imprint laser-etched into the interior of a fusion reactor. In essence, it was a serial number for the reactor and could conceivably be tracked by any number of databases, military and otherwise. Cherenkov shot Duncan a glance, then pulled out a sheaf from among his thick stack of papers.

"Yes, we thought of that," he said, laying the sheet before Trane and Duncan. "But the stamp tells us only that the 'Mech was originally part of the Armed Forces of the Federated Commonwealth and was sold for scrap to a mercenary unit, Lennox's Longriders. The Longriders tried to make it in the games on Solaris VII after falling on hard times about five years ago, but they weren't successful. The 'Mech surfaced again on Galatea and was officially listed as sold for parts a year ago. No trace of it since."

"Mercenaries then," Trane said, his voice dripping scorn. Duncan had heard that tone so many times in his own mercenary days that he resented it even now. Rod Trane obviously viewed mercs as second-rate, and beneath contempt.

Cherenkov shook his head. "Not necessarily, Captain. Whoever is behind these raids was simply smart enough to use a 'Mech like this rather than one that's more traceable."

"I think we can rule out the other Houses of the Inner Sphere, Captain-General," the elder Kalma put in.

Cherenkov sat back and removed his glasses. "Are you privy to some special information, General? Some special source I know nothing about?"

"No, Director Cherenkov. I've merely been analyzing the situation logically. Victor Davion has the biggest motivation to attack and discredit us, but he's got his hands full at home, let alone trying to trigger another war he can't hope to win."

"Perhaps he wasn't seeking to trigger a war but merely to discredit the Knights," Trane said.

"What could he hope to gain from that?" Duncan couldn't help putting in. "So what if the Knights are discredited? It doesn't reflect on the Free Worlds League as a whole, just on them as a unit."

"Not true," Thomas Marik said. "Ruining the reputation of the Knights hurts them, the League, and the rest of the Inner Sphere more than you can imagine, my boy. But perhaps I don't really know how the common man views my Knights. What would you say, Duncan?"

Duncan was sorry he'd opened his mouth, and looked quickly at his father, who was nodding for him to speak. *Fine,* he thought. *I'm as good as any to be the mouthpiece of the common man.* "I'd say many people view them as a kind of personal toy for you, sire. Yes, the Knights are good MechWarriors, but they also get the best equipment and the best training. I suppose some may also be wondering whether they might be the start of a private army, but I always figured you would probably turn them into an elite unit like the Death Commandos or the Combine's ISF."

Marik shook his head. "The reality is that the Knights of the Inner Sphere have very little to do with the military per se."

"I don't understand, sire."

"You've studied history, Duncan. You've surely read about the Star League and how it came to be. No, it wasn't a purely peaceful era and some problems could only be solved militarily, but what truly held the Star League together was not force of arms but a social ideal. A rise in the moral fiber of every person in the Inner Sphere. People began to value honor and the common good, not just power and national self-interest. That is what I hope to do with the Knights of the Inner Sphere, plant the seed for the founding of a new Star League."

Duncan blinked, realizing he didn't understand any of this at all.

"I did not forge the Knights as my sword," the Captain-General went on. "No, I intend them as a model of how humankind can find our proper relation to technology. In the past humanity's greatest challenge was to find our proper relation to Nature. In our day the challenge is to create a new relation between man and technology. Technology is soulless. Weapons—the technology of war—exist only as a means of destruction.

"And that's where the Knights come in. The Knights of

the Inner Sphere are a way to bring ethics and morality to bear on war and its technology. Instead of technology being the instrument of mindless destruction, it becomes the protector of mankind. The rise in moral character that I hope to see develop in my people, beginning with the Knights, can lay the foundation for the resurgence of a new Star League. Maybe not in my lifetime, but one day in the future. Another magnificent golden age." As Marik spoke, his eyes seemed to look far beyond this room, as if seeing the great day he imagined.

Harrison Kalma broke the long silence that followed. "If I understand you correctly, Thomas, you're suggesting that Victor Davion might want to destroy the Knights because of their potential as a movement for social change rather than because he wants to spark a war."

Marik nodded, obviously pleased that the General had caught his meaning.

"It's a possibility, sire," Cherenkov said, "but I have found no evidence to support it. Davion wouldn't have let one of his own prized units like the Sixth Crucis Lancers RCT get hurt so bad. They took significant damage in the attack, and lost key officers and troops."

"So that leaves Theodore Kurita and Katrina Steiner," Harrison Kalma said. "But Kurita is too preoccupied with the Clan threat and Katrina Steiner wouldn't sacrifice her own Twenty-fourth Lyran Guards. That shortens the list considerably, and leaves the Capellan Confederation. The Capellans are the only ones who haven't been attacked so blatantly." The General paused, obviously choosing his words carefully. "This is a difficult question, Thomas, but is it possible your future son-in-law might be behind these raids?"

Thomas shook his head. "I might have suspected Sun-Tzu, except for one thing—he has nothing to gain. He and my daughter will be married soon, so why would he begin creating problems with me now?"

Rod Trane spoke almost under his breath. "He is a Liao, sire."

"Yes, he is. But he's not like any Liao we've seen in the Inner Sphere for a long time. He has given me personal assurance that he was not involved. He has even provided SAFE with intelligence reports his own people gathered after the raids on their shipments of refit kits. No, Sun-Tzu Liao is not the individual behind this."

"It's my guess we're not facing any known government or foe, Periphery or otherwise," Harrison Kalma said.

Cherenkov nodded. "And I must concur, sire. We can't identify a connection to any of the Periphery governments, and the logistics involved with these attacks would also seem to argue against it. Given the timing of the raids we've got to be dealing with three companies or more of 'Mechs. Getting them in and around the Inner Sphere, even disguised as the Knights, is no small task."

"What about the Clans?" Trane asked. "Perhaps one of them wants to use these raids to turn the other Houses against us so they can hit us more easily."

"Don't forget Cumbres," Thomas said. "A Steel Viper unit also took a beating from these raiders."

"Perhaps it's the Clan they tried to purge, the Wolverines," Cherenkov said. "We know they showed up once in the Inner Sphere as the Minnesota Tribe. Perhaps some more of Kerensky's legacy has surfaced to haunt us again."

"That's not likely if they were using 'Mechs bought and refit on Galatea," Duncan said. "And no kin of the Wolverines would get that near the Clans."

The room went quiet for a long moment before Harrison Kalma again broke the silence. "We're looking at this the wrong way."

"What do you mean?" Cherenkov said.

"We're trying so hard to figure out who's behind these raids that we're forgetting it simply doesn't matter. What's important is how do we stop the attacks? How do we expose the true origins of the raiders? Sitting and guessing about who might be behind the raids is like aiming a gun into a crowd and hoping that we hit the guilty party."

"Don't you think we've been trying to determine that, Harrison?" Wilson Cherenkov said. "I've made this Priority Alpha for every SAFE agent in the field. We've gotten some leads, but nothing solid. Even our operatives on Outreach and Solaris haven't turned up anything solid. Rumors mostly, and

othing that points even remotely at who is behind these at-
acks."

"What rumors have surfaced, exactly?" Harrison Kalma
sked, knowing Cherenkov would hate having to reveal in-
elligence a rival hadn't been able to get on his own. But it
vas too late. The SAFE man had spoken up in front of the
Captain-General and would now have to show his hand.

"One of our operatives on Outreach reports rumors of
omeone doing major recruiting on Galatea, far from the
Dragoon hiring halls on Outreach. We got no details except
hat it was for a raid against a Periphery world known as
Herotitus."

Duncan knew both Galatea and Herotitus well. Herotitus
vas a world dedicated to the pursuit of sensual pleasures, a
place relatively untouched by the ravages of time and the
enturies of war that had devastated the rest of human space.
The old saying was, "On Herotitus anything goes, and usually does." He looked around at the little group gathered
ere and wondered how they'd fare on the highways and by-
vays of such a place.

The same went for Galatea. Though it had once been the
ub of mercenary hiring in the Inner Sphere, all that had
changed after the Mercenary Review and Bonding Commission had been established on Outreach. Now virtually all legal and legitimate hiring was done on Outreach under the
eyes and ears of the famous mercenary Wolf's Dragoons.
Galatea's economy had virtually collapsed, and what passed
for law and order was dealt out on its streets with guns and
knives. The only mercenaries who went there were tough,
desperate types who couldn't get the time of day from legitimate employers. Duncan had gone there himself looking for
work more than a time or two.

"Have you sent operatives to either of those worlds?"
Thomas asked.

"I have stationed several on Herotitus to learn whether a
raid actually occurs, but so far things have been quiet. If the
raid comes, we'll send a team to Galatea to track down
whoever's doing the hiring. But this is just one of hundreds
of leads, sire."

"Perhaps we could post the Knights along the jump routes

a raiding force might travel," Trane suggested. "Inspection of transports in our region of space might stumble across them, though it would probably be only blind luck if we actually found them."

Duncan couldn't resist. "With all due respect, gentlemen, I suspect that neither the two of you nor the whole rest of the entire Free Worlds Militia will uncover who is behind these raids."

Cherenkov shook his head angrily. "I don't know what your father has been telling you, son, but I'd say this situation is a bit beyond your experience. This is a matter for experts in intelligence and military operations."

"And that is why you will fail," Duncan said.

The Captain-General's face showed irritation mixed with curiosity. "If you have something to say, Duncan, I suggest you do so now."

"You're all looking at this up from here, at this level"—Duncan held his hand in the air horizontally at the height of his own head. "The problem is that the people you're dealing with are working down here"—he waved his hand just slightly lower than the table surface. "They can see you, anticipate your reactions, and counter them easily. But you're too far removed from their world to do the same.

"These raiders are desperate people, not honorable warriors like the Knights of the Inner Sphere. Oh, they're probably skilled enough—hell, they took on some pretty sharp units and did them serious damage, but they aren't the kind to get work from any known agency or government.

"They operate the backwaters, probably out in the Periphery, more like pirates than warriors. Many of them probably served in our militaries and know the routines we'll use to search them out, so they'll be able to dodge those approaches right off the bat. You've been looking on Solaris and Outreach and wasting time. Anyone involved in raids like these doesn't hang around civilized places like that."

"Sounds like the scum of the galaxy," Trane said.

"Not scum. We're talking about professional soldiers who have, for whatever reason, become outlaws or desperate, or both. Scum would never have been able to pull off impersonating the Knights. Scum couldn't have managed to ambush three elite regiments and a Trinary of Clan Warriors and survived without leaving so much as a trace of their true origins."

Cherenkov had been listening thoughtfully. "Interesting," he said, "but it's just more conjecture and doesn't get us any closer to stopping these raids."

"Wrong," Harrison Kalma said. "There are ways to deal with this kind of element of society." He looked to Thomas, who nodded for him to continue.

"You've heard the old saying, it takes a thief to catch a thief. If Duncan's right, we're dealing with renegades who associate only with their own kind. So if we want to catch them, we should manufacture our own team of renegade mercenaries, then infiltrate their ranks from within. From the inside, we can learn how to put an end to this dangerous game."

"I volunteer the Knights of my company to pose as such a unit," Trane said eagerly.

Cherenkov laughed softly. "My dear Captain, you and your Knights could never pose as rough and ready mercenaries living on the edge of the law. You'd be spotted light years away."

"I assure you that my people are qualified for any mission, especially one as important as this. It's not just the Captain-General's honor at stake."

Harrison Kalma held up his hands for peace. "Director Cherenkov and I are not often on the same side of any issue, Captain Trane, but in this matter I have to agree. On their own, the Knights of the Inner Sphere could not pose as outlaw mercenaries.

"However, what if the leader of such a unit were someone who had lived in the Periphery as a mercenary and knew his way around? Someone who could take even the spit and polished Knights and turn them into a team able to infiltrate whoever's running these raids." As he spoke the elder Kalma eyed his son squarely.

Duncan started to protest, but Cherenkov beat him to it.

"You can't be serious, Harrison. What this mission needs is a SAFE operative, an individual trained in intelligence and espionage. If it's your son you've got in mind, the only thing he's done until now is wander around the Periphery getting into trouble."

Thomas Marik smiled. "Actually, Wilson, you've just made a splendid case for Duncan Kalma. His experiences and knowledge of the Periphery should make him able to blend in easily with the element we're looking for."

"Sire . . ." Once again Duncan was interrupted, this time by Trane.

"Captain-General, you would see fit to place my Knights under the leadership of this man?" He pointed a finger at Duncan.

"No, not yet anyway. We don't know whether or not our information about a raid on Herotitus is accurate. But what if I sent you and Duncan there to investigate and be on hand should the raid materialize? In the meantime the rest of your company will come here and await word. If there is a strike in the Periphery, we'll send a team under cover to Galatea to find out who's behind the hiring and try to infiltrate them."

Marik studied Duncan's face for a moment. "I would never force you to do this," he added.

It wasn't being sent to the Periphery that bothered Duncan. No, the issue was that he wouldn't be working for himself. He'd always been his own master. Now they wanted him to do his bit for king and country.

He stared back at the other four men who were watching him intently. Marik and his father waited expectantly, Wilson Cherenkov looked skeptical, and Trane showed that he wanted no part of Duncan. If anything, that was what finally decided Duncan.

"I will do as you ask, Captain-General, but only on the condition that I'm in charge. Period. We go to Herotitus, see if anything develops, and report to you here. Meanwhile the Knights gather here on Marik in case we need to follow up more leads on Galatea."

Trane looked nearly ready to burst with anger and frustration, yet he managed to maintain his courtly composure. "My liege, I beg you to reconsider. Duncan Kalma is not the right person for this mission. He had the chance to serve you once, but he abandoned the Free Worlds League and went off to seek his fortune in the Periphery. Now you place the future of the Knights in his hands? Surely there are others better suited than he?"

Thomas Marik seemed unmoved. "Gentlemen, I realize that this is a gamble, but right now it's the best shot we have. There may well be men better suited than Duncan Kalma for this kind of operation. But none of them are here right now. Furthermore, this mission must remain secret. I don't want to take the chance of revealing the plan to still more people. Besides, bringing in someone else would take weeks of searching and travel that we simply do not have.

"You and all the other Knights made a solemn pledge to me, Captain Trane. What I'm asking of you now is no different from any other service you have undertaken in my name."

"Of course, my liege," Trane said, bowing his head.

"Excellent," Thomas Marik returned, standing up to show that the discussion was over. "You will depart for Herotitus as soon as possible. I can put my family's own merchant ships at your disposal, plus a code that will authorize the captains of those ships to cooperate with you one hundred percent. This will also keep my enemies in Parliament from trying to interfere with the plan. In the meantime a contingent of Knights will travel here to be on hand in case you learn something there."

Duncan wasn't sure if he should be glad or sorry at the way this thing had turned out. Suddenly he was involved in affairs far beyond his ken, and he had been brash enough to ask for leadership of the operation. At the very least this little caper would take him back to the Periphery and would surely offer an adventure or two to add to his belt.

"Duncan," Thomas Marik said, startling the younger man back to reality. "Your father and I have been friends a long time. I trust you as I do him. I'm sure you would never violate that trust."

Duncan leaped to his feet and quickly bowed. "You can count on me, sire," he said, wondering what in the name of Gaffa he'd gotten himself into.

7

Cavern of the Skull
New St. Andrews, The Periphery
Rimward of the Circinus Federation
18 April 3057

The office deep in the bowels of the Cavern of the Skull was empty except for Stefan Amaris and Varas seated at the desk where they had done so much of their planning until now. Laid out before them was a boldly colored map of the Inner Sphere showing the governments and territories that had once been united under the banner of the Star League. The room was dimly lit, making it difficult to read the map. But that did not matter to Varas. They'd been over all this dozens of times. Nothing had changed—not in his mind anyway.

"The First Company of the Republican Guards is one jump from Herotitus, my lord. They can jump in, carry out the raid, and have the ship recharged within two weeks."

The self-proclaimed Star Lord was studying the map as if he could see something invisible to other eyes. He stared at the arrangement of stars in and around Herotitus, fingers drumming on the table. Amaris slowly raised his head and looked at Varas. "I am concerned."

Varas felt his anger rise immediately, but he did not give into it. *He is not a military man, yet constantly questions my orders. He is a scholar, a dreamer. Military operations are my area of expertise. One day, I will not have to curb my anger. One day, I will command.* "What is your concern, Star Lord?" he said mildly.

Stefan Amaris pointed to Herotitus on the map. "Security.

We've been planning this raid for so long, how can we be sure the plan won't be leaked in some way? Perhaps it would be best to reschedule the attack or select another target."

"Your concern is well placed, lord," Varas replied carefully. "But I can assure you that the name of our target has not gone beyond a small number of our staff. Our recruiter on Galatea had to know since it was his job to find troops with the necessary transport. I know him well and have utmost confidence in his discretion. Also we have seen no' large-scale troop movements on the part of any of the House governments.

"If someone were anticipating our action, we'd be seeing at least a regiment of front line troops moving toward Herotitus. Our operative on the planet has thus far reported no troop arrivals on-world. It is safe to assume, for now anyway, that no one has learned of our intentions." What Varas did not say was what he had expressed so many times before, albeit unsuccessfully. Sooner or later the leaders of the Great Houses would begin to look for them. Fortunately, he had provided a number of contingencies for when that day came. The key was to have their forces organized and well-trained by the time they came hunting.

"I have your word then. This strike will be executed like the others?"

"Of course, my liege."

"A man's word is his bond, eh, Varas? Do not fail me."

"I will not fail, lord. Herotitus is only lightly defended. The raid can't help but be a stunning success. Once again the rest of known space will blame the Knights of the Inner Sphere."

"Good." Amaris began to study the map again. "Any word from our other agents?"

"It's been several weeks since we lost contact with our team on Luthien. They've picked up none of our encoded messages."

"Do you think they've been uncovered?"

"It's possible. The ISF is everywhere. They've either been detected or are under such tight surveillance that they don't dare communicate. Either way, though, they can be assumed to be neutralized, at least for the time being."

Amaris frowned deeply. "That bodes ill for us."

"Yes. Fortunately the team that was sent in knows nothing about our base of operations or your identity. Even if tortured, there is little they can reveal. But this does hurt our timetable. It will take considerable time to recruit and prepare another team. The news from Sian, however, is very good. Our team sent a coded message that they've managed to set up operations in a small apartment only a short distance from the Celestial Palace. On New Avalon, our squad has found employment and are blending in with the locals."

"And the team on Atreus?"

"Oddly enough they report that Thomas Marik has not been seen in public for ten days or so. Official reports indicate that he is still on-world, but I suspect he's taken a trip or is sick."

Amaris laughed. "He's gone into hiding. He knows that his precious Knights are in peril. The pressure is starting to build. Soon he'll be forced to make a stand politically to defend his precious Knights. In the end, they will be sacrificed on the altar I have created."

"If I may, Star Lord, ask a question of you?"

Amaris tilted his head slightly to one side, his balding head reflecting the dim yellowish light of the room. "Proceed."

Varas chose his words carefully. "We could have struck at any one of the Inner Sphere governments. We could have discredited any one of the elite units belonging to any of the Houses. You chose the Knights of the Inner Sphere. If I may, what is your quarrel with House Marik and the Free Worlds League?"

Amaris stared at him for a long moment, leaving Varas listening to each beat of his heart as he wondered whether he'd crossed the fine line. Slowly, Stefan Amaris leaned back in his chair and smiled at his officer. "Ah yes, the Knights," he said, and his smile grew even broader. "Thomas Marik's bold experiment. Most people see them as an elite military unit. Isn't that the case with you?"

Varas nodded. It was true, they were simply another elite house unit.

"Well, they are more than just a regiment of MechWarriors. The Knights pose the greatest threat to my new vision of a Star League. Of all the regiments of BattleMechs poised throughout the Inner Sphere, they alone could stand in my way. Because of that, they must be disgraced and ruined, utterly destroyed."

"How—"

"I know what you're thinking, Varas. How could they pose a threat to a movement like mine? But remember, I am a scholar of history. Thomas Marik did not create these so-called knights as a military force so much as a force for change. He, like I, realizes that empires can be forged in one of two ways, and we have each chosen our own approach. His is a ground swell. He hopes to use the Knights to create a new social order.

"I, on the other hand, have based my plans on leadership. It is leaders who create empires, who inspire movements. It is the leader who uses his power to generate confidence in his people, to keep them united around him and their common purpose so that they can rise to great deeds. I will strip the Inner Sphere of its tired old rulers. Then, in one fell swoop, I will forge an empire that can stand against and crush even the might of the Clans. The people will flock to me because I offer them a future, a vision, a dream. Tell them what they want to hear, and they will follow." His voice trailed off in a way Varas found almost chilling.

"We must destroy the reputation of the Knights so that their movement dies and cannot stand against you, is that correct?"

Amaris nodded. "With my understanding of the forces of history and your military prowess, we now stand on the brink of freeing mankind from the tyranny of the House Lords and the misery of centuries. At last humanity can look forward to freedom."

Galaport
Galatea
Skye March, Federated Commonwealth

Hermann Bovos stepped off the transport DropShip's landing ramp onto the tarmac of Galatea's primary spaceport and drew a long breath of the planet's air. It was heavier than the processed air he'd been breathing aboard the DropShip during the journey, damper, and more heady. It was hot too, Galatea warmed by its fiercely brilliant white sun. His nostrils stung slightly at the smell of rotting trash and garbage, his eyes watering slightly as he looked around.

In its prime nearly half a century before, the city of Galaport had been the hub of activity on busy Galatea. What Bovos now saw framed against the purple evening sky were buildings left abandoned and decaying, with smoke rising from the city prime. Where the spaceport had once been bustling with the coming and going of dozens of mercenary units who traveled to Galatea to find and negotiate new contracts, now there were only tall weeds growing through cracks in the tarmac's edge.

When Wolf's Dragoons took over the planet Outreach and the governments of the Inner Sphere shifted their mercenary-recruiting efforts to that world, Galatea nearly collapsed. The mercenary trade had been the basis of its economy, but the only units who came here now were those too inferior to compete on Outreach, or those who would not or could not go through legal channels to be hired. Where Galatea had once been the Mercenary's Star, it was now a virtual den of desperate men and women who didn't care whether or not they lived within the law.

Following the other two DropShip passengers across the tarmac, Bovos had no idea what the decrepit spaceport might offer in the way of security. His only weapons were a knife and his father's laser pistol, but he had no wish to surrender either one. On the way out he passed what might once have been a security checkpoint, but it was unmanned and looked as if it had been that way for years. Hermann Bovos could have carried a light anti-'Mech rocket off that ship and with him into the city. And that meant the people he met here could also be armed with almost anything.

The streets outside the spaceport were in no better repair. Many of the buildings were abandoned or boarded up. Those still functioning tended to be bars, pawn shops, and what appeared to be houses of prostitution, or worse.

The few locals Bovos picked out were recognizable by their scrubbed and neat appearance. Mostly he saw every kind of mercenary, from the dangerous to the down and out. Some stood leaning against the facades of various taverns and bars. Their uniforms were often tattered and soiled and much the worse for weeks or months of neglect. Some bore the patches and insignia of rank, though Bovos seriously doubted that any of these individuals had ever been officers during their legitimate military careers. The assortment of patches were more often the insignia of long-forgotten and disbanded mercenary units. Most did not even have that much, only the darker places where the insignia had once been, now torn off and discarded.

As Bovos passed one such group, one of the men stepped directly into his path. He looked like he hadn't shaved in at least a week and was rank with the odors of beer and sweat. Bovos stopped dead, immediately on guard.

"Can I help you, stranger?" he said, half expecting the man to start a fight for no good reason.

"You new around here?" the man asked.

"Yes, friend. Is there a problem?"

"I'm the guy you're looking for. Black Jack Barton. Best 'Mech jock in a hundred light years." Black Jack Barton extended his hand. Bovos shook it, not fully understanding.

"I wasn't expecting to meet anyone here," he replied.

"Sure you were," Barton said. "You're here to hire, ain'tcha?"

Bovos ran his eyes quickly over the man's uniform, wrinkled and dirty in contrast to his own clean and well-creased green fatigues of the Second Oriente Hussars. "You've got me wrong, friend. I'm not here to hire, I'm looking for work myself."

Barton's face went from hopeful to angry. He looked

Bovos over from head to foot. "Good luck," he said as he turned to walk away. "You're gonna need it."

Bovos watched him go, feeling a cool breeze over his face as the first splatter of a storm moved over the dank and dingy city. He adjusted his shoulder pack and stepped into the street, hoping the hotel across the way would offer him clean but cheap quarters. For the first time in many years, Hermann Bovos felt very much alone.

8

Hermann Bovos took a seat in the booth and checked his surroundings. The patrons of the Lazy Lighthorseman looked far from reputable, but seemed totally uninterested in him one way or the other. The woman he was to meet had insisted on a place where she wouldn't be recognized. Bovos figured the Lighthorseman was as good as any because it was a haunt of techs rather than MechWarriors.

The waitress came over to his table, her jaws continually moving as she slowly chewed her gum without closing her mouth. Her arms were bare, tattooed with the names of what Bovos guessed were former paramours—probably long gone or dead or forgotten while she toiled on in this broken-down bar in the proverbial armpit of the Inner Sphere.

"Whatcha want, big guy?" she asked, letting some leg show through the high slit in her well-worn skirt.

"Northwind Red," Hermann replied.

"Big spender," she said, returning with his mug less than a minute later.

"Run it on a tab," he told her as she laid the bill on the table.

"No tabs, good-lookin'. We got enough problems with people don't want to pay for one drink, let alone a whole night's worth. Cash on the barrelhead." Bovos nodded and slapped down a C-bill.

It had taken him a week to arrange a meeting with one of

the dozen or so mercenary recruiters who operated on Galatea. Unlike Outreach, those who came here recruiting did not want their presence advertised. And usually with good reason. Most of their contracts were for jobs well beyond the law of any Inner Sphere government. Piracy, assassinations, subversion, kidnapping—every dark twist of mankind's tortured id could be bought and sold in the bars and streets of Galaport. His contact that night, Clare Lieb, was one of these.

Bovos knew the odds were against her being the person who would lead him to the raiders who had struck Shiro III. But he was so new at all this, the life of an outlaw mercenary. He was going to have to learn the ins and outs if he was to survive and find out what he'd come to learn.

The woman entering the bar wore a long hooded cloak against the nightly rains common on Galatea at this time of the year. As she pushed back the hood, Bovos saw that she was in her early fifties, worn and weathered, tanned from years in the fiery climate of Galatea. Her hair was a shocking white, worn short. She also wore thick glasses and an expression that told the patrons bellied up against the tarnished rail of the Lighthorseman bar that she was not someone to be toyed with. The shoulder holster exposed as she unfastened her cape further erased any lingering doubts.

Lieb walked over to where Bovos was sitting in a dark corner of the place. She stood there for a moment staring at him, then asked curtly, "You Bovos?"

"Lieutenant Hermann Bovos," he said, extending his hand. She looked at it, ignored the formality, and dropped into the chair opposite him. Bovos slowly withdrew his hand. "You must be—"

"Yeah, I'm her. Don't use my name here. The last thing I need is someone overhearing you. I'd never offer a job to any of the trash in this place, but they'd swamp me if they knew I could. I'm pretty particular about who I hire."

"So I hear," Hermann said. According to the grapevine that twisted its way through the bars and streets of Galatea, Clare Lieb was looking for a few mercenaries to pull off a mission in the Draconis Combine. That was all the detail he had, but he was hopeful. Perhaps, just maybe, this was the same group that had hit Shiro III. If not, she might know who was hiring for those jobs.

"Your background is one of the few around here that checks out," she said, tossing his data disk across the marred table top. "I have some friends who have some friends, and they confirm that you really were a Lieutenant in the Second Oriente Hussars. Not bad. So, let me be blunt, what are you doing here?"

Bovos's eyes narrowed. "Personal reasons."

"You're going to have to do better than that, Bovos."

"I'm looking for work. I want a job with some challenge. The stuff you can pick up on Outreach is too easy. I want something with some meat to it." He took a long draw of his Northwind Red, licking the excess from his lips.

Lieb sat back and took her time crossing her arms, then chuckled, probably the one thing he wouldn't have expected her to do. "Just what I thought, a digger." She pushed the chair back from the table and stood, obviously about to walk out on him.

"What in the hell is a 'digger'?" Bovos demanded.

"You really are a newbie, aren't you? A digger, a mole, a plant. Spy-boy. We see them here on Galatea all the time. Plants from any one of the intelligence agencies of the Inner Sphere. I must admit you're the only one I've met from the Free Worlds League who stood out so badly though. You better let your boss know he needs to do a better job in cover-up training."

Hermann stood. "You think I'm a spy?" He was stunned.

"Of course. But a pretty sorry one. A guy like you won't last long in a place like this. If I were you, I'd be seeking a way to get my tush off this rock before somebody decides to take revenge for some old wrong out on your young head."

Bovos reached out and gripped her arm to keep her from walking away. "You're wrong. I'm no spy. I'm just looking for work."

Lieb looked pointedly at his hand on her arm and opened her cape wider to give him a clear view of the pulse laser pistol sitting in its holster. "Listen here, Bovos, or whatever your real name is, your story doesn't hold water with me."

Several of the other patrons looked up briefly, also caught sight of the gun, then quickly returned to their drinks. "I've got some serious business to conduct with some mercenaries who aren't spending their time squealing to some spy-agency."

"I'm not a spy," he said through gritted teeth, keeping hold of her arm despite the threat of the Sunbeam pistol.

"Prove it," she replied.

That caught him off guard even more than the accusation. The last thing he'd expected was to be taken for a SAFE agent. How in the name of Gaffa's Ghost did you refute something like that? He stared at her and felt his face grow warm with frustration and anger.

"I—I can't. No matter what I say or do you're not going to believe me, are you?"

"No."

He swallowed his anger, which seemed to burn its way down though his chest and into his belly. "Fine then. Go— leave. But before you do, let me ask you this. This town is bulging with 'Mech pilots who haven't had half the career I have. You checked me out, you know I'm legit on that score. Can you really pass that up?"

Clare Lieb listened carefully, then stared back at her arm. Hermann released his grip and she sat down. He wasn't sure what part of what he'd said had gotten to her, but at least she was still willing to talk.

Lieb planted her elbows on the table and cradled her chin in her hands. "Why don't you tell me first why you're really here, Bovos? Try the truth this time. I'm a good listener if the story is good."

"All right, I did lie about that much," he confessed apprehensively. "I'm here looking for a recruiter, somebody who ran a mission against my old unit before I mustered out."

"Go on," she said.

"I've seen them in combat and I want to sign up with them." Bovos could tell by the wincing expression on Lieb's face that she wasn't buying it. But she didn't get up again and seemed to be waiting for him to say more.

"I didn't do the hiring for anybody heading for Shiro III," Lieb told him. "There's not many of us in the recruiting racket here on Galatea, not anymore. The job I was hiring for was a little Periphery op. And you can drop that line about trying to hire in with these bandits because they impressed you, Bovos. You've got something else written all over your face."

Bovos shook his head, realizing he was no closer to finding the raiders who had ambushed and killed his lancemates. "You're right," he said finally, realizing he was going to have to tell her the truth. "I don't want to work with them, I want revenge. They lured us into a trap and wiped out my lance, one by one. I almost bought it myself. Somehow I survived, but I was the only one out of my command." There was a ripple of bitterness in his voice, anger as he couldn't help remembering the day of the attack.

"I've heard about the raid. Hell, everyone's heard something about it. According to the reports it was old man Marik's Knights."

Bovos shook his head again. "They were painted up that way, but I don't think so. The Knights get new, top of the line 'Mechs, but these guys all had refits. Besides, nothing can make me believe that the Captain-General would use the Knights against his own countrymen."

"The press doesn't see it that way."

"Damn the press to hell and back. I was there. I saw them."

Lieb gave him a pencil-thin smile, the closest thing she ever got to a full grin. "Listen to me, Bovos. Spending your life looking for revenge can be pretty lonely. Most of 'em like that just seem to dry up, get mean, and then get old and sloppy before they go off to die. I need 'Mech jocks and I'd say you're one who was in the wrong place at the wrong time. Sign on with me. Within six months you'll forget all about going after revenge."

Bovos was listening hard. Maybe she was right. Would he become just a bitter man looking to right a wrong that he never could or would? No. This wasn't just a matter of simple revenge. The men who'd died in his command had been murdered, the deck stacked against them from the start. He took a sip of his Northwind Red, then sat staring at the mug for a while before turning back to Clare Lieb. "I wish I could, but this is something I've got to do."

She nodded slightly. "What will you do next?"

"I'm not sure. But I believe that whoever hit my unit must have been recruited here. No legitimate mercs would undertake that kind of mission, posing as a friendly unit and all."

Lieb's face drew tight as she rubbed her chin in thought. "If you're gonna make it here there's a few things you can do to flush out whoever *is* doing the hiring for those kinds of raids. Galatea runs a series of games, tournaments."

"Yeah, I saw a poster for one. Looks like the kind of 'Mech duels they run on Solaris."

Lieb chuckled at his comment. "Son, what we've got on Galatea hasn't got a shred in common with what you see on the holovid from Solaris. Those are formal matches in specialized arenas. This here is the minor leagues. These guys play for keeps. Nasty stuff too. A lot of MechWarriors never make it out of the arena. Those that do find their 'Mechs blasted apart and have little in the way of funding or spares to keep them going. Still, if you fight well and stand out, somebody's going to want to hire you. Get hooked up with some of the mercenary units that are forming here, and eventually you might find the people who did your unit in."

"Sounds good," Bovos said, his spirits suddenly rising. "How do you get into these games?"

Lieb looked around the bar to make sure no one was listening. "I don't do this for just anybody, but I do have a few contacts who might be able to help you get started—with a good word from me."

Hermann Bovos leaned forward, hanging on every word that she said.

Commercial DropShip **Levine's Star**
Orbital Entry Approach
Herotitus, The Periphery

Duncan walked up to the stateroom and knocked on the door. The trip to Herotitus had taken over two weeks, thanks in part to a command circuit of JumpShips the Captain-General had put at their disposal, a circuit that would await their return as well. This trip would normally have taken much longer, with the JumpShips needing at least a week to recharge their solar batteries at each stop.

Now that they were only a few hours from Herotitus, Duncan knew he had to try and speak with Rod Trane again. It was a matter of necessity, not just small talk.

The two always seemed to rub each other the wrong way, and had from the minute they'd met. A part of Duncan wanted to put an end to it, even if it meant beating the hell out of the high and mighty Sir Knight of the Inner Sphere. Another part of him almost enjoyed the tension. It wasn't hard to figure out why Rod Trane disliked him so. Trane was nothing if not proud of being a knight. To him Duncan must seem like so much mercenary scum, and he must deeply resent having to work under him. *Regardless,* thought Duncan, *we're going to be operating on my turf, the Periphery. I don't want this white knight to get the both of us killed because his little ego is sensitive.*

At his knock, the door to Trane's cabin opened a crack, letting Duncan peer in. He was impressed at how pristinely clean and orderly the tiny stateroom had been maintained. Even the two books on the tight drop-cot bed seemed to be laid out symmetrically. Duncan laughed to himself, thinking about the contrast to his own cabin.

"Yes," Trane said, still not opening the door all the way.

Duncan gave the door a little push. "We need to talk. We're only a few hours from planetfall and I thought I'd fill you in on what I know about Herotitus."

"I've thoroughly scanned the intelligence data SAFE provided," Trane said. "I doubt you could add anything to those reports."

Duncan grinned and stepped into Trane's room, just fitting past the other man's attempt to block his entry. "Oh really?" He walked over to the meticulously made bed and slouched down onto it.

"Did those SAFE reports tell you how the casinos are rigged? Did they tell you that the police chief in New Hedon is on the take from three different gangs and often sets up travelers like us on trumped-up crimes to extort money from their families? Did those SAFE reports tell you about the illegal slave market they run there?"

Trane closed the door, crossed his arms and leaned against it. "No, they didn't."

Duncan gave a short laugh. "And that's just the tip of the iceberg."

"Why didn't the reports mention any of this?"

Duncan shrugged as he scanned the hardcopy books. One was by someone named Patton and the other by a Chinese author he'd never heard of. "SAFE doesn't know everything."

Trane frowned. "Well, what you've just described is barbaric. Apparently everything they say about the Periphery is true."

"Like what?"

"It's a place beyond the pale. Uncivilized. Lawless. The people are barbarians, with living conditions to match. The technology's years behind what we've got in the Free Worlds League. And its people are often fugitives from the law with no ties to moral decency."

Duncan felt a pang of pity for Trane. "You're an odd man, Trane. I heard Thomas Marik describe his vision, one that you share, a vision that the Knights are a social force rather than a military one. Yet now I find you to be someone who lacks faith in what he's allegedly dedicated his life to."

"Lacks faith? I resent that remark, Kalma, especially from someone who's only here because of who is father is. Lacks faith indeed."

"Let me say this and say it only once," Duncan said, curbing his urge to punch Trane in the mouth. "I'm here because of me, not my father. The Captain-General invited me personally. And on my original point, yes, you're judging these people on where they live rather than who they are. I'm willing to bet you've never even been to the Periphery."

"Never. And the sooner we leave the better, as far as I'm concerned."

"For someone who's part of an elite legion bent on changing the social structure of the Inner Sphere, you sure have a limited view of things."

"What do you mean?"

Duncan had obviously struck a nerve. *Good,* he thought. *Let him simmer.*

"I'll grant you, the Periphery is a frontier of sorts, but you don't have to look down on the people and their way of life. These folks may be working with inferior technology, but they make up for it in sheer bravery and determination. Sure, some are criminals, but a lot of them are farmers and miners and other kinds of honest working people who hope that one day their children will prosper because of their hard work.

"You studied the history of the Star League. Remember it took twenty years and the entire Star League Defense Force to bring the Periphery under the League's rule. These people are proud and independent. With an attitude like yours, they'll kill you as surely as look at you."

Trane was, for the moment, speechless, but Duncan knew that winning a battle wasn't the same as winning the war. He sprang to his feet almost nonchalantly and reached past Trane for the door tab. "I'll see you when we touch down." To his surprise Trane reached out and grabbed his wrist tightly.

"Not yet," he said. "Our discussion isn't over."

Duncan reached down and gave the skin of Trane's wrist a vicious pinch. "I think it is." Trane's reflexes kicked in and he let go of Duncan's hand. Both men stood holding their sore wrists.

Duncan looked at Trane squarely and firmly. "You hate me, don't you?"

Trane surprised him by shaking his head. "No, not hate. But I don't respect you."

"Same thing."

"No, it's not."

"Regardless, Captain Trane," Duncan said, "on this mission you report to me. We don't have to like each other at all, but I do expect you to follow the orders of Thomas Marik." With that he reached out and hit the switch to open the door.

This trip might just be worth my while after all, he thought as he pushed past the Knight of the Inner Sphere.

9

New Hedon
Herotitus
The Periphery
30 April 3057

The spaceport in New Hedon was little more than a big black tarmac surrounded by a small scattering of warehouses. From the spaceport at its center the city sprang outward in all directions. With the morning sun beaming down on them, Duncan Kalma and Rod Trane descended the ramp and were immediately approached by a man handing out pamphlets. Duncan nodded and took one, as did Trane.

"What's this?" Trane said.

Duncan took the leaflet and carefully folded it before putting it into his back pocket. "Advertisement for the Mother Lode Casino. Great place, from what I remember."

Trane wadded his into a small ball and stuffed it into a pouch in his carry-on bag. "We won't have time for such foolishness."

Duncan grinned broadly. "Like hell. I plan to make time. Besides, we're here to see if this planet gets hit by the fake Knights. According to my calculations, we have a day or so before they were supposed to hit, according to the SAFE report anyway."

"You can go to a casino and waste your time and money, Kalma. But right now we need to find customs, get cleared, and find a base of operations."

"Already taken care of," Duncan said.

"Oh really?" Trane reverted to the arrogant tone that served to cover his surprise or annoyance whenever Duncan managed to get the better of him.

"Yes. I took the liberty of booking a room at The Bismarck, a hotel not far from here. I've stayed there before. It's an older place, but isn't totally lacking in either amenities or charm, and it's got a great bar. And, as for customs, there aren't any."

"No customs office?" Trane asked in surprise. "How do they keep people from smuggling in personal weapons or other goods?" As he spoke, Trane's eyes scanned the surrounding area, apparently hoping to spot a customs official simply to prove Duncan wrong. But, except for the maintenance crews, they were quite alone.

Duncan gestured in a wide sweep that took in the whole of New Hedon like a ringmaster opening the circus. "Welcome to the Periphery," he said.

At one time the Bismarck Hotel had probably been a showplace, even in a city on a frontier as remote as Herotitus. It had obviously been built centuries before, when mankind had been expanding outward from Terra and still in the first flush of colonization. An era when men and women of the Periphery believed that their backwater worlds would one day be thoroughly developed as the frontier of the Inner Sphere continued to expand outward.

Then came the collapse of the Star League and all that changed.

The outward expansion died as the dreams of the Star League went up in the flames of the Succession Wars. No longer a way-station on an expanding frontier, Herotitus became frozen in time on the border with the great unknown. The Bismarck showed the signs. Even decades of obvious neglect could not totally diminish the splendor of what must once have been an elegant lobby. Remnants of past eras, paintings and other ornamentation, intricate carvings near the main staircase, the stunning mirrors in the lobby, all spoke of another, perhaps more innocent, time.

Duncan and Trane shared a room on the fifth floor, neither one commenting as they entered and took in their surroundings. Seeing that it was small but immaculately clean seemed to surprise Trane, who looked relieved. Duncan tossed his bag on one of the beds while Trane carefully unpacked his and laid each piece of clothing, neatly folded, in a drawer of the small dresser.

"We should go down, get something to eat, then stop by one of the casinos," said Duncan, by now reclining on the bed with his head propped on one elbow as he watched Trane.

Trane looked over his shoulder with a rare smile. "Good idea, Kalma. After a diet of ship's food I could go for a real meal. I think I'll pass on the casino, however."

"Why's that?"

"It wouldn't be fitting, but I won't object if that's how you want to pass the time."

Sitting up straight at the response, Duncan was dumbfounded. "Are you telling me you wouldn't go into a casino because you're a Knight of the Inner Sphere?"

"Affirmative," Trane returned, sounding quite proud of himself. Almost unconsciously he stood at parade rest during this exchange with Duncan.

"Why?"

Trane paused, obviously marshaling his thoughts. "When we were on the DropShip you accused me of lacking vision. But that's where you're wrong about me. I've been to plenty of pubs in my time, but now I place a higher code of conduct and honor above personal wishes and desires."

"But all we're talking about is a little innocent amusement," Duncan parried. "I'm not inviting you to a lynching or a human sacrifice."

"You just don't understand. No matter where I go, no matter what I do, I'm a Knight of the Inner Sphere. I've sworn to uphold the honor of House Marik and the Free Worlds League. What would people think of the Knights if they saw me frequenting bars, maybe having a cup too many or perhaps gambling like a fool?"

They might think you're human, Duncan thought, but all he said was "We're just talking about the things every soldier does, at least once in awhile."

"Those things would offend some people. The only way I can hope to represent the best of the best, the epitome of what a MechWarrior and a person can become, is to try to live beyond reproach. To live as though my honor were one and the same with that of the Free Worlds League and my liege lord."

Duncan thought he understood, but it was hard to grasp such depth of commitment. "No one knows you're here, Captain. No one will know you're a Knight, so I don't see how you can tarnish your image or sully the good name of Thomas Marik either."

Trane smiled, unshaken in his conviction. "You simply don't understand. *I* will know. That's enough. If I can't be true to myself, then who or what can I be true to?"

Duncan nodded. What Trane said made a crazy kind of sense, and he was starting to seem not so much a prig as a man who knew his place in the scheme of things. Duncan didn't like him any better, but couldn't help but respect the strength of his convictions. He didn't like admitting to himself that Trane had something he lacked—a purpose in life. *I left the military and wandered around, as a mercenary, gambler, and what not. No regrets. I lived my life for me and wouldn't change any of it. What's different is that Trane would lay down his life for the Captain-General or the League without giving it a second thought. I'm not sure I could do the same—for anybody or anything.* Trane's last words struck him the hardest. *Am I true to myself?*

"Captain, I think this round of our fighting is over and I concede the victory to you," Duncan said, bowing in mock salute.

"Very gracious of you, Kalma," Trane returned.

"Lunch then, and a walking tour of the city. I want to check out the possible targets and avenues of approach. If these raiders do show up, let's see if we can figure out what they might do and where they might attack."

"Good thinking," Trane said. He opened the door, gesturing to Duncan with a mock "after you." Duncan chuckled at this rare show of lightheartedness, then the two men walked out of the room, down the stairs and out onto the street, headed toward the outskirts of New Hedon.

Galaport
Galatea
Skye March, Federated Commonwealth

Garth Hawkes had discarded his former Lancers uniform for one of studded leather. He'd also removed the spurs he'd worn as a MechWarrior of the Armed Forces of the Federated Commonwealth in favor of plain high boots. His hair had grown even longer, and he'd begun a dark beard that was in a stubbly uneven phase that made him look more disreputable than rugged.

He'd been on Galatea for nearly a week, long enough to make numerous contacts, but he still had not made the one he'd come for. In fact, he'd realized after only a few days that any employer wanting to put together a raid by false Knights would be doing his recruiting at the 'Mech games. So now he was concentrating on finding a local sponsor who would let him compete and show off his 'Mech piloting skills. And that was why he was seated in this little office at the end of Delancey Street, near the center of town.

Trying to win a slot in the games was a positive diversion and kept him busy, kept him from thinking too much about how the men and women of his unit had died while he'd been sipping Northwind Red in town. It was only at night that the memories came back to haunt him—the sights and sounds of the battle already in progress when he'd finally arrived on the scene. He wondered if he'd ever put those demons to rest.

"You Hawkes?" The deep raspy voice startled Hawkes from his reverie.

"I'm him," he said, trying to look as casual and tough as he dared without overplaying the role. The man who'd spoken looked like he weighed in at no less than 350 kilos, half of which had to be pure muscle. Thick, curly body hair tufted from his open shirt and across his thick arms.

"Former Davion jock, eh?"

"You got it."

"What're you doing here then?"

"Let's just say I didn't leave on the best of terms."

"Let's just say you tell me why you left or you get out of here," the big man rumbled.

Hawkes paused as if trying to decide whether or not to trust him with his tale. "I was the officer in charge of payroll for the company. Let's just say my books didn't exactly jive with what command thought they should. When they decided to run an audit, I decided I didn't want to spend the rest of my life in a stockade."

The man chuckled slightly, wiping at the sheen of sweat on his shaved head. Either the room had gotten hotter or Hawkes was getting more nervous. "Pretty damn cocky. Stealing funds from the Fed-boys takes some moxie."

"Where do you think I got the money for a 'Mech?" Garth returned, telling himself to *relax*. Showing up with a BattleMech on Galatea was a prudent move. His father's connections had helped him get a good price, but the 'Mech was an older model that had been over-customized in its career. It was a *Crusader,* long ago mustered out of active service, but it was his and his alone.

"Afraid to go to Solaris 'cause they'll spot you and arrest your butt, eh?"

Hawkes nodded.

"Well, maybe you came to the right place. I don't know if you're any good, but I need somebody with a 'Mech. My best fighter skipped out a few days ago, and I need to keep up my end of this match."

"What's the deal?"

"You fight, kick the guy's tin butt. I get any and all salvage and sixty percent of the take on the bets."

"No way," Hawkes said boldly. Galatea was a dangerous place to go around bluffing, but if he gave in too quickly they'd see right through him. Word would get around and he'd never find the people behind that raid.

"What do you mean?"

"I put my head on the line and get forty percent? Uh-uh. Fifty percent and you pay half the repairs."

"You're dreamin'," the huge man said, shifting his bulk behind the small desk.

"Like you said, you need me. There are plenty of Mech-Warriors in Galaport, but from what I've seen, most are Dispossessed. I'm here now with a 'Mech. And I promise you I've got the skills to beat any comers. Take it or leave it."

The man stared at him. "Fifty-fifty, but you pay for your own parts."

Hawkes nodded. "You just got yourself a 'Mech jock, friend." Now all he had to do was win a few victories so he could flush out whoever was doing the hiring for those raiders.

Commercial DropShip **Blitzen**
Orbital Approach
Galatea
Skye March, Federated Commonwealth

"Hey," the *Blitzen*'s cargomaster said, prodding the hanging hammock. "We're on final approach, sleeping beauty. Time to rise and shine."

The hammock swung quickly and deposited its occupant on two legs in front of him. Dawn eyed the DropShip's cargomaster blurrily as she ran her fingers through her cropped hair. She hadn't spoken to anyone during the whole trip, accepting whatever rations they brought her and only leaving the small cargo bay to shower. The rest of the time she'd spent working out her muscles or practicing her mental exercises.

"We are landing, *quiaff?*"

"We're about twenty minutes from touchdown at Galaport. For you, the end of the ride."

She stared dully at the man. They had not executed her, but Dawn wished they had. What would she become now that she'd been stripped of her caste, stripped of her welcome among her Clan and her kind?

"Fine, don't talk," he said, stuffing his hands into the pockets of his dull gray jumpsuit. "Listen, little lady, somebody paid a hefty price to get you out of the Clan Zone. I don't know why, and I don't wanna know. You can be a Clan spy, assassin, or whatever you want. I'm just being paid to deliver you to Galatea."

"I am not Clan," Dawn said, but her voice sounded disembodied, as if she were listening to a recording of herself instead of speaking the words.

"Sure you are. You look Clanner, talk Clanner, and those clothes. People will spot them a mile off. Just do me a favor, pretend you never heard of me or this ship."

"I am no longer Clan," she repeated dully.

"Whatever," the man said, shrugging to show his utter disinterest. "Just don't tell anybody I smuggled you out. They'll want to tar and feather me."

"Others would harm you because you helped me?"

"Of course they would," he replied, moving past her to check some cargo nets.

"Explain," Dawn said, clasping her arms overhead to stretch out her shoulders while the man went about his work.

"What's there to explain? You and the rest of your Clan gang show up one day and start invading three of our governments without even so much as a 'hello'. Rasalhague is gone almost altogether and you Clan-heads have taken over a big piece of what was the FedCom and the Combine. If the locals knew I'd voluntarily transported a Clanner here, they'd hang me high, right after they got ahold of you."

"We came to restore the Star League," she returned.

"More like force it down our throats," the cargomaster said, making notes on his electronic pad of the goods that were tethered along the walls of the bay. "What makes you think that's what any of us wants?"

Dawn stopped what she was doing and stared at the man. "Of course you do. We are the descendants of General Aleksandr Kerensky, a man that even your people revere. He and his son Nicholas foretold of our return, commanded us to one day come back to the Inner Sphere to restore what your people had carelessly destroyed. We came to restore the hope of the future."

"Not from where I'm sitting, sister," the cargomaster returned. "All I've seen of your so-called vision is an invasion force that brutally wiped out whole regiments. I don't think the Kerenskys would have wanted it that way, not at all."

"You must not speak of the great Kerenskys in such a manner," she said fiercely.

The cargomaster of the *Blitzen* glanced up quickly. Being

trapped in small quarters with an angry Clan warrior was not how he'd pictured his day or life going.

"I meant no harm," he said, gulping slowly. "I forgot how you Clansmen are sensitive about the Kerenskys."

Her fury waned slightly. "As I said before, I am no longer Clan."

"You keep sayin' that."

Dawn felt a rush of mixed emotions. She was no longer a Steel Viper. That was Clan law. But in her own heart she would always be one. What they had taken away was just words. They could not strip her of who she was. One day, Dawn would win back her place, restore her honor. *I must. It is our way.*

Dawn stared blankly across the room, remembering the Judgment. "It was"—she chose her words carefully—"a misunderstanding. It is not something I wish to discuss."

"Well, like I said, somebody was willing to pay a bundle to have you hauled away, and to here."

"You speak as if Galatea were an evil place."

The cargomaster shrugged. "No, not evil. Galatea used to be known as the Mercenary's Star. But that was a long time ago. Now it's just a rough, tough place where washed-up MechWarriors or those living outside the law can find a place."

She sensed Brett Andrew's hand in sending her to Galatea. The Clans viewed the mercenary warriors of the Inner Sphere as an icon of the corruption of the former Star League. Paying some member of the merchant caste to bring her here, a place that sounded like a trash heap for the worst of the Inner Sphere's mercenaries, was his way of sealing her fate. Dawn knew that, and drew strength from her anger. *You believe you are grinding salt into an open wound, Star Colonel Brett Andrews, but instead you only make me stronger. One day you may be sorry.*

"I do not know your ways or customs, only those that have shaped me. I will survive because of who I am."

"Your people threw you out, did they?"

"Aff. They have banished me from my caste."

"So, what will you do now?"

Dawn tipped her head slightly. She had not thought much

about her future. In her meditations, her thoughts had been of the past, of her shortcomings and perceived failures. She had relived Tukayyid a thousand times during the trip from Jabuka. She had also replayed the battle of Cumbres over and over again. Dawn had even tried the tactics she was accused of neglecting and found no change. Only senseless death and destruction as she had run through each scenario in her brain. Her fate had been sealed even before she set foot on that Kerensky-forsaken planet.

Now she was going to have to deal with the present and the future. For a Clan warrior, doing that usually took no thought. A warrior served her Clan and sought to win a Bloodname, the highest honor, the greatest glory to which a warrior could aspire. A Bloodname guaranteed that one's genetic legacy became part of the Clan breeding program to create future generations of warriors. That was lost to her now. All the rules were suddenly changed. She was in the Inner Sphere, a place of barbarians. Worse, a place populated only by *freebirths*. Castes meant nothing to these people. Dawn was no better than the lowest member of the Labor caste, the most humble gardener or waste remover. No, perhaps even lower because as yet she had no means of survival. The concept was hard to understand, as difficult to grasp as the need for money in order to survive.

"I do not know what I will do," she said, some of the vigor draining from her voice as she contemplated the unknown, a darkness as mysterious as the deepest space.

"You'll do all right. You're a 'Mech jock. Someone will hire you."

A mercenary? For Dawn the thought was nearly alien. *Is this what I have become? One day I am living with the vision of the great Kerenskys to lead me. The next I am fallen lower than even a bandit.* Her mind balked at the thought that her people had denied her so completely that she was not even as good as a member of the despised Bandit caste.

"Yes. I will do what I must to survive." As she walked over to pack her carry-on, Dawn was remembering the story of two water snakes so often repeated to her and her sibmates during their cadet days in the sibko. One snake lived in the marsh, happily enjoying its natural watery habitat.

The other lived in the lane, where it had to content itself with puddles occasionally left by the rain. The first snake implored his cousin to come to the marsh where life was not only more pleasant but safer. The second snake refused, saying he could not leave a place to which he had become so accustomed. A few days later a heavy wagon came down the lane, crushing him to death under the wheels.

Dawn knew she could not cling to what she was accustomed because it was gone, stripped away. If she was to survive, it would be by striking out into the unknown. And survival was all. It was her only hope of proving herself, of finding a way to restore her honor, of one day finding the way back to her Clan.

10

New Hedon
Herotitus
The Periphery
1 May 3057

Duncan leaned up against the old chain-link fence and looked beyond it as Rod Trane studied the city map they'd purchased from a street vendor. A lone BattleMech, a worn and weary *Warhammer* dating back at least two centuries, stood on the other side of the fence. In its time, it had probably been a good war machine even though much of the high technology of the Star League had disappeared or been destroyed in the Succession Wars at the time of its construction. Its technology was antique and primitive by current Inner Sphere standards, and almost childish against the mighty weapons of the Clans. The proud *Warhammer* had probably fought on dozens of worlds before ending up retired on Herotitus, never having to face the juggernaut of the Clans, whose captured technology had helped the Inner Sphere recover some of the technology lost since the fall of the Star League.

Nearby was a pair of Galleon tanks that were probably even older, still pock-marked from damage they had taken in some old fight or war. Instead of being repaired, the laser scars had simply been painted over. The *Warhammer* showed similar old damage, and seemed to carry more paint than armor.

"This is it?" Rod Trane asked.

"Yessir, the lead element of the First Herotitus Defense garrison. Impressive, isn't it?" Duncan glanced over at some nearby buildings, which were little more than makeshift barracks. The mercenary in him noted that the communications lines were exposed and unshielded, and that the garrison didn't even boast a bunker for protection should they need defense. A properly organized strike could take out this facility in a matter of seconds.

"If the raiders hit this place, the city won't stand a chance. The weapons on that 'Mech are a decade out of date."

Duncan squinted at the old *Warhammer,* impressed that Trane knew his weaponry well enough to tell at a glance that the 'Mech's PPCs were outdated models. "They'll be grossly outnumbered and outgunned. The other lance we saw at the south edge of town had only three light 'Mechs. Given their positioning and the layout of the roads and buildings, they'd be lucky to even have time to power up before they get toasted."

"We could warn them," Trane said.

Duncan nodded. This was one of the few times the two had seen eye to eye. "But if we did that we'd be tipping our hand to the raiders. They might go to ground, hide out, and it'd take months to track them down again."

"I know that," Trane said. "But how can we let innocent people die when there's a chance to save them?"

"Well, if it makes you feel any better, warning them wouldn't make much difference. So far these fake Knights have always struck in at least company strength. Even with their infantry, the garrison around New Hedon couldn't fight, much less survive, that kind of firepower. The best they could hope for is a running battle or to take out a few of the raiders. In the end the results would be the same."

Trane nodded. "The SAFE briefing said the planet's detection gear doesn't provide full coverage. If I were planning a raid, I'd drop outside their scanning area."

"My thoughts exactly," Duncan replied. "They're posing as the Knights to stir up trouble for the Captain-General or the Free Worlds League. I'd have them hit the city from several angles, using the main avenues to converge near the spaceport. That would create the illusion that there are even more of them." He walked over to Trane and pointed to the most logical routes on the map.

Trane took his pencil and circled the spaceport. "The garrison probably wouldn't have a chance to rally. And by the time they did they'd be facing a full company in the center of town. The confusion of an attack from so many angles would keep them from being able to concentrate their efforts. They'll come piecemeal and die that way, one by one."

"How about the escape route?"

"I'd have the DropShips land at the spaceport and pick us up as soon as the defense had been knocked out, or meet us outside the city for a fast getaway."

"My thinking as well. When I was running a merc unit I always went for the fast getaway on raids. Stick around too long and the cowboys show up with the cavalry in tow. So, where do you think we should position ourselves?" Duncan said.

Rod Trane looked around the massive lot where the *Warhammer* stood silent guard and then out at the city beyond and around them. "If we're right most of the fighting will be at the spaceport. Let's head that way."

No sooner had he spoken than a rumble shook Galaport's warm, humid afternoon air. Duncan looked around and then up into the sky, thinking it was thunder. But all he saw were thin white clouds blocking the world's white sun. No sign of what caused the sound.

And that scared him.

Glancing over at Trane, he saw him also scanning about for the origin of the sound. "It's happening, isn't it?" Duncan said.

"Those were explosions, autocannon rounds going off," Trane replied, stuffing the map into his belt.

"Damnation!" Duncan spat out, but neither sound nor movement came from the garrison force even as another rumble and roar tore the white sky over the city. This time it seemed closer, like a summer storm sweeping toward them, only this was no rainstorm, it was a torrent of war and destruction. *It's happening too fast. Hell, they might never even get the call to mount up if they're caught too much by surprise.* "Trane, we've got to do something."

"Yes, but what?"

Duncan looked over at the *Warhammer,* then slowly back at Trane.

"Steal the *Warhammer?*"

"We can at least get closer to the fighting and observe," Duncan said, looking for a place to climb over the fence. "If we're lucky, take one of them in the process."

"I'll pilot," Trane said, and without another word both men began to climb the fence. It swayed and buckled slightly under their weight, but held until they cleared the top and dropped down on the other side.

In less than thirty seconds the two had sprinted to the *Warhammer* and climbed the footholds up to the cockpit. Duncan squeezed into the tight space first, and was nearly overcome by the stale odor of centuries of sweat. The bulky cockpit panels and gear protruded forward into the cockpit, not leaving much room for Trane as he bent his long frame to fit into the small space.

Duncan wished he were at the controls, but this wasn't the time to argue with Trane, especially given the condition of this 'Mech. Trane was fitting the bulky, old-style neurohelmet over his shoulders and looking for the sensor tabs that would attach it to his body as Duncan hit the preheat switch on the 'Mech's reactor. "Wonder if they have security protocol in place."

"Never realized just how creaky these old models were," Trane said, manually adjusting the neurohelmet contacts. Under them the fusion reactor of the *Warhammer* started to throb to life. A low hum filled the cockpit and the entire 'Mech seemed to vibrate. "Blast it, they've got security in place." Both men knew what that meant. The 'Mech could be started up, but it couldn't move or fire until the proper security code and movements were fed into the 'Mech's computer system.

Even as Trane was uttering those words, Duncan was wasting no time. He'd crawled around to the front of the cockpit and begun to work under the 'Mech's foot pedals. Trane was trying to activate some of the switch controls in the cockpit, but more out of frustration than any hope that he was wrong about the security system. "What are you doing?" he said irritably.

"Working on the security box," Duncan said from under Trane's feet. Duncan knew that sometimes BattleMechs stored the encrypted security code sequence in a small box under the cockpit controls.

"If you pull the box, the 'Mech will lock out and we won't be able to move." It was a standard security feature and one that had prevented the theft of more than a few 'Mechs in the history of warfare in the Inner Sphere.

"I know that," Duncan said, finding the box and examining it under the glow of the few cockpit control lights that were on. "But I also know a few tricks." He pulled out a small object from his pocket and wrapped his hands around the top of the box near its juncture with the computer system. "Try it now!" he grunted, straining from the position.

Trane attempted to move the 'Mech and suddenly found that he could swing the right arm with its massive PPC. As he continued to work the controls, the huge machine lurched with a screeching of metal like an old machine protesting being roused from its slumber. So much for security, Duncan thought with satisfaction

"How did you do that?" Trane asked, switching on the heat-sink system and revving the fusion reactor to even higher levels of output. The humming that filled the cockpit increased and all the control-system lights flickered to life around him.

"One of the things you learn being a merc in the Periphery is how to work with this older equipment." Duncan held up the small object, revealing it to be a magnet. "Put this on the feed line at the same time you try to startup and there's a thirty-second lag in the security system loading. That buys enough to time to start, and the protocol won't load once the 'Mech is up and running."

"I've never heard of such a thing," Trane said as Duncan squeezed back into the space behind him. Trane's hands were a flurry of motion across the control panels, stirring the machine to life. Every 'Mech cockpit was similar, but placement of gear was always slightly different. This being an older model of *Warhammer* made finding everything even harder, but he quickly mastered the controls.

"Of course not. It only works on these antique 'Mechs

and it's not the kind of thing guys like you ever need to know."

"Are you riding shotgun?"

Duncan squirmed back behind the command seat, barely fitting and forced to kneel in the tight space. "Not by choice," he muttered, wedging his body in even more tightly than before. The heat level in the old *Warhammer* rose slightly as the 'Mech began to lumber forward. Though they'd been lucky to find the neurohelmet sitting in the dank cockpit, neither one of them would have a cooling vest. In a prolonged battle, he and Trane could roast if they fired everything they had. The old 'Mech's technology pre-dated the invention of double heat sinks and more efficient weapons. "Activate the short-range sensors," he said.

"I know what I'm doing," Trane snapped.

"Right. Well, then, better run a check on our long range." Duncan wished he was at the controls. What if these Knights weren't as good as they were cracked up to be? Worse yet, what if Trane didn't know how to pilot an antique like this in battle?

"Tactical feed up," Trane said as the secondary monitor flickered on. His voice was muffled by the neurohelmet, and the external cockpit speaker enhanced it only slightly, making it even more staticky. There was a permanent ripple on the screen from feedback and lack of maintenance. "I have a force at about two kilometers from here on Murphy Boulevard. It looks like they're doing just what we thought they would."

Duncan leaned over the seat back and saw the battle computer's readout in greater detail. The small iconic dots representing the raiders were moving toward the spaceport in the center of New Hedon. They were just under a company in size, and Duncan was sure the city's defenders would never be able to fend off their assault. From what he saw, however, they were attempting to do the impossible.

Trane pivoted the 'Mech just as it ripped through the chain-link fence. Behind them the tiny garrison forces were running, looking frantic and confused. Duncan saw them through the small side window of the cockpit, shouting and waving at the errant *Warhammer. At least they'll get those*

*tanks in motion to pursue us and hopefully engage the raid-
ers. Not that it'll do much good.*

Trane broke the *Warhammer* into a trot down the street,
ripping through three sets of power lines as if they were
mere spider webs in his path. The heat level in the cockpit
began to creep even higher, and Trane unbuttoned his shirt
and squirmed out of it as the *Warhammer* entered a straight-
way. Duncan could barely move in his tiny space, so mostly
he just concentrated on watching the controls and the tactical
readout.

"Problems," he said, loud enough for Trane to hear in his
neurohelmet.

The Knight looked down at the secondary monitor and
saw the images himself. Two of the raiders, tentatively identified as a *Vindicator* and a *Rifleman,* had stopped their drive
toward the spaceport, turning to intercept the *Warhammer.*
Either one alone would have been fair game for the older
'Mech, though the odds were not as good against the *Rifleman.* Together, however, there was little hope for the old
Warhammer against the kind of technology these raiders had
wielded previously.

Trane switched on his targeting gear, and a dim red light
came on inside the cockpit. He slowed the 'Mech to a walk
as he surveyed the area. A city was both good and bad for
fighting, depending on how a 'Mech pilot made use of it. At
the moment the *Rifleman* was coming straight at them down
the wide avenue while the lighter *Vindicator* was making its
way along their left flank. It was only a matter of seconds
before the *Rifleman* began to open up.

"I'm going to engage the *Rifleman,*" Trane said.

"The *Vindicator*'s going to be on your flank any minute."

"I know," Trane shot back. "I don't have any choice."

Suddenly the air around the *Warhammer* seemed to erupt
with explosions and flames as a blast of autocannon fire
scored huge hits on the old Leviathon Plus armor covering
the 'Mech's chest, ripping some of it away as the machine
rocked ponderously at the impact. Duncan hit his head hard
on the rear wall of the cockpit as the 'Mech jolted backward.
His ears rang slightly, but he managed to stay conscious.

"I'll teach him," Trane said just loud enough for Duncan

to hear as he locked on to the target. Then he thumbed the trigger for the 'Mech's two Donal PPCs. Duncan, still somewhat dazed from the head-banging, saw the error and reached out, grabbing Trane's arm.

"Let go!" Trane shouted.

"You'll kill us," Duncan screamed back, his words followed by two laser beams from the *Rifleman* stabbing through the smoke of the autocannon attack. The red beams reached out like deadly searchlights, just missing the *Warhammer* as Trane sidestepped their glancing attack.

"Let me fire," Trane insisted, moving the weapons joystick to a lock on the approaching *Rifleman.*

"You've got both PPCs on line. We'll fry in this cockpit. This old *Hammer* can't vent heat like the ones you're used to piloting!"

Trane's face went white when he realized what he'd almost done. "Damn!" he said, removing one of the PPCs from the target interlock circuit, then firing the other with a ferocious stab at the trigger button. The PPC bolt cracked like lightning from the *Warhammer*'s left arm, the heat in the cockpit instantly rising to where Duncan's throat burned with every breath, but he knew the shot was true. The bolt slammed into the right leg of the red and silver *Rifleman,* the sickly gray-green smoke showing that the PPC had hit deep, probably damaging a heat-sink coolant line.

Trane zigzagged the *Warhammer* from one side of the avenue to another, moving backward in uneven diagonal lines. The *Rifleman* kept closing the distance, firing its Imperator autocannons in a raking fire. Shells ripped across the *Warhammer*'s upper chest, penetrating the torso and right arm. What was left of the old armor sprayed off in every direction, and once again a wave of heat poured up through the cockpit.

At the maximum range of his Holly six-pack, Trane fired the SRMs. The *Warhammer* only carried three more reloads, and if he didn't use them they would simply explode should the 'Mech be destroyed. The missiles streaked down-range, one of them wobbling off course and slamming into the side of a building midway in flight. The others plowed into the *Rifleman*'s lower chest, sending up plumes of white smoke.

"Where's that *Vindicator*?" Trane asked, his bare chest and arms drenched in sweat from the heat in the cockpit.

"He's closing in. You've got another couple of shots and then he's on us," Duncan said, the sweat stinging as it dripped into his eyes. Just then another blast of laser fire streaked out and hit the left leg of the *Warhammer.* There was a slight shudder as the armor plating boiled away, and the secondary monitor told them that the leg could not take another hit.

Trane moved the 'Mech forward slightly and hard to the right, taking it into a narrow street surrounded by higher buildings, one of which blocked a second laser blast. For now the *Warhammer* would be out of reach of the *Rifleman* and away from the *Vindicator.* Even as the cockpit began to cool slightly, both men knew the heat would spike again as soon as they had to open fire.

"He's not fighting the heat we are and he's got the firepower to do us in."

"His leg is hurting. Take out the leg and you take out the 'Mech."

"Got it. I need a stable firing platform," Trane said. "And it's going to get very hot in here." Trane stopped the *Warhammer* and methodically began to target the *Rifleman* as it came into view.

Seeing Trane switch the short-range missiles and the right-hand PPC to the same target interlock circuit, Duncan knew the heat produced would be worse than before even though the *Hammer* had cooled considerably. "Let him have it," he said, bracing for the unbearable heat to come.

Trane fired. The blue bolt of the PPC lashed out first, its accelerated particles sizzling like lightning. The shot hit the *Rifleman*'s lower hip region as the 'Mech rounded the corner. Its arms tilted upward at the impact, their aim disrupted and discharging a massive blast of autocannon fire into the air.

The short-range missiles did the most damage, digging into the hole in the *Rifleman*'s right leg. The explosions went off inside the already badly damaged leg, eating it up. The knee actuator exploded outward as the leg from the joint down erupted in flames, smoke, and shredded myomer. The

Rifleman pilot fought to maintain his balance, but it was no use. The 60-ton 'Mech swayed backward and to the right, plunging into the building behind it, blocking the narrow street and crushing most of the structure it fell onto. It was still at a considerable distance, but Duncan doubted the pilot had much chance of getting his 'Mech operational again.

"That's one," Trane said.

"That *Vindicator* is still—" Duncan was interrupted by a bright blue flash filling the *Warhammer*'s cockpit. The *Vindicator* had scored against the *Warhammer*'s left arm with its extended-range PPC, hitting it so hard the 'Mech's torso twisted under the impact. Duncan's arms ached as he gripped the back of the command couch even while being tossed about the cockpit.

The secondary display told the story. The armor had weathered the assault, but what was left was more imagination than protection. The reinforced plating had been charred off and several thick bundles of myomer hung exposed. Duncan looked down and saw them sparking and smoking as Trane tested the arm, trying to realign it for firing. The arm was still operational, but even small-arms fire could take out what was left at this point. They'd been lucky to make it even this far in this old war-bucket.

Trane backed up the *Warhammer* as fast as he could, but unlike the wide avenue where they'd first engaged the *Rifleman,* here there was no room to dodge or evade the enemy. The buildings were five stories tall or higher over intersecting streets so tight Trane would have a hard time getting the 'Mech and its long PPC arms through. He was running out of space and ideas.

The *Vindicator,* at the far extent of their vision, fired its jump jets to leap over the fallen *Rifleman.* A glimmer of silver paint caught the light as it went. "Now!" Trans said, triggering the PPC in the *Warhammer*'s damaged left arm.

The weapon made a snapping sound as it discharged its azure bolt at the *Vindicator.* The air seemed to crack with thunder as the shot found its mark, ripping into the raiding 'Mech's left torso, just under the long-range missile rack. The *Vindicator*'s movement had ceased, but only for an instant as the pilot reeled from the attack. Duncan licked his lips; the air stank of sweat, heat, and the smell of burning insulation from somewhere in the 'Mech. Only the steadily humming throb of the fusion reactor seemed to deaden the sounds of war around them.

Obviously angry, the *Vindicator* pilot let go with a blast of long-range missiles in response. Duncan and Trane could see the missiles coming, but there was little they could do to avoid the incoming fire. Two of the missiles missed, hitting the ground just in front of them. The others dug into the legs of the *Warhammer*, the impact rattling the 'Mech and increasing the discomfort inside the cockpit.

"We've got to take him out or our mission is a scrub," Duncan said loudly and firmly. *We're not here to win a battle, just to confirm their attack and regroup on Marik. With all this fighting, we're losing sight of our real mission.*

"One PPC shot at a time?" Trane said. The sensors showed the *Vindicator* barely damaged and keeping its distance while firing its long-range weapons. The tactical readout was clear enough: the attacking 'Mech's center torso was damaged but not enough to stop it or force it to disengage.

"If you can fire both PPCs at once, can you hit him with both?"

"Yes, but how—"

"Open the cockpit hatch manually. It will give us the cooling we need when you fire."

Even through the narrow protective plate of the neurohelmet, Duncan could read the look on Trane's face. With the forward cockpit hatch open they would be totally exposed, with no protection against anything the *Vindicator* might throw at them. But surrender was the only other option, and they knew that thus far the raiders had taken no prisoners.

The *Vindicator* closed in to where even the short-range missiles could be brought into play. "Do it!" Trane said.

Duncan contorted his frame and cycled the side access door to the cockpit. It opened and almost immediately a wave of cold air bathed his sweat-soaked skin. Rising to his knees, he manually cranked open the overhead hatch nearly four feet. The *Vindicator* was now even closer, moving in for the kill. *He's cocky. He thinks we won't open up with everything because we'll fry in this old* Hammer.

Duncan saw Trane combine the short-range missiles and the two Martell medium lasers on the same target interlock circuit along with both PPCs. With one press of the firing stud, the *Warhammer* would let go with almost everything it had, short of the machine guns. Under normal conditions the 'Mech would either shut down or blow from such overheating. But Duncan and Trane were hoping that the open hatches would at least keep them from cooking alive as the temperature in the cockpit soared.

"For the Captain-General . . ." Trane said, hitting the trigger on the joystick at the same time the *Vindicator* pilot opened up with his own PPC. The air in the close quarters of the narrow street burst into sparking, showering, blinding life like a star being formed. With the cockpit open Duncan felt the hairs on his arms and head stand on end as the shots passed and struck. His ears ached from the roar of the missiles racing out of the rack only two meters from his head, their flames lapping at the open cockpit's glass viewpoint.

The *Vindicator*'s PPC struck a full milisecond before the *Warhammer*'s, hitting the *Hammer*'s already crippled left arm just after its PPC there discharged. The elbow joint buckled under the hit, snapping off with a noise like bones breaking. The entire *Warhammer* swayed to the left, tipping under the impact until Duncan thought they might be crushed when it fell into a nearby building. But somehow Trane managed to keep the huge machine upright. The steady crackle of frying myomer filled the air, and the heavy taint of ozone and the sooty taste of burnt insulation coated his tongue and mouth.

The cockpit panels flickered out for a moment as a wave of long-range missiles slammed the legs of the *Warhammer,* vibrating the 'Mech in mid-list. The secondary display popped, imploding as the heat in the cockpit spiked upward. Duncan strained to get near the hatch for even a breath of cooler air. Suddenly the throbbing under him from the fusion reactor stopped, accompanied by a sick grinding of metal against metal and a steady hiss like steam venting somewhere in the distance. The emergency lights in the cockpit came on, and through the smoke and haze Duncan knew the reactor had shut down, either from heat or damage. *No mat-*

ter what happens now, this BattleMech is dead—at least for this battle.

He looked out, but instead of seeing the *Vindicator* fallen, he saw the raiding 'Mech still upright, looking more like a statue than a weapon of war. With no readout possible, Duncan visually surveyed their foe. Its frontal armor was charred black—what was left of it anyway. Several missile craters showed near the cockpit, which probably explained why the 'Mech was not pressing further attack. The pilot was either injured, dead, or somewhere in between. Even though the 'Mech was still a distance away, the small pockets of smoke rising from the torso told the story. The 'Mech had been badly damaged, maybe enough to buy them enough time to escape. The extended-range PPC hung limp as Duncan checked Trane's condition.

The Knight was alive, sucking in air as fast as his lungs would allow. He struggled to remove the neurohelmet, then let it fall to the floor of the cockpit. His dark hair sparkled with sweat and his face was red from the heat inside the helmet. He looked stunned, almost in a daze.

"You all right?" Duncan asked, releasing the restraints holding Trane into his seat.

Rod Trane nodded. "You?"

"Alive," Duncan said. "We've got to get out of here in case that guy comes to and decides to finish the job he started."

Trane nodded. Slowly, as if each joint and muscle ached, the two men climbed out the hatch and began to descend the footholds down the side of the *Warhammer*. Now they could see the 'Mech's damage up close and personal. Massive plates of armor torn like paper. Internal structural supports of foam aluminum melted like wax. Several of the rungs were missing, making the descent even slower. They skipped the last few rungs, jumping down onto what had been a sidewalk before the battle. Now it was blackened, cracked, and reduced to worthless rubble, thanks to the weight of the *Warhammer* standing on it.

Duncan looked down the street and saw the *Vindicator* moving slowly backward, almost staggering. "Looks like our friend is moving on to other opportunities," he said. For all intents and purposes the *Warhammer* was no longer a threat to the *Vindicator.* "Let's check out that *Rifleman.* See if we can find the pilot or any evidence."

Trane nodded, still drawing in long, deep gulps of air. "We must also render assistance to the people." Duncan wanted to protest, but he knew Trane was right. He'd seen the damage the raiders had already done just from his little corner of the attack. These people were definitely going to need some help.

The two men moved across the tarmac near where the Herotitus militia were cleaning up the remains of one of their Galleon tanks. There was a crowd of on-lookers, some looking stunned, others huddling to see what had happened. The tank had been gutted from the top through to the interior. 'Mech fire at very close range, Duncan realized. The Galleon never had a chance, none of the local militia did. Most of a day had passed and the sun was finally setting over New Hedon. The two men were tired, near exhaustion, having pressed on throughout the battle, hoping to find some clue to the origins of the raiders. There was none. As with the previous raids, the attackers did their damage to the place and to the reputation of the Knights, and then escaped. Trane and Duncan had destroyed the *Rifleman,* but the pilot had gotten away. No other enemy 'Mechs had been felled in the fight, but the press was already portraying the attack as the work of the Knights of the Inner Sphere.

"Did you get the message off?" Duncan asked as they watched the recovery crew try to pry the tank's melted metal off the tarmac with heavy picks and bars.

"Yes, but Herotitus isn't a Class A station, so it will take a few days for our people to get the word." Trane was careful not to mention the name of Thomas Marik. They'd been careful to encrypt their message as well.

"We did pretty good today," Duncan said.

Trane shook his head and wearily pointed to the tank where one of the crewman, burned to death in a contorted position of pain and death, was being hauled from the remains of the Galleon. "No we didn't."

Duncan wanted to argue the point, but was too tired from

the battle and the mop-up. There was a bitter taste in his mouth and his nose was clogged with dust and smoke debris. He, like Trane, was running on his last reserves of energy.

"We should get back to the hotel," he said, rubbing at the stiffness in the back of his neck with both hands.

"While I was sending the message, I had our bags delivered to the DropShip," Trane told him.

"You think we should leave right away then?" It didn't matter to Duncan that Trane had acted without consulting him, even though Duncan was technically in charge of the mission. He was just too tired.

"There's nothing more for us to do here. The raiders got away and the damage is already done."

Duncan looked around him. Smoke from several fires still drifted into the evening sky, marking where the raiders had struck. They were still out there, somewhere, laughing at everyone. They'd pulled off raids on four worlds, taken on major and small units and waxed them at every turn.

But he and Trane had accomplished something here on Herotitus. *We got close this time, we were one step ahead of them and we saw what they did. We also know that the source of this information is on Galatea. Go there, to the old Mercenary's Star, and maybe we can learn the truth and find out who is behind these raids.*

"Let's go," Duncan said. The two men began to walk across the long stretch of tarmac back to their DropShip. They had a long journey ahead.

═══ 11 ═══

Galaport
Galatea
Skye March, Federated Commonwealth
5 May 3057

Dawn had known the pains and pounding headache of hunger before, but not for many years. The last time had been during a survival training exercise in her sibko days. As a test of their ability to live off the land, she and the other cadets had been sent for a week into the deadly jungles of Arcadia. Several of her sibkin nearly died in that place of killer beasts and poisonous vegetation, but Dawn had learned that all she needed to survive was her wits.

In some ways coming to this place called Galatea was a similar test. She was no longer among her own people and must understand and adapt to whatever were the limits and laws and customs of this alien society. It wasn't the first time Dawn had encountered freebirths of the Inner Sphere, but she'd never observed them so closely. She'd spent most of the past five days wandering the streets and markets, watching people, observing their manners, their ways, their speech, their clothing, even the way they walked. It was truly alien, this life, and Dawn sometimes imagined herself regaling her comrades with tales of these Inner Sphere barbarians. How the others would laugh, how they would scorn, how they would pity these freebirths.

But she must not waste her thoughts so idly. Hunger she could survive for a while longer, but Dawn knew her biggest dilemma was coin—or the lack of it. No Clan warrior needed money, for all basic needs, from food and shelter to education and medical care, were provided. Not so here in the Inner Sphere.

She had been sleeping in alleys, where she saw others picking through the garbage bins for scraps of food before also bedding down there for the night. But Dawn was no stranger to sleeping out of doors, nor did she find it particularly uncomfortable. What did shock her was how many of these freebirths were gray-haired, stooped, and wrinkled. Dawn had seen very few aged people in her life, for the Clans had no use for the old. At twenty-nine, she was already past the age when most warriors won a Bloodname—if they were ever going to do so. The sight of people who'd survived beyond the age when they could possibly be useful disgusted her. It was a fate worse than death for a Clan warrior, who hoped to die in combat long before he or she became too old for battle.

Jabuka and other planets in the Clan Occupation Zone were much different from Galatea. Their cities were controlled by the Clans, the conquered populations governed by Clan laws and traditions. It was difficult to grasp, but Dawn was finally beginning to understand that life in the Inner Sphere was not ruled by caste. Among the Clans there was no easy mixing and conversation between members of the various strata. Such encounters were rare, at best, and usually determined only by the needs and desires of the ruling warriors.

This was important for Dawn to learn. Until now, she had avoided speaking to people. Though her appearance was probably strange, the streets of Galaport were full of mercenaries wearing all manner of uniforms and everything in between. But she knew her speech would give her away instantly. Dawn couldn't be sure how people might react to her. She was, after all, from the enemy.

This morning Dawn was walking down a street she had not explored previously. All around her she saw people setting up displays and outdoor stands and tents, probably getting ready for a local market day. Young laborers with bandannas around their foreheads and sweatbands around their necks were bringing in loads of fresh vegetables, fruits, spices, and other food items she could not identify. Others were unloading racks of clothing from several big trucks, while further up the street she saw still others carrying huge flat pans filled with loaves of bread high over their heads. The bread must be just baked and warm, for its tantalizing scent carried all the way down the street.

Thoughts of food were suddenly interrupted by a rough voice. "Say, girl," the man said, "how do you like Galaport?"

Dawn turned quickly, instantly assessing the possible threat. She saw none in this man wearing high leather boots and soft trousers belted at the waist, so overweight his belly actually hung over his belt-line. He was also nearly bald except for a few strands of gray-white hair draped across the top of his head in a foolish attempt to make it look like the hair still grew there. As he smiled, Dawn winced at the sight of his yellowed teeth.

The man laughed. "You're a Clanner, aren't you?" His eyes ran from her short-cropped hair to her leather jacket, to the place where her unit insignia had been torn off, to her tan jump trousers and leather boots.

"I am no longer of the Clans," she said curtly. "Perhaps you should go, *quiaff*?" She wanted this freebirth to leave her alone.

"That so?" He held out his hand. "Well, I'm Edel Mordoc."

Dawn looked down at his hand, not sure what he expected her to do. "I am Dawn."

Mordoc dropped his hand. "Dawn what?"

"My name is Dawn."

"I heard that. What's your last name?"

"I do not have a . . . second name," she said. Among the Clans people were born with only one name. To win a second name, a Bloodname, was very difficult, and the honor went only to the most elite warriors. Dawn had competed in several Trials of Bloodright and had just missed winning her last one. She'd been confident she'd win the next time, but now that would never happen. The Judgment had ended her life in the Clans.

"Come on," Mordoc insisted, "everybody has a last name."

"Neg, I have none."

Mordoc looked her over from head to toe once more, but this time with obvious suspicion. "Let me be sure I'm getting this right. You're not Clan now, but you were once, eh? I've never heard of anyone leaving the Clans before." He did nothing to mask the suspicion in his voice.

"I did not leave, I was removed." The words were hard to say but stung with the truth. She made her face hard and closed, defying him to pry further.

Mordoc saw the look, and must have guessed that getting deeper at the truth would take time. "What were you, a MechWarrior, a technician?"

Dawn drew herself up in pride. "I am a warrior." She did not speak in past tense. Her Clan had cast her out, but they could not take from her who she was in body and mind. She was Dawn, a warrior, and would always be that.

"You got a lot of guts coming here."

His comment surprised her. "Explain."

Mordoc looked around and pointed to a small cafe across the way. "The street isn't exactly the place to talk. You eaten yet?"

"Neg. Not for several days." Dawn did not say it in shame or weakness, but with pride.

"Listen," Mordoc said. "I might be able to help you. Let me buy you some grub and I can fill you in on anything you want to know about Galatea."

Dawn looked at him warily. "I do not know you. I should not trust a stranger who comes up on the street offering me help and a meal, *quiaff*?"

The big man smiled again. "Well, Dawn, some food might do you good. All I'm asking is for a few minutes of your time, a chance to make you a very interesting business proposition."

Dawn drew back in disdain. Business proposition? She was a warrior, a member of the Steel Vipers, an elite. Even outcast from her Clan, the Viper blood ran through her veins. Now she was consorting with merchants and beggars. As much as she wanted to believe that things hadn't changed, it finally hit her that they had. She was in the Inner Sphere now, and all the Clan pride and honor to which she wanted to cling so fiercely would neither feed nor clothe her.

The time had come for her to face reality. It was the only way to survive.

Mordoc took a seat at the empty counter of the small cafe, and Dawn sat beside him as his extra bulk settled down around him in rolls. He ordered for them both without consulting her, but Dawn did not care. She wouldn't have known what to ask for, and she was still reeling a bit from her first encounter here in this alien place.

"You know, you're the first Clanner I've ever met," he said as the waiter poured them each a steaming cup of dark liquid.

"That is not so strange. Not many of us have ventured beyond the occupation zone."

"Treaties do that," Mordoc said. His reference to the Treaty of Tukayyid touched the painful place in Dawn's heart, but she steeled herself against the memories. This was no time for dwelling on Tukayyid, the losses, the humiliation. No, right now she needed all her courage and strength.

"You spoke of a business proposition," she said. "You wish to offer me work, *quiaff?*"

Mordoc looked a little confused, but apparently understood the gist of her query. "Work? In a way. I like to think of it as a great opportunity—and you should too. You see, I run a small stable here on Galatea."

Dawn tilted her head slightly to one side. "I have no skill with animals. I am of the warrior caste. You misunderstand my capabilities, *quiaff?*"

Mordoc waved his hands and shook his head. "You're thinking of the wrong kind of stable, Dawn. On Galatea and a few other worlds like it, a stable refers to a group of MechWarriors who join together to fight in 'Mech duels. In arenas. Have you heard of that?"

Dawn nodded. She knew of the 'Mech games on Solaris VII, where MechWarriors squared off in combat, sometimes even to the death. The games were viewed as corrupt by many in the Clans, though Dawn thought she understood their purpose. The Steel Vipers often performed such training between units.

"You have such a group of MechWarriors then, *quiaff?*"

"Yes. And I would like to hire you for my little stable."

"But you know nothing of me or my skills."

He shrugged. "It's a risk I'm willing to take. You're a Clanner, which means you're a very good warrior. So maybe they threw you out from some reason, but all that genetic tinkering probably gives you a hell of a head start over most of the other 'Mech jocks on this rock. I'd rather have that working for me than for one of my competitors."

"What must I do?"

Mordoc took a sip from his steaming cup. "I'm paid if my stable wins a match. But for that I need good MechWarriors. Fight for me and I'll pay you well—in hard currency. You'll get to climb into a BattleMech again—nothing like the ones you Clanners have, but a good old girl anyway. You say you're a warrior. Well, here's a chance to show your stuff. Besides, you being such a total unknown ought to get me some great odds, for the first few fights anyway."

Dawn said nothing because she didn't know what to say. She picked up the mug in front of her and lifted it to her lips, then immediately spat out whatever brew the thing was filled with.

Mordoc tried to hide his smile as he handed her a handkerchief. "You're on your own now, Dawn, and it sounds like you haven't got any money. Clanner or not, you're going to need it if you plan to stick around Galaport or any other place in the Inner Sphere."

Dawn dabbed at her face with the handkerchief, now fully realizing what Mordoc had in mind. A mercenary. He wanted to pay her to fight, he wanted to make her into a mercenary. To a Clan warrior, there was no lower form of existence than a warrior who sold his skills.

Anger roared in her ears and her face burned red. The Clan hatred of mercenaries ran deep. After the fall of the Star League, Stefan Amaris had depended heavily on them. Some lived on in Clan history as despicable villains, especially the members of the infamous Greenhaven Gestapo. The idea of joining such a group was appalling.

"You have erred. I will not fight for money. That is the way of the mercenary and I would not stoop to it. I may no longer be of the Steel Vipers, but I cannot be other than what I am and always have been." She rose to leave.

Edel Mordoc reached up and tried to grab her arm, only to have Dawn jerk it free. The look in her eyes told him he was dangerously close to a fight he couldn't have won even in his prime. "Wait. What if I didn't pay you?"

Dawn was still staring at him. "Explain."

"I provide you with whatever you need; food, clothes, you name it. No money need change hands. Just an arrangement between friends."

Dawn was thinking hard. Mercenaries were warriors who sold their services for profit, but if she accepted Mordoc's offer she would earn nothing by her actions. She would simply be able to survive. But was that not the same thing as being a mercenary? Was it not a twisting of her beliefs? Dawn could not be sure of the answers to those questions. What she did know was that sooner or later she must cease living on the streets, that she must find some kind of safe haven from which to plan her next moves.

"Aff," she said finally, "I accept, but I will have nothing to do with money. You will never offer me coin in return for fighting in your . . . stable. Do so, and I will leave. But not before we settle the matter in a Circle of Equals."

Mordoc hadn't the faintest idea what a Circle of Equals was, but Dawn's tone made him hope he never had to meet her in one.

"Deal," he said, not believing his luck. He had just recruited a Clan warrior to his stable. Better yet, one who demanded that she *not* be paid for doing her work. Ha!

"Well bargained and done," she replied. "This stable has a name, *quiaff*?"

"Yes, we call it Mordoc's Minutemen."

Dawn nodded. For now they would be her Clan, her home. It was a start, a beginning. From here she might begin to see the road back to what she had once been and might still become. For the first time in weeks Dawn had a sense of purpose, a reason for being. She was no longer lost among the stars.

Winter Palace, Dormuth
Marik
Marik Commonwealth
Free Worlds League

As with so many things associated with Thomas Marik, his study in the Winter Palace on Marik was like a visit to the past. Rich mahogany wainscoting lined the walls, two of which were hung with real oil paintings of sailing ships and early spacecraft, and the other two given over to built-in bookcases filled with hardcopy books dating back five centuries, or more. The beautiful rugs laid down over the gleaming wooden floor also seemed to speak of another time. The patterns were hand-loomed, obviously dating back centuries as well.

The centerpiece of the room was the Captain-General's carved mahogany desk set near the massive stone fireplace. Standing behind it, striking in his white uniform of office, was Thomas Marik. The Marik eagle formed the clasp of the rich cape thrown back from his shoulders. Seated opposite him were Harrison Kalma and Wilson Cherenkov, both of whom turned at the sound of footsteps.

"Welcome back," the Captain-General said, a smile of real pleasure on his face.

Rod Trane bowed slightly, which Duncan forgot to do. "Thank you, sire," he said quickly, trying to cover his embarrassment. "We sent our report on ahead. Have you had a chance to review it?"

"Yes," Marik said. "We were just discussing it." He gestured to two dark red leather chairs set between the elder Kalma and Cherenkov. "Please, gentlemen, have a seat."

"You two had quite an adventure, Captain Trane," Marik went on. "But wasn't stealing a BattleMech and actually taking on these impostors a bit beyond the scope of the mission?"

"I accept responsibility for what happened, sire. We did not see our mission at risk, and we thought it might be an opportunity to capture one of the raiders."

"Which you were unable to do," Cherenkov said.

Duncan spoke up quickly. "That's true, sir, but we still learned some interesting things about them."

Duncan took Marik's calm silence as a cue to continue. "This was the fake Knights' first strike against a major metropolitan area and they pulled it off by the book. And with plenty of skill. The *Vindicator* we tangled with got out of there as soon as we got toasted. But up till then he stayed his distance and just kept pummeling us at long and medium ranges. A green warrior would have rushed in for the kill. No, these attackers are trained."

"We also learned that SAFE's information regarding contacts on Galatea is accurate," Thomas said, with a nod at the intelligence chief.

"Thank you, milord." Cherenkov's usually stern expression softened slightly.

"Well, the Knights have arrived and are bivouacked here on Marik, but how we proceed from here is tricky politically. After the attack on the Twenty-fourth Lyrans I can hardly send them to Galatea without risking the charge that I'm again using my Knights to invade Federated Commonwealth space. Secrecy is the key, gentlemen. My son Joshua is under the care of Victor Davion's people, and he may be refraining from making an issue of this matter to keep from looking like a continual warmonger to his people. I wouldn't want to give him any cause to believe the strike on Valexa was anything other than it was, the work of imposters. The two of you making a run to the Periphery to glean confirmation of a rumor is one thing, sending a fully functional unit into another government's space is quite another."

Marik paused, choosing his words carefully. "Your next step is to return to Galatea with a company of Knights, posing as mercenaries. But should the operation become exposed, I will not be able to protect you. And even if I could, it would only add fuel to the argument that the raids really *were* conducted by the Knights."

"Understood," Duncan replied.

"Good. Now, gentlemen, how soon can you leave?"

"In a few days time. I want to make sure the unit is ready," Duncan said.

His statement seemed to rub Trane the wrong way. "We're

Knights of the Inner Sphere, not some vagabond mercenary unit. We can be ready within the hour if you so desire."

Duncan rubbed his chin in thought. "Captain Trane, I don't doubt a word you say. The Knights are probably one of the best MechWarrior units in the Inner Sphere. That's not the issue. The problem is that they aren't really prepared for the special demands of this mission, and that's where the extra time comes in. My estimate stands."

Harrison Kalma leaned forward slightly in his seat. "What do you mean they're not prepared?"

The younger Kalma pulled a tightly folded sheet of paper from his jacket pocket and unfolded it. "I went over the Knight's TO&E on the trip back. Look at their 'Mechs." He handed the hardcopy to his father.

The General looked at the sheet for a moment before handing it back. "I see what you mean."

"I'm afraid you've lost me, gentlemen," the Captain-General interrupted. "I don't understand why there should be any concern about the 'Mechs assigned to the Knights. I assure you they field only the best the Free Worlds League has to offer. They also get to test prototypes of new 'Mechs. They can beat anything these raiders might throw at them—if it comes to that."

Duncan stuffed the paper into his pocket and shook his head. "But that's exactly the problem, sire. We're going to Galatea with the express mission of infiltrating the ranks of whoever is behind these raids. To get hired we're going to have to prove ourselves as skilled MechWarriors, which the Knights will have no problem doing. But we've got to remember that Galatea isn't like Outreach. Units operating out of there are a much seamier bunch. And they'd never have top-of-the-line BattleMechs or prototypes. I doubt that many of them can even spell 'prototype'."

Rod Trane still had a head full of steam. "Are you saying we have to get rid of our 'Mechs?"

Duncan nodded very calmly, very deliberately. "Yes, I've checked. The Marik First Planetary Militia is equipped with a hodgepodge of older 'Mechs. Some are customized, but most are too old for front-line duty despite being refitted with new technology. I suggest we swap them out with 'Mechs the Knights currently field."

Wilson Cherenkov's next words took Duncan completely by surprise. "I completely agree, sire. The team would stand out like a sore thumb if they showed up with new 'Mechs on Galatea. I can put some of my special operations teams to work on their machines. Remove any and all trace that might connect them back to the Marik Militia, burn off the paint, and give them fresh coats so that even tight thermo scans won't reveal anything of their origins."

"Excellent," Thomas Marik said. "Anything else, Duncan?"

"Actually, sire, there is. I want to leave some of the Knights here, at Captain Trane's discretion. Three to five, to be exact."

"Why is that?" Trane demanded sharply.

"Simple, Rod. We're going to have to blend in with the scene when we get to Galatea. I plan to hire a couple of additional mercs once we arrive. That will give us some contacts on the planet right off the bat as well as helping you Knights learn how to talk, think, and act like anything but Knights of the Inner Sphere."

"What are you spouting off about now, Kalma?" Trane groused.

"It isn't just mercenaries that this little team of Knights has to learn to become. They've got to act like the kind whose careers are shady enough to end them up on Galatea in the first place. We need a few days here for them to train in their replacement 'Mechs and to start getting used to more informality. We've also got to come up with a cover history for where we've been. Stories we'll tell the various people we run into so that we're all singing the same song. Otherwise, whoever is hiring for the fake Knights will see through us in a second and this whole mission will be a wash."

Trane appealed to Thomas Marik. "Captain-General, the good name of my men is being smeared by the actions of these false Knights. Any one of them would give his life to put an end to these raids. I strongly protest this decision. My people deserve the chance to defend their honor themselves."

"Captain Trane," Marik said, "the Knights of the Inner Sphere are a regiment strong, and most of them won't have the opportunity to participate in this mission. Though I understand your sentiments, in this case I feel obliged to defer to the expert. I'm sure if you give it a little more thought, you'll see that his reasoning is actually very sound."

Rod turned to Duncan angrily. "So you're going to teach my men to behave like cutthroat mercenaries?"

Duncan half-expected Thomas Marik to speak up again. When he did not, Duncan decided to set the record straight once and for all.

"Trane, these are not your men, not on this mission. They report to me. I know you don't like it, but if you can't deal with it, I suggest you bow out now. And if you're in, then you'd better become one hell of an actor. Because pulling off the role of a 'cutthroat mercenary' is exactly what you're going to have to do.

"The other thing is that none of you will enjoy any rank while on this mission. From this point on, if you're still with us, you're simply Rod Trane—mercenary. I'm in charge and you follow my orders."

Trane was infuriated, but all he said was "Yessir!" while giving Duncan a kind of mocking salute. "Request permission to be dismissed and meet with the unit."

Duncan saluted back. "Dismissed." Trane bowed to Marik, then fairly stomped out of the room.

There was a long silence before Thomas Marik spoke. "He's a good man, Duncan. One of my best Knights. I understand why you had to be rough on him, but he's still a member of the Knights of the Inner Sphere and deserves your respect."

"I had no choice, sire. You've stressed the importance of this operation and also that you wanted me to lead it because my experience could be the key to our success. I've seen Trane in combat, and believe me, I want him with me. He's a fine 'Mech pilot. I've seen it with my own eyes. But he's got to get over wanting to be in charge. He's not a Captain now, he's a mercenary. If he can't play the game, then let him be one of those who stays behind."

═══ 12 ═══

DropShip **Farragut's Folly,** *Attached to FWL*
JumpShip **Janos**
Nadir Jump Point
Bordon
Silver Hawks, Free Worlds League
8 May 3057

Duncan stepped into the cargo bay of the old *Union* Class
DropShip and saw the small contingent of MechWarriors
gathered near the massive 'Mech doors. Next to them stood
the BattleMech replacements he'd ordered. Older models,
most having seen plenty of action during their careers, were
carefully strapped and lashed into position in their cocoons.
The men, when they saw him enter, went to parade rest,
though some more quickly than others.

Duncan looked around at them, thinking it had been a
while since he'd felt so much excitement and anticipation.
Not since running his own mercenary unit out of the Periphery. He went to stand before them and nodded for them to
relax. Only Rod Trane, standing dark and sullen in the back,
did not.

Duncan let his gaze travel over all their faces as he spoke.
"Most of you don't know me very well, but by now you're
aware that this mission is far from typical, to say the least.
That's why I thought it would be good if we all got together
to clear up any questions and to be sure everyone under-
stands what we're supposed to do and how I think we should
approach it.

"It won't be long before we reach Galatea. You all received the SAFE briefing with your orders, though I'm sure

most of you already know something about the place. Our team will be posing as a mercenary unit in order to find the recruiters who're hiring the mercs impersonating you Knights in raids against the various other Houses. Once we find them, we infiltrate their ranks, learn their mission, and put an end to the raids. I don't have to tell you that both the Knights and the Captain-General have a lot riding on this operation."

One of the men stepped forward. "Permission to speak freely?"

Duncan gestured affirmatively. "By all means. And that applies to all of you."

"It's about the 'Mechs, sir." It was one of the younger Knights, Karl Villiers. "We've always had top-of-the-line models and now we get these rust buckets. Only half the heat sinks on mine have been upgraded to doubles and one of the lasers only works when it's in the mood."

Duncan had expected this. "If you think about it, we really had no choice but to swap out your 'Mechs with older refits. From now on none of us can forget our cover—we're supposed to be a mercenary unit. Not an elite bunch like Wolf's Dragoons or the Kell Hounds, but one a lot lower on the spectrum. That kind of merc unit simply doesn't have top-line models."

Ben-Ari, who'd been posted to the Command Lance, spoke up next. "These imposters are fielding nearly a regiment of 'Mechs, sir. Even if we find them they'll vastly outnumber us. I'm proud to be a Knight of the Inner Sphere, but three to one odds or worse in substandard 'Mechs doesn't sound like we've got much chance of winning."

"Good point," Duncan said. "But the plan is to have the rest of the Knights ready and waiting to assist when the time is right. The Captain-General is covertly pulling the rest of your comrades together. When the time is right either Captain Trane or I will transmit the codeword to bring the Knights en masse. That should more than equal the odds."

This time Derek Hasson spoke up. "Sir, I checked my quarters and the shower isn't working. As a matter of fact, none of the showers on this ship are functional."

This part wasn't going to be easy, Duncan thought. "I know. I ordered them shut off."

"You did what?" Trane demanded.

"If we don't blend in when we get to Galatea, then we fail before we even begin. I've temporarily confiscated your razors and shut off the showers so we'll all look and smell like the kind of mercs who come to Galatea looking for action. I've also stocked up on the kind of clothes we'll need from one of the local surplus stores. Just think of this as one of those field operations where you go for days or even weeks without bathing or shaving. This is just like that."

One of the taller Knights, Jon Blix, looked over at Rod Trane. "Captain, are you behind all of this?"

Duncan didn't give Trane a chance to respond. He had to make these men understand that he was in command for now. "I've been given command of this operation by your liege lord Thomas Marik. Yes, when this is all over and done with, Rod Trane will be your Captain again. But for now you must behave as though neither he nor any of you have rank. The only one with rank will be me. The rest of you are warriors, mercenary warriors and hard cases, at that. For the duration of this mission, you will refrain from any use of rank. You can call me Duncan or Kalma—I'll answer to both. You can even call me Captain, since technically I'm in charge"—Duncan gave a short laugh—"but you don't need to overdo it. Formal titles and I don't get along very well."

Trane had been listening hard, standing with arms folded across his chest and head cocked to one side. "Hear me out," he said, raising one hand for attention. "I think we all agree on the importance of this mission. And it's true that the Captain-General made Kalma the head of it. That's because Duncan knows so much about the ways of the people and places where we're going. He knows what we need to do to convince people we are what we seem—a tough band of mercs who are skilled but hungry for work. We'll follow Duncan Kalma because that's what our honor dictates. The future of the Knights of the Inner Sphere depends on it."

Many nodded their acceptance as Trane spoke. He'd calmed their fears and reassured them that there was honor in what they were about to do. But Duncan knew that in his heart Trane believed he should have been given command of the operation. He could only hope that the the issue wouldn't cause trouble later.

"Thank you, Captain Trane," Duncan said, as the gathering turned back toward him. "During the next three days we'll be traveling to Galatea via a command circuit the Captain-General has set up for us. Some of these ships are commercial haulers, but none of them know anything about who we are or where we're going, so let's keep it that way. Once we're on our way I'll be meeting individually with each of you and also holding some informal sessions to brief you on our cover stories as a unit and as individuals and so on. Remember, you're no longer Knights of the Inner Sphere. That part of you must be hidden from this point on.

"You will adopt new identities and histories for this mission. Learn them inside out. Our lives may depend on it." Duncan knew that last was no exaggeration. Every time he'd been to Galatea the place seemed to take another step backward on the evolutionary ladder.

"In the meantime we still need to check security on our 'Mechs one last time and run through the docking checklists. You all know the drill, so let's shake, rattle, and roll."

Ben-Ari stepped forward with his hand up. "Captain Kalma, before we break, just one more question."

"Fire at will," Duncan said.

"What are we called?"

Duncan had given plenty of thought to the same question from the moment he'd accepted the mission. "From now on we're known as Kalma's Mercenary Company Incorporated—unless we come up with something better." He'd wanted to keep it simple, but also hoped this group would be more successful than the last one that had gone out under the banner.

With that Duncan walked over to where his own 'Mech was slung into its cocoon and began to check that the bracing was secure. All around him the others followed suit, each one finding reassurance in the familiarity of routine.

13

Galaport
Galatea
Skye March, Federated Commonwealth
15 May 3057

Dawn adjusted the sensor tabs on her neurohelmet for what seemed like the tenth time and made sure she still had good contact. The neurohelmet, which provided a neural interface between the 'Mech pilot and the BattleMech's gyro, was the key to piloting a 'Mech. The pilot used his or her own sense of balance to adjust the balance of the 'Mech, lending the machine what often seemed like human movements.

She looked around the cockpit with a sense of frustration. Dawn had been weaned on Clan battle technology, which was significantly more advanced than even the best the Inner Sphere could boast. She could not help having misgivings about the fact that some components of this ancient *Shadow Hawk* were technologically *behind* the Inner Sphere's current capabilities. This neurohelmet, for one thing, was nearly twice the weight and size of the kind used by the Steel Vipers.

And that was only the beginning. Though this was no OmniMech, Dawn thought the 'Mech could and should have been better than it was. It had ferro-fibrous armor, which would let it withstand a lot more than most 'Mechs its age, but its weapons array was a shambles. Apparently the weapons had been heavily modified at least several times by previous warriors who'd piloted the machine. Its last refit had gained it some of the more contemporary systems, but Dawn was used to the Clan's more powerful and penetrating pulse lasers, which this machine sadly lacked. That didn't mean the *Shadow Hawk*'s essentially long-firing beam weapons were not deadly, just that they didn't offer nearly the firepower. Perhaps her biggest concern was that some of the 'Mech's heat sinks were so old and decrepit that they barely worked.

Among the Clans, the technician in charge of maintaining this 'Mech would have been punished severely. As for the 'Mech, it would probably have been consigned to a solahma unit of over-the-hill warriors or even dismantled for parts. Dawn had to remind herself sternly that she was *not* of the Clans now and that this equipment was all that was available to her now. In some ways it made her wonder that the barbarians of the Inner Sphere had managed to hold off the Clan invasion as well as they did.

She had complained to Mordoc, but the stablemaster had simply thrown up his hands. The Minutemen were out of money, he said, which was why he had such high hopes for her. Every one of them, including Mordoc, had bet his or her last C-bills on her victory. He also said that even though she considered the *Shadow Hawk* to be hopeless, the rest of the Minutemen had been mightily impressed when they saw how skillfully she piloted it in practice.

Her teammates were aware that Dawn was of the Clans, but Mordoc had not passed that information on to their opponents, Carmody's Cavaliers. All he'd let slip was that this new warrior was also fighting in the Games for the first time. It was a blatant deception, but one Dawn understood. The ritual of bidding often included exaggerating or undervaluing one's force.

She hadn't known what to expect of the "arena," but wasn't disappointed to find that it was nothing more than a large open area with massive dirt embankments standing nearly twenty-five meters high. It could easily have been a Circle of Equals for an honor duel between Clan warriors. The field was well over a kilometer long and half that distance wide. Much to Dawn's chagrin, stands full of spectators were positioned on the edge of one rampart. There was little protection, and Dawn wondered how many spectators of previous matches had been killed accidentally. The Clans never wasted the smallest thing, and this carelessness struck her forcefully.

The mud and muck of the arena were dotted with the ruins of several buildings, indicating that this had been a battle zone for decades, perhaps even longer. It was here Mech-Warriors came to fight, in battles one-on-one. Again Dawn was reminded of a Circle of Equals. Memories of losing her Trial of Refusal stung, but she held on. She must make her way down this new path, without regret, without excuses, without faltering.

Her headset crackled to life, producing as much static as message. "This is Mordoc. Are you ready yet?"

"Aff," she replied.

"I assume that's a 'yes,' " Mordoc said. Her speech was one of the hardest things for Dawn to change, but this little exchange reminded her once more of the necessity. "You remember the plan, Dawn. Your opponent's piloting a *Griffin*. With that PPC he's going to try and keep you at a distance and whittle you away from there."

"I understand, Mordoc," she returned, almost irritated at his comments. She was a warrior, born and bred. She had known many battles in her time, including the one on Tukayyid, the biggest battle in the history of mankind. What advice would this overweight freebirth have given her there? she thought angrily. And now he wanted to tell her how to go one-on-one against another warrior. *Ah, well,* she told herself, *her victory would show him who she was.*

He spoke again as the lights on the starting pole changed from green to yellow. Dawn throttled the old *Shadow Hawk*'s fusion reactor to maximum power and opened the heat sinks all at once. "One more thing," he said.

"Aye? What is that?" Dawn gripped the joystick firmly, readying to charge at the *Griffin*.

"Carmody's Cavaliers are known to cheat," Mordoc said, his voice almost drowned by the sound of the *Shadow Hawk* roaring to life. "Good luck, Dawn!" Just then the light on the pole turned red. The moment of battle had come and she was ready.

Outside, the voice of the announcer blared, but Dawn could not hear it and opted not to tune in on her command frequency. She was in her element. She wanted to shout or sing or scream with the power of it. *This is what I do. This is what I am, a warrior. This is the one thing that no one, not even the Khans of the Steel Vipers can take from me. It is the one truth I can hold onto no matter what. I will win here today and that will be only the first victory in restoring my honor.* She leveled the Armstrong J-11 autocannon at the *Griffin* and began to run, breaking slightly to the right. She needed the weapon, but not now, in a few moments.

The Carmody pilot was moving at a very slow walk, hugging the back corner of the arena to keep her at a distance. Dawn understood the tactic and knew that within three seconds he could lock onto her and open up with his deadly PPC. The particle projection cannon would rip her *Shadow Hawk* apart if she did not take him out or close the range to where he could not safely use the weapon. In tight quarters she would stand a better chance and have much better odds in her favor.

On the third and critical second of his attempt to lock on to her, Dawn ignited the old *Shadow Hawk*'s jump jets, leaping almost five meters into the air by the time her opponent fired his PPC and long-range missiles. Three of the missiles found their mark in the *Hawk*'s leg armor, but more important was that the bright blue flash of the PPC missed her.

Having piloted jump-capable 'Mechs only a few times before now, she had some difficulty in handling the *Shadow Hawk* as it rose over the smoke and weapon blasts. To Dawn, as to many Clan warriors, jump jets were weapons of a coward. Freebirth warriors of the Inner Sphere used them to fight unfairly, to get behind a true warrior for a rear shot. She would never stoop to that, but using the jets for simple movement did not violate any code or honor. Even though she had been thrown into the world of freebirths, Dawn found comfort in being true to the Clan way.

He will expect me to close to medium range where my weapons are best. I will not give him the satisfaction or the opportunity. Instead of moving laterally across his field of fire and taking up a firing position of her own, Dawn guided the low-flying *Shadow Hawk* straight at the *Griffin*. The heat in her cockpit began to rise, but she ignored it.

Her 'Mech landed in the soft mud, its feet sinking in slightly under the impact. Her heads up display blared a warning that she'd finally achieved a lock with her autocannon. She thumbed the trigger, sending a stream of shells into the body of the *Griffin*. There were flames and smoke as the other 'Mech reeled under the hits.

The Cavalier pilot recovered quickly, letting go with a salvo of LRMs just as Dawn was trying to adjust the heat sinks manually to bleed off the heat building up in the old 'Mech's cockpit. The missiles slammed into the *Shadow Hawk*'s chest and both arms, shaking it like a doll. Gripping the joystick as a brace, Dawn weathered the hit.

She responded by firing her lasers, which sent javelins of red, yellow, and green light ripping across the space between the two 'Mechs. Some missed, others dug deeply into the *Griffin*, hitting it low in the torso. The Cavalier 'Mech twisted under the hits and began to run to her right, the pilot trying to maintain his distance. Again Dawn outguessed him. Also breaking into a run, she raced the *Shadow Hawk* across the field of mud and death, heading directly for the *Griffin*. *He does not understand, this Cavalier. He does not know that I will fight to the death if need be. In the end, it will be his undoing.*

The Cavalier swung the massive PPC in her direction. For a moment everything seemed to move in slow motion for Dawn. It had happened this way once before, back on Tukayyid. From her cockpit she saw a flash of light and a wave of impact striking her *Shadow Hawk* like a massive stake being driven into its heart. The 'Mech tottered back slightly under the hit, losing some of its speed and momentum as the PPC blasted a huge hole in its chest.

A wave of heat washed over her as the temperature in the cockpit suddenly spiked. But Dawn kept her concentration, bearing down on the *Griffin*. When the targeting and tracking system squealed again, she opened up with the autocannon and a barrage of short-range missiles. *We are too close for him to use the PPC. Now it will be settled in the way of the Clans, warrior to warrior.*

The missiles rippled the armor plating off the *Griffin*'s right arm like a fruit being peeled. Some of the autocannon rounds missed their mark altogether while others slammed into the chest and other arm of the Cavalier 'Mech. The pilot hesitated slightly, unsure whether to break and run or turn and fight. That pause would cost him dearly.

Dawn suffered no such hesitation. She charged, plowing into the *Griffin* at more than 80 kph, the impact sounding like something between a hovercar crash and massive bones breaking. The noise was all around her as the *Shadow Hawk*'s shoulder dug into and through the *Griffin*'s torso. She was thrown back into the command seat with incredible fury, but kept her 'Mech upright, spinning to the left slightly as the Cavalier lost his balance. The *Griffin* seemed to fly backward and down, burrowing into the muck and spraying mud in every direction.

Dawn's damage monitor told her what the charge had cost her. The *Hawk*'s right arm was nearly exposed raw, stripped of its armor. Her shoulder actuator seemed to be sending the battle computer mixed signals that it was both on and off line at the same time. Either way, she didn't trust it. The heat in the cockpit was so stifling that the air seemed to sear her lungs. Drawing every breath was a battle, but she prevailed. Taking a few seconds to let the 'Mech cool slightly, she gathered her wits and her sense of where her foe was.

The *Griffin* was only a few scant meters distant as she locked her cross hairs onto its mauled form. While the laser began to preheat, she told herself that one good volley would end this contest, leaving her the victor. She waited, hoping to cool the *Shadow Hawk* a bit more before opening fire again, when suddenly her targeting system began to crackle.

She reached for the controls as a flickering wave of snow came off and on again and again. In the next few moments Dawn tried numerous combinations of adjustments as the *Griffin* pilot attempted to rise, but she couldn't get the system to clear. Out of the corner of her eye she saw a yellow light on her communication panel and understood.

Mordoc told me they cheated. She had seen the same kind of pattern on a targeting and tracking system once before, on Tukayyid when she had faced off against two platoons of Com Guard infantry. A jamming device with very limited range was being used on her 'Mech, interfering with her ability to fight. *Whoever it is, they must be close, in the bleachers or the technician pits.*

Not waiting for a weapons lock she manually eyed up a shot and fired her short-range missiles. Only one of them hit, burying itself in a hole her charge had already opened in the *Griffin*'s armor. For a millisecond Dawn wondered if the warhead was a dud, when suddenly it erupted from inside the superstructure of the other 'Mech. There was a deep groaning, then a flash of flames and huge billows of smoke from the hole. Dawn ignored it, still trying to adjust her targeting system to compensate for the jamming. It was a failing effort.

Despite the hit, the *Griffin* pilot was still trying to get his 'Mech back on its feet. The parts of his machine not covered in mud spewed smoke and fire as he attempted to rise in the muck of the arena. Dawn knew she had to act, and act quickly. Bringing the *Shadow Hawk* to point-blank range, she drew back the massive reinforced foot, and kicked the *Griffin* with everything she had.

The kick mauled some of the armor on her own 'Mech's foot, but she'd dug a massive gouge in the *Griffin*'s leg. The Cavalier once again lost control of his 'Mech, which fell on its side, facing her. Dawn could see the damage and knew there was little the pilot could do, even with her targeting system being jammed.

Then came the lightning-like flash of the *Griffin*'s PPC.

The blast hammered her torso hard, the armor shattering like ice under the blow. Her ears rang from feedback to her neurohelmet, and her eyes felt as if they wanted to push out of her head. She fought the wave of the impact, leaning into it to kill its momentum and push. The restraining straps dug into her chest, and the cooling vest felt as if it was being ripped off her by the force of the hit. In an instant Dawn knew what had happened. The Cavalier had cut off the field inhibitors that prevented the PPC from firing at close range. There was a good chance the weapon would be destroyed in such an attack, fused into a massive slug of ferro-titanium, but it did allow him to fire at incredibly deadly ranges.

And this time it had paid off. A glance at the secondary

monitor told her that her left-side armor was all but gone and that the autocannon normally slung there was now missing, ripped off and tossed behind her into the mud. *He fights like a filthy bandit, jamming my weapons system from the crowd. I offered him a fair trial, a contest of equals, and this is how he respects the rules. This man is no warrior. He has no honor. What I do now, I do for the betterment of his stable.*

Dawn closed the ten-meter distance in less than a step and a half of the *Shadow Hawk*'s massive feet. In front of her was the *Griffin,* trying to stand or line her up for another shot, both efforts doomed to failure. She was near the helmet-like head of the fallen 'Mech, out of reach of the PPC. Again, she raised one of the *Shadow Hawk*'s feet over the *Griffin*'s cockpit. She could imagine what it must feel like to be on the other side of that foot, looking up and seeing tons of metal about to drive in on top of you.

But still the Cavalier fought back, opening up with his long-range missile rack. Fortunately for Dawn, the warheads did not have time to arm. Most shot up past the *Shadow Hawk,* missing totally. The small number that hit did not explode, but simply nudged her as she stood.

Then Dawn drove the 'Mech's giant foot down into the *Griffin*'s cockpit, smashing through it.

Nothing could have survived the attack. Dozens of tons pushed to incredible speeds flattened the cockpit of the Cavalier. From high up in the her own cockpit Dawn watched it all—the small fires that broke out around her foot, the different colors of smoke that drifted out of the hole where the Cavalier warrior had piloted the 'Mech. He never had a chance.

Dawn had never intended for him to.

To her it made perfect sense, was completely logical. This freebirth was inferior. Jamming her and preventing her from using her weapons systems, he did not fight fair. Even had he tried to surrender, Dawn doubted she would have accepted it. This warrior was not worthy of survival. Yet she had given him something he didn't deserve, a death in combat. In doing so she had served Carmody's Cavaliers as much as her own stable. His destruction meant that his genes would not pass to another generation. Still, he had died with some degree of honor—on the battlefield—as all true warriors dreamed of doing.

Mordoc met Dawn as she jumped to the ground from the leg of the *Shadow Hawk*. Some cheers rose from the nearby stands, but she also heard the sound of booing and hissing. Dawn was unsure what to make of the gathering, the lower castes coming to pass judgment on her prowess as a warrior. She looked up at them and then back at Mordoc, hoping that the stable master could tell her how to respond.

"I wanted you to win, but I didn't think you'd kill the guy in the process," he said, patting her on the back.

"One of his comrades was jamming my targeting and tracking system. He continued to fight in an effort to take advantage of that. It was a mark of dishonor. That is why I destroyed him."

"I suspected that old man Carmody might try something like this," Mordoc said. "Are you all right?"

"I am ready to serve."

"You've already done quite enough tonight, Dawn. The biggest problem we're going to have from this point on is keeping the Cavaliers from killing you out of revenge."

"They would do that?"

"Yes, in a heartbeat. That was no ordinary pilot you offed back there. That was Jay J. Carmody, son of the old man. He's lost his boy, and after tonight, half his funds. He's going to be gunning for revenge in a big bad nasty way."

To Dawn, the concept of revenge killing was something to be handled in a ritual manner, between warriors in an honor duel. How different was this new world she'd entered, how alien. If they even had the concept of honor, they viewed it far differently from the way of the Clans.

Hermann Bovos rose from his seat in the stands and watched as the drunken crowd went wild. The man next to him stood too, looking down on the shattered and mud-covered remains of the *Griffin*. He rolled up the betting sheet and stuffed it into his coat pocket.

"Thank you for meeting me here," Bovos told him. "Claire said you might have some information for me."

The man did not answer the question. "Claire doesn't usually do favors of this kind."

Bovos smiled slightly. He hadn't really understood why Claire Lieb decided to help him, but he wasn't about to question it. "Let's just say that she and I are friends."

"Sure," the other man said, looking around as the crowd thinned rapidly around them. Reassured that no one could overhear, he spoke again. "Claire said you're looking for somebody who's been doing some serious recruiting here recently. Well, I think I've got a line on someone like that. The word on the street is that they'll be back in a week or so looking for more warriors. I also hear they want to hire several companies worth of troops, full units if they can find them."

Bovos's heart raced. These were probably the same people who'd hit the Hussars, who'd wiped out his lance and left him for dead. Finally, he would get a chance at them, a chance to get inside their operation. His mind danced with the possibilities.

"I appreciate the tip," he said.

The man shook his head. "Listen to me, kid. If I was you, I'd stay away from these guys. I hear they're bad trouble."

"Out of the question."

"Then you'd better get tied up with a lance or company of 'Mechs real quick-like. Otherwise you ain't going along."

14

Galaport
Galatea
Skye March, Federated Commonwealth
15 May 3057

From the stands Duncan Kalma and some of his men sat watching the 'Mechs preparing for the coming bout. The one down below and in front of them was a late-model *Crusader.* Judging by the patchwork of armor replacements that were unpainted but in place, the 'Mech had obviously been refitted several times in its career. Technicians crawled over, around, and under it, quickly opening small access panels, checking them, then securing them shut. The pilot, a virtual unknown on Galatea, was already inside the cockpit. Duncan said little, taking occasional sips from a bottle of beer.

He was thinking that the Knights had, for the most part, adapted well to their mission since arriving on Galatea. He'd spent a few days bringing them into the city in small groups, staying close until he was sure they could hold their own and maintain their cover. Then he left them to the task of frequenting various MechWarrior haunts to learn what they could and make their presence known on Galatea. They'd also gotten rooms at the Starspan Hotel, which would give them a base of operations other than the DropShip.

Trane, at Duncan's bidding, had begun to spread the word that Kalma's Company was looking to hire three MechWarriors to fill out its last lance, a rumor that was making them something of local celebrities among the many unemployed MechWarriors in Galaport. Duncan didn't jump too quickly to hire any of them. He was looking for certain kind of people—ones that seemed trustworthy and might fit in well with their current mix.

Duncan glanced up as someone he didn't know extended his hand in greeting. The newcomer was a big man, but by his combat gloves and the way his head was shaved in several places to allow neurohelmet contacts, he was obviously a MechWarrior.

"You Duncan Kalma?" the man asked.

Duncan nodded and shook the man's hand.

"I hear you're hiring. That true?"

"Maybe," Duncan said.

"Well, if it is, I'm looking to sign on."

Duncan studied the man's face for a moment. "Where'd you serve last?"

"Free Worlds League."

Duncan knew when to play his cards close to his chest, and this was one of those times. "You don't say? What unit?"

"Hussars. Second Oriente Hussars."

Duncan recognized the unit, having read all about it in the SAFE briefings prior to Herotitus. Again, he didn't let it show. "Have a seat," he said as Karl Villiers shifted over slightly on the bench to make room.

"You got a name?" he asked.

The man smiled, "Bovos. Hermann Bovos."

"I'm Duncan Kalma, CO of Kalma's Company. How'd you hear we were hiring?"

Bovos shrugged. "Word gets around. They say you've got close to a company of 'Mechs but still need a few more jocks."

Duncan nodded. "That's right. And once we're up to speed, we'll be looking for some contracts. You say you were with the Second Oriente Hussars?"

Bovos nodded warily. "I was a Lieutenant and lance commander."

"Pretty tough unit. They practically wrote the book on fast recon operations, if my memory is on target."

"One of the best, Mister Kalma."

"Call me Duncan, Hermann. Mister Kalma is my father. How long were you with the Hussars?"

Bovos smiled. "Eight years." Then he added, "And you can call me Bovos."

"Pretty good stint. Why'd you leave?" Duncan took a long drink on his beer, which was growing warm.

"Personal reasons," Bovos said.

Duncan nodded, but his mind fidgeted with the information and wondered if it were true. If it was possible this guy had actually tangled with those raiders on Shiro III, Duncan was sure he wanted him. "Well, Bovos, you might just fit the bill. Why don't we meet later, somewhere where we can sit down and talk? Listen, do you know a place called Lulu's near the old hiring hall?"

Bovos nodded.

"Good. I'll meet you there at twenty-three hundred hours."

Bovos stood up, a smile widening across his face. "Thanks, Mister—er, Duncan. I'll be there."

As Hermann Bovos turned and made his way down from the stands, Duncan followed him with his eyes. When he was out of sight, Duncan pulled a small communicator from his breast pocket.

"Rogue One to Tin Man," he said, relishing the call sign he'd picked for Rod Trane.

"I read you," came back the voice.

"Run a check on the DropShip's computer files on Shiro III. See what you come up with on a 'Mech pilot name of Hermann Bovos with the Oriente Hussars. Give me a buzz when you've got something."

"Understood and out," Trane said, his tone wooden. Duncan knew that Trane was still struggling with his resentment over command of the operation going to a knockaround like Duncan instead of to him. Trane was just going to have to get over it, and Duncan wished he'd hurry up and do so.

The light on top of the old wooden pole went from yellow to red as Duncan watched the *Crusader* move forward. Its opponent, a bright green *Thunderbolt*, stood at the opposite end of the muddy embankment that marked the arena. Both weighing in at 65 tons, the 'Mechs were equally intimidating. The stocky *Thunderbolt* displayed an imposing solidity, looking as difficult to knock over as a deeply rooted tree. The *Crusader,* with its Lindblad anti-missile system protruding from the center of its head, resembled the fabled unicorn of the ancients. The spotlights from towers surrounding the area cast odd shadows in the night, making the 'Mechs seem even more menacing.

The *Crusader* closed cautiously on its opponent, while the *Thunderbolt* pilot wasted no time opening fire with his large laser and long-range missiles. The laser sliced through the *Crusader*'s right arm with surgical precision, burning through the armor and destroying myomer muscle and sensor equipment as it went. The missiles also found their intended target, most slamming into the *Crusader*'s boxy chest. Watching these first few minutes of fighting, Duncan wondered if this match was going to be any contest at all. The *Thunderbolt* was mauling its opponent, whose armor was already pitted with gaping holes and severe burns.

Despite the damage he'd taken, the *Crusader* pilot hung in with the fight, answering the *Thunderbolt*'s attack with a wall of thirty long-range missiles. A few missed, but the rest punched into the *Thunderbolt*'s green armor, turning its chest into a bed of small explosions. A wave of fire and smoke engulfed the *Thunderbolt,* but when the smoke cleared, it emerged still functional and in the fight.

Facing the slow-moving *Crusader,* the green 'Mech released a trio of medium lasers from its left shoulder and a deadly large one from its right arm. Duncan cringed. He knew the heat generated during such a salvo was tremendous, and in an instant saw the results. The *Crusader* took two of the laser hits on its lacerated right arm, the last of its armor sizzling and then falling into the mud with a giant splash. A secondary explosion finished the arm off while the large laser ate into the *Crusader*'s chest like a voracious electrical beast.

Duncan was shocked that the *Crusader* pilot didn't give up, despite the heavy damage to his 'Mech. This, he knew, was a critical moment. Any more damage and the *Crusader* was a goner, while the *Thunderbolt* was hanging tough. It was almost over.

The pilot of the burn-marked *Thunderbolt* apparently decided to toy with the *Crusader*. He moved in close, venting heat and getting ready for the final blow. The *Crusader* seemed to waver, and for a moment Duncan thought it was all over for him.

But, just then, bright blue, red, and yellow flames streaked from the 'Mech's lower torso. The *Crusader* had fired its jump jets, lifting sixty-five tons of death and destruction up into the air. Duncan could hear the whooshing roar of flames all the way up to where he and the others sat in the stands. The *Thunderbolt* was racing to reposition, but the *Crusader*'s flight was rapidly picking up speed. At a height of about fifty meters, it suddenly began to descend on a collision course with death—and the *Thunderbolt*.

The pilot of the green 'Mech tried to defend himself, firing a salvo of long-range missiles upward at the *Crusader*, but every warhead fell wide of the plunging battle machine. Duncan knew why. At that close range it was difficult to aim the missiles accurately at a moving target—there wasn't enough time. The besieged *Thunderbolt* drifted back, trying to evade the *Crusader*. But the jumping 'Mech anticipated the *Thunderbolt*'s tactics like some massive bird of prey. The *Crusader* sailed just over the *Thunderbolt* . . . then dropped.

The move was known as Death from Above and was considered one of the most deadly attacks a 'Mech could perform in full-contact fighting. The one-armed *Crusader* drove feet first into the back and shoulders of the *Thunderbolt* with a grinding and screeching that was terrible to hear.

The *Thunderbolt* doubled over at the waist, then collapsed under the *Crusader*'s weight. The *Crusader* almost toppled too, a risk in such an attack. But the pilot somehow managed to keep the 'Mech on its feet. The two 'Mechs were motionless for ten long seconds as both pilots regained their bearings and their wits.

As if to emphasize its victory, the *Crusader* fired one of its short-range missile packs downward into the mangled form of the *Thunderbolt*. The missile pair ripped up the armor on the 'Mech's muck-covered back, but Duncan was sure the pilot took the shot more for dramatic effect. Suddenly the lights of the arena flashed once off and back on. The light on the wooden pole went from red to yellow. The *Thunderbolt* had signaled surrender. The match was over.

"Villiers," Duncan said to his nearest companion.

"Yes, Duncan?"

"Who's that *Crusader* pilot?"

Villiers studied the program sheet for a minute, tracing his finger down to the match they'd just witnessed. "His name is Garth Hawkes. There are the letters 'DPI' after his name."

Duncan's brow wrinkled as he tried to remember the term, then he recalled that it stood for Damn Proud Independent. "That was one hell of a move. You don't see Death from Above too often in your career, let along this close."

"You interested in him?"

"Let's meet him first," Duncan said. "Tell him we'd like to talk. We can meet at the arena entrance."

As Villiers went to do his bidding, Duncan took another sip of his beer. This Garth Hawkes DPI looked like just the kind of man he needed. Not only a skilled pilot, but one willing to take extraordinary risks.

Cavern of the Skull
New St. Andrews, The Periphery
Rimward of the Circinus Federation

Outside, morning was breaking, but deep in the bowels of the cavern it was always night. Kemper Varas sat at the desk waiting. He didn't like to bring his lord bad news, never sure what form his anger might take. As Stefan Amaris VII entered, Varas rose and bowed slightly. "You look well today, Star Lord."

Amaris lowered himself into his chair slowly and carefully, leaning his forearms on the desk. "You have received word from our forces who hit Herotitus?"

"I have."

"Tell me, Varas, were they successful?"

"We lost no personnel, but three of our 'Mech pilots were injured enough to end up in sickbay on the return trip. Our BattleMech losses, however, were unacceptable, sire. One 'Mech was a total loss, and two others suffered enough damage that the Captain says they should be scrapped for parts rather than repaired."

The Star Lord's nostrils flared and he balled his hands into fists, slamming them into the table with such force that it seemed the heavy wood would crack under the blow. "I am building an empire, Varas! You are my general and you keep telling me of losses. Do you have any idea what all this costs? I've already funded the formation of the Republican Guards. Now, with these losses and those of the other raids, we're down several lances worth of 'Mechs."

"But, lord, the raids thus far have all been successful." Varas wanted to stem the tide of rage rising at him from across the table.

"Victories that are costing me a fortune. I want you to contact our recruiters and tell them to send us at least two companies worth of mercenaries. Make sure they have their own equipment, though—ships and BattleMechs. I'm growing weary of having to build this army one stick at a time. Caesar ... Alexander ... McKenna ... none of them ever had to deal with the difficulties I've been forced to endure. If not for the noble blood flowing though my veins, I'd have given up long ago."

Amaris was ranting rather than speaking, his thoughts and words seeming to wander with each sentence. There was a dark fire burning in his eyes, and Varas couldn't help but wonder if it was the same rage that had maddened Amaris the First. He cringed, knowing he had yet to conclude his report.

"I will order the recruiters on Galatea to sign up more troops. We'll replenish our ranks and equipment and bring the Republican Guards to well over regimental size."

Amaris smiled suddenly. "Yes, my Guards. They are the key to the victories we must forge. I am the hammer, and the Guards are my anvil. Between them lie the Clans and the House Lords. They will perish, swept away by the people of the Inner Sphere. They will follow me because I offer them an age of enlightenment, an era where wars and petty lords do not exist. No invaders, only liberators. That is what I bring to them."

"Of course, Lord," Varas said, being careful not to meet Amaris's eyes. "But there is another matter I must bring to your attention."

"Yes?"

"I spoke with the Clave Lords last night—"

"And?"

"They expressed their displeasure at our presence on their world—again. They claim we have not lived up to our promises for the use of this mountain base and that they may revoke their permission. They say they will be forced to remove us from New St. Andrews."

The laughter that came from Amaris startled Varas, who had expected another tide of fury. "Remove *me* from New St. Andrews? Don't they realize who they are dealing with?"

"They know who you are, Star Lord."

The laugh stopped and changed to a twisted, crafty expression. "They know me, yet they do not fear me? They will, though. They will, or my name is not Amaris. When we came here, they had nothing. I clothed and fed them. Now they want more. Well, they won't get it, not from me. New St. Andrews is my world now. I rule here as I will rule the entire Inner Sphere. They must be made to understand their position in relationship to me. Don't you agree, Varas?"

Varas nodded slightly, not sure where this discussion of the Claves was going.

"Good. Who is the strongest of their leaders?"

"Markelonis Kav of the Red Dog Clave."

"Excellent. Send one of my Guards there tonight to poison their precious water supply. Let them drink and die in their beds. When the others see the price of resistance to my will, they will fall to their knees before me."

"This will harm many innocents, Star Lord. The wells are used by the entire community. It would be easy enough to dispose of Kav."

Amaris's face grew even darker, a storm cloud ready to

burst. "You have your orders, Varas. Make it happen. No one will interfere with the forging of my empire, especially not these petty little shepherds. New St. Andrews is mine, I tell you. I claim it, just as I will lay claim to the whole of the Inner Sphere!"

Galaport
Galatea
Skye March, Federated Commonwealth
15 May 3057

Standing in front of Duncan was a man with his hair tied back tightly into a pony tail and wearing a black leather vest. Though a few gray hairs were visible, the face was one of those boyish ones that seemed perpetually young. The man hadn't shaved in a while, but was otherwise well kept.

"Garth Hawkes?" Duncan said, extending his hand.

"The same. And you are?"

"Duncan Kalma." He gave the man a firm handshake, then gestured toward his companions. "And some of my people." Garth saluted them with a slight wave of the hand, then turned back to Duncan.

"Your man Villiers says you're here looking to hire."

"Possibly. I was impressed with your work in the arena tonight. It was damned gutsy, especially at the end. Death from Above can often backfire on a pilot. You took a big risk taking out that *Thunderbolt.*"

Hawkes nodded slightly.

"Why?"

"Because I wanted to win," Hawkes said simply. "I've only lost one battle in my life and I have no intention of ever losing another."

Duncan could tell there was definitely a story in all that, but this wasn't the place or the time to pursue it. "We're three men shy of a full company, but we've got a full complement of 'Mechs and our own DropShip."

"Equipment isn't my concern," Hawkes said.

"That so?" Duncan studied the other man for a moment. "Where have you served?"

"I've been around. I just finished a stint with the Federated Commonwealth. I was a company commander."

"And now you're here on Galatea looking for work."

"That's right. My unit was attacked while I was away from my post. They were caught totally off guard—hell, half of them were in for equipment upgrades. They went into the fight without me. By the time I got there it was too late."

"So what happened?"

"They cashiered me." Hawkes shrugged. "Maybe some of my men would still be alive if I'd been there."

"What unit?"

"I'd rather not say."

Duncan could understand why Hawkes preferred to keep that to himself, but he also needed to know more about him. "Where did all this happen?"

"The Capellan March. So now you know something about me. But what about your little unit? Like who are you going to try to hire on with?"

"That's an odd question," Duncan said slowly, still trying to feel the other man out, "but I guess I don't mind. We've met a few of the recruiters on this rock so far, but we're waiting for the right job. We'd like to sign with someone who's putting together a private army or a large-scale raid. A bigger unit, none of this single-run stuff. Does that answer your question?"

Hawkes nodded. "Sounds right up my alley."

"So, what do you say? I think we could use someone like you."

"Could be. How's about we iron out some of the details over drinks?"

Duncan nodded. He was sure Hawkes would sign on, and he took it as a good omen. Just as he'd been going down to meet with Hawkes, Trane had transmitted word that Hermann Bovos had checked out. The big man would be a valuable addition to their ranks and Duncan was sure he'd stay on even if he learned the truth. Now along came Hawkes.

Two down and one to go to fill out the last slot. After that it was only a matter of time . . .

Still exhilarated from her match, Dawn had decided to walk part of the way home, and was rounding the corner toward the hotel where Mordoc had rented her a room. He'd invited her to a celebration with the other members of the Minutemen, but she had declined. *They celebrate victories here, but we of the Clans know better. We honor victories by adding verses to* The Remembrance *and the passing of our genetic legacy to another generation of warriors. These Inner Sphere freebirths live only for the now. They do not look to the future of our species, to what would serve the good of all, even the generations to come.* The imbibing of alcoholic drinks was a rare experience among the Clans. Dawn had tried it only once, and the memory of the sickness that followed was enough to cure her of the desire for a lifetime.

Rounding the corner she came suddenly and unexpectedly upon a group of men who seemed intent on blocking her path. There were five of them, each with some kind of hand weapon, ranging from blackjacks to a section of chain. Their uniforms told a story as well. All showed the insignia of Carmody's Cavaliers, one of whom she'd defeated earlier that evening. Now it looked like they wanted to fight her again, with the odds stacked to boot.

"Lookie what we got here," said one of the men. He was holding a blackjack. "The bitch that killed Jay."

"I hear she's a Clan-head. Hey, blondie, you really a Clanner?" another one mocked. Dawn had trained since her earliest years in the arts of war, had survived test after test until the final Trial of Position that had finally made her a Clan warrior. After a lifetime of learning to master fear, these trashborns did not frighten her. Instead she was assessing each one, their weapons, the terrain, possible exit routes they might take, anything and everything about the situation. It was the mark of a warrior to understand and use whatever was at hand. The idea of retreat never crossed her mind.

Also hanging about a little ways off were three or four more Cavaliers. Seeing how they kept their distance, she dismissed them scornfully as freebirth cowards who only fought when they didn't fear getting hurt.

"Aff," she said proudly. "I was once of Clan Steel Viper."

Another one of the men came up along her right side, holding a blackjack. "This is going to be even more fun than I thought. I'm from Rassalhague and I haven't seen or heard from any of my family since the planet fell to you Clan bastards. We're gonna get you good, Clan girl, but not just for Jay—this is for everybody who's had his life cranked over by you and your friggin' Clans."

Dawn dropped into a fighting stance. "There are five of you. Do you wish to bid away your numbers or shall I take you on all at once?"

"This isn't one of yer frigging batchalls, baby. You're gonna fight all of us. And we'll give you plenty to remember us by, except you'll be too dead to do it." The man laughed harshly and grabbed at his crotch, leaving Dawn no doubt about what he had in mind. So it was true what the Crusaders said about the Inner Sphere, she thought. These freebirths were truly barbarian.

"You will not kill me," she said, her voice cold and utterly confident. "But some of you will surely die."

One of the men held up a knife. "Time to pay, bitch," he said, rushing forward with the blade lifted to strike.

In one fluid sweep Dawn spun to the left on one leg and threw him a hard kick to the groin. The man dropped the knife in mid-swing and literally flew backward into the dark street. By now another of the Cavaliers was swinging a heavy club at her, but she was too quick, ducking and jumping back. The move also gave her a chance to grab the first man's knife off the ground. Dawn had become totally alert, every fiber of her being tuned to this moment, this fight, these opponents. A lifetime of training had honed her reactions to the sureness of pure instinct. She did not fight with logic, but with the deadliness of any creature that knows its own power.

Hermann Bovos had just come up the street toward Lulu's, but almost forgot the reason he happened to be on this street at all when he ran straight into a brawl unlike any he had ever seen. He stopped to watch. The woman was obviously outnumbered, yet so far she was more than holding her own. Two of the men were downed already, one with a kick to the groin that would probably end his blood line forever and the other stabbed with a knife intended for use against her. Bovos didn't know how this fight had begun, but seeing more men begin to encircle her, he knew it was only a matter of time before she was overwhelmed.

As other attackers moved into position around her, a chain whizzed through the air, just missing her head by centimeters. Eight against one certainly wasn't a fair fight, especially when the one was a woman. But judging from the way she fought, this was no ordinary female. Definitely a Mech-Warrior.

Bovos threw himself into the melee, his target one of the men just rearing his club back to strike the woman from behind. Bovos jerked the arm backward, throwing the man off balance and sending him sprawling. Now the one with the chain was swinging the thing at Bovos instead of the woman. It struck him across the legs, knocking him to the ground. But Bovos was fast enough to grab the chain even as it was swinging away. He ripped it out of his attacker's hands.

The woman had by now seized a club from one of the others and was slamming it into the back of the neck of the man attacking Bovos. The blow snapped the club as well as the man's neck, and his body fell like a sack over Bovos's legs. Everything was happening too fast for thought, but he couldn't help being amazed that she was fighting to kill. Another one of the men was swinging a chain now, this time grazing the woman in the head and ripping her ear.

"Hang on!" Bovos shouted, throwing a punch at the man closest to him.

"Neg!" the woman hissed. "This is my fight. They belong to me!"

Duncan was on his way up the same street to Lulu's when he too came upon the street brawl. "What's going on?" he asked a Galaport local shouldering his way closer.

"The Cavaliers got them a real Clan warrior," the man said."

Duncan spotted Hermann Bovos in the middle of the fight and his heart raced. *Blast it! I need him!*

Almost without thinking, Duncan also began pushing through the crowd to where Bovos was grappling on the ground with a wiry, bearded man. A woman, the side of her face and neck slick with blood, was locked on the ground with another man. Glancing around, Duncan noticed a man holding his groin, apparently doubled over in pain. But when the same man suddenly straightened up, he was holding a laser pistol. It was leveled directly at the woman, who now had her hands wrapped around the throat of the man she was wrestling. With a flying leap, Duncan knocked the man with the gun backward, slapping at his hands even as the weapon fired.

The shot seemed to shake the air and stun both the crowd and the combatants. Everything stopped suddenly as if time had frozen. The man Duncan had tackled dropped to the ground, apparently unconscious. The woman stood up, her eyes flicking from Bovos to Duncan. She looked exhausted and was already showing bruises where she'd been punched, hit, or kicked.

"The fight . . ." she began, her voice wavering, ". . . was mine." She took a step toward Bovos, then looked over at Duncan again.

Then she collapsed onto the wet, cold sidewalk. Blood was everywhere. Those who weren't dead moaned in pain.

Duncan had no idea how this woman had gotten herself into such a brawl, but she could obviously take care of herself. Bending down to see what he could do for her, he couldn't help thinking that maybe he'd just found the final member of Kalma's Company.

If so, he promised himself, he'd better be damn careful never to get on the wrong side of her.

Galaport
Galatea
Skye March, Federated Commonwealth
16 May 3057

"**D**uncan, I think she's waking up," Bovos said, seeing her eyes flutter. Duncan quickly stood and walked over to the bed. After another few minutes the woman's eyes opened. She stared curiously up at the two men hovering over her.

"Where am I?"

"We brought you to our hotel," Duncan said, but her look was one of utter bafflement. "Don't you remember? We got into that fight you had with the Cavaliers who ganged up on you."

She started to sit up, then quickly fell back against the pillow as a look of pain flashed over her face.

"You've been out since last night. One of Carmody's Cavaliers plastered you with the butt of his pistol. But we had a doctor in and he said there's no concussion. You'll be all right."

"Who are you?" she asked, almost angrily.

"Duncan, Duncan Kalma. And this is Hermann Bovos."

"But why did you interfere? I do not know either of you."

"Well, let's just say it looked like you needed some help."

"Help?" She blinked, tried to sit up again. "But it was my fight, *quiaff*?"

"It sure was," Duncan said. Her speech was strange, almost like listening to someone born centuries ago. "People in the crowd were shouting something about you being a Clanner. Is it true?"

She looked him in the eyes. "Yes," she said finally. "I was a Clan warrior, a Steel Viper."

"You say 'was'...?"

"I am now *dezgra*—disgraced, cast out."

"So you came here ... to Galatea."

"Being a warrior is all I know. I met a man who offered me a place in his stable."

"You're talking about Edel Mordoc, right?" They'd done some checking on her, which hadn't been hard at all. A blond, blue-eyed Clan warrior competing in the Games of Galatea definitely stood out from the crowd.

"Mordoc, yes, an odd little man. So ugly he could make an onion cry. I won him several matches, but in the last one I defeated the son of the man who owns Carmody's Cavaliers."

"You killed him, to be precise," Duncan said. "Which is why they came after you. But you sure can hold your own in a fight."

Duncan kept talking quickly to keep her from interrupting. "That's why we brought you here. I came to Galatea to fill out the ranks of my company. In the past couple of days we've signed on two." He looked at her pointedly. "We still need one more."

This time she sat up without flinching, eyes flashing anger again. "I may be disgraced, freebirth, but I'm no mercenary."

"Then what are you doing in Galaport?" Bovos asked. "And why were you fighting in the games?"

She shook her head stubbornly. "Too long a tale."

"You're right. You don't know us, we don't know you," Duncan said soothingly. "How about starting with something simple? I've told you my name. I'm from the planet Marik in the Free Worlds League. I trained as a MechWarrior but decided I wanted to see the galaxy first. How about you?"

Dawn did not answer immediately. The location of the Clan homeworlds was a secret, but not the name of the planet where she'd been stationed in the Steel Viper occupation zone. "I came from Jabuka."

"What's your name?" Duncan asked, touching her shoulder gently so that she dropped back against the pillow once more.

"My name is Dawn," she said, pushing his hand away roughly.

"Trane, look at this star chart. She says she's from Jabuka."

Duncan had gone down the hall to Trane's room, leaving Dawn to get some more rest. He had the chart spread out on the room's single small table.

"So?"

"Remember the SAFE report on the Cumbres raid? It said the Twenty-fourth Lyran Guards were attacked first by a company-sized unit from the Clans. The report also said the unit was testing new 'Mechs. So the Clanners had to slug it out with 'Mechs equal to their own. Then the fake Knights arrived and finished off the Guards after they'd been mauled by the Clanners. The Clan force had to withdraw because they took so much damage—first from the Guards and then from the fake Knights."

"I see what you're driving at, Duncan. Jabuka is close enough to Cumbres for the Steel Vipers to launch a raid. Do you think she could have been part of the Clan strike on Cumbres?"

"I don't know. She said she's 'deshra' or something like that—means they threw her out and don't come back. I assume it also means she was dishonored in some way. But I don't know much about the Clans."

Trane shrugged. "Nor I. But from some of the briefings I've seen, the greatest dishonor a Clan warrior can suffer is poor performance on the battlefield. That's what comes to mind first."

"Dishonored, as in losing a battle against Inner Sphere forces, perhaps? What if she was a part of the Clan company that hit Cumbres? Those Clanners were expecting to find a regular Lyran Guard unit and they walked smack dab into a force of new 'Mechs. Would something like that be enough to get her thrown out of the Clans?"

Trane shrugged. "I'm not sure. I'm no expert either."

"Well, at the moment we're all she's got. I guess that's

what made up her mind. I told her Mordoc would have nothing more to do with her now that she's made so many enemies here."

"You're incorrigible," Trane said.

"And get this," Duncan went on, "she made me promise not to pay her. She says she could never honorably sell her warrior skills, but that it's all right for her to accept food and board. From what I've heard of the Clans, I'd wager she's a damned good MechWarrior. We can cobble something together for her once we win some salvage. Having a Clanner ought to be a big help with our cover."

Trane studied Duncan a moment. "How do you propose to use her?"

"Well, Bovos and Hawkes already have some experience in one-on-one matches, so the four of us will form up the Command Lance. Dawn's got experience too, so we'll put her in the Fire Support Lance with Villiers, Blix, and Goto for backup in case one of us gets injured. She's certainly a high-profile item. The rest will make up the Recon Lance."

Duncan had spoken quickly, anticipating an objection. He was sure Trane would have preferred to put all the Knights in two lances, with Duncan and the rest of the pick-up recruits in the third.

But all Trane said was, "So, now we're a full company. All we need are some matches."

"Exactly. What did you find out?"

"With the Galateans so desperate to keep the economy going, they schedule contests pretty regularly."

"The Arena where we fought last time is called the Field of Combat, right?"

Trane nodded. "The other is the Combat Range. A fifty-square-kilometer area complete with mock town, bridges, and different terrains. From what I've seen, here's how it works. There will be nine matches. The first four are lance-to-lance, the second four are one-on-one, and the final match is fought by what's left of the whole company."

"We're going to be at a disadvantage in the lance fights," Duncan said thoughtfully. "We've never fought together as a unit. And we've got precious little time to train. We're going to have to do it right ... the first time out."

"From what Hawkes and Bovos have said, it doesn't sound like they're big on following the rules around here either. They say you can break off a fight at any time by setting off a signal flare. Your opponent is supposed to honor it, but maybe he will, maybe he won't."

"Our goal is to establish a reputation ... and quickly," said Duncan. "Losing a match because we withdrew from the fight wouldn't do much for us in that department, not to mention the salvage rights that go to whoever beats you. We can't afford that either individually or as a unit. For us, it's going to be do or die."

"That's right," Trane said gravely. "To the death."

"And now the big question—when do we start?"

"Tomorrow. It seems there's an opening in the schedule. No one wants to be the first to take on last month's champions."

"And who might they be?"

Trane flashed a rare grin. "None other than Carmody's Cavaliers."

"Good," Duncan said, grinning back. "Dawn'll love that."

=== 17 ===

Galaport
Galatea
Skye March, Federated Commonwealth
22 May 3057

Duncan sat looking at the secondary screen in the cockpit of his *BattleMaster,* suddenly wondering what he was doing here. Piloting a BattleMech in a series of murderous combats in a place like Galaport had certainly never been one of his dreams in life. But it had seemed like the only way to get into the circle of warriors where leads to the bogus Knights might be found. They'd known going in that Carmody's Cavaliers were cutthroats and bullies, but they'd also proven relentless in combat. Not only that; they had the advantage of being familiar with the Combat Range, where lances engaged lances. Despite that, Kalma's Company had won their first three matches against the Cavaliers.

"Demon, do you see anything?" It was Hawkes on the line.

"Not a thing, Gunner," Duncan returned.

It was Trane who'd suggested the call sign of "Demon" for Duncan, apparently getting in his licks where he could. But Duncan didn't object to either the nickname or to how well four 'Mech pilots who barely knew each other were fighting together.

"I hear the bookmakers are now giving us even odds against the Cavaliers," Trane said to no one in particular, and Duncan could have sworn he heard a note of pride.

"Did you put a few C-bills down on us?" Duncan asked wickedly, knowing Trane wouldn't dignify the question with a response. Smiling to himself, he returned his attention to the tactical display. Still no blips indicating contact with their opponents. In the three previous matches the Cavaliers had seemed to depend on variations of a single tactic. After locating the most vulnerable 'Mech in the opposing lance, all four Cavaliers would attack it. Then they worked their way through the rest, always four against one. Neither brilliant nor original, which was why Duncan's team always found some way around it.

Having won the coin toss for the match, the Cavaliers had the right of choosing their entry point on the fifty-kilometer Combat Range. To the north was a rise of rocky hills, then a desert plain typical of most of Galatea's bakingly hot climate, and what passed for a forest to the south. The Cavaliers had elected to enter from the north among the rocky hills and were now playing a waiting game.

"I'm getting bored," said Bovos.

"Me too, Ox. What about you, Paladin?"

"Same here," Trane said. "I'm on my way." In their first match against the Cavaliers, luck had been on their side. When Carmody's Lance had converged on Hawkes in his *Crusader,* Duncan in his *BattleMaster* and Bovos in his *Warhammer* had wound up on the same path and come up behind the Cavaliers quite by accident.

Thinking the Cavaliers might try something similar in the second match, Duncan and company came up with a plan of their own. Trane's *Valkyrie* wasn't the fastest light 'Mech available, but it did boast six tons of armor that let it keep fighting even while absorbing a fair amount of damage. It also had a jump-jet capacity of 150 meters and good armament. On its own the *Valkyrie* was no match for a medium or heavy 'Mech, but could be very effective as part of a lance.

Trane had used his speed to find the Cavaliers and then taunt them until they attacked, believing him to be alone. The second match ended as abruptly and violently as the first, with Duncan, Bovos, and Hawkes swiftly hitting the Cavalier lance from the rear. Another variation on the theme was also successful in the third match. As he watched the *Valkyrie* disappear in the distance, Duncan hoped the Cavaliers would think they wouldn't try the same trick again.

Trane gazed at the low-slung mountains ahead. Somewhere, he assumed, in those rocks an *Assassin,* a *Hunchback,* and a *Dragon* should be waiting for him. He made a slow, steady approach to give the Cavaliers plenty of time to spot him. It also bought him time to think. Clinton Carmody's unit was supposed to be company-size. But in three days Carmody had lost three lances to Kalma's Company. Three lances constituted a company, yet here they were trying to ferret out yet another lance of Cavaliers. Approaching the foothills he throttled back the *Valkyrie* to just over ten kilometers per hour. He was looking for signs of heat-sink exhaust rising above the stone outcroppings.

Still thinking about the Cavalier numbers, his mind flashed quickly over the last three matches. Trane was sure there was something he was missing. Perhaps he'd been so eager to climb into his 'Mech that he hadn't properly studied his opponent. Carmody had the usual assortment of battered 'Mechs often typical of a mercenary company, but it wasn't till he thought back on yesterday's match, when a *Javelin* had come bearing down on him, that it hit him. All of Carmody's 'Mechs had the same white and gold crest painted on their chest armor. The *Javelin* displayed no such crest. And now that Trane thought of it, neither did at least half the 'Mechs they'd destroyed so far. He and Duncan had been using these fights to establish a quick reputation. Was it possible that Carmody was using the matches as a testing ground for potential recruits? If so, he would still have the better part of his original company intact.

Trane stopped the *Valkyrie.* Ahead was a deep arroyo and a trail from the foothills of the mountains leading into it. The arroyo looked plenty big enough to conceal a lance of 'Mechs. Checking his sensors for the heat signatures of hidden 'Mechs, Trane nudged the *Valkyrie* forward to the edge of the deep gully. There were no Cavalier 'Mechs in the stretch of slough he could see, but it was obvious that they *had* been there. Directly below him in the soft dirt of the arroyo floor were the distinct impressions of giant 'Mech feet, and they were heading south . . . away from the mountains.

Trane eased his 'Mech down the slope leading into the arroyo. Calling up the topographic map of the Combat Range on his display, he could see that the arroyo meandered in a general southeasterly direction ending just outside the mock town of empty buildings. That's where they were heading—toward the town—not the forest where Duncan and the rest of the lance waited hidden among the trees. So predictable till now, the Cavaliers had suddenly changed their tactics.

The Cavaliers were fielding three mediums and a heavy against the Kalma Company's heavy, medium, light, and assault 'Mech. Carmody's crew were only forty tons lighter in overall weight, which made for fairly even forces. As Trane moved the *Valkyrie* slowly down the arroyo, he punched up the specs on the Cavalier 'Mechs from his computer ID program. The *Assassin.* Designed for close-range fighting and originally intended to replace the lighter *Wasp* and *Stinger* 'Mechs. The *Centurion.* With its autocannon, missiles, and medium lasers, best at close range. The *Hunchback.* A solid reputation as a streetfighter. *The Dragon.* A short, squat, sixty-ton monster made for brawls in tighter quarters. The specs told the story. Trane knew what they were up to now.

The floor of the arroyo began to rise slightly. Most of the turns had been gradual, offering no sharp bends around which an enemy 'Mech could hide . . . until now. Trane could see the arroyo making a tight turn to the left ahead, and his warrior instincts told him that danger lurked less than a hundred kilometers away. Almost without thought, he fired his jump jets. As the *Valkyrie* lifted out of the deep trench he could see what had been waiting for him. It was the *Centurion.*

"Demon, they're in the town." Trane was shouting into his mike even before his 'Mech had settled on the rim of the arroyo. "I jumped over a *Centurion* in a trench north of it."

"Do tell. Nice to hear from you, Paladin," came Duncan's voice over the commline. "We were beginning to think you'd decided to sit this one out."

Seeing a cloud of dust spraying up from the arroyo, Trane kicked the *Valkyrie* into a full run. The *Centurion* didn't have his speed, especially with the narrow confines of a deep ditch to negotiate. If he could manage to be a respectable distance behind the *Centurion* when it came up out of the arroyo, he might get off a few back shots with his LRMs.

From the dust rising out of the gash in the ground Trane knew the floor of the arroyo was ascending. The *Centurion* would be back on the surface in a few minutes. Ahead of him he saw a steep rise. Shooting a quick glance at his topographic display he noted that the rise was just a few kilometers north of the mock town. The arroyo ended on the other side of the rocky knoll. As his 'Mech started up the rise he could see smoke billowing above the crest and hear the concussions of SRM explosions. *Centurion*s didn't have SRMs. Who was shooting at who?

Trane brought the *Valkyrie* to a stop. Standing in a semicircle a half-kilometer from the slope leading out of the arroyo were Duncan, Hawkes, and Bovos in their 'Mechs. Hawkes was firing another SRM barrage into the *Centurion*, whose right arm—along with its autocannon—was already ripped off. The 'Mech's torso also showed a gaping hole where the Luxor LRM 10-rack had once been. Myomer bundles were snapping and showering sparks from the joint of the severed limb. More fire from Hawkes, this time his missiles blasting into the *Centurion*'s torso, and the Cavalier 'Mech died.

"He was probably sent out to lure us into the town," said Trane. "It just dawned on me a few minutes ago that their lance is a perfect bunch of streetfighters. But, wait a minute. How come you're up here instead of in the forest?"

"Well, I had nothing to do but sit around and think while you were out cruising the countryside," said Duncan, "and I came to the same conclusion about the 'Mechs they're using in this match. If I was right I figured they'd have a scout out trying to draw you to the town. When I saw this arroyo on my topographic I knew that's how they'd get from the hills to the town without us seeing them. Sooner or later I knew you'd find it and come this way."

"Hey," Hawkes cut in, "don't forget we've got three more hiding over there in the town."

"My guess is that the *Centurion* was supposed to draw us

in, then the *Assassin* would appear and try to split us into pairs," Duncan said. "I'll bet anything the *Hunchback* and *Dragon* are well concealed and waiting to get us with a back or side shot. What do you think, Paladin?"

"I'll trot down the main street and Ox can follow me. You and Gunner look for another way in. This is the kind of fight you make up as you go along."

"I agree. Good luck, guys." Duncan watched Trane move the *Valkyrie* directly toward the town. No matter how much the man might be a pain in the butt at times, Duncan had to admit he had courage when it counted.

Rod Trane entered the mock town on its main street. Duncan was right. Five or six blocks ahead the *Assassin* was pretending to cross the main thoroughfare from a side street. Supposedly detecting Trane's presence, it turned and raised its right arm, firing two bursts from the medium laser encased in that limb. The beams of energy shot past Trane's 'Mech, missing him by a wide margin. But, then, the *Assassin* wasn't really trying to score a hit. It continued across the main pavement and down a side street.

"Demon, you were right," Trane said into his neurohelmet mike. "The *Assassin* is trying to pull me down an alley. Looks like it leads generally south."

"Roger that, Paladin. Take it easy. Demon is off the comm for a while," came Duncan's response.

Trane didn't have time to speculate about why Duncan suddenly wanted to run silent. He guided the *Valkyrie* down the street and into the narrower lane. Seeing the twists and turns it made ahead, he knew the *Assassin* and its chums could be waiting for him around any of those corners.

"Paladin, this isn't good." Even over the commline the apprehension in Bovos's voice came through. And it was valid. The Cavaliers had the advantage. They had fought on the Combat Range before and they would know its every nook and cranny, including the town. Kalma's lance had only fought three matches on the range so far, and not one of them had been in the town. Bovos had every right to feel apprehensive. They were in a tight spot.

As Trane came around the next corner, the alley opened

up into a circular plaza. Across the plaza he could see the *Assassin* starting to enter another side street. There was just barely enough room for it to turn around and launch a barrage of SRMs. Again, Trane realized the *Assassin* pilot wasn't trying to hit him but to tease him into continuing the chase. Looking around the plaza he could see why. Two other streets entered the square, but were at an angle away from him. The other Cavalier 'Mechs were probably in those streets, but he wouldn't be able to look down them until he was past where they entered the plaza. Another SRM whizzed into a building to his right.

"Impatient, isn't he?" Bovos's question indicated he wanted to move.

"Let's do it, Ox." Trane began to cross the plaza toward the *Assassin*, which now began to target him in earnest. Another SRM grazed the left shoulder of his *Valkyrie*, but didn't detonate until a second later. The blast rocked his 'Mech slightly, but he pressed forward undamaged. Then it happened.

Trane could see the exhaust trail from the *Assassin*'s left torso, but only two of the missiles left their tubes. The others remained jammed there. The *Assassin*, bless its computerized head, was demonstrating one of its flaws—an unreliable ammo-feed system—and the 'Mech's safety mechanisms weren't allowing the jammed missiles to fire. Trane targeted the 'Mech's hip joints and began to launch his own SRMs one after another. The *Assassin* pilot apparently panicked, laying out a pattern of medium-laser fire in hopes of slowing Trane down or even deflecting a missile. It didn't work. Trane's missiles were beginning to chew the *Assassin* to pieces.

"Paladin . . ." Trane heard Bovos over the commline a split second before he felt the impact, like someone was jabbing at his 'Mech from behind. The sounds told him it was autocannon fire, and from the reports on his damage monitor he knew it had to be that big Tomodzauru cannon on the *Hunchback*. He was losing control of his 'Mech and there wasn't much he could do. He tried to turn the *Valkyrie* to the right, but just then the right hand of the *Hunchback* suddenly came crashing down on his 'Mech's right shoulder, missing the cockpit by less than a meter. A second later the medium 'Mech slammed its fist into the *Valkyrie*'s torso just behind the head. The punch was so violent Trane's seat restraints gave way and he was hurled out of his seat. Then his head slammed into something and the whole world suddenly went black . . .

Galaport
Galatea
Skye March, Federated Commonwealth
22 May 3057

Even before he opened his eyes Trane knew he had one hell of a headache. He wasn't a religious man, but just in case he was dead instead of alive, he hoped there was some place of everlasting life for warriors who died in battle. But then he recalled that the places for the good were supposed to be free of mortal woes ... and pain! Since his head was splitting maybe he was dead but had ended up somewhere reserved for those not so good.

"I think he's coming around."

Trane groggily recognized Hawkes's voice.

"Well, finally. First he lollygags all over the Combat Range and then gets the bejesus stomped out of him. It's about time for him to wake up and get going." That was Duncan. Either they were all dead or they had survived the match. Trane opened his eyes.

"How are you feeling, Rod Trane?" Trane turned to look at Dawn, who was sitting on a chair beside his bed. Looking around the room he finally noticed that Villiers, Blix, and Goto were also gathered around.

"Fill me in," he said weakly.

"A most impressive battle, Captain," said Jon Blix. "We saw it on the field monitors in the spectator's gallery."

"Captain?" Hawkes instantly picked up on Blix's slip of the tongue.

Duncan laughed nervously. "He and Trane once served together," he put in quickly, realizing it was a pretty lame effort to cover over the slip.

"Well . . . *Captain*," said Hawkes, "you owe your hide to Duncan. When your 'Mech went down, that *Hunchback* was about to stomp you into scrap metal. Duncan came down the same street where it had been hiding and sneaked up behind it. When the *Hunchback* tried to duke it out, Duncan showed him what those big fists on a *BattleMaster* can do."

"And the *Dragon*?"

"He came looking for me," said Bovos, "but when he saw the *BattleMaster* he started to back up. He clipped me with an autocannon burst, but then Hawkes came up from behind and crushed the cockpit with one big downward punch. I carved him up with my PPCs and finished off what was left of the *Assassin*."

"They're talking like it was an easy fight . . . Rod," said Karl Villiers, a note of pride in his voice. "It wasn't. Everyone was shot up and injured in some way. It was 'Mech to 'Mech, and it was dirty, but we won." Like the rest of the Knights, he'd had his doubts about how well this ragtag lot would do, but he couldn't help but admire their tenacity in battle.

Trane glanced around the room. Duncan, Bovos, and Hawkes looked cut up or bruised, or both. "How badly did I get it?"

"The *Valkyrie* is history, Rod," said Duncan, "and you've got a mild concussion. We're all pretty lucky really."

"I've fought with a concussion before. I can do it again. When's our next match?"

"Not for another two days," Duncan said. Obviously, nothing was going to keep Trane out of the fight.

"Good, I'll be ready then for sure." Trane was feeling better just knowing that his injuries weren't grave. "In the meantime, I'm starved."

"Let's go to The Gardens," suggested Blix.

Trane looked at the young Knight in amazement. "That's the most expensive restaurant in Galaport."

"No problem . . . Trane. My treat," said Blix expansively. The young Knight seemed to stumble over Trane's name every time he spoke to him.

"Your treat? Where did you come up with that kind of money, Blix?"

"Well, I, uh . . ." Blix was trapped. He was going to have to confess. "I made a wager on the match . . . on you, of course. It paid off rather well."

Trane said nothing for a moment. Then the humor of it hit him and he began to laugh. Duncan, Hawkes, and Bovos began to chuckle, too, until the four of them were fairly roaring with delight. Dawn looked from one to the other, then over at Jon Blix, who gave her a shrug. She understood the concept of the wager, but for the life of her she didn't know what these freeborns found so funny.

"Jon, if you keep winning wagers big enough to pay for meals like this, we're all going to get fat!" Duncan was feeling very content at the moment.

"I do not wish to dampen this mood of self-satisfaction," said Dawn, "but we should tell Rod Trane about the attacks, *quiaff?*" She had eaten very little, just enough to keep up her strength. The only food available on this world was vile, either too rich or so obviously lacking in nutrition that Dawn could barely get it down her throat.

"Attacks?" Trane said, putting his fork down so sharply that it clattered loudly on his dish, drawing looks of alarm from some of the other diners sitting near them.

"This afternoon," said Duncan. "Someone threw a knife at Bovos when we were coming out of the 'Mech bay area. Fortunately, it only grazed his collar bone and bounced off. But there was such a crowd gathered around us that we couldn't see who it was. It had to be one of Carmody's flunkies, though. Who else?"

Bovos picked up the thread of the story. "Then, while we were waiting for the medic's report on you at the dispensary, someone took a shot at Hawkes through the window of the waiting room. It's a wonder no one else got hurt."

"It would seem the Cavaliers mean to win these matches one way or another," said Dawn. "They are without honor."

While the staff was clearing away their dinner plates, Trane told them what he'd been thinking on the field that afternoon. "Something occurred to me in the middle of the match today," he said. "For a unit that's supposed to be company-size, there are an awful lot of those Cavaliers. And they just keep right on coming."

Goto nodded, but waited to speak until Trane was finished ordering a honey-based liqueur for dessert. "Duncan asked me to check into that yesterday," he said. "I found out that the Cavaliers have been busy recruiting new members ever since becoming last month's big winner. They've been telling people they've got a new contract, but have to build up to at least one more company . . . or two. I think they're trying to get up to battalion strength."

"And they've been testing their new recruits against us?" Trane was irritated not only at the Cavaliers, but at the fact that Duncan had thought about this matter a full day before he had.

"Sounds logical," said Bovos. "They've got little love for us ever since we jumped in to even up the odds against Dawn that night. By pitting their new recruits against us they can't lose. Either we die or they eliminate recruits who can't win matches. Actually, it's not a bad program."

The waiter returned with Trane's drink and he took a swallow of it. The fiery liquid stung his palate a bit more than he remembered, but it was still very good. "By my calculations the Cavaliers should have enough pilots and 'Mechs for the rest of the matches," he said. "Karl, you and Jon and Goto start spreading the word that the Cavaliers are afraid to come out and face us and are using 'ringers' against us. That ought to guarantee Carmody and crew showing up for future bouts."

"Good idea," said Duncan. "The next four matches are one-on-one in the arena. The final one is the free-for-all of whoever is left. They should have at least a lance or two of the original Cavaliers for those fights. And make no mistake about it, they'll be out for blood. Especially after Karl and company start wondering out loud if they're afraid to face us. We've all got to stay very, very, sharp."

Trane took another sip of his drink. It was less inflammatory this time. "I've got a question," he said. "How did you manage to come up behind those Cavaliers in the mock town on the range?"

Duncan shrugged. "I just decided to try it," he said simply. "That's why I dropped off the net. I didn't want anyone to know I was coming that way, and I couldn't tell you what I was going to do. I looked in the direction you were going and picked out what I thought was the likeliest spot for an ambush. Hawkes and I just snuck up on 'em."

"Well done," Trane said, standing up. "Given our successes to date ... I propose a toast." He raised his glass, looked around once at this group of unlikely comrades, and then pitched forward facedown onto the table.

19

Galaport
Galatea
Skye March, Federated Commonwealth
23 May 3057

Once again Trane was waking up to a nuclear-class headache. It seemed a bit much for less than two ounces of strong drink.

"Rod, can you hear me?" It was Duncan's voice.

"I can hear you." Trane opened his eyes slowly. He was waiting for Duncan to begin chiding him about a Knight of the Inner Sphere drinking enough to pass out, but instead Duncan looked serious.

"You were poisoned," said Duncan. "It was Goto who picked up on it. The poison was in the drink you ordered."

Trane nodded. "I remember now. It tasted a bit too strong, but I didn't think anything about it at the time."

"At first we thought you'd drunk too much, but then Goto said we'd better get you some medical attention because you already had a concussion."

Trane looked sharply over at Duncan. "It had to be Carmody's work again, yes?"

"We can't say be sure, but we haven't made any other enemies around here. The poison is a paralytic type. It paralyzes body organs. We got you to a medic before it killed you, but it will be several days before the effects wear off."

"Nonsense. I'll be up before you know . . ." Trane started to raise himself up in the bed, but fell back instantly, barely able to control his muscles. Duncan was right. He was going to be out of action for awhile.

"It's a good thing you didn't get to finish that toast, Rod. If you'd drunk the whole glass, you'd be dead now." And that would have been one humdinger of a report, Duncan thought. Try explaining to the Captain-General that one of his Knights died from making a toast.

"When's our next match?"

"Tomorrow. And then a match each day until all five are completed . . . assuming any of us make it that far. I'm going to have to replace you, Rod."

"Replace me? What are you talking about?"

"Yes. I want to give Dawn a shot. She's a crack 'Mech pilot, and from what we've seen of her so far, she's not afraid of anything."

"That's not fair," Trane protested. "The place belongs to one of my Knights. This mission is about them. They have the right."

Duncan started to argue, then thought better of it. Trane had a point. Whether he liked it or not, this *was* the Knights' fight. It was their good name being smeared.

"All right, Rod. But consider this. The next four matches are one-on-one. Let Dawn and the rest of the Fire Support lance take them. We've cobbled together a *Shadow Hawk* from what we've won, and she's already familiarized herself with it. You, Hawkes, Bovos, and I will take a breather."

It was a good suggestion and Trane knew it. Between the matches so far and the various attacks on them, the so-called "Command Lance" of Kalma's Company was weary. He was too weak to debate the issue, and three of his best Knights would still get a shot at the Cavaliers. "All right," he said. "Do it."

There was a soft knock on the door and Duncan went to open it. Hawkes was there. "There's a messenger here from the Arena Master," he said, trying to keep his voice down for Trane's sake.

"Get some sleep," Duncan told Trane, then followed Hawkes out to meet the young man dressed in the uniform of an arena page. "I'm Duncan Kalma. What can I do for you?"

"Sir," the page said, "the Arena Master would like to see you and your team."

* * *

As Duncan and his six companions walked down the hall to the Arena Master's office, several men approaching from the other end began to talk excitedly to each other and point in their direction. When the two groups got close enough to speak, one of the men called out, "Congratulations. You guys fight like demons!"

Duncan gave them a courteous nod and smile as they passed. He knew they meant it as a compliment, but he was glad Trane wasn't here to hear it. What the others thought, he'd never know because just ahead was the door to the Arena Master's office. Duncan knocked, then went in, trailed by Hawkes, Bovos, Dawn, Karl Villiers, Goto, and Jon Blix.

"Welcome," the Arena Master said, spreading his hands wide.

Glancing around the room, Duncan was amazed at the luxurious appointments. He'd had no idea the games on Galatea were so profitable. No one would guess it from the purses. Yet here it was displayed in abundance, even to some furnishings being inlaid with gold.

"My name is Alfonse Vreeken. And may I congratulate you on your success in the Games to date. Quite honestly, few of us thought you'd make it this far."

"Thank you, Mr. Vreeken, but I doubt you've summoned us here just to extend your felicitations," said Duncan.

"I see you are a man who likes to get right down to business, Captain Kalma. Very well, let's do that. Your team has fought four matches so far, and public interest has grown with each contest. This interest has been fueled by gossip concerning your rescue of the young woman from the hands of Carmody's Cavaliers, the attempts on your lives, and so on. The wagers on your matches are expected to rise more rapidly than any I can remember since the Games began here. If you make it to the final match, I expect the betting to reach astronomical heights."

Duncan was pleased but puzzled by this speech. "Is that a problem?" he asked, but the news was giving him an idea.

"No, no, this is indeed not a problem," said Vreeken, "but your lack of a recognizable name is."

"Our lack of a name?"

"My friends, one of the reasons the Games on Galatea have grown is the fact that we respect some people's desire for ... shall we say ... privacy? We do not require documentation of anyone's identity, background, and so on. It's actually one of the strong appeals of doing business here. We permit independents to participate all the time. But surely you've noted a certain sensational quality to the names of the competitors ... Carmody's Cavaliers. Beck's Beasts, and such. You've entered the Games listed solely as 'Kalma's Mercenary Company, Ind.' "

"So that's why you asked to see us?" Duncan said. "You want us to adopt a catchy name?"

"Precisely. It's simply a matter of good business."

Duncan did not respond immediately, but looked around for a chair and sat down. The others remained standing behind him and along the back wall. Up to this point he'd resisted a flashier monicker for the unit. Now it was going to be forced on them.

The others weren't so reticent. "How about 'Kalma's Tigers'?" Bovos said.

"Wait a minute," said Hawkes. "What was it that fellow in the hall said just a few minutes ago?"

"He said we fought like demons," Dawn said proudly.

"Well, there's an idea. How about calling ourselves 'The Demons'?" He looked around at the others, seeing approval from Duncan and Bovos, but no reaction whatever from Villiers and Goto. Blix, however, showed the hint of a smile.

It was Dawn who stepped forward. "May I suggest ..." she began, but suddenly stopped when everyone turned to look at her. She had said so little to anyone till now, still grappling with her new life. But she understood the value of a name, for wasn't the hope of winning a Bloodname the fierce dream of every warrior?

"A demon is a being with one great thought, one great desire—to succeed. I find honor in the name. May I suggest," she went on, a little less shy now, "that we be known as Duncan's Demons?"

* * *

Still unsteady on his feet, Trane stood only by leaning against the shoulders of Karl Villiers and Jon Blix for support. He watched in silence as the burial container was carried aboard the DropShip. No flag draped the container. No proud symbol showed. But inside, in the dress uniform of a Knight of the Inner Sphere, lay Goto-*san*. He was making his last voyage through the cosmos. His mortal remains would return to Atreus to take their eternal rest in a place the Knights had established with their own personal funds.

Trane and the Knights could give no salute to their fallen comrade. They stood stiffly, not moving an inch as the bay door of the DropShip closed. A coded message had been sent to the Knights headquarters on Atreus. They would arrange for Goto's body to be picked up.

"Let's go," said Trane. Supported by Villiers and Blix and followed by the rest of the Demons, he began the walk out of the starport. Villiers and Blix had triumphed in their matches, but the victories had not been easy. Villiers's match, especially, had been gruesome, with hand-to-hand fighting between his *Wolverine* and a *Thunderbolt* in the final moments. The Cavaliers and their recruits seemed to be fighting like madmen for something more than a large purse and unit acclaim. Goto in his *Commando* had held his own against a Cavalier *Javelin,* but in the end both 'Mechs had been fatally damaged. In a last desperate charge the *Javelin* pilot locked the arms of his 'Mech around Goto's *Commando* and fired his chest-mounted SRMs, killing both 'Mechs and their pilots. Trane was saddened, but still proud of his Knight.

"He was a fine warrior," said Bovos as they left the starport.

It was colorful. Trane had to admit that. The maintenance technicians had labored for days to come up with the design and get it painted on the chest armor of Dawn's 'Mech.

"It's perfect," said Duncan.

The entire mission team, including Morneau, Hasson, Auramov, and Ben-Ari of the Recon Lance, stood looking up the 20-meter-height of the 55-ton *Shadow Hawk.* There, smack dab in the middle of the 'Mech's chest on a flat armor plate was the image of a demon. It was a devil's head with a blood-red face, white slits for eyes, the mouth partially open with white teeth and fangs clearly visible, and two white horns—one at each temple. The effect was most menacing. For a few moments no one spoke.

"Warriors to their 'Mechs." The Arena Master's voice was loud and distinct over the public address system.

"Good luck, Dawn. From all of us." Duncan put one of his hands gently on her shoulder. Dawn smiled faintly, then went to the right foot of her 'Mech and began to climb the mounting rungs to the cockpit. She was still struggling to calm her emotions, as a warrior must before combat. But the conflict was too great. She was of the Clans. She should hate these Inner Sphere barbarians—the Minutemen, the Cavaliers, even the Demons. But she did not despise her comrades. They treated her well and were far different from the other disreputable trashborns she'd encountered up till now.

Once inside the cockpit, Dawn stripped down to her fatigue shorts and T-shirt, then pulled on the cooling vest that would keep her from frying in the intense heat generated once the 'Mech started moving and firing its weapons. It would get hot, but she knew that the *Shadow Hawk*'s Sparrow 300J life support system provided more protection and comfort against heat buildup than most 'Mechs. This was a later model whose armor plating had been overhauled to prevent damaging the myomer bundles that controlled the 'Mech's movement. It also had an Armstrong autocannon mounted on the left shoulder and a Martel Model 5 medium laser affixed to its right arm.

"Yes," she had told herself after her first ride in the *Hawk*, "this 'Mech will do just fine." And this match was just the kind of fight a Clan warrior relished. One on one in close confines, with no quarter given. She was ready.

"MechWarrior Dawn of Duncan's Demons. Enter the Field of Combat, please," the Arena Master said.

Dawn pushed her throttle forward, taking the *Shadow Hawk* into a slow walk. As she passed through the gate leading to the field she could hear the cheers and applause of the spectators even through the armored body of her 'Mech. Outside, she thought, the din must be deafening. As she took her place at one end of the field she noticed the crowd beginning to fall silent. At the other end she saw the reason why.

The Cavalier entry was a 'Mech named the "Enforcer." She quickly called it up on her 'Mech ID program. The 'Mech was five tons lighter than her *Shadow Hawk* and was a good brawler with jump capability. Its combination of a Class 10 autocannon and Chiscomp 43 Special large laser gave it a terrific punch.

"Dawn, listen up." It was Hawkes, but his voice wasn't coming over the commline. She looked around the cockpit until she spied what looked like a small, hand-sized communicator. Picking it up she noted that it had no transmission controls.

"Have you found it yet? You can't talk to me. It's a receiver only. Duncan got one for each 'Mech yesterday so we can get info to 'Mechs on the field. I'm in the stands about halfway down the field close to the referee's booth. You're up against an *Enforcer*. That scrappy little SOB was born in the Federated Commonwealth. I know it well. He'll try to get in close and hit you with the autocannon or large laser. You can't survive more than three hits from either one."

That much I know, Dawn thought irritably. *Now tell me something I can use.*

"It has two weaknesses, Dawn," Hawkes said as if reading her mind. "The ammo-feed system for the autocannon is subject to jamming and it can only carry ten bursts. He'll be trying to husband those salvos. The 'Mech is also vulnerable from the rear. The armor is very thin there. Gunner out."

"Let the match begin," came the Arena Master's voice over the commline. It was followed by the loud report of the signal cannon.

Dawn could see the *Enforcer* charging down the field toward her at high speed. This freebirth's idea of how the order of battle should go wasn't hard to discern. He wanted to get within point-blank range and cut loose with his autocannon. Well, two could play at that game. She hit the *Shadow Hawk*'s throttle hard, and began to run a collision course toward the other 'Mech. It looked like the match was going to begin as a test of nerves.

At 500 meters Dawn launched a spread of SRMs. A good hit at this distance would be pure luck, but the sight of eight SRMs heading one's way could give the hardiest warrior food for thought. The *Enforcer* slowed, and when Dawn got to within 200 meters she veered her 'Mech to the right, turning the *Shadow Hawk*'s torso slightly and thumbing the autocannon. She could see the explosive shells slamming into the left side of the *Enforcer.* Even as the fire was hitting him, the Cavalier pilot raised his 'Mech's left arm and triggered three bursts from the large laser. His first two shots missed, but the third hit the *Shadow Hawk*'s left forearm. The ferro-fibrous armor buckled and sparks flew out of the hole that had been gouged. Dawn gained an immediate respect for the power of that large laser. Had she been any closer the big red beam of electron energy would have sheared her arm off completely. She swung the *Shadow Hawk* to the left, trying to get behind the *Enforcer.*

The Cavalier sensed what she was up to and twisted his 'Mech violently to the right. When Dawn stopped to what should have been his rear, the *Enforcer* was already coming round to meet her with autocannon firing. Hits began dancing across her 'Mech's torso while warning lights flashed and alarms wailed.

"Dawn, look at his arm. You made a hit against his left shoulder joint," Hawkes was yelling through the small communicator, which she'd set on a utility shelf beneath the command console.

Dawn turned the *Shadow Hawk* to her right and began to put some distance between the two 'Mechs. The *Enforcer* remained stationary as the pilot continued pumping autocannon fire at her. She felt one or two bursts striking the back of her 'Mech, but judged any harm to be minimal. She was far more concerned about the blast holes in the 'Mech's chest and lower torso. The battle computer's secondary display painted a grotesque picture of the damage. Her primary heat sinks had ruptured a coolant line and it was flowing out of the hole like blood from a ripped vein. The myomer gel used to reduce friction in the older-model 'Mech also mixed with the bright green fluid, smoke, and stain. The secondary monitor told her the *Enforcer* was holding his position. She stopped and turned to face him.

Now she could see what Hawkes was talking about. The *Enforcer*'s left arm wasn't completely out of action, but it could barely move. By her count he had expended seven of his ten autocannon bursts. Right now he was trying to get the large laser raised to at least a hip-firing position.

It was now or never. Dawn locked her targeting system onto the *Enforcer*'s left arm and charged him. Again closing to 200 meters she concentrated her SRMs on it. It was still not a good range for the small missiles, but the *Enforcer*'s pilot took them seriously, dodging his 'Mech right and left. She saw one hit the *Enforcer*'s upper arm and then, suddenly, the *Shadow Hawk*'s missile-feed system jammed. Not only was that system out, but other systems were closing down from the heat buildup. The explosive shells from the *Enforcer*'s autocannon had ripped through her 'Mech's chest armor and done more damage than she'd realized.

Seeing Dawn slow to a walk, the *Enforcer* stopped darting about and tried to get its left-arm large laser up for firing. Dawn meanwhile was bringing up her right arm with its medium laser. Drawing a bead on the *Enforcer*'s left arm she waited until her targeting cross hairs glowed gold, then pressed the trigger.

The muzzle of the laser flared, and 100 meters away the beam of pulsed energy sliced into the *Enforcer*'s shoulder. The left arm dropped away, hanging by the few remaining strands of myomer. Sparks and fluid poured from the shoulder joint. Dawn squeezed the trigger of the laser again but nothing happened . . . it was dead.

"Dawn, move away!" Hawkes was practically screaming at her through the small communicator. "He's still got some autocannon loads."

What did that matter? Dawn retorted silently as she began walking her 'Mech straight at the Cavalier 'Mech. Not fast, just a steady gait, but headed in a direct line toward the other 'Mech. The *Enforcer* could see her coming. His first autocannon burst missed her by less than a meter. At 50 meters the second burst tore into the *Shadow Hawk*'s left leg. Armor plates popped off as the shell exploded within. The third burst hit the torso of her 'Mech dead center. As the *Shadow Hawk* began to overheat, it was nearing shutdown and the heat in the cockpit was suffocating.

Seeing her slow down, the *Enforcer* made no attempt to move away. His sensors told him her 'Mech would shut down at any moment. Then he would use the autocannon in his right arm to finish her off. As Dawn brought the *Shadow Hawk* to within a few meters of her foe, he raised his arm and pointed the autocannon at her cockpit. But nothing happened. He was out of ammo. Knowing she was only moments from shutdown, Dawn had cut off the lights and other unnecessary systems. She raised her machine's right arm and then brought it down with brutal force on the *Enforcer*'s cockpit. Metal screeched and the interior bulkheads snapped as the *Shadow Hawk*'s powerful armored fist crushed the life of the pilot who'd given life to the machine. An instant later the *Shadow Hawk*'s reactor shut down completely.

"Excellent shooting, Dawn," came Duncan's voice over the receiver in her neurohelmet. His disembodied voice seemed to surround her head as she watched the *Enforcer* collapse in front of her. "You've avenged, Goto-*san*."

"Warriors do not fight for revenge," Dawn said just before passing out from the heat.

Dawn did not like beer, but it was cold and cold was what she needed. Hawkes and Bovos had rushed out onto the field, reaching her 'Mech even before the arena's fire-control squad. Their shouting awakened her enough to pop the cockpit hatch, and then they got her outside and to the ground quickly. She was groggy and disoriented until the cooling packs they applied began to bring her body temperature down.

"The referee ruled it a victory for Dawn."

Dawn looked up to see Jon Blix coming into the area where the Demon 'Mechs were parked. "There was a doubt?" she asked.

"The Cavaliers wanted it ruled a draw because your 'Mech shut down," Hawkes explained. "They insisted a winner had to be able to leave the field."

"They truly are swine." Dawn's vision was beginning to

clear and she felt better. Looking around, she saw all the Demons standing over her . . . except Duncan.

"Well, what do you think, good people?" It was Duncan's voice.

As the others turned around, Dawn stood up shakily. Seeing Duncan, her eyes opened wide in astonishment. There he stood, obviously very pleased with himself, dressed in a light gray duty uniform. The epaulets and bibbed front were outlined with red piping. A red stripe ran down the side of each trouser leg. The red belt had a buckle in the shape of the House Marik black eagle. On the bib of the jacket was the symbol of their company . . . the horned, fanged, fearsome face of a demon.

"How do you like it?" Duncan stepped to one side as a delivery man rolled a clothing rack up alongside him. "I had a local haberdasher begin whipping these up after our talk with Vreeken. There's one for each of you."

Trane stood staring at Duncan, hands on his hips, gaping in dismay. At this moment he wanted to shoot Duncan Kalma so bad it hurt.

= 20 =

"**D**emon, the *Stalker* got Hasson." Hawkes's voice sounded grim and he had every right to sound that way.

The final match was an exercise in total madness, with Trane still too weak to fight as the match began on the 50-kilometer Combat Range. Competing companies were allowed to enter whatever 'Mechs were still functioning, up to but not exceeding company strength of twelve 'Mechs. The Demons had lost three 'Mechs: Trane's *Valkyrie*, Dawn's *Shadow Hawk*, and Goto's *Commando*. Five more, Duncan's *BattleMaster*, Hawkes's *Crusader*, Bovos's *Warhammer*, Blix's *Archer*, and Villiers's *Wolverine* had been shot up in their matches. Where the repairs would normally have been easy, on Galatea prices were inflated and often other stables deliberately bought up the few parts that were available in order to place their foes at a disadvantage. The Demons had four undamaged 'Mechs; Morneau's *Rifleman*, Hasson's *Griffin*, Autramov's *Wasp*, and Ben-Ari's *Stinger*. Nine 'Mechs against the ten fielded by the Cavaliers. Now Hasson was dead.

The fighting had been furious from the moment the match began. The Cavaliers were scum, but boasted good 'Mech pilots among them. It was Clinton Carmody piloting the *Stalker*, and he knew how to wield its massive firepower. It was time for a head count.

"Hawkes, what have we got left? Can you tell?"

"Bovos is on my right," Hawkes replied. "Looks like he's about got that *Thunderbolt* whipped. I saw Villiers a few minutes ago hot on the heels of a *Phoenix Hawk*. And I finally got that *Vulcan* when his jump jets ran out of reaction mass. I haven't seen Blix, Morneau, or Ben-Ari lately, and they're not on my tac screen. They're probably west of us over the horizon."

"So, we should have eight left?"

"That's the way it looks to me until we hear from the others," said Hawkes. "The Cavaliers started with ten. You and I and Bovos have put one each out of business, and Villiers got a *Whitworth* before he wandered off. So now they're down to six. Hey, Duncan. Carmody is moving his *Stalker* back north. I'll bet he's headed to the foothills."

"If he gets back among those rocks it'll be hard to force him out," said Duncan. "I'm going after him. Bovos, can you hear me?"

"I read you, Duncan."

"What shape are you in?"

"I've taken some bad hits. I need to cool down before fighting again." Duncan called up the topographic map on his secondary monitor.

"There should be a small creek between you and where Villiers and the others are fighting. Use it to cool down as best you can and then go help them."

"Will do."

"Hawkes, you want to help me stalk a *Stalker*?"

"Yeah, let's end this thing," came Hawkes's reply.

Duncan brought his *BattleMaster* to a northern course and kicked it up to cruising speed. That should have been nearing 44 kph, but with the damage he'd taken in the last ten days it was down to less than 40. The *Stalker* was still slower at just over 30 and Carmody wasn't pushing it that fast, so Duncan knew he could overtake the 85-ton titan before it reached the foothills. The question now was what would he do when he caught it? The *Stalker* was made to stand fast and use its awesome array of weaponry to bombard opponents in a long-range fire-fight. It had LRMs, whereas he had only short-range missiles. He needed a plan.

Duncan checked his computer ID program, which told

him a *Stalker* carried twin 10-racks with 24 LRM reloads each.

"Got any idea how many of those LRMs he's used so far, Hawkes?"

"He must have drained one rack dry early on trying to scatter us, and another dozen before he made some hits against Hasson. He's not a good shot, but he's persistent!"

"I remember he took some shots at Morneau's *Rifleman*, and I think he lobbed a couple of Villiers's *Wolverine*. He ought to be running low on his long-range stuff."

"So what's your plan, Demon?"

"Let's tease him into using up his LRMs. Then I'll move in close and snipe at him until he begins to burn those heavy lasers."

"I get it," said Hawkes. "You distract him and I'll do the rest." His *Crusader* was on its way to its maximum speed even before he'd finished speaking. Duncan's plan was sound, he thought, but it depended on Carmody being overzealous. The *Stalker* boasted a lot of lethal power. In the days of the Star League it used to have a versatile computer that could identify a target, determine its range, and select the optimum mix of weapons for an attack. The early Succession Wars destroyed the technology for building that computer, and now *Stalker* pilots had to depend on their own estimates. In the fervor of battle many overused their multiple weapons systems, quickly overheating the 'Mech to the point of shutdown despite its twenty heat sinks. Duncan was going to try and pressure Carmody into such overuse.

Two LRM salvos zipped to either side of Duncan's *BattleMaster*. "I think I've found him, Hawkes."

"I saw on my tactical display," Hawkes came back. "He's just saying hello."

"Guess I'll go over and see what's on his mind." Duncan was still a good 400 meters from the *Stalker*, but Carmody was sending another spread of LRMs his way. They, too, flew past, with only one getting close. Then, no more long-range fire from the *Stalker*.

Duncan increased his speed until the *BattleMaster* was in a full run. He could see Carmody just standing there waiting for him. At 250 meters, he stopped and squeezed off a few PPC shots to get Carmody's attention focused on him. Inside 300 meters Duncan knew he was in dangerous territory. As he expected, his PPC fire was ineffectual against the heavy armor of the *Stalker* at this range. It was time to get bold. He accelerated the *BattleMaster* back to its running speed and made an irregular zigzag course toward the *Stalker*.

At 150 meters the laser fire was murderous. Armor was exploding off his 'Mech's arms, torso, and legs in a billow of fragments and smoke. Duncan could feel the heat beginning to rise in the cockpit. At 90 meters he decided to take a risk. He brought the *BattleMaster* to an abrupt, sudden, stop as laser beams crossed in front of him 30 meters ahead. Carmody had been leading him as he made his run. Duncan sighted his PPC on the *Stalker*'s left knee joint and fired the instant his targeting cross hairs glowed with a lock-on.

It was a solid hit. The *Stalker* had powerful, well-armored legs, but the knee joints were its weakest points. As the knee gave a little, Carmody would know it might collapse and must have vowed to finish this contest in one salvo.

The better part of the barrage hit Duncan's 'Mech dead on. So much smoke and fire spewed up from the searing wounds in the *BattleMaster*'s torso and right arm that he couldn't see out the viewscreen. Another barrage would kill him. But it never came.

As he moved the *BattleMaster* forward, the smoke began to drift aside. Ahead, the *Stalker* was fighting to stay on its feet. The constant barrage of fire that Carmody had laid down from both his medium and large lasers had made the 'Mech overheat. If Carmody could get the *Stalker* cooled enough, even a little, to fire one of those large lasers, Duncan knew he was dead.

Duncan heard Hawkes's gleeful shout as he crested a small rise behind the *Stalker*, only 100 meters away. He targeted the *Stalker*'s left leg with his torso-mounted medium lasers and poured laserfire into it. The leg splintered and the 'Mech fell over on its side. Carmody was helpless.

"What now, Hawkes? Shall we show the man a little mercy?" Hawkes made no reply. He simply walked a few meters closer and began to fire one SRM salvo after another into the *Stalker* until it was nothing more than a steaming heap of white hot metal.

After Hawkes had destroyed the *Stalker,* Bovos, followed by Blix, Morneau, Auramov, and Ben-Ari, had arrived on the scene to help defeat the remaining Cavaliers. Though the Demons took a beating in the Games, the Cavaliers were now an extinct species. Duncan's Demons had survived, and survival in the Games meant offers of employment by a host of patrons. Duncan could hardly leave the hotel room without being beset by agents wanting to contract the Demons' services. Such a reversal of fortune was most gratifying.

Trane and his Knights were at the DropShip assessing the damage to the company's 'Mechs and setting up a plan to get them back in repair, and Duncan was just returning to the hotel after running a most interesting little errand. In one hand he carried a briefcase stuffed with stiff new C-bills. He couldn't help gloating over the way his life had changed in a mere six weeks. Piloting a 'Mech had been the farthest thing from his mind while facing long-term servitude on Herotitus. Yet, here he was with half a million C-bills in prize money from the Games, plus a hefty sum from his own personal wagers. Duncan wasn't a gambler by trade for nothing.

The lock clicked slightly as the door to his room popped open easily, and he had his laser pistol out almost as quickly. Standing there in the middle of the room was a man whose slender body, thin neck, and sharp, pointed nose made him look like a human version of a weasel. Duncan's pistol was pointed at his head.

"This would be an excellent time for you to tell me what you're doing in my room," he said, "and don't delay your explanation. I haven't killed anybody today and it's got me depressed."

The man seemed totally unperturbed. "I, sir, am Count Sessa Lottimer." He gave an oily smile. "I apologize for my unorthodox entry. But I wanted to make an impression. So many others are bidding for your attention. I have come with an offer of employment."

"As you say, my dear Count, the Demons have had many offers since our success in the Games, but most agents have used a more traditional approach. That is to say, they haven't broken into my quarters."

"I'm here to make you a very unusual proposition," the Count said slowly, watching Duncan carefully. "An offer of work and a chance to be a part of a world ruled by Mech-Warriors. The Houses of the Inner Sphere use mercenaries like you and your people as so much cannon fodder to expand their own empires and bloat their own treasuries. I offer you more than a contract to serve at the whim of these despots. I offer you not only wealth . . . but power!"

Duncan's felt the hairs rise on the back of his neck. This was it, he was sure of it. The man had spoken only in generalities so far, but they were the right generalities. This was the contract they'd been waiting for. He knew it. "Let's get back to the basics first. How much are we talking about it?"

With Duncan's pistol still aimed at him, Count Lottimer reached slowly and carefully inside his loosely draped tunic and withdrew an envelope, which he handed to Duncan. After holstering his sidearm, Duncan removed a single sheet of paper from the envelope. Examining what was written on it, he saw that Lottimer wasn't kidding. The amount being offered the Demons was substantial.

"The riches part meets what I require," said Duncan, "but what's this about 'final approval'?"

"When one is building a new and sovereign state, one must use a certain amount of caution. You must meet with the personal representative of the one we call lord. Please note that you will be well paid just to meet with my master."

"When and where would this meeting take place?"

"On Kyeinnisan, in the Free Worlds League. I will arrange for a meeting upon your acceptance of the offer."

"You have it. Or a tentative acceptance at least. And tell your 'master' we're a bunch of impatient souls. This meeting occurs soon or it doesn't take place at all."

Lottimer bowed slightly and left the room. Duncan closed the door behind him.

"A world ruled by MechWarriors, is it?" he said half-aloud. "This little weasel could be just what we've been waiting for."

21

Luck City
Kyeinnisan
The Protectorate Border, Free Worlds League
8 June 3057

A few days after the meeting with Count Lottimer, Duncan's Demons left Galatea bound for Kyeinnisan, an independent Marik world lying between the Protectorate and Regulus provinces. The capital of this planet known as the Gambler's World was Luck City, and it was a place Duncan knew well.

The rooms booked for them in a downtown hotel were comfortable and clean, if not terribly plush, but their mysterious "host" had yet to appear. Standing at the window of his room, Duncan looked out at the city and marveled that it existed at all.

Like Herotitus and Galatea, Kyeinnisan offered a wide-open society where every imaginable—and unimaginable—pleasure was for sale. And yet the serious-minded, idealistic Thomas Marik had not tried to shut it down. Perhaps he realized that such a world in his own backyard offered a place where certain kinds of information could be exchanged and a wary eye kept on potential threats to the security of the Free Worlds League. SAFE agents haunted this prosperous planet.

It was ironic that Kyeinnisan, lawless as it was, had the lowest crime rate of any Free Worlds League planet, including Atreus. The planetary government maintained law and order—after a fashion—by means of a highly efficient, well-trained, Security Force. It was said that death was preferable to imprisonment in Kyeinnisan's infamous penal colony. The Security Force was maintained by a tax imposed on casino owners and the various other merchants involved with supplying the world's gaming and other entertainments. Such people might not have been motivated to pay those taxes, but not doing so meant a serious drop in profits when their premises were no longer patrolled or monitored and became too dangerous for most patrons. Duncan had also heard it said that individuals with enough wealth and power could engage the Security Force for their own purposes.

Unlike the worlds of Solaris VII, Galatea, or Hardcore, Kyeinnisan offered no blood sports. This was mainly a mecca for those who enjoyed games of chance. Knowing the place well, Duncan should have felt at ease in this milieu, but he didn't. Their "Host" had yet to contact him.

He had been amazed at the JumpShip circuit set up for them by their prospective employer. Instead of having to wait a week or more for their starship to recharge at each jump point along the route between Galatea and Kyeinnisan, they had simply transferred to a fresh ship awaiting them at each stop, drastically cutting the transportation time. But that relay had also meant leaving their own JumpShip at the first jump back into Free Worlds space. Their ship would, of course, get a message to Atreus about their destination. Equally disconcerting was their "host's" insistence that only the Command Lance, minus its 'Mechs, could be transported to Kyeinnisan's surface. The reason given was that government policy forbade the landing of large 'Mech forces on the planet.

Duncan had persuaded Trane, still suffering some lingering effects of the poison, to remain on the DropShip. Trane had reluctantly agreed to let Dawn take his place. If anything went amiss on Kyeinnisan, Duncan wanted him where he could get his Knights into action. A knock at the door interrupted these reflections.

Duncan went to the door and opened it, letting Hawkes, Bovos, and Dawn into the room. He could tell from the looks on their faces that something was wrong.

"They took our weapons," Bovos said with a growl.

"They? Who's they?"

"A Security Force Patrol," said Hawkes. "They claimed they'd heard there was going to be a riot, or a fight, or something, and were confiscating all weapons. They got everything but this." Hawkes reached around behind his head and withdrew a long, thin throwing dagger from a sheath resting between his shoulder blades under his shirt.

"But we were the only ones who were stopped," said Dawn. "The street was filled with people wearing sidearms."

"I don't suppose you have a little something hidden away for a rainy day?" Duncan asked her. Seeing Dawn's baffled look, he tried again. "Maybe you have a weapon they didn't get?"

"But, of course." Dawn reached inside the red belt of her Demons uniform, where Duncan could see a small pouch sewn to the backside. From the pouch she removed a laser pistol.

"What about you, Bovos?" Duncan asked. "Any little hidden treasures the Security Forces overlooked?"

Bovos shook his head glumly.

"I guess it's a good thing I dropped by to see my old friend Roy this afternoon to pick up a few things," Duncan said. He went to the closet and brought out a small valise, which he opened to display four small-caliber-slug-throwing pistols. "Help yourselves. They're small, but the slugs have a mercury tip that makes a nasty internal wound. They'll also be easy to conceal."

"So, we've partially solved one problem," said Hawkes, "but this whole setup still makes me edgy."

"Me, too. Whoever is behind this contract offer and recruiting new citizens for their brave new world is going to be super-cautious. I think we can assume we're being watched—watched very closely."

"What now?" Dawn asked.

"A while ago I got a message from the manager of one of the casinos inviting us to visit his establishment this evening. We've even been given a small line of credit as an enticement. So . . . we do as Count Lottimer suggested—relax, enjoy ourselves, or pretend to, until we're contacted. Most of all, don't ask questions, don't make any waves. Keep a low profile and just do what everybody else is doing."

Dawn looked dubious. "And if trouble does come, what then?"

"We'll be on our own, but I did take out a little insurance." Duncan reached inside his jacket and took out a compact two-way commlink until. "Kyeinnisan's jump point is only two days away. Trane has one of our people monitoring communications traffic around the clock. The friend who provided me with these pistols has a private, very powerful, narrow-beam transmitter. If we get in over our heads I'll use this to contact him and he'll get a message to Trane on the DropShip."

"And . . . ?" Hawkes asked.

"Trane and the others will commandeer the JumpShip and stand by to deploy here if needed."

"So if big-time trouble comes our way we go it alone for two, maybe three days, until Trane gets here."

"That's about the size of it, Garth. For now, though, let's rest a few hours and then get out and see the town." Duncan pulled out a false bottom to the valise that had held the pistols. Stacks of C-bills sat in neat rows in the hidden compartment. "Each of you will get ten thousand C-bills. That should be enough for you to flash around looking like cocky champions of the Games and . . . to have some fun at the same time."

"Do we go separately or as a group?" Bovos asked while fitting his pistol into the inside pocket of his uniform jacket.

"Let's stay together," said Duncan.

"Civvies or dress?"

"Uniforms. If the invitation to this casino is a pretext for setting up a time and place for our 'host' to contact us, we want to be visible." Duncan looked around at the other three. "If there's nothing else, then—"

"There is," Bovos said, glancing quickly at Hawkes, who nodded as though by some previous arrangement.

"We need to talk, Duncan," the big man said. "And Dawn too."

"Of course," said Duncan. "What's on your mind?" Dawn looked curiously from one to another, then sat down again at the foot of the bed.

Bovos stood up and cleared his throat, apparently putting

his thoughts together. "Hawkes and I started to wonder what was going on when you turned down so many of the contract offers on Galatea. Some of them were quite lucrative."

"Lucrative, yes, but I thought we could do better."

"Well, that wasn't all," said Hawkes, picking up the thread. "We also started wondering about Trane—and why some of the others call him 'Captain' and why they act more like professional soldiers than mercenaries. Bovos and I have both been military regulars. Soldiers move differently, talk differently, think differently than mercenaries. A merc sells his services for profit and maybe a little fun. They aren't known for strong loyalties to their unit. But it's obvious Villiers, Blix and the others are totally loyal to Trane. Don't try to deny it, Duncan. Bovos senses it too."

Duncan exhaled slowly. Given some of Jon Blix's verbal blunders, he was surprised this hadn't come up sooner. The whole mission suddenly felt like a house of cards in a violent windstorm. There was no time to consult Trane or anyone else about what he should do now. He'd already been through a lot with these three, and his gambler's heart told him to take the risk.

Duncan looked from one man to the other, than at Dawn. "We've known each other only a short time," he began slowly, "but we've fought some hard fights and lived to tell the tale. Hawkes ... Bovos, I know you've heard of the Knights of the Inner Sphere, but maybe Dawn hasn't." In a few sentences he told her how Thomas Marik had in recent years formed the Knights from some of the best warriors in the Inner Sphere.

"Well, there's something else about them you should know," Duncan went on.

He took his time, leaving out very little of the story while the others listened without interruption. When he was done, no one spoke. "And while we're on the subject of who acts like a merc and who doesn't," Duncan added, "I've got to say that I've known a few in my time. And you don't seem very much like one either, Hawkes."

Hawkes shrugged and then smiled faintly. "I'm Hauptmann Garth Hawkes, Commander of the First Company, First Battalion, of the Sixth Crucis Lancers. Or I was until those raiders destroyed my command on Valexa. I'm still a Lancer. My commanding officer sent me here to see what I could find out.

"Neither of us bought the fake Knights impersonation, but our intelligence boys are so up to their eyeballs in what's going on with the Skye March and the Sarna March and god knows what else that we couldn't get them to pay attention. Sending me to scout around seemed like the only way to find out what was really going on. Galatea was the logical place to begin hunting for whoever was behind the raids. Sooner or later they'd have to find replacements for their losses." Hawkes paused. "I'm disappointed you saw through me. I thought I was playing the role pretty well."

"And you, Bovos, I suppose you're going to tell me you were with the Oriente Hussars company that got hit on Shiro III. I've wondered about that since the day we met."

Bovos nodded. "My story's almost the same, except that I resigned my commission and went to Galatea on my own. The only way I'll ever be able to live with what happened to my people is to track down whoever did it and pay them back."

"That brings us to an interesting point," said Hawkes. "What if this 'lord' is here on Kyeinnisan? Even if Trane comes roaring in with his Knights, that still leaves us with nine warriors and eight 'Mechs against however many troops he's got, the local Security Force, and whatever else is on this chunk of rock."

"True, but Trane will get off a coded message to the nearest HPG station. From there it relays to the Second Regulan Hussars on Tiber, which is only a jump away. The main body of the Knights is standing by on Marik, but that's too far for a rapid response. All Free Worlds League military units have been ordered to render immediate, unquestioning, assistance to this mission. There's nothing on Kyeinnisan that can stand up to them."

"I know the Regulan Hussars," Bovos said. "They're one of the best regiments in the League."

"I don't think it will come to that," Duncan said. "Kyeinnisan isn't the kind of place the raiders would need for a baseworld. I suspect this is some kind of intermediary stop in their plan to recruit new units. All we can do for the moment is just play along and wait."

"Let's hope the wait won't be long," said Bovos.

Duncan looked over at Dawn. "What about you, Dawn? You've been all eyes and ears, but haven't said a word. When Trane and I first met you, we wondered if you'd been involved on Cumbres."

Dawn lifted her head proudly. "I was driven from my people and my Clan because of what happened on Cumbres," she said. "I led the Steel Viper raid on that world, and now I know it was the raiders you describe who surprised us there and destroyed my Trinary. I survived where nearly all the rest fell. I failed as a commander. That is my shame.

"A warrior without honor is nothing. Though the Steel Vipers drove me out, I will not rest until I can reclaim my honor. How I will do that I do not know, nor whether the warriors of my Clan would acknowledge such a claim. For now, I am neither of that world nor of your world, but your mission has merit, Duncan Kalma, and I would assist you in it if you will still have me."

Duncan walked over and offered Dawn his hand. "You're one of us now, Dawn."

She bowed her head, then shook it slightly. "Neg, Duncan. I fight with you and I respect you. But I am not one of you. We walk the same path at the moment, but this is only for now."

Duncan turned to the others, still clasping her hand. "That's good enough for me. How about you other two freebirths?"

"We're a team," Hawkes said, laying his hand on top of Dawn's and Duncan's.

Bovos added his big paw to theirs. "A team."

22

"The lady wins again!"

Dawn understood the concept of gambling, but not the fascination. Compared to the thrill of combat, it offered only a glimmer of entertainment to her. Still, the ritual was one she decided to master should the skill be of use to her at some point in the future. She'd handed some C-bills to a young man standing beside a table, and in turn he'd asked her to pick two numbers. Her selection was duly recorded, and after other players had similarly registered their choices, the man gave a yank to a large wheel mounted on a stand behind the table and set it spinning. The wheel had numbers from 1 to 100 on it, and clacked as it spun, rhythmically catching at a ratchet that gradually slowed and then stopped it. At the top of the wheel was a lighted arrow. As best Dawn could figure it, whatever number the arrow pointed to when the wheel stopped was the winning number. However this game was played, she had now won twice.

"I don't believe it. Luck and looks all in one lovely little package." A swarthy man standing just behind her was the one who spoke. Dawn was about to tell this freebirth where he could stuff it when she remembered Duncan's admonition to keep a low profile. She gave the filthy rodent a withering glance, then quickly turned on her heel and strode away.

Duncan, meanwhile, was seated at a gaming table, feeling very much at home. There were many casinos on

Kyeinnisan, but the most popular, and his favorite was this one ... The Cave. Looking around, he thought it hadn't changed much since his last visit. Despite its name, the place was as ornate as the casino's vast profits could make it. And the drinks were free to those actively gambling. Duncan motioned to a scantily clad young waitress that he needed a refill.

Bovos stood quietly behind a velvet rope strung between brass stands that circled the table where Duncan was playing cards. Each table or major gaming space was cordoned off by such a soft rope to keep onlookers, called "The Gallery," at least a meter from the game. Watching Duncan playing Four Card Drax, one of the most popular in Marik space, was a sad reminder to Bovos of many nights he'd passed playing Drax with his comrades in the barracks, amid the jovial telling of tall tales, reminiscing, and good-natured joking. From what he could see, Duncan was winning ... a lot. Hawkes, who wasn't much a gambler, wandered over and also stood by watching idly.

"Are you ready for the fourth card?" the dealer asked nervously. He was so edgy and inept that Duncan couldn't figure out how he'd ever gotten the job—or managed to keep it.

"Deal." The man who spoke was a textile merchant from Tamarind. He was a disagreeable-looking person with a sullen face full of pockmarks and several teeth capped with gold. His losses in the game so far had not improved his attitude.

The dealer cringed when he saw that he'd dealt Duncan the Lancer of House Marik. Of itself the card was worthless, but its possession increased the value of every House Marik card in Duncan's hand by one. The two Marik nines he already had showing thus increased to a value of ten. Duncan set the Lancer card aside—in plain view, in keeping with the rules—as the dealer dealt him another card. It was another nine of the House Marik suit.

"I'm out." The fellow who threw in his cards had a five, six, and seven showing face up on the table, the seven being the last card dealt. All three cards were of the same suit. He'd obviously been trying for the next to the highest winning hand in the game, which was called the "Drax"—a numerical sequence of four cards all of the same suit. Whatever his "hole" card was, the first card dealt to a player face down, it wasn't going to make his other three cards into a successful hand. He claimed to be some sort of bush-league bureaucrat from Atreus on vacation. Hearing that, Duncan was glad none of the Knights were with him. What if this man had somehow recognized Trane or one of his men?

"So, it's down to you and me . . . again," said the Tamarindian. "I'm showing three nines and so are you. But . . . have you got another nine in the hole? That's the question."

"You'll have to pay to see," replied Duncan. If the man's hole card was a nine, he would have four of a kind, a winning hand, unless Duncan's hole card was also a nine, in which case they would both have four of a kind. With his Lancer card increasing the three House Marik cards in his hand by one to a value of ten, Duncan would have the winning hand by virtue of numerical superiority. Of the four suits in Drax—Marik, Steiner, Kurita, and Davion—Duncan thought it ironic that the House Marik suit might prove a winner for him.

The Tamarindian seemed to be caving in under the pressure. During the two hours of play he'd lost a hefty number of C-bills. Sweat was forming on his brow, and the pot now approached 5,000 bills. After lengthy consideration, he apparently decided to cut his losses. "I fold," he said.

Duncan raked the pile of currency over to his place at the table. His luck had been exceptionally good tonight . . . maybe too good. He noticed the nervous dealer looking furtively about. It was time to leave "I thank you for your contributions to my financial welfare," he said, "but I've only recently arrived after a long journey and now it's time to retire. I bid you all a good night and—"

"Wait," the Tamarindian barked. "You haven't shown your hole card."

"Nor am I required to do so," Duncan said politely. "You folded." Before he could react, the man reached out and turned his hole card over. It was a three.

"You're a cheat," the man cried. "In every hand you've

had a ranking card. You and the dealer—he's giving you what you need. It's a set-up." While he continued to complain loudly, calling for the manager, the dealer began to blubber a confession, saying that it was all true, yes, Duncan had paid him off. Two security guards in The Gallery stepped over the velvet rope and moved up protectively behind the Tamarindian. "Get him," the man told the pair.

In an instant Duncan realized that the Tamarindian and the dealer were plants to create an incident. One of the bodyguards started to draw his pistol, but not before a knife flew through the air and embedded itself almost to the hilt in the man's chest. Duncan recognized the blade as the one Hawkes had showed him earlier that day. The second bodyguard managed to get his pistol free of its holster, but he never got to fire it either. First came a sharp *crack,* followed by a small hole appearing in his forehead. He fell backward without a sound. As people nearby began to shout and shriek in fear, Hawkes and Bovos were pushing their way roughly through the panicked crowd to where Duncan stood.

"Where's Dawn?" Hawkes shouted.

"No time now," Duncan said, gesturing in the direction of the door. "She'll find us."

"Just stand real still, little lady." Dawn felt the muzzle of a pistol pressed against her right side. The voice belonged to the man who'd spoken to her at the table with the rotating wheel. "They told me to kill you, but if you behave—"

Dawn quickly spun to her left. Coming about, she jabbed back with her left elbow, knocking the gun away from her ribs. Facing the man now, she drove the heel of her right hand into the end of his nose. She could feel the bone breaking and being driven back into his brain. The man stood motionless for a few seconds as if frozen in time and then dropped to his knees. Dawn almost pitied him. These freebirths seemed itchier to fight than an Arcadian rat, but they didn't do it much better.

As the crowd in the casino scattered before them, Duncan, Hawkes, and Bovos made their way toward the main entrance of the casino. Duncan looked around for the

Tamarindian in hopes of having a very short and violent conversation with him, but the man had disappeared. As they neared the door, it suddenly opened as two Kyeinnisan Security Force Patrolmen entered brandishing gyroslug carbines.

"Dandy, just dandy," Duncan said under his breath. As the pair of Patrolmen aimed their rifles at Duncan and his companions, Duncan stopped and raised his hands.

"Don't these nitwits even ask who the bad guys are first?" Hawkes said peevishly.

"I suspect that knife in your hand may have something to do with it," Duncan said. Hawkes had retrieved his knife from the body of the Tamaridian's bodyguard, but hadn't wiped it clean. Blood still dripped from the blade. Still, with the mad flurry of bodies trying to get out of their way, Duncan doubted that the Patrolmen had even seen the weapons in the hands of his companions or that they'd actually known who they were looking for. He smiled when he saw Dawn pushing her way toward them, her pistol in one hand.

"Lady, get out the way," snarled one of the Patrolmen.

Dawn triggered the weapon. There was a loud report, the Patrolman dropped his rifle, clutched his abdomen, and fell.

The second Patrolman made the fatal mistake of turning his head to see what had befallen his partner. Bovos's small pistol sounded more like a loud *pop* than the bang of a slug-throwing weapon. That Patrolman crumpled too.

"Let's move it!" Duncan yelled, then darted out the door, the others trailing closely behind. People running, screaming, and shouting in every direction provided them cover. Outside, the small Security Force transport sat empty in front of the casino.

"Shall we?" Duncan looked at Bovos.

Bovos pulled the door open and threw the driver to the ground while the others piled in. "Where to, Duncan?"

"Hell, I don't know. Just get us out of here." Duncan reached into the side pocket of his uniform jacket and pulled out the small communicator. When Bovos had driven about dozen blocks from the casino he began to transmit.

"Roy, do you copy?" For a few seconds there was nothing but static on the frequency.

"I gotcha, D.K. What's up?"

"Call the ship. Tell Trane to get ready and to stand by."

"Roger that, D.K. I'll be standing by, too." Duncan and his friend had prearranged to keep their commlink contacts brief just in case the Security Force, or anyone else, would be monitoring such message traffic. Short and sweet would give the eavesdroppers no time to get a fix on their locations even if they were lucky enough to be listening on the right frequency.

"I repeat, where to, Duncan?" said Bovos.

"Head west if I remember right, there are some heavy woods out that way. We need to ditch this transport."

"And then?"

"Damned if I know."

"Someone's been setting us up ever since we got here," Hawkes said. "Why?"

"Perhaps it's some kind of test. Right now all we know for sure is that we're fugitives—unaffiliated mercs who're going to be accused of cheating and shooting up a casino. From here on it's likely to get a lot hotter."

"I hope things are going better with Trane," Dawn said as Bovos leaned forward at the wheel, scanning intently as he drove westward and out of the city.

23

Kispiox Forest
Kyeinnisan
The Protectorate Border, Free Worlds League
8 June 3057

Duncan, Hawkes, and Bovos sat on the trunk of a fallen tree and watched Dawn struggling with her boot. After they'd abandoned the transport at the edge of the forest she'd fallen down an incline, her left leg becoming entangled in a sharp rusty wire that sliced long gashes in the leather. She was now trying to effect repairs without much success.

Sitting there thinking about how they'd ended up in this fix Duncan berated himself for not being sharp enough at the casino. True, he'd noticed the young dealer's nervousness, but hadn't guessed that his own exceptional luck with the cards was due to the young man's double-dealing. But now it all fit. The manager had met them at the door and steered Duncan to that particular game. The dealer dealt him exceptional hands and the loser cried foul.

Duncan was staring off into space, pondering the strangeness of their experiences since arriving on Kyeinnisan when a rumbling at the edge of the woods made them all come alert and instinctively dive for cover in the underbrush. It was just past dusk, but enough light remained in the field beyond the forest to silhouette the shape of a wheeled armored personnel carrier. The ten-ton vehicle was sweeping the forest and adjoining fields with powerful searchlights. Inside, they knew, seven well-armed Security Force troopers were ready to pop out and begin spraying automatic fire at a moment's notice. The sounds of other APCs could be heard all along the forest edge.

"Looks like they don't want to risk coming in," whispered Bovos to Duncan.

Duncan nodded. "Whoever planned this evening's little entertainment hadn't counted on us being armed. The idea was to arrest us and charge us with some local violation. Maybe even confiscate our DropShip and prize money from Galatea. Then our 'host' could offer to intercede on our behalf if we agreed to accept his contract . . . or something like that. But we blasted our way out. Those troopers should be itching to get in here and pay back the folks who killed their buddies, but instead they're making a feeble show of searching for us."

"You may be right, but those troopers in the city were carrying gyroslug carbines. You can bet the ones in the APC are toting heavy gyrojet rifles."

"And wearing flak vests and maybe even a whole armored suit," said Duncan, "so pass the word to the others to keep still. If I'm right, they've been told not to try too hard to find us. Let's not give them a target so they have to start shooting."

Bovos knew Duncan was right. The risk to the troopers of coming into the woods after them was acceptable. The flak vests would repeal most small-arms and laser fire. And by now the troopers would know the little group had only small-caliber pistols. The gryojet rifles were more rocket launchers for five small, highly explosive missiles than a standard rifle. In this terrain the gyrojet ammo would have fragmenting tips that would disintegrate, sending out shards in a 180-degree arc. Even with all that going for them, the Kyeinnisan Security Force wasn't hunting them too hard. Flashing spotlights across dense undergrowth wasn't going to find them either unless Duncan and the others were stupid enough to get up and start running. Bovos used hand signals to tell Hawkes and Dawn to stay down.

The Kyeinnisan APCs continued to cruise the area for another hour, but not once did any trooper climb out of a carrier to look for footprints or other signs that their quarry had been in the vicinity. To Duncan that said the troopers knew they couldn't have made it very far on foot from where they'd abandoned the patrol transport. No, the troopers seemed to be satisfied just making a lot of noise and light. Finally, they began to move back toward the city to the east.

"You're the one who knows this place, Duncan," Hawkes said. "Where to now?"

"We'll continue heading west. As far as me knowing my way around, I'm familiar with the city, but that's it. About all I know of the surrounding area is that there are a few villages out here somewhere—I think—and some private estates. Come first light we'll try to find some country roads where the APCs can't travel. We'll just play it by ear." Duncan laughed softly. "Which is what we've been doing all along anyway."

"I was hoping one of those troopers would come in here so I could kill him and take his boots," said Dawn. She had managed to wind some thin, tough vine around her torn boot, but it didn't look like it would hold together for long.

"Let's get some sleep," Duncan said. "Then we'll move out at daybreak." He watched by the light of Kyeinnisan's single moon as each of his comrades began to make a little nest for him or herself. In the moonlight he could still make out enough to see Dawn. He was glad to have her; she could handle a 'Mech and fight and kill as good as any man. Probably better, Duncan corrected himself with a smile.

"Looks peaceful enough."

"See any antennas or land lines for communications, Bovos?"

"Nope, looks like about ten buildings in all. My guess would be it's some sort of commercial center for folks who live out here in the wild. There's no real way of telling if news of us has reached them or not."

"We need food and different clothing, Dawn needs boots, and it would help to look at a map and learn where the hell we are," said Duncan, "So I guess we'll have to chance it."

"How do you want to play it?"

"We'll just stroll in and, if asked, say our vehicle broke down while we were touring the countryside. I'll wait here while you go back and get the others."

* * *

"Good day to you, sir." The older man seemed friendly and not at all alarmed to see dishevelled strangers somewhat worse for the wear.

"And a pleasant day to you," said Duncan. "Is there a place in this town where weary travelers might find food and maybe buy a few things?"

"Down toward the end of the street. Look for the General Merchandise Store."

As Duncan and his companions walked in the direction indicated, villagers passed them with barely a glance. "You know," said Bovos, "if four people walked into my home town, all of them wearing warrior uniforms and on foot, I'd be as curious as all hell."

"Well, I've known plenty of frontier towns where people go out of their way to mind their own business," said Duncan. "This could be one of those, considering how close it is to Luck City, but you've got a point. There. That must be the store up ahead. Let's stay sharp."

The store had a quaint, rural flavor to it. All the necessities of life, from food to clothing to cooking utensils, were for sale—but neither weapons nor maps were on display. Duncan thought that strange. He wouldn't expect the proprietor to carry Class II Intek laser rifles, but he was surprised not to see weapons for hunting and self-protection this far out from the city—however far that was. Of immediate interest were the small tables in the rear of the store next to a refrigeration unit containing food items that looked like they were sold for consumption on the premises.

"What be your pleasure, warrior?" The portly man behind the cooler unit looked like he must have sampled the contents of the cooler case a little too often. He was wearing what reminded Duncan of a butcher's apron.

"A plate of meat, cheese, and bread for my companions and I would do nicely," he said.

"Coming right up. Have a seat and I'll bring it over. And we have some nice, cold beer."

"Beer will be fine."

"Do you sell boots?" asked Dawn. "Something similar to what I am wearing?"

The man pointed toward the front of the store. "My wife will help you find whatever you need."

While Dawn went off in search of boots, Duncan, Hawkes, and Bovos chose a table that gave them a view of the front door of the store, the man behind the food counter, and Dawn. They munched hungrily on the meat and cheese, washing it down with large gulps of beer, while Dawn tried on several pairs of boots.

Apparently satisfied with one of them, she rejoined them, holding a boot in either hand to display her selection. "These should serve very well, *quiaff?*"

"Anything you—" Hawkes's mouth was still open as his eyes rolled back in his head and he pitched forward onto the table.

Duncan's head began to swim too. He tried to stand and could see Bovos also passing out. "Dawn, we've been drugged . . . run!" As his body collapsed under him, the last thing Duncan saw was the proprietor's wife coming up behind Dawn holding what looked like a Nakjama laser pistol. "So you do have weapons here," he gasped and then blackness overtook him.

= 24 =

Kispiox Forest
Kyeinnisan
The Protectorate Border, Free Worlds League
9 June 3057

Duncan was surprised. As consciousness began to return he expected to have a roaring headache. He'd been drugged a few times in his checkered past and knew that most knockout potions left behind a blinding headache. What they'd been given was either some local concoction or a sophisticated chemical. Whichever, he was grateful for the lack of pain. Opening his eyes he could see Hawkes and Bovos lying on the floor near him. They, too, were beginning to come out of it.

"We are in a storeroom at the back of the building."

It was Dawn's voice. Duncan sat up and pushed himself backward across the dusty floor until he could lean against a wall. Looking around in the dim light, he noticed that the room was about three meters long by two meters wide. In the wall opposite him were a window and a door apparently leading outside. The other three walls were lined with shelves stacked with what looked like boxes of merchandise. Hawkes and Bovos were also struggling to sitting positions. As his vision cleared further, Duncan made out Dawn sitting under the window. Her hands and feet looked to be tied with strips of cloth. It was odd that they'd bound her hands in front rather than behind her back.

"Are you all right, Dawn?" he asked hoarsely.

"I am fine. I thought it foolhardy to resist someone pointing a wide-dispersal beam laser who seemed prone to fire rather than fight."

"I thought you Clan types never passed up a chance for a fight."

Dawn shook her head. "You misunderstand the way of the Clans. We did not prosper as a people by rushing blindly into death. Attacking a shopkeeper with a pistol would not have been honorable combat. I made the choice of any thinking warrior."

"I approve of your prudence. I guess we can assume the local gentry did know the Security Force was looking for us. But I don't understand why you're still tied up. With your hands in front of you like that, couldn't you have gotten at the knots with your teeth?"

Dawn smiled. "Observe this." She strained at the cloth bands around her wrists. The cloth gave easily, apparently some kind of elastic material. "Now, you are wondering why, if I could escape with so little effort, I have not done so, *quiaff*? But you three had not awakened from the drug, I had no place to go without you, and if I got free of these comfortable bonds our captors might have returned and seen fit to make me less comfortable. So I decided to wait for you to wake up. Pity. My dislike of beer, which is where I imagine they put the drug, has robbed me of a refreshing nap."

"A refreshing nap?"

"You do look rested."

Duncan smiled. Dawn was actually showing a sense of humor. Perhaps the big truth session they'd had yesterday had relaxed her guard some. "Has the store owner or his wife been back to check on us?"

"Not once since they put us in this room. Odd, *quiaff*?"

Duncan stood up with some effort, still feeling a little dizzy. He walked over to the door, saying, "Bovos, check the door into the store. Listen for anyone coming. Dawn . . . get yourself loose!"

Hawkes, meanwhile, was checking the window. "It's not even nailed shut," he said.

Duncan rattled the knob of the door. "And this door is so flimsy Bovos could open it with one kick. Hell, I could open it with one kick."

Duncan turned to look over his shoulder. "Bovos?"

"I don't hear a thing. No one's in the store—or else they're not making any sounds."

"How about outside, Hawkes?"

"Twenty meters of open ground, some storage buildings here and there, then more forest. Can't see anyone."

"A sophisticated drug that knocks you out with no ill effects, Dawn bound with elastic cloth, a room that wouldn't hold a child captive, no guards, and a clear escape route. What do your powers of deduction tell you now, Dawn?"

"Someone wants us to escape, Duncan."

"Let's oblige them. Bovos, would you be so kind?"

"What?"

"The other door, please."

Bovos walked the length of the room. With a single hit of his double fists the latch sprang open, the lock thrown from its casing.

"C'mon, people, let's go," said Duncan, but he hadn't taken more than a few steps through the door before freezing in his tracks. He heard something, and the sound was unmistakable . . . a BattleMech!

"I hear it too," said Hawkes.

"Dawn, you and Bovos wait for us over at the edge of the woods. Hawkes and I will go check this out."

The two men eased along the rear of the store until they came to a side road leading to the main street. Keeping close to the side of the building they stood and watched for a few moments.

Down the road, in the same direction from which they'd entered the village, stood a light 'Mech—a *Wasp*. Next to it was a ground transport. Both bore the markings of the Kyeinnisan Security Force. The troopers were chatting sociably with some locals, who were providing them with cold beer.

Duncan winked at Hawkes. "I wonder if it's drugged?"

"I'm hungry," said Bovos, but Duncan knew he spoke for them all.

It had been two days since he and Hawkes had slipped back into the store and grabbed some clothing plus a few loaves of bread and some tins of vacuum-packed meat before rejoining Dawn and Bovos at the forest's edge. That meager fare was now long gone. Since then they'd continued traveling, just to keep on the move, sticking to narrow woody trails where vehicles couldn't maneuver. Occasionally, they heard a 'Mech or an APC behind them on the main road.

"This is getting stranger and stranger," Duncan said. "If any of you were in command of the Security Force trying to find us, what would you do?"

"Disperse my troops to box you into these woods and then tighten the perimeter until I was on top of you," said Hawkes.

"Exactly. With all the troops and vehicles the Kyeinnisan Security Force is fielding, they could have surrounded us by now and then closed in. But they haven't tried that or anything like it ... not once. They keep to the south of us, to the north of us, and behind us. But the west is always open. They could have had us back in that village while we were still out cold. Instead, they dawdled around drinking beer, giving us time to wake up and escape.

"The village must have been just a means to find out where we were," Duncan mused. "They didn't know precisely where we'd entered the woods or what direction we were going. So they alerted little villages like that to sound the alarm when we showed up."

"Precisely. The locals got all hyped up and slipped us a drug. They let us escape because they wanted to get us heading west. They've kept on three sides of us for two days."

"They're herding us like cattle," said Bovos, "but to where?"

Before Duncan could answer, they heard the sound of someone approaching. A few seconds later Dawn came into view, moving carefully up the little trail toward them. Duncan had been so involved in the discussion that he hadn't even missed her. "Dawn, where the hell have you been?"

"I found something," she said. "A large wire fence about a hundred and fifty meters from here."

"A government installation of some kind?"

"I do not think so. There are signs at regular intervals.

And there is a symbol but no words. A short distance inside the fence is an orchard." Dawn reached into the pocket of her jacket and produced three pieces of fruit.

"Well, Bovos," Duncan said, "breakfast is served, courtesy of Dawn." He turned back to her. "I guess the fence wasn't electrified or you couldn't have climbed it."

"Neg, the fence is not electrified nor did I have to climb it. A hole has been cut in it big enough to walk through without having to bend over."

"Sounds like an invitation to me. Dawn, lead the way. Gentlemen, shall we continue our morning stroll?" Following Dawn back up the trail, they were nearly out of the woods before catching sight of the fence. It was a heavy-gauge linked-mesh type not quite two meters tall. As Dawn had said, someone had cut a meter-wide flap in the wire and pulled it back so a person could step through without effort.

"There's the sign," said Hawkes.

Duncan looked to the right of the opening in the fence. The sign was a half-meter wide by a meter in length. On it was the representation of a deep blue shark against a sea of red resting on top of a staff. "What in the hell is that?"

"Beats me. I've never see it before," said Hawkes.

"I have," said Dawn coldly.

"So ... give ... what is it?"

"It has not been seen in many hundreds of years," said Dawn. "Not since the time of the Star League."

"The *Star League*?" Hawkes virtually whistled the words under his breath.

Bovos suddenly pointed toward the trees. "We have company," he said.

Duncan looked beyond the fence and saw some troops or guards trying to conceal themselves among the trees where Dawn had apparently gotten the fruit. He didn't recognize the pale green uniforms the men were wearing. Whoever they were, they were definitely not Kyeinnisan Security Force Troopers.

Dawn's eyes had narrowed to angry slits as she stared from the symbol to the guards and back again. "They have no right," she was muttering angrily.

"Now what?" Hawkes fingered the small pistol stuck into his belt.

"Let's go introduce ourselves," said Duncan, ducking through the opening in the fence, then heading straight for the half-concealed soldiers. The others followed.

Duncan walked slowly but confidently in the direction of the orchard. Hawkes moved up along to his right. Dawn and Bovos came up on his left. They stopped less than ten meters from the orchard and looked at the soldiers, who suddenly realized their presence was no secret. One of the soldiers came forward. Unlike the others he carried no rifle or large weapon, just a holstered sidearm. He also wore what Duncan figured was officer's rank on the epaulets of his jacket.

"Hello there," Duncan said cheerily. "Looks like you've been expecting us . . ."

"Our ship is clear of guards, Captain."

"Very good, Lieutenant," Trane told Auramov, but he couldn't help worrying about Duncan and the others. He kept telling himself it was because the success of the mission depended on their well-being, but it was more than that. Duncan might be an amateur, but he was one damned talented amateur. He could have stayed out of the Games on Galatea, but he'd fought bravely and well. As had Hawkes, Bovos, and Dawn.

But he couldn't dwell on those worries now. He had a JumpShip and its crew to capture. "Where's Lieutenant Blix?"

"He's already on his way to the JumpShip's comm center, Captain," replied Auramov.

"Then we will proceed to the bridge." Trane stepped through the door to the bridge of their DropShip, followed by Villiers and Auramov. The two Knights had put all the guards on their ship out of action . . . permanently. Blix had taken Morneau and Ben-Ari with him. At the airlock between the DropShip and the JumpShip they found the body of a JumpShip crewman who'd been acting as a guard. His throat had been cut ear to ear.

"Ben-Ari's work," said Auramov. "He's good with a blade."

Trane led the two Knights through the air lock and into a secondary passage of the JumpShip. As they neared the entrance to the starship bridge the passageway split into two wider walkways. To the right, in the direction of the comm center, a female steward lay on the deck unconscious. A tray of empty food containers lay toppled next to her body. It was evident she'd run into Blix and his party.

They continued quietly down the passage and stopped in front of the door to the JumpShip bridge. "Ready?"

Auramov and Villiers nodded. Trane pressed the wall switch and the door slid open smoothly. The captain and his bridge crew were seated at their stations, the forward port wide open to a view of the recharging station, which seemed to hang motionless in space. As Trane and his men entered with drawn pistols, the captain quickly swiveled his command chair around to face them.

"Captain Trane, you and your crew were under orders to remain on board your DropShip. What do you want here?" In the subdued greenish glow of the bridge the Captain had yet to note the three pistols pointed at him and his crew.

"What do I want, Captain?" Trane said coolly. "Your ship—and your life, if you don't do as I say."

Jaggoda Estate, Kyeinnisan
The Protectorate Border, Free Worlds League
11 June 3057

The man Duncan had guessed to be an officer had identified himself as a "Major Javitz" of the "Estate Guards." Polite but not terribly communicative, he offered Duncan and his companions places in a large transport vehicle, asking that they accompany him to "the Estate." As the transport approached the large and luxurious edifice that Duncan guessed to be their destination, he could see fortifications surrounding the main compound on every avenue of approach. From the hangars and 'Mech bays that were also plainly visible, he estimated that whoever owned all this must have at least a battalion at his beck and call.

The group of buildings surrounding the opulent main house, which Duncan assumed was the dwelling of their "host," looked like storage houses, a garage, an armory, and a munitions bunker and what had to be a barracks. Whoever their "host" was, he had considerable resources at his command. Once the transport came to a halt in front of the main house, the driver and Major Javitz disembarked and disappeared inside. Not long after, the rear door of the transport opened.

"Ah, Kalma, my good friend," said Count Sessa Lottimer, climbing into the vehicle. "I heard about your trouble. I'm delighted you found your way to our humble abode."

"Bovos, if you please," Duncan said.

The big man reached out to grip Lottimer's tunic near the

throat and threw the man bodily to the deck, where he landed face down with a muffled thud. Before Lottimer could get up Hawkes had grabbed the back of his tunic near the nape of the neck and hauled him up on his knees. He held the blade of his knife across the man's throat.

"My dear Count," said Duncan, "you look like a weasel, you sound like a weasel, and you act like a weasel. My companions and I are not stupid. Our 'trouble' was arranged by you and our 'Host.' You will note that my friend Hawkes absolutely insists you start talking. You know . . . little things . . . like where we are, why all this business of setting us up to look like criminals, and so on? If you don't, he's going to air-condition your vocal cords by cutting a big hole in your scrawny neck!"

"Patience, gentlemen, patience. Please. All will be explained to you. Your host is Master Jaggoda and he awaits you inside. He will tell you what you want to know."

"Lead the way, little man."

Hawkes let Lottimer go and pushed him toward the transport door.

As Lottimer led them into the big house, Duncan noticed that the place was richly and elegantly appointed with the pride of various worlds in fine art and furnishings. They traveled through several such rooms until eventually coming to a large one that seemed to be some kind of reception area. At the far end was an ornately carved wooden bar. Bovos and Hawkes walked over to it.

"Hey, this thing's got a cooler unit, crystal goblets, and looks fully stocked—the best money can buy," Bovos said appreciatively.

"I take that as a compliment."

Duncan and Dawn turned around to see who had spoken. Hawkes and Bovos also looked up from their search for food and drink at the bar. Standing at the entrance to the room was a slightly rotund man of medium height. He had the heavy black brows, full head of dark hair, and dusky skin of some of the desert worlds, but his voice betrayed no accent. An impressive mustache curled around the sides of his mouth. He was wearing an ablative flak vest over a jumpsuit and a sleeveless calf-length coat. All were the same pale-green color as the uniforms of his Estate Guards.

"Your guests have many questions, Master Jaggoda," said Lottimer. "And they are a bit impatient." He rubbed at where Hawkes had roughly abraded his throat with the knife.

"I'm sure they do," Jaggoda said. "Let us not waste either their time or mine." Jaggoda gestured for them to sit. "Please, my friends, make yourself comfortable. You are wondering why I have brought you here, but I'm sure you realize it has to do with the considerable skills that won you victory in the Games on Galatea. Now I offer you the chance to play a different game. A much bigger game."

"We're listening," said Duncan, who had not taken a seat. He remained standing, hands clasped behind his back.

"As you know, the leaders of the Inner Sphere are preoccupied with the fear of the Clans and with their own petty squabbles. Their military forces are stretched thin. For those who are bold it is a time of great opportunity. I represent just such an individual, a visionary who is establishing a new empire . . . or should I say, one is about to be reborn."

"A new empire?" From the sound of the scheme, Duncan was suddenly certain they'd come a step closer to finding their prey.

"Yes, a republic . . . one that will be ruled by Mech-Warriors. If you're as good as your reputation, I am prepared to offer you a commission in the New Republican Guards."

"We're mercenaries," said Duncan, "not state soldiers."

"Ah, Captain Kalma, that is precisely what is different about this offer. If you accept, you will share equally in all the power and wealth we achieve. But, my friends, all that will be explained to you in detail in good time. For now, take your ease and restore yourselves. Tomorrow, we will talk more and . . . I will ask a small favor of you."

"If he wants you to play cards, forget it," said Bovos.

"No, no, I ask only that you evaluate some new 'Mechs I've just acquired. I know you need to replace several lost in the games. You may find some of them acceptable. And while doing that, you can also see more of my little estate."

"If we can be of assistance . . ." said Duncan, giving Jaggoda a slight bow of the head.

"Splendid, splendid. Until the morrow then." Jaggoda returned Duncan's bow and left the room.

"Well, friends," murmured Duncan. "I think we're finally there."

The hour was late. Jaggoda paced back and forth across his study. He stopped pacing at a soft knock on the door.

"Enter."

"You sent for me, Master Jaggoda?"

"Yes, Kolus. I would like to discuss our new arrivals with you."

Kolus entered the room, closing the door softly behind him. He was a large, sinister-looking man in his early fifties, his appearance made more so by the stern brush cut of his silver-streaked hair. He wore the uniform of an Estate Guard, and it was obvious that age had not diminished his muscular physique.

"Have you turned up any more background on these so-called Demons?"

"So far we only have information on Kalma and those who accompanied him here. The Kyeinnisan Security Force has verified their stories. Kalma is a mercenary and a gambler who lost heavily on Herotitus. He apparently went to Galatea to try to recoup. The others were in trouble of one kind or another and met Kalma while he was forming up a merc company to compete in the games."

"And the others? At least six on their DropShip. What of them?"

"By their accents some may be from the Free Worlds League, and they say the girl is a fugitive from the Clans. Otherwise, we don't have much to go on. They kept pretty much to themselves in Galaport."

"This disturbs me. Somewhere between being a big loser on Herotitus and arriving on Galatea, Kalma picks up two full lances of MechWarriors no one has heard of before. We need to be cautious but . . ."

"There is a problem, Master Jaggoda?"

"Somewhat. The Star Lord is pressuring me for new recruits. Says he needs a regiment or more. I must also consider the price tag for keeping these people here at the Estate. And, sooner or later, the rest of Kalma's company on their DropShip could prove a difficulty—or at least an embarrassment for us with the Kyeinnisan authorities."

"How shall we handle it, Master?"

"We will watch these ... Demons ... for several days. That should give the KSF a little more time to get us more information. I'm still disturbed that we have no hard facts on what Kalma did between the time he left Herotitus and arrived on Galatea. If no other information becomes available we'll send only these four to New St. Andrews. I'm sure Varus will be able to verify their backgrounds before placing them in active service."

"And what of the six others and their DropShip?"

"You will instruct the captain of our JumpShip to jettison them if they become a problem. They have only one place to come ... here to Kyeinnisan. We can warn the KSF that a hostile 'Mech force is arriving and offer the assistance of our Estate Guards to deal with them. There will be no explanations needed. I pay the Security Force well to assist us in such matters. These rogues are part of a company that cheated in one of the casinos and then killed two KSF troopers while escaping."

"The deaths of those troopers may well be of value," said Kolus.

"We have not had such a problem before because we always disarm potential recruits before beginning out little test of making them fugitives on this world. It gives them an incentive to accept a contract with us. But these 'Demons' showed up with weapons. I was worried for a while that the KSF would want revenge and would kill them in the forest. It appears the troopers value profit over comradeship."

"I will notify the JumpShip captain of your wishes, Master Jaggoda," Kolus said. "Will there be anything else this evening?"

"Yes, what is the status of our next 'Mech shipment to the Star Lord?"

"Truthfully, our suppliers seem to be scraping the bottom of the barrel. The model types get older, and most are in an abysmal state of repair. We do not have the maintenance resources to do adequate refits on many of those we send to New St. Andrews."

"The Star Lord is pressing me for more 'Mechs as well as recruits," said Jaggoda. "Send him whatever we have on the next ship out ... regardless of condition."

"I will see to it."

"Good, good, then let us retire. Tomorrow should be a most interesting one."

The morning mist was beginning to burn off the plain that lay west of the Jaggoda estate. Duncan, Hawkes, Bovos, and Dawn were moving their 'Mechs in the direction of the foothills of what Jaggoda had called the Madeira Mountains. They were supposed to be evaluating new 'Mechs Jaggoda had received and refitted. The "master," as Jaggoda was called, had told them the machines were part of a shipment he was sending to his "lord." He asked Duncan to certify, in writing, that the 'Mechs were battle-ready.

They were an odd assortment of battle machines. Dawn was in an *Ostsol*, a fast 'Mech with long spindly legs and medium lasers. The 'Mech could be useful for tactics such as delaying actions to cover the retreat of heavier 'Mechs, but this particular variation hadn't seen wide use in years. Hawkes was given an old, slow-moving, 65-ton *Catapult*, a 'Mech designed as a second-line, fire-support platform. This version was equally rare on the field these days. Bovos, on the other hand, had a familiar powerhouse of the battlefield, the well-armed *Thunderbolt*. Duncan's old *Quickdraw* also had fantastic firepower, and though not a 'Mech known for illustrious victories, it was a popular one in the Free Worlds League.

"There's a canyon just on the other side of these foothills," Duncan called to the others. "From there we can get a better look at the terrain." It wasn't the most brilliant pretext he could have invented, but it was a good enough excuse to halt their 'Mechs, just in case they were still in range for Jaggoda's Command Post to monitor their radio traffic. Dismounted from their 'Mechs, he and the others could converse freely.

* * *

Ten minutes later they were standing in the shadow of their giant machines and further surrounded by the jagged walls and rocky spires of the canyon.

"We have to certify whether these 'Mechs are ready to fight when we return," Duncan said. "I suspect Jaggoda doesn't want a negative report."

"And if they aren't battle-ready?" Hawkes asked.

"Then Jaggoda can always tell his supplier I'm the one responsible for sending him some junk that walks."

"My 'Mech has many problems," said Dawn. "A lot of little things, minor systems that do not function well."

Hawkes nodded. "Same here, Duncan. Little stuff, but things that might set you back in a fight. What I'd like to know is how do we test the armament? None of these 'Mechs are armed."

"A head-on approach, I think," said Duncan, "but let's talk about something else first—this new empire Jaggoda described. Dawn, you said you recognized the symbol on the signs around Jaggoda's estate. Something about the Star League?"

She nodded. "Every Clan warrior is raised learning about that time. It is the reason the Clans came to the Inner Sphere in the first place—to restore the Star League and to rescue mankind from a dark age."

Duncan held up a hand to still Bovos and Hawkes, both of whom looked ready to dispute this outrageous statement. "Go on," he said.

"The symbol we saw is infamous. It is the symbol used by Stefan Amaris, the monster who brought about the collapse of the most glorious age in history."

Duncan just stared at her. "Is it possible that this empire Jaggoda speaks of is some person's wild plan to invade and conquer the Inner Sphere?"

"It's as good a time as any for someone to try and start trouble and then grab something for himself in the aftermath," Bovos said. "With every state's military spread so thin these days, it would be easy to grab off an outlying world or two and go unchallenged."

"Every state except the Free Worlds League," said Duncan. "I don't believe there's any doubt now that the raids by those impersonating the Knights were made to divert the Captain-General's attention from his borders by creating the possibility of reprisals from within and without the League."

"We're on the right track, Duncan," said Hawkes.

"I agree. Let's kill another hour here and head back to the Estate for a little heart-to-heart with Jaggoda."

"Let's cut the bull, *Master* Jaggoda," Duncan said. He and the others had just returned to the compound and were standing at the foot of their 'Mechs near the big open doors to the 'Mech bay. "It's time for some straight answers. First you set us up with that nonsense at the casino. Then you ask us to evaluate 'Mechs you know are defective. So listen up. My people and I are good at tinkering with 'Mechs. While we were out there in these relics we rigged three of them to self-destruct in seconds. The combined blast will destroy you and just about everything else for half a kilometer around." Duncan noted that the Estate officer next to Jaggoda began to fidget nervously at these words.

"Colonel Kolus?"

"It is possible, Master Jaggoda. The lasers. Perhaps if they—"

"Very well, Kalma," Jaggoda cut in impatiently. "Maybe this is a good time to continue our talk. It's true I arranged the unpleasantness at the casino. Despite your successes in the Games, we knew very little about any of you. Accept it as a crude test and forget it. I asked you to evaluate the BattleMechs to see how well you know them."

"So where does all this intrigue leave us, Jaggoda?"

"It leaves you with a commission as the newest unit in the New Republic Guards. After resting up a few more days you will leave Kyeinnisan to take your place at the side of our lord. I congratulate you." Jaggoda turned and walked away, motioning for Kolus to follow him.

"I wonder if he really bought the bit about us rigging these 'Mechs to self-destruct?" Hawkes said.

"Dunno. Maybe." Duncan looked around the parking area where they'd brought the test 'Mechs and saw maintenance personnel scattering. They weren't taking any chances that the Demons hadn't booby-trapped their 'Mechs. "But Jaggoda needs MechWarriors for the army his so-called 'lord' is building and, unless you've seen any other merc outfits around, we're all he's got to send right now. We're safe . . . for the moment. We've got to find out where we're going and get word to Trane so he can alert the Knights on Marik."

"That isn't going to be easy, Duncan," said Hawkes.

"Easy or not, we do it or end up dead!"

26

Jaggoda Estate
Kyeinnisan
The Protectorate Border, Free Worlds League
11 June 3057

"**W**e're in luck," Duncan said. "It's a Krueger Model 1200."

"Does that mean you know how to get it open?" Hawkes was nervous. It had taken Duncan almost half an hour to figure out the alarm system to Jaggoda's study and disarm it. Looking around, they'd noticed the safe and thought it might be the place Jaggoda stored papers or other information on what was going on and where he was planning to send them. It was a large vault with a standard size door tall enough for a person of average height to enter without stooping over. A tapestry that slid to one side was the only attempt at concealment.

Hawkes went to the door of the study and listened for sounds in the hallway outside. Hearing none, he moved to the only window in the room and carefully peered out. From this vantage point he could see the roving patrol of Estate Guards making their rounds. He adjusted the heavy drapes so that they would not see the flashes of illumination from their hand-held lights. Though there were surprisingly few Guards in Jaggoda's house there was always the chance one of them might check the study at any time. Hawkes wanted to get out of there. He looked over at Duncan, busy trying to discover the electronic combination.

"Where'd you learn all this?" he asked.

"At the Allison MechWarrior Institute, believe it or not,"

Duncan laughed softly. "But that's another story." He threw a glance over his shoulder. "While you're waiting, have a look around and see if you can find anything interesting."

What was of interest to Hawkes at the moment was the thought of crawling into a bed and getting some sleep. They'd risen early to go out on the 'Mech evaluation that morning. Then they'd spent a tense afternoon swiping the electronic components Duncan said he needed to make a device to overcome Jaggoda's alarm system. It seemed logical that Jaggoda would have information on the base for this "new republic" in his office. But it was now two in the morning and Hawkes's energy was flagging. Glancing idly over the surface of Jaggoda's desk he saw nothing of interest. A small comm console sat to one side and two document baskets, one on top of the other, sat on the other. There were several vidpads in the basket marked "Out."

"I guess everyone, including bad guys, has paperwork," muttered Hawkes.

"What?" Duncan wasn't really paying attention.

"Nothing, Duncan. Just talking to myself." Hawkes picked up one of the vidpads and switched it on. Displayed was a list of invitations to ceremonies and celebrations both on and off Kyeinnisan. Picking up another at random, he flicked its switch and watched the screen glow faintly, then become brighter. He pressed the Display button and words began to appear.

"It couldn't be this easy," Hawkes said out loud.

"What now?"

"Forget the safe, Duncan, Jaggoda dictated a transportation order this afternoon to be transmitted to the captain of a JumpShip tomorrow. It instructs him to take four passengers and a company of 'Mechs to the New Rim Worlds Republic baseworld."

Duncan turned around suddenly, almost dropping his tools. Whether it was Jaggoda's carelessness or the arrogance in thinking no one would dare search his office, Hawkes had found what they'd come for. "Is there a specific destination, Hawkes?"

"Just a sec, there are several jump points to get there . . .

here it is . . . yes. He's sending us to New St. Andrews—in the Periphery."

"I was allowed to send Trane a message," said Duncan, "but all they'd let me say was that we're leaving tomorrow. Jaggoda wouldn't let me mention where we were going, only that Trane would receive further orders shortly. In fact, Jaggoda didn't tell *me* where we were going except to say it was to the 'New Rim Worlds Republic.' "

"What reason did he give for not letting all of us go at once?" Dawn asked.

"His line was that the Command Lance would go on ahead to meet our new 'lord' and officially receive our commission in the New Republican Guards. From there we prepare for the arrival of Trane and the others."

"Do you believe this?" Bovos's voice was husky and betrayed his trepidation.

"It doesn't matter whether I do or not. I tried to insist we travel as a unit, but Jaggoda wouldn't budge. I think he's buying time. This lord of his wants more troops. So Jaggoda's going to send us. Our background stories apparently checked out enough to pass inspection so far. But the lack of information on Trane and the Knights bothers him. By delaying their departure he gets more time to investigate."

"Do you think he'll find out the truth?"

"SAFE put out a cover story, but there's always a risk."

"Then we still need to get a message to Trane?"

"That's the way I see it. And Hawkes, my boy, I give the job to you. We also need to leave an explosive charge to take out Jaggoda's transmitter after we leave."

"And should I manage this feat, what's the message?" Hawkes wanted to know.

"Follow us. New St. Andrews. The Periphery."

Keri Yansosha was one of the most beautiful women Hawkes had ever seen. Of Euroasian ancestry, she had the dark straight hair and almond eyes of the Orient, but the fairer skin of Terra's European stock.

He had spent most of the day learning all he could about

Jaggoda's Communication Center, including the fact that Yansosha was its Chief Tech. Next he contrived several "accidental" encounters as she made her rounds of delivering messages to the various offices of the Estate. Turning on the well-bred manners he'd been raised with, he'd wangled a date to meet for a drink after her shift. She had her own quarters in one of the support personnel buildings around the big house. Now they were sitting close together on her small sofa.

"Some more wine please, Garth."

"Are you sure? Don't you have to make evening rounds?"

"No. We shut the Center at night. Any incoming messages are relayed to the Estate Guards Command Post. I'm free to enjoy myself . . . and you."

Hawkes poured her another glass. For something made from rice the wine seemed strong enough to melt the enamel on his teeth. Keri, on the other hand, had consumed most of a bottle and was showing no effects.

When they'd first come in, Hawkes had leaped at his chance when she got up to go into the other room to change out of her uniform. She was on her way out, already unbuckling her utility belt, when he jumped up and caught both her hands in his. That gave him the pretext to take the belt and toss it lightly onto a chair. "Hurry back," he said, lifting both hands to his lips and gallantly giving them a kiss.

She laughed, and as he hoped, left the room without giving another thought to the belt. Hawkes knew he had to work fast, but he was in luck. The belt contained a computer code key, which he assumed would allow him access to the Comm Center and its transmitter. Now if he could only ply her with enough wine that she would pass out before he did.

When she came back into the room dressed in a real silk kimono that Hawkes guessed must have come all the way from the Draconis Combine, he was pouring out two more tiny glasses of rice wine. He handed her one, and raised his own. "To us," he said, watching as she threw back her head and consumed the wine in one long swallow. Keri Yansosha was still smiling sweetly and holding out her glass for more when suddenly she toppled over, her head falling into his lap.

* * *

"Captain Trane, a message from Duncan Kalma."

"Read it, Lieutenant Blix."

"Follow us. New St. Andrews. The Periphery. Departure in twelve hours. Do not reply."

Rod Trane felt an unexpected calm come over him. Something told him this was it—they'd found the imposters, and New St. Andrews might even be their baseworld. It was a moment of intense satisfaction. The captain of the JumpShip, his bridge officers, and crew would be no problem. They had been confined until needed. Andre Morneau was manning the sensor station, Jon Blix was handling communications, Ben-Ari had the helm, and Villiers and Auramov were in charge of engineering.

"Captain."

"I heard you. Contact the HPG station on Kyeinnisan. Use the code given us by Precentor Blane and tell them to send the same message to the Captain-General, except for the last sentence. Also, send a message to the garrison commander on Tiber. Tell him to set up a JumpShip circuit to New St. Andrews, ready to go upon our arrival."

"Aye, sir."

Trane was feeling better with each passing minute. Ever since Thomas Marik had given sanctuary to the ComStar dissidents calling themselves the Word of Blake they had taken over virtually all the interstellar communication centers in the Free Worlds League. Their loyalty to Marik, at this point, bordered on the fanatic. He was sure the Captain-General would receive his message in good order in the shortest amount of time. Marik would deploy a force of Knights to New St. Andrews, where they would rendezvous. United, they would crush those who had dared to impersonate the Knights of the Inner Sphere.

"Lieutenant Villiers."

"Yes, Captain."

"It will take two days for Kalma and his party to reach either of the standard Kyeinnisan jump points. I want to leave for Tiber twenty-four hours after their departure. Will this vessel be ready to jump?"

"It's an old ship, but I believe we can have it ready, Captain." Of all the JumpShips that had been used in the command circuit to bring them to Kyeinnisan this one seemed in the worst shape. All were independent ships under contract to ferry cargo for a "Jaggoda Enterprises" on Kyeinnisan, but Trane had learned from the Captain that only this one was under exclusive contract to that firm. The Captain's computer files had also revealed that this Jaggoda Enterprises provided funds for maintenance as part of that contract. From the condition of the ship it looked like the Captain had been skimming off some of those funds into his own pocket. The normal recharging time for a JumpShip averaged eighteen hours, but this one badly needed maintenance before it could be recharged. The Captain had begun recharging three times before Trane and the Knights had taken over the freighter, only to have to abort when the drive core refused to accept the energy. But Villiers swore he would have this old space buggy ready to go on time.

"Lieutenant Morneau, any sign of another JumpShip in our area?"

"Aye, Captain. One just arrived."

"Have you hailed it?"

"Aye, Captain. But read-out only. I told them our audio was on the fritz."

"Think they bought it?"

"I think so. They're under contract to ferry cargo for that Jaggoda Enterprises the Captain of this boat told us about. They chided us for not spending enough C-bills on maintenance."

"Did they say what they're doing here?"

"Aye, sir. They're dropping off some cargo and picking up some passengers. Said they'd be leaving in twenty-four hours or so."

"Lieutenant Ben-Ari, raise the shields on the viewing port." Trane watched the protective shields open to reveal the blackness of space all around them. In the distance he could just make out the outline of the other ship. It had to be the one that would carry Duncan and the others on the first leg of their journey to New St. Andrews. His mission was at a critical phase now. If he failed to get the Knights to New St. Andrews when they were needed, Duncan and the others might not leave that world alive . . .

27

Marik Palace
Atreus
Marik Commonwealth, Free Worlds League
12 June 3057

General Harrison Kalma approached the office of Thomas Marik, lost in deep thought. The palace had been plunged in gloom for weeks now, ever since Sophina Marik had fallen ill. Though the Captain-General spent much time at her side, Kalma admired his ability to retain a firm hold on the reins of state. The General wasn't sure he could have mustered the same strength of will in Thomas's place, but no one close to Marik could ever doubt either his love for his wife or his concern for his people.

In the weeks since Sophina had fallen mortally ill, there'd been no further news of Duncan and Trane after a message from the captain of the JumpShip they'd been forced to leave behind at Galatea. The communique said merely that they'd accepted a contract as mercenaries for a patron on Kyeinnisan and were enroute to that world in one of his ships. But that was not the reason for General Kalma's visit to Thomas Marik today. He'd been summoned because Magestrix Emma Centrella had sent a personal envoy to Atreus.

Kalma paused at the door to Thomas's study while a guard in a Knights uniform announced him. A moment later, he was ushered in.

The Captain-General was studying the computer screen before him, head tilted slightly to one side in concentration.

"Excuse me, Thomas, you seem occupied. Am I intruding?"

"No, Harrison, not at all. I was just contemplating why Emma Centrella has seen fit to send us an envoy."

"As have I, sire."

"An interesting woman, isn't she? As popular as ever with the Canopians since taking over from her mother."

"Yes, and her vigorous efforts to attract foreign investment has brought a wide range of consumer goods to her people, making her even more popular."

Marik seemed about to comment, but stopped at the sound of a knock on the main door to his study. "Enter," he said.

The doors were opened slowly by two Knights of the Inner Sphere. "Captain-General," said one of them, "Colonel Norbert Kingelt of the Magistracy of Canopus."

"Show him in, Captain Reiter." The Knight saluted and turned to one side, taking a step backward. Colonel Kingelt entered the room, pausing a moment to survey his surroundings. He was a middle-aged man who looked to be in excellent physical condition. His uniform was immaculate, which, Harrison Kalma opined, was an improvement over the last time he'd seen any Canopian troops. Kingelt walked directly up to Thomas Marik and saluted.

"Captain-General, I am Norbert Kingelt, Senior Aide to the Magestrix of Canopus."

"Colonel Kingelt, a pleasure. And allow me to present Harrison Kalma, an old friend and trusted advisor." Marik gestured his visitor to a seat. "Now, tell me, Colonel, what brings you to Atreus?"

"Officially, I am here as part of a trade delegation visiting a number of League worlds. Unofficially, I've been entrusted with the serious matter of preserving the peace between us."

"Most interesting," said Marik. "You have my undivided attention, Colonel, and my curiosity. Please continue."

"Captain-General, toward the end of last year and into January of this one our Military Chief of Staff informed the Magestrix of rumors that some of our mercenary companies might be planning to abandon their contracts with us. Details were sketchy. We didn't know which units or where. In an attempt to contain any problem, the Magestrix began to shuffle regular Canopian forces to various worlds in the Magistracy."

"A show of military might, so to speak," said Marik.

"Exactly. We noted that your military responded by moving its units around as a counter-balance in the event our intentions were hostile. As the months passed our merchant vessels began to pick up stories of small, company-size, or smaller, units leaving domains such as the Lothian League, Astrokazy, and the Circinus Federation."

"Now that is interesting, Colonel," Marik said. He glanced at Kalma and his eyes were hard. Neither SAFE nor the Directorate of Intelligence in the League Central Coordination and Command had advised him of such activity. Harrison Kalma knew that General Cherenkov at SAFE and Matt Sederholm at the LCCC were going to catch hell.

"Captain-General, the Magestrix has entrusted me with a holotape that will help you understand our situation," said Kingelt. He handed the tape to Thomas Marik, who in turn passed it to Harrison Kalma for placement in the holotank. Kalma adjusted the controls, and the image of Emma Centrella flickered into view. She was not as tall as was sometimes reported, and her long hair curled darkly around the tawny skin of her face. After a few seconds, her strangely accented voice could be heard.

"Captain-General, news reaches the Periphery more slowly than you might think. I did not know of the attacks on Shiro III, Valexa, and Cumbres until after the raid on Herotitus. You can appreciate our concern, I'm sure, when we were told it was your Knights of the Inner Sphere who attacked Herotitus and when we learned they were credited with attacks on three other worlds. It was another month before we found out it was a company from our Captain Highlanders Regiment named Long's Light Lancers who were the real perpetrators of the attack on Herotitus disguised as your Knights."

Marik quickly arose and went to the holotank, pressing a button to pause the recording. "Colonel Kingelt, the raid on Herotitus was in early May. You became aware that it was one of your mercenary companies who struck that world impersonating my Knights not long after. It is now June. Why the delay in getting this information to me?"

"I understand your dismay, Captain-General. But the Magestrix addresses this issue if you will allow her message to continue." Marik restarted the holotape, but he was obviously disturbed, even angry.

"Captain-General, you are now asking yourself why I failed to contact you sooner. The answer is twofold; simple economics and intelligence. There is something of a trade imbalance between us. Canopian industries feel threatened that they will be put out of business by the richer firms of the Free Worlds League. To keep the peace between us I must first keep the peace at home. I cannot afford to seem a mere lackey who runs to the League at the first sign of trouble. Also, I do not benefit from the same extensive intelligence network you do.

"Even now, I continue to receive reports of some clandestine group seeking recruits to build an army. I lack the resources to check out these reports. I certainly have not been able to gather enough facts to engage in an all-out war with lunatics like the Crimson Reapers on Astrokazy. So the situation is this . . . I know something is going on in the Periphery and I don't think it's good for either one of us, but I don't know what it is. Though belated, I send what information I have via Colonel Kingelt. He will extend full cooperation in this matter to your military."

The image of Emma Centrella flickered and disappeared. Thomas Marik said nothing for several minutes before finally turning to Kingelt. "Well, Colonel, if there's anyone who can appreciate the fragileness of politics it's a Captain-General of the Free Worlds League. Is there anything else?"

"No, Captain-General. Per the wishes of my Magestrix I stand ready to assist you in any way you deem appropriate."

The door to the office swung open without warning and a Knight in full battle dress entered. Marik recognized him as being from the Operations Center of the Knights Headquarters.

"Captain-General. Pardon the interruption. An urgent message for you."

"Colonel Kingelt, please forgive me for cutting this

meeting short," Marik said. "I'll see you again before you leave Atreus." Marik waited until the Canopian had left the room before addressing the Knight. "And the message?"

"My liege, it's from Captain Trane. Somehow the message was distorted in transmission. The World of Blake people think that one of the HPGs may have been sabotaged by ComStar. All they could receive were the words Andrews, Periphery, Trane."

"Just those three words?"

"Yes, my liege."

"Thank you, Captain. You are dismissed." The Knight turned with a smart click of his boots and left the office. Marik looked at his old friend. "Harrison, what shall we make of this?"

Harrison Kalma got up and began to pace about the room. Suddenly he stopped, then turned back to the holotank and began searching through the programs stored in its database. Finding what he sought, Kalma called up the holographic map of the Inner Sphere and the surrounding Periphery.

"Thomas, St. Andrews ... It has to be New St. Andrews in the Periphery. I think our boys are telling us that the planet is the baseworld of the criminals we seek."

Marik came over to the holotank and looked at the colored globes floating in the air before him. "How can we be sure, Harrison? They could be advising us of the next stop in their quest to find these outlaws."

"That's a real possibility, but let us consider the information just given us by Emma Centrella. From Dainmar Majoris in the Magistracy of Canopus to Circinus in the Circinus Federation she hears persistent rumors of someone, or some world, trying to raise an army. I'm not trying to defend our intelligence agencies, Thomas, but it takes time for such information to be gathered by operatives, forwarded to us, then analyzed. Our people probably have the information but simply haven't yet pieced it together to form a picture of a larger operation. If 'Mech companies are being recruited in this region of the Periphery, or wherever, they need a staging area. New St. Andrews is close enough to launch raids into the Inner Sphere and to seek converts to their cause in the Periphery."

"Harrison, I have long valued your counsel. What are you saying?"

"Send out the Knights, Thomas. Send them in full strength, all of them."

"And what if we're wrong? What if New St. Andrews isn't the baseworld of the imposters? Our arrival in that sector will not go unnoticed. Instead of helping we might barge in and destroy all that Trane and Duncan have accomplished in these last few months. Not only that, my sending such a large force would bolster the false notion that the Knights are a private army for the conquest of neighboring states."

"I don't disagree, Thomas. If we're wrong all those things could happen."

Thomas Marik stood looking at the map in the holotank, then turned slowly to face his old friend.

"I am a politician and ... yes ... sometimes a soldier when need be. I make no pretense at being a military strategist like you, Harrison. No matter which way I go we will lose some good Knights. I could also be risking setting off an even bigger interstellar war. Against this, you could lose a son. I ask you again, my old friend, how do you advise me in this matter?"

Harrison Kalma hesitated for the first time in his life. And for the first time he wondered if he was getting too old for this business. Also, for the first time in a very long time he wanted to see his son again.

"Send the Knights, Thomas."

28

Cavern of the Skull
New St. Andrews, The Periphery
Rimward of the Circinus Federation
8 July 3057

"**D**o you have any questions now that you are officially members of the New Republican Guards?" Varas asked. He could see the shock in the eyes of Duncan Kalma and his Demons, but it was a typical reaction to the revelation that they'd been recruited to fight for a new empire ruled by a man who intended to take over the Inner Sphere and claimed the right by virtue of his blood connection to Amaris the Usurper. Even Varas had never fully recovered from the news that Amaris the First, perhaps the most hated figure in human history, had managed to leave behind an heir. History taught that General Aleksandr Kerensky had destroyed Amaris and every trace of his line after the liberation of Terra. Who would have dreamed that a bastard son had escaped the fate of the rest?

Stefan Amaris the Seventh was very persuasive, however. His speeches about creating a MechWarrior republic, about finally ending the squabbling that had brought centuries of war and destruction to the Inner Sphere, his claim that his ancestor was falsely reviled by history soon overcame any lingering resistance. After all, the kind of warriors willing to be recruited to their new army were more interested in plunder and power than history or honor.

These four were different, though. Varas sensed it, but couldn't put his finger on what it was. He made a mental note to keep a close eye on them.

"Just one," Kalma finally said. "When will the rest of our company arrive?"

"Soon. In the meantime you can prepare accommodations for the whole unit in an area we designate. Also, I understand you lost three 'Mechs in the games on Galatea. You may select replacements from among those sent here by Jaggoda."

"Uh, actually, one could say we lost four 'Mechs on Galatea," said Duncan. "We had to cannibalize a 'Mech to repair the five heavily damaged in the fighting. If you want us at full company strength when our other two lances arrive, we'll need a fourth 'Mech."

"Very well, you may have it. My lord, do you have anything else for our new recruits?"

"Yes, Varas. I want to assure them that we are actively continuing to build our army. I trust Captain Kalma will not be deceived by what still appears to be a small force. There are six companies here now and two more due in shortly. When the rest of the Kalma company arrives we will have a full regiment plus a good contingent of ground troops. We will be ready to make our move in less than a month."

"In that case, we have much to do," said Duncan.

"I agree," said Varas. "Unless the Star Lord has anything further, you are dismissed. One of my aides will show you to your quarters."

Varas pressed a button on the comm console of the Star Lord's desk. A young officer entered the room and motioned for Duncan and the others to follow him. He led them back across the walkway from the Star Lord's office to the tunnel leading to the Cavern of the Skull, and then to the surface.

Outside the Cavern a small transport waited to take them to their encampment. As they rode past the areas occupied by other mercenary companies Duncan noticed that some had yet to remove the insignia of previous employers from their 'Mechs. He nudged Hawkes.

"See the Snow Bear on top of a ski and skipole? I think that's the Lothian League. Ever hear of them?"

"The name and that's about all," said Hawkes. "What's the one over there? A ship?"

"The Illyrian Palatinate. They draw mercenaries from all

over the Periphery and the Inner Sphere by staging games like the ones on Galatea but on a smaller scale. These aren't crack troops, Hawkes. I've been to these worlds and I know.

"But I think this so-called Star Lord was right. It won't take him long to put together four or five regiments from all the various units in and around the Periphery."

"And that will be enough to begin capturing worlds," said Hawkes.

"That's how I see it. The people of the Inner Sphere will be too busy fighting each other and defending the Clan border to spare troops to recapture a few insignificant planets far out in their realms," said Duncan. "The worst of it is, this plan of his could work."

"Do you really believe that, Duncan?" Dawn asked. Duncan knew that it had taken every bit of her impressive discipline to keep from leaping up and killing the man who boasted of his relation to Stefan Amaris and called himself Star Lord.

"It's a crazy scheme, but stranger things have happened in history. He's an Amaris. He calls himself Star Lord. If he really does manage to assassinate every House Lord, in the confusion people might turn to him and his wild dream of restoring the old Star League with an Amaris as its First Lord."

"Savashri!" Dawn spat out the word, her face cold with anger.

"Whatever that is, I second it," Hawkes said.

"Duncan, that *Rifleman* is a piece of junk. The bottom half is from a *Warhammer*. It works . . . but just barely." Hawkes was steamed. "These aren't the 'Mechs we tested out on Kyeinnisan."

"Same story here," Duncan said. "The one I just checked out was an *Ostroc,* an old Marik experimental job with jump jets. They don't work, of course. Not much on it does. Though the ones we had to 'certify' on Kyeinnisan weren't much better." The Demons had spent the rest of their first day on New St. Andrews going over the 'Mechs Jaggoda had sent on the same JumpShip that had brought them to this world. The search wasn't going well. Duncan had looked at two and Hawkes had gone over two others, with no good candidates so far. Seeing Dawn and Bovos approaching, they guessed from the looks on their faces that their luck hadn't been much better.

"We haven't found a single 'Mech that's in good condition," said Bovos. "I checked out an old *Firestarter.* Only two of its flamers and one of its lasers were working."

"The one I tested was called an *UrbanMech,*" said Dawn. "Neither its heat sinks nor its autocannon looked like they could be counted on in a fray."

Duncan shook his head in dismay. "I'm beginning to see something here. Jaggoda gets a fee for finding recruits for the Star Lord. He also gets a goodly sum for providing the New Rim Worlds Republic with 'Mechs for those warriors who don't have one and to replace those lost in battle."

"And what he's sending here are old relics that couldn't be sold anywhere else. The exteriors are made to look in fair shape, but everything else from engine to armament is in a lousy condition," added Hawkes.

"Talk about a sting operation," said Duncan. "The question is . . . how do we turn this information to our own advantage?"

"We could always offer to assist our fellow Republican Guards," Hawkes said.

"Assist?" Bovos said. "To do what?"

"Well, first we fix up four of these heaps as best we can so we'll have a full company when Trane arrives. Next, we visit some of the other merc units and tell them about the 'Mechs Jaggoda sent."

"I see what you mean," Duncan said. "We take a second look at these 'Mechs . . . and if we should be having a bad day and accidentally loosen a few connectors here and there . . ."

"It means eight of these beasts will go out to different companies," Hawkes said. "And then we go to other merc outfits and tell them what we've discovered about the Jaggoda 'Mechs. These can't be the only ones he's sent here. We can accomplish two things, I think. One, they'll pull those 'Mechs offline to check them out. That puts some out of action for awhile. Two, we offer to check out their

'Mechs to see if we find problems akin to this latest shipment. We do as much damage as possible to any 'Mechs we can get into so they'll either have to pull them offline or else we make it so they'll malfunction in battle."

"Hawkes, this is a deceitful plan completely lacking in honor. If Trane were here he'd hate it," said Duncan. "But I love it."

"What about Trane?" asked Dawn.

"All I can do is guess, Dawn. Trane would have waited at least twenty-four hours before leaving Kyeinnisan space. Hawkes set the timer on the explosives he hid in Jaggoda's comm center to go off about the time we thought Trane would make his jump. From there he was going to Tiber where the Regulan Hussars would have set up a relay of JumpShips to whatever our destination might be. I'm sure he also forwarded our message on to the Captain-General."

"Then he should be one to two days behind us."

"If everything went smoothly. That's what I'm counting on, Dawn. It takes a week for a DropShip to get here from the jump point. If I'm right on all this, Trane and his Knights should be enroute in the DropShip now."

"I've got an idea of what we can do in the meantime," Bovos said.

"Let's hear it," said Duncan.

"This Star Lord has infantry. Not many and possibly not very good, but they must be dealt with. I've heard some gossip that some of the local Claves have defied the Star Lord and he sent people to wipe them out."

"Did they succeed?"

"No, the Clave Lords led their people into the high mountains where 'Mechs can't fight very well. If we could get them to attack Amaris's ground troops when the time is right . . ."

"Why should they be willing to help us, Bovos?"

"These are simple folk who want nothing more than to raise their families, herd their sheep, and breed their horses. My own family back home is a lot like that. Perhaps I could speak to them in a way they'd understand."

"Do it. We'll fix up one of the 'Mechs for you, and then we'll get to work on Hawkes's plan."

"I suspect not all the Claves on this world are in revolt," Hawkes said. "Some may even elect to fight for the Star Lord. How do we tell the 'good' Claves from the 'bad'?"

Duncan thought a minute and then smiled. "Tell the ones who agree to help us to make a Demon's head and wear it ..."

═══ 29 ═══

Cavern of the Skull
New St. Andrews, The Periphery
Rimward of the Circinus Federation
11 July 3057

Kemper Varas considered that he had many virtues as a military man. One of those was not letting himself become overconfident. Though all seemed to be going well, he had arranged for a JumpShip to be standing by, just in case.

"Captain Varas," Amaris was saying, "sometimes I don't understand you. Within days we'll have built our force to a regiment or more of 'Mechs, within weeks we'll be on our way to conquering the Inner Sphere. Yet I sense you have doubts."

Varas looked at the man who called himself Star Lord as he sat in his desk endlessly studying the map of the Inner Sphere. He relished the thought that one day this fool would no longer be needed.

"It's not the plan that concerns me, my lord. It's the quality of recruits to our cause. The best we have are the Black Warriors of the Circinus Federation. Some, like the Crimson Reapers from Astrokazy, show promise if they can be disciplined. Many of the others are questionable."

"Questionable—who?"

"The so-called Praetorian Guards from the Marian Hegemony, for one. They're a mixed lot of ex-nobles, impoverished merchants and farmers, and just plain scrum. They may, if someone points them in the right direction, actually find the battlefield."

"We shall replace them as our agents continue to seek out more capable warriors."

"That's just it, my lord. We can't count on Jaggoda anymore. He's our main supplier of recruits and 'Mechs, but the man is defrauding us. In the past three shipments of 'Mechs form him, the machines were old and poorly refitted. Many were nowhere near battle-ready. Such treachery must not go unpunished."

"Then by all means you must deal with him," Amaris said impatiently. "I have other matters of even greater import to resolve. For one, our raids on the Inner Sphere have resulted in a most surprising lack of response among the leaders of the Great Houses. Much of what I hope to do rests on seriously discrediting Thomas Marik both within and without his state. Marik should certainly have done something by now . . . or has he?"

"An excellent question, lord. Those new recruits Jaggoda sent us, the Demons, there's something about them— something odd, suspicious . . . I still haven't been able to confirm what Jaggoda told us about the rest of their company. I don't trust them."

"Trust is primary, Varus. You know that," Amaris said. "There are plenty more where they came from. Get rid of them."

"Yes, my lord."

"This is our third day here, Duncan. Where the hell is Trane?" Hawkes looked toward the late afternoon sun. There wasn't much of their third day on New St. Andrews left.

"I don't know, Hawkes. But once he does get here, we'll be able to receive in either our 'Mechs or on our portable links. I've tuned our commlines to the DropShip's frequency."

"Any idea where he might land?"

"My best guess is that he'd touch down near the mountains and call for us to rendezvous with him there." Duncan looked out across Brannigan Plain, pensively scanning the mountainous area to the west, then turned his attention back to the four 'Mechs they'd labored so hard to get refitted. He'd chosen one of the most menacing ever built—the *Atlas*.

It was an ugly, brutal piece of machinery, famous in history as the 'Mech used by General DeChavilier, who had spearheaded the assault on the last stronghold of Stefan Amaris the First. It was poetic justice that one would now be used against his descendant.

Dawn emerged from her *Orion*. It was another older model, but this 'Mech too was symbolic. After DeChavilier's *Atlas* had knocked down the wall surrounding Amaris's Canadian palace, it was General Aleksandr Kerensky in an *Orion* who began the triumphant liberation of Terra by kicking open the palace gates and capturing the Usurper. She climbed down to the ground and walked toward the heavy *JagerMech* they'd chosen for Bovos that was standing near the lighter *Hatchetman* Hawkes had tinkered with.

"I have done all I can do, Duncan."

"I'm sure you have, Dawn."

Dawn had not participated in her comrades' efforts to sabotage as many mercenary 'Mechs as possible. It was something her Clan would never permit her to do. From what they could make of her explanation Clan warriors believed that deception should not be necessary to vanquish an opponent. Instead she'd spent all the previous day and most of last night working on the 'Mechs the Demons had selected. With still no word from Trane, Duncan and Hawkes had left her around mid-morning to visit other Republican Guard units and do what damage they could.

"I got to three companies who needed new 'Mechs. Between them I suspect they snapped up the remaining eight 'Mechs Jaggoda sent along with us," Duncan said.

"Add another four 'Mechs that I was able to get into and cause some grief. We've robbed Amaris of a company of 'Mechs—numerically speaking," said Hawkes. "It's not much, but it's better than nothing . . . Well, look who's coming."

Bovos walked into their camp area. He looked tired. "I'm back," he said simply.

"Any luck?"

"I think so, Duncan. A leader has arisen among the Claves that revolted against the Star Lord. I was able to meet with him, and explained that we were here to stop Amaris. He said he would consult with his Clave. I don't know for certain, but I think they'll help us."

"Duncan, down the road, NOW!" said Hawkes.

Duncan turned to see an *Archer* approaching in the distance. It was painted in the totally black scheme of the Black Warriors of the Circinus Federation. "Dawn, get your 'Mech powered up. I'm not taking any chances." Dawn was climbing the rungs up the *Orion*'s side even before he'd finished speaking.

"There's a small patrol car leading the way," Duncan said. Even as he spoke, the vehicle stopped and the driver and another man got out. They were armed. "Have your sidearms ready."

The *Archer* halted behind it as its arms moved to the side, a prelude to its massive missile hatches springing open. The forty gleaming black-tipped long-range missile warheads were poised like the stingers of a deadly scorpion ready to strike. Duncan, Hawkes, and Bovos dove for cover as Dawn swept the *Orion* into position as if it were an extension of her own thoughts.

Just a heartbeat before the other 'Mechs's missiles leaped free, Dawn opened up with the medium lasers in the *Orion*'s massive tubelike arms. The shots sliced across the torso of the open misile bays and torso of the *Archer* with the skill of a surgeon. A handful of the warheads went off as the massive 'Mech tried to fire its loads. The internal explosions set off a ripple effect of secondary blasts that gouged out the heart of the *Archer*.

Plumes of flame roared upward and outward as the missile launches went wild. The *Archer* was no more, its engine and gyro gutted by the internal fires. Duncan saw the pilot in the cockpit desperately attempting to eject while the jet-like flames inside the head of the dying BattleMech consumed her.

Dawn, unmoved by the death, strafed the patrol vehicle. The laser shots cut off a fender and sent its two passengers running. Bovos stood up, took aim, and cut them down even before they realized how close he was standing to them.

"Let's get the hell out of here!" Duncan was already moving to his *Atlas*.

As he popped open the cockpit and climbed in, he wondered what had made Amaris send out his personal guard to murder his newest recruits. But it was no crazier than anything else he'd seen and heard since arriving on this forgotten world. If anyone had asked him five minutes before whether he'd ever be truly glad to see Trane and the Knights again, Duncan would have said no. But right now that was *all* he wanted to see—Knights . . . lots of Knights . . .

"How long do you think it will take them to send someone after us?" Hawkes asked from his *Hatchetman*.

"Not long, Hawkes. I'm hoping they'll send some units over to where we were encamped. They keep their best companies closer to the Cavern of the Skull so the odds may be more even for a while."

"Which way do we go?"

"West, to the mountains. If any of them catch up to us before sundown the sun will be in their eyes. It didn't look to me like Amaris had many units ready for pursuit. If we can find some rocks or woods to hide in until morning we can rest and figure out what to do next."

"I read three 'Mechs coming fast, very fast," said Dawn in her *Orion*.

Duncan looked at his tactical screen. The three 'Mechs were exceeding 100 kph. "They're scouts. Light 'Mechs out looking for us. I'm going to drop back and let them catch me. Hawkes, you and Bovos give me a hand."

While they were catching up to him, Duncan identified the pursuing 'Mechs were *Locust*s. Though lightly armed, they were fast and hard to hit even with a good targeting system. Individually, they were no match for most 'Mechs. Any weapon could destroy or cripple a *Locust,* but in a formation of three they could harass the heaviest of 'Mechs until reinforcements arrived.

The advancing *Locust*s lost no time employing that tactic. After slowing for several minutes they picked up speed and started a circling action around Duncan's *Atlas*. The *Atlas* had a reputation for endurance, and as the first *Locust* darted in to use its medium laser Duncan hoped the 'Mech's reputation was accurate.

Hoping to save the valuable ammo for his Class 20 autocannon or missile racks, Duncan tried to get a lock onto one of the *Locust*s with his lasers, but the targeting system was just too old and too slow. It was like trying to swat gnats with your bare hand. Time for some help.

"Hawkes, Bovos, your presence is requested," he yelled into his commlink.

So intent on Duncan, the *Locust*s didn't spot the *Hatchetman* and *JagerMech* until it was too late. Hawkes pushed his *Hatchetman* to within arm's reach of one of the *Locust*s. It must have been a terrified pilot who looked up to see the gigantic axe descending on his cockpit. From Duncan's viewpoint it looked like a metal man squashing an oversize bug.

"That's one, Demon."

The two remaining *Locust*s broke off their attack and turned to move away. The first turned directly into the path of Bovos in his *JagerMech*. Bovos cut him down with simultaneous bursts from the 'Mech's torso-mounted medium lasers.

"That's two," Bovos chortled.

The last *Locust* topped a small rise a hundred meters away. Hawkes took a shot, but he missed.

"Got him," Duncan said, locking on to the retreating 'Mech and launching a spread of SRMs. Two lost their lock but a third hit the remaining *Locust* squarely in its unprotected back. After the flash of the explosion only the 'Mech's legs remained standing. Then, they too, fell to the ground.

"More on the way," came Hawkes over the commline. Duncan looked at the rise where he'd just downed the *Locust*. His tactical display showed at least a company of 'Mechs painted in the colors of the Lothian League.

"Dawn, you're about to miss one hell of a fight!" Duncan felt the sweat stinging his eyes. Once again he wondered if he should have stayed in jail.

"Three to one odds. That seems about right for us," Hawkes said through what sounded like clenched teeth.

"Paladin to Gunner," came an unmistakable voice over the commline. "You may recompute those odds."

Duncan looked at his tactical screen. What his monitor showed coming up behind him were the blips not only for Dawn's *Orion,* but for six other 'Mechs as well. It was Trane and the others. Finally.

"My lord, we have problems."

"What now, Captain Varas? Can't you see I was just about to dine?"

"It's about the new recruits, Duncan's Demons. I sent some Black Warriors to take care of them."

"And?"

"I don't know all the details yet, but the Demons killed them. Then they fled west to the mountains."

"Why do you plague with me this, Varas? Send out another unit to do the job right this time."

"That's not all, my lord. A DropShip has also been reported landing in the direction the Demons are headed. We could be under attack."

Amaris leaped to his feet. "Notify all the Republican Guards. Form an assault team and attack at once. But ... keep at least a battalion here for my personal guard."

"Your safety is always of paramount importance, my lord." Varas bowed and left to do what he was bid. It was, he was sure, the beginning of the end.

30

Brannigan Plain
New St. Andrews, The Periphery
Rimward of the Circinus Federation
13 July 3057

"**H**ow's Duncan?" asked Trane.

"He's in a lot of pain," said Hawkes. "But I suppose you could say he's lucky. The shrapnel went all the way through his left side. The damned thing was white hot and it seared shut a lot of blood vessels. Otherwise, he might have bled to death."

"Is he conscious?"

"Somewhat. He's refused to take anything that would put him out. He told me to find him a 'Mech and he'd be ready to fight again."

"He can't be serious," said Trane. "But it's true we might still need his Mech. Hawkes, why don't you take Dawn and Bovos back to the DropShip and bring back Duncan's *BattleMaster* and your *Crusader* and anything else we can use."

Hawkes nodded, but he made no move to go. "Trane . . ." He paused. It was time to get things out in the open. "Trane, we know the whole story. Before we left Kyeinnisan Duncan told us that you and your men are Knights of the Inner Sphere. It didn't come as any great surprise. Bovos and I had already begun to suspect."

Trane sighed. "Frankly, I'm surprised we got away with it as long as we did."

"I've got a little confession to make, too," Hawkes said, then gave Trane a quick rundown of the events that had brought him, Bovos, and Dawn into this mission to track down the impostors who'd been giving the Knights a bad name.

"Stranger than fiction," Trane said, shaking his head.

Hawkes laughed softly as he turned to walk away. "You can say that again."

Trane watched as Hawkes headed toward the small, wheeled scout vehicle they'd captured yesterday. What was left of the Praetorian Guards from the Marian Hegemony had abandoned it and fled on foot after the Demons all but destroyed their company. Hawkes motioned to Bovos and Dawn to join him in the light transport, and then the three drove away.

"Captain Trane." Trane turned to see Jon Blix approaching.

"Yes, Lieutenant, what is it?"

"We're down to eight 'Mechs. Ben-Ari will be all right, but his *Stinger* is totaled. We're also low on autocannon reloads and missiles. We'll be down to energy weapons soon."

"All right, Lieutenant. Tell the men to get what rest they can. I'll be with Duncan."

Blix headed back to where the Knights were making what repairs were possible on their 'Mechs. Two days ago the Demons had gleefully made mincemeat of the Lothian League company. Afterward, Ben-Ari, in his *Stinger,* had made a fast recon of the general area and found this small clearing in a dense forest that ran along the foothills of a mountain range. As night fell the various other mercenary companies that now formed the "New Republican Guards" had returned to their encampments near the Cavern of the Skull.

The next morning the Demons had left the forest, but decided the site would serve well as a secondary camp if they managed to survive the fighting. Though grimly determined, their mood was far from dark. And it was boosted after their engagement with the Praetorian Guards.

The Guards were hardly up to their namesake in terms of equipment and organization. From what Duncan could tell, either their communications systems were down or they were simply too inexperienced to make use of them. Instead of fighting as a unit each Guard seemed to operate in isolation, letting the Demons pick them off piecemeal. A part of Duncan had hoped they would break off after their initial losses, but their inexperience showed. They assumed something like the posture of Custer's Last Stand, meeting the same ignominious fate.

Just as the last of the Guards were being cut down, their reinforcements finally arrived. By their markings Duncan recognized that the unit had once served the Oberon Confederation, in ages past part of the Rim Worlds Republic of Amaris the Usurper. That had been before the arrival of the Clan invaders, who had eaten the tiny pirate kingdom like a ravenous monster. The company of older 'Mechs had been on a raiding mission when the Clans had stolen their homeworlds. There had been rumors of their survival, but Duncan had discounted them until now. The Oberon warriors had nothing to lose by throwing in their lot with Amaris. They had already lost their homes, kin, and their future, and seemed to fight today as if this battle would determine their entire fate.

The Oberon troops tried to engage the Demons up close, but Duncan knew better. Using a series of fading attacks and feints, he had managed to maintain a distance from them as his Demons' long-range weapons inflicted their terrible damage. The battle lasted for most of the day, but in the end the tactics had paid off. The Oberon forces were defeated, but for most of the day, and though the Demons were the victors, they took a beating.

Andre Morneau had died about midday when a *Thunderbolt* caught him with a salvo of LRMs. In the afternoon, a *Griffin* snagged Ben-Ari's light 'Mech with a PPC burst. Everyone had taken damage of some kind before the few remaining Oberon 'Mechs retreated. That was when Hawkes had found Duncan's *Atlas* standing motionless in the middle of a wide plain with a gaping hole in its head. It was one tough 'Mech. In spite of the internal damage to the cockpit, they had managed to get it back to their camp in the forest.

Trane walked across the clearing to where Duncan was sheltered under the rocky overhang of a mountain wall. He lay on a blanket taken from the captured Praetorian Guard vehicle.

Duncan did not open his eyes, but must have sensed Trane's presence. "Is it morning already?" he asked weakly.

"Almost. I just wanted to check on you."

"Thanks, I was beginning to feel a little out of the loop right now . . . if you know what I mean. Where are the others?"

"Hawkes, Bovos, and Dawn have gone to the DropShip. If the ship hasn't been captured they'll bring back your *BattleMaster* and Hawkes's *Crusader* and what supplies they can. The DropShip is a good bit south of here and well camouflaged, so there's a chance it hasn't been found yet. We're keeping our eyes open for the Republican Guards, who are north of us."

"How'd we do yesterday?"

"We lost Morneau. Everyone else took some lumps. You got the worst of it."

"That leaves nine of us. Roughly two lances against two battalions, if the two companies the Star Lord was expecting have arrived. How do you compute the odds now, Rod?"

"Are you kidding? They haven't got a chance. They're up against Duncan's Demons!"

Duncan tried to laugh but it only made him cough in pain. "Rod . . . there's something I need to tell you about Hawkes and the others. There wasn't time with all the fighting."

"Save your breath. Hawkes filled me in."

"They're good people, Rod. Take care of them . . . if that's possible in this situation. By the way, I'm more than happy to relinquish command of the Demons to you."

"It is. And I gladly assume command. And don't worry, I'll do my best to take care of our people . . . all of our people. Look, this probably isn't the best time, but I'm going to speak my mind anyway."

"Timing has never been your long suit, Rod. Fire away."

"We've all changed during this mission. You, me, the Knights, all of us. It's not easy saying this, but I've got to admit I'd be proud to fight with you again . . . anytime . . . anywhere."

Duncan opened his eyes and raised his head a little. He

smiled. "My god, Trane. I would have never believed it of you. Humility!"

"Captain Varas. I trust you've taken care of our little problem?"

"Hardly, my lord. The DropShip that landed contained the rest of the Demon company. In less than two days they've destroyed the better part of three companies."

"Three companies? Which ones?"

"Those from the Lothian League, the Marian Hegemony, and the Oberon Confederation. The Demons were able to engage them individually and defeat them. From the battle reports I've seen, the Lothians and Praetorian Guards fell like matchsticks. The Oberon pirates were a different matter. But the Demons have been bloodied too."

"So? Why do you trouble me? Finish them off."

"I intend to do exactly that, my lord. I'm sending out every unit we've got except for the Black Warriors. The problem is finding them. These mountains are several thousand kilometers long, which gives the Demons a vast area in which to hide and then fight when it suits them. We've got no aerospace fighters for recon, but I've sent out everything else to scout for them."

"And when they're found?"

"We'll attack with every unit in the field and obliterate them. Otherwise, they'll continue to pick us off a lance and a company at a time."

"Have you considered making them an offer to surrender?"

"No, my lord."

"Why not?"

"I can't prove it, but I'm sure they're not mercenaries. The presence of a Clan woman threw me at first, but it's probably all part of some plan."

"Not mercenaries? A plan? What are you talking about?"

"I believe the Demons are agents from one of the Successor States—House Marik would be my guess since we've been giving the Knights a bad name. These Demons are no run-of-the-mill mercs. They're superior warriors. They . . ."

Varas paused as the idea hit him. "They could even be Knights of the Inner Sphere!"

"What? That's madness, Varas."

"That's got to be it. The only way the rest of them could have gotten here from Kyeinnisan so quickly is by JumpShip relay. Mere mercenaries wouldn't have those resources. It must be Marik . . . he put it together. He knew whoever was behind the raids would be seeking replacements for those lost in battle. So he sent out his precious Knights disguised as these mercs."

"If what you say is true, Varas, they must be stopped before they can reveal what they know about us."

"If that is still possible, my lord. If that is still possible. I will alert one of our DropShips we have to stand by should we need to depart in haste. We must prepare all documents and communications relative to this operation for destruction or transport as necessary."

"It will be all right, Varas. My Republican Guards will rally to their Star Lord. You'll see."

"Yes, my lord. As I have said before, the brilliance of your leadership inspires us all . . ."

31

Brannigan Plain
New St. Andrews, The Periphery
Rimward of the Circinus Federation
13 July 3057

Duncan felt better than he thought he would, considering the wound he'd sustained. He was a little shaky but managed to get to his feet and walk across the clearing.

"Duncan?"

"Morning everyone. Anything to chew on around here?"

"Some battlefield rations and that's about it," said Hawkes. "How you feeling?"

"I feel rotten, thank you. What's happening?" Duncan took the ration pack Hawkes handed him and began to pop it open.

"We'll know in a few minutes. Trane sent Blix in that scout car to the edge of the forest. Sooner or later one of their scouts is going to see our tracks and follow them back here."

"I thought I heard rifle fire a few minutes ago," said Bovos.

Duncan moved slowly to a tree stump and sat down to chew on some rations. Hawkes and Dawn had found seats on the trunk of a fallen tree and were also gnawing on their bars. "What's the line-up for today?"

"Dawn will stick with the *Orion* and Bovos will keep the *JagerMech*. We got your *BattleMaster* and my *Crusader* from the DropShip earlier this morning. Trane's got the *Warhammer* Bovos piloted on Galatea. Villier's *Wolverine* is in good shape, Auramov plugged up some holes in his *Wasp*,

Ben-Ari is going to take over the *Archer*, and Blix swears he can keep the *Atlas* going a while longer."

"Listen, if anyone wants to talk me out of fighting today I want you to know it's perfectly all right with me," said Duncan.

His three companions looked at each other and smiled, but then went back to munching on their rations and said nothing. The clanking sound of the small transport returning got their attention. Several minutes later Trane came walking up, followed by Blix.

"So ... what's happening out there?" Hawkes asked.

"They've got scouts out all over the place. Both ground troops and 'Mechs. One of the scout cars found the road leading into these woods," Trane said.

"I heard rifle shots," said Bovos.

"Blix got one of 'em."

"Good."

"Not good," said Blix. "There were two."

"The fat's in the fire now," said Bovos.

"Let's mount up," said Duncan, then added sheepishly, "I think I'm gonna need some help."

As they moved out onto the plain, Auramov, Ben-Ari, Villiers, and Blix took up flanking positions to the right and left of Trane a hundred meters apart. With Trane in the lead, it was a somber line of 'Mechs that lumbered out of the forest,

"My 'Mechs are in the best shape," Trane called to Duncan. "Why don't we move forward about half a kilometer? The plain dips down there. We'll go about halfway down and set up a skirmish line. The rest of you stay on the crest for bombardment."

"Sounds good to me." Duncan knew the combined weaponry of the *BattleMaster*, *Orion*, *JagerMech*, and *Crusader* made for firepower of Herculean proportions. The *Orion*'s Death Bloom missile system could launch 15 LRMs in a concentrated pattern, the *JagerMech* had its awesome autocannons, the *Crusader* a full spread of 42 missiles, and the *BattleMaster* its big PPC. They could unleash a lot of lethal force—as long as their ammo held out. Trane was right. They would make a good bombardment line.

"Auramov, why don't you scoot over the hill and see what's coming?"

"On my way, Captain ... uh ... no need. I see infantry coming our way."

Even before Auramov had finished speaking Trane caught sight of the advancing ground troops, including assault teams carrying portable SRM launchers—potent anti-'Mech weapons. "Hold your positions," he said. "Wait until they get well within range. Villiers and I will use our machine guns first, then Duncan and Dawn will back us up with their energy weapons if necessary. No autocannons or missiles."

It was a suicidal attack. No sane commander would throw infantry into a first-wave assault against nine 'Mechs. The only explanation was that the enemy commander hoped to force the Demons to expend their remaining explosive ammo. The ground soldiers broke ranks and began running toward the Demons. The SRM squads moved slower, unable to set up to fire until they were within 300 meters.

"Trane, I'm going to move down closer. This *BattleMaster* has two machine guns and you're going to need them. That looks like a battalion of bodies out there."

"Good idea. Let's concentrate on the SRM squads and knock them out before they get in range. Commence firing. . . NOW!"

Even in the daylight, belches of flame could be seen shooting out a meter from the muzzles of the machine guns. Every tenth round was a "tracer" that gave off an eerie glow as it sped to its target, helping the Demons pinpoint their firing pattern. Duncan saw three bodies catapulted through the air when he hit an SRM squad's reload case. In less than two minutes the withering barrage of bullets forced the attacking infantry to fall back.

"Think they've had enough, Trane?"

"No. I think they'll keep it up until there are none left or we run out of ammunition. See what I mean?"

Duncan looked out toward the crest of the small hill. Infantry officers were shooting at their own troops, forcing them to turn back and attack the Demons again. His finger began to tighten on the trigger.

"Who's firing explosive rounds?" Trane's voice was angry.

Duncan looked to the south, where small explosions were popping up all over the plain. "It's not us. Those are grenades."

"It's the Claves. They've decided to join us." There was exultation in Bovos's voice at the sight of the banners of the New St. Andrews natives fluttering in the air above the charging Clavesmen. Though poorly armed, they were rushing at the New Republican Guards infantry with wild abandon. For every Clavesman that fell dead to the ground, ten seemed to take his place. By sheer weight of numbers they drove the Guards back to the north, passing directly in front of the Demons.

"Do you see them, Trane?"

"Yes, I see them." Trane smiled. The images were crudely drawn on a piece of white cloth tied around each Clansman's chest, but they were still identifiable representations of a demon's head.

"Captain, you won't believe what's coming." It was Jon Blix calling from his position south of Trane and the other Knights.

Trane's mouth gaped open at the sight. At least two hundred horsemen were galloping northward after the retreating Guards. Most had rifles and pistols of various makes, but Trane saw a few wielding nothing more than swords and spears. Horsebreeders, the Clavesmen had formed a mounted unit.

"I guess you could say the cavalry's arrived," Duncan said.

"And more company on the way," called Hawkes.

Duncan looked back to the east. At this distance they were little more than dark sticks on the horizon. But there were a lot of those dark, slender shapes. They weren't close enough for the tactical screens to give a total readout, but he could tell it was at least a battalion. Duncan felt a chill run over his body. It could be fever from his wound, but more likely it was because he was watching death slowly coming at them. He and the rest of the Demons sat waiting silently for what seemed like a long time before they could actually make out their new foes.

"The bastards!" Trane's cry was one of pure indignation. The advancing line of 'Mechs stopped at 300 meters. The Crimson Reapers from Astrokazy held the center of the formation directly opposite the Demons. On one of their 'Mechs they were flying the tattered remains of a battle standard bearing the shield of the Knights of the Inner Sphere. It was a crude boast that they were one of the raiding parties who'd impersonated the Knights, and now flaunted their flimsy disguise before real Knights.

"Attack," screamed Trane.

The ground trembled as both sides opened fire. The light and medium 'Mechs in the Reapers' front ranks began to splinter from the bombardment laid on them by Dawn, Bovos, and Duncan. But more 'Mechs from other companies of the Republican Guards could be seen coming up to either side of the Reapers.

"Dawn, to your left. A *Rifleman* is trying to get behind you," Hawkes warned.

Dawn saw the *Rifleman* making a run some hundred meters south of her. The pilot was attempting to give himself covering fire by rotating the 'Mechs torso as it moved to keep its weapons bearing on her. It fired twice more before the torso began to rotate 360 degrees without stopping.

"Ha! That's the one with the bottom half of a *Warhammer*," Hawkes gloated. "Did I bugger up that baby or not? Don't waste your ammo, Dawn. He's going to be dizzy for quite a while."

"The Reapers are moving up their heavy stuff," called Duncan. He could see heavy and assault 'Mechs taking the place of their fallen, lighter comrades in their front ranks. An 80-ton *Zeus* began pumping large laser bursts into Auramov's *Wasp*. The light 'Mech erupted into flame and then exploded.

Trane barely had time to register the loss of the young Lieutenant.

"Ben-Ari to Trane. I'm hit. I'm hit." Trane had seen the *Marauder* open up with its two Hellstar PPCs, firing first one and then another. The high-energy bolts tore into the armor of Ben-Ari's *Archer* and there was little he could do but watch. His two Doombud LRM racks were empty. Trane got off a PPC shot that looked like it hit one of the *Marauder*'s arms, but it wasn't enough. The next two shots from the *Marauder* plowed into the *Archer*'s lower torso, and Ben-Ari vaporized into history.

Again, Trane had no time but to bid a silent farewell.

"I'm out of ordnance," Duncan said over the commline.

"And me," echoed Bovos.

"It's over. Let's make a run at 'em and do what we can with our lasers," said Hawkes.

"Captain Trane, look!" Jon Blix had a tone of awe in his voice.

Trane looked to the north. It was a single 'Mech. There was no mistaking its configuration. There was only one 'Mech whose round cockpit windshield made it look like a one-eyed metal man—the *Cyclops*! It was a 90-ton behemoth whose advanced communications and information network made it a natural battlefield command center. But a command center for whom? Trane wondered.

The *Cyclops* did not move. Slowly, one at a time, more 'Mechs came into view. The Reapers' barrage began to slacken as they caught sight of the newcomers. Trane could recognize the shape of the 'Mechs—an *Anvil*, a *Tempest*, a *Cerberus*, and a *Grand Titan*—all heavy and assault 'Mechs, and they kept coming.

"I don't remember the Republican Guards having that much heavy hardware, do you, Hawkes?"

"Negative—unless they're a part of those last companies Amaris said were scheduled to return."

Another massive 'Mech strode forward of the new 'Mechs still assembling to the north of the Demons and Crimson Reapers. At 200 meters the sun glittered off its silver and red armor. The awesome machine continued to move steadily toward the battlefield. At a hundred meters a symbol on its chest armor became visible.

"It's the Knights, the Knights of the Inner Sphere!" Trane yelled exultantly over the commline. There was no mistaking that 95-ton battle monster. It was an *Albatross*, one of several new designs exclusively assigned to the elite Knights.

For the next two hours they watched as the Knights' fury swept over not only the Crimson Reapers but every Republican Guard company in the field, all the way back to the encampment area near the Cavern of the Skull. It was the kind of battle not seen in the Periphery for many centuries. Duncan listened as Trane made contact with the Knights commander in the *Cyclops*. The man's orders were to leave no survivors among those who'd impersonated the Knights.

The few times Duncan had met Thomas Marik he had seemed benevolent, reflective, perhaps even fatherly. And he'd heard the elder Kalma describe him often enough as everything from a statesman to a philosopher. Now Duncan knew something else about the Captain-General of the Free Worlds League. His enemies no doubt underestimated him. Few would guess how ruthlessly Thomas Marik could order their destruction.

Trane stood watching as Garth Hawkes helped Duncan down the last few mounting rungs on his 'Mech. The Knights were mopping up all across the plain, and the sounds of distant explosions told him the fighting in the Republican Guard encampment area below the Cavern of the Skulls was winding down.

"Captain Trane."

Trane turned around to see a Knight approaching him. "I am Trane."

"A message from the Captain-General, sir."

"Yes?"

"I quote, sir. 'Well done. Well done.' "

Turning back around to face the others, Trane suddenly noticed that one of them was missing. "Where's Dawn?"

"I didn't see her 'Mech go down," Hawkes said. "Last I remember she said something about destroying the blood of Amaris. I didn't know what she was talking about at the time, but I'll bet she's headed over to the Cavern."

"Let's get going. She's still a Demon until this thing is over," said Duncan. As he turned to climb up the side of his *Atlas* once more, he saw Trane already scaling the rungs of the *Warhammer* to its cockpit.

═══ **32** ═══

Cavern of the Skull
New St. Andrews, The Periphery
Rimward of the Circinus Federation
13 July 3057

Trane pushed the *Warhammer* up to its maximum speed. The old 'Mech had taken some heavy damage during the games on Galatea, but the power plant was holding up well. It was making almost 60 kph. Dawn's *Orion,* from Jaggoda's shipment of 'Mechs, probably couldn't reach anywhere near that speed, not having benefitted from all the refits Trane and his Knights had made to their machines while she and the other Demons were down on Kyeinnisan. The problem was, Trane wasn't sure how much of a head start Dawn had on him in her race to Amaris's headquarters in the Cavern of the Skull. A bolt of energy from a large pulse laser suddenly shot across his path. Checking his tactical screen he saw that it came from an *Anvil,* one of the new, heavy 'Mechs that had arrived for service with the Knights just before this mission had begun. It took him a second to recall the pilot's name.

"Lieutenant Zinsky, this is Captain Trane. Why the hell are you shooting at me?" Trane could see other 'Mechs here and there on the plain leading to the foothills of the mountain containing the Cavern. Zinsky was probably checking for survivors of the battle that had just taken place out here.

"Sorry, Captain. I didn't stop to ID you. Guess I was spooked. An old *Orion* just shot past here, ignoring my challenge. I assumed you were with it."

"I am. Pass the word that some of our battlegroup is on

the field. Three more will probably show up in a matter of minutes. Make damn sure who you're shooting at, Lieutenant. How long ago did that *Orion* come through here?"

"Couldn't be more than ten minutes, Captain. It was slow, but my lasers virtually bounced off all that armor."

"Where was it headed? I can't see it on my screen."

"There's a trail in the foothills dead ahead of you. It leads up to a cave in that mountain, from what I've heard."

"Stay here, Zinsky, and let the rest of my group know I'm headed up there when they show up."

"Aye, Captain, will do. And Captain, be careful. One of our recon 'Mechs reported that it's a hell of a place to try to fight in."

"Understood." Trane saw the trail into the hills becoming visible ahead of him, but not Dawn's 'Mech. The high rocky outcrops plus the metallurgic content of the hills were probably creating a communications and sensor blackout. This so-called Star Lord had chosen his command center well. Without a highly accurate topographic map of those hills, it would be suicide for attacking 'Mechs to use jump jets in here. No telling where a 'Mech might land. But neither he nor Dawn had jump-jet capability, so that was not an option in finding her. If the Star Lord had his headquarters deep in the mountain, even aerospace bombardment would have a hard time rooting him out. And all manner of defenses, including 'Mechs, could be hidden along the trail leading up to the Cavern.

The trail was so narrow in places that the high stone walls almost grazed the *Warhammer*'s shoulders at times. Recklessly, Trane plunged up the slope trying to close the distance between himself and Dawn so he could communicate via radio.

Then, just ahead, he saw the *Orion*. "Dawn, this is Trane. Do you read?"

"I hope you have not come to try and stop me, Rod Trane." Her transmission crackled and popped on a few words, but it was getting clearer.

"I probably should, but I think I know what you're up to. Hold up and wait for me. This trail could become our grave if we're not careful."

It took only another minute or so for him to catch up to her. The trail widened some and he could see a short, level stretch ahead. Still, there were so many huge outcrops of rocks lining the trail, and any of them could conceal a 'Mech waiting to ambush them.

"I read 'Mechs ahead," he heard Dawn say, the excitement coming through even over the commline.

"This trail is probably crawling with them, Dawn. Let's get the hell out of here!" Backing a 'Mech down a narrow mountain trail wasn't easy under the best of conditions. These were not the best of conditions. To his left, Trane saw a *Wasp* and a *Javelin,* both light 'Mechs, using their jump jets to leap to the top of the gullies that had been hiding them.

"Black Warriors!" Dawn shouted.

The *Javelin* targeted him, triggering a salvo of SRMs from one of its six racks. Two flew past, missing Trane completely. Probably a miracle, under the circumstances. A third slammed into the *Warhammer*'s left arm, and the damage display immediately told him it was out of action for now. Trane tried to lock onto the *Javelin* with his PPC, but he wasn't able to hit.

While the *Wasp*'s medium laser was cutting gashes in the *Orion*'s left arm, Dawn managed to get her right-arm laser lined up, scoring multiple hits to the light 'Mech's vulnerable torso. It exploded, pieces of the 'Mech showering like confetti down onto the trail. The *Javelin* meanwhile had landed and begun advancing on Dawn. Her lowered 'Mech made a nice, compact target.

Dawn suddenly made a break for it. "I claim the right to Amaris. He is mine."

"Dawn, abort. They've got this trail covered on all sides. Hold back, I say!"

"Neg. The time is now." As Dawn bolted the *Orion* forward, a wall of fire suddenly rained down on her. Dozens of missile explosions, the azure bursts of PPC fire, and the stabbing and probing red and green beams of laser light showered down as she rushed ahead. In horror Trane saw her pivot mid-stride and fire, catching the Republican Guard *Javelin* in the leg, nearly severing the limb from its hip as her own 'Mech was bathed in exploding autocannon rounds from a *Rifleman* on the opposite ridge. Trane tried to scan her *Orion,* but in the seemingly endless wall of death and destruction, his contact with her was intermittent at best.

He silently cursed the bastards. If only she hadn't charged in headlong.

In the swirling cloud of smoke he could see the charred wreck of Dawn's *Orion.* All that remained were the legs and part of the upper torso, listing almost at a 90-degree angle. The paint that covered the legs was gone, burned off. The ground around the remains was a wasteland of craters and smoking debris. He saw no evidence that she'd been able to eject before the 'Mech died.

Dawn couldn't have survived that rain of death and destruction, he thought. No one could.

"Trane, slow down," Bovos was saying. "These Clavesmen are shooing at anything that moves." Duncan, Bovos, and Hawkes had caught up just as Trane made it to the Cavern entrance. Then the four had climbed down from their 'Mechs and gone in to find a scene of gore and destruction. The Clavesmen were venting their wrath on anything that smacked of the Star Lord and that was everything in sight. The bodies of Black Warrior infantry were shrewn about both inside and outside the Cavern of the Skull.

"Trane, to your left!"

One of the black-uniformed bodies had risen and was aiming a machine gun at them, but the obviously wounded man was moving too slow. Trane whirled and began firing his needler pistol. The Black Warrior clutched his chest, the machine gun discharging as the soldier pulled its trigger in his death throes.

"Bovos, wait." Trane saw the big man already darting ahead to a tunnel entrance in the back of the Cavern. He began running after him, with Hawkes and Duncan close on his heels. The emergency lighting system in the tunnel provided dim illumination as they ran its length toward the command center. Smoke could be seen billowing upward near the end of the tunnel.

As they came to the walkway overlooking the command

and communications center, they found a scene of complete devastation. Every shred of the complex had been attacked and destroyed.

"Look at the positions of the technicians' bodies," said Hawkes. "These people were destroying their own records. Then, either the Clavesmen or their own people killed them. It's hard to tell which."

"I checked Amaris's office," said Duncan. "It was empty. Unless the Knights catch him on the ground our Star Lord may have escaped."

"We've got to get out of here. This whole place could blow up any minute," said Trane.

Moving at a run they headed back up the tunnel and toward the Cavern entrance. Not only had they lost Dawn, but it looked like all evidence connected with Amaris's wild dream of conquest had been destroyed.

"Captain Trane?" A Knight in battle dress was standing at the end of the tunnel waiting for them.

"I am Trane."

"Sir, I was told to find you and tell you that a Clavesman reported a small DropShip lifting off just minutes ago."

Trane turned back to the Demons. "Well, I guess now we know where our Star Lord is."

33

DropShip **Good Richard**
Pirate Jump Point, New St. Andrews System
The Periphery
Rimward of the Circinus Federation
14 July 3057

"**C**aptain Varas."

Kemper Varas stood at a view port on the observation deck, looking in the general direction of New St. Andrews, just barely visible as a speck of light in the celestial night. The DropShip had just docked with the starship that would soon take it light years from this system. He turned around to see an older man with graying but well-groomed hair. He was wearing an immaculately tailored uniform. "I am Varas."

"I am Captain Kulhane, captain of this JumpShip."

"What can I do for you, Captain?"

"Do you expect pursuit?"

"I think not, Captain. I'm the only one who knew your ship awaited us at this pirate point. Before I left, our comm center was just beginning to get messages that our ships at the primary jump points were under attack by Knights aerospace fighters. Only one ship had made a jump at that time. Of those left, how many will survive I do not know. The Knights will be fighting their way past them to the planet's surface. They'll be busy for some time."

"I suspect not many will survive the Knights attack, either in space or on the ground."

"And I suspect you're right, Captain."

"What went wrong? From what I know of the plan it seemed strategically sound."

"It was ... up to a point. Time became our enemy. We

should have made our move months ago. The delay allowed the Knights, or their agents, to use our own tactics against us."

"What do you mean?"

"We had units posing as Knights, they had one posing as mercenaries. A strange lot, though. They didn't act like Knights, but they didn't seem like hardened mercenaries either."

"Who were they?"

"I don't know. We may never know."

"Just give the word and we're ready to go," Kulhane said.

"A few minutes more, Captain? There's one last matter I must attend to before we leave this system . . ."

"Varas, where have you been? I have had need of you."

"I am here, my lord," Varas said, hefting his pistol upward. "Be assured you have my full attention." He held the pistol leveled at Amaris. "Your death will be my salvation."

There was a hint of fear in the face of Amaris, a contortion of surprise and shock, but his voice betrayed none of it. "You're mad if you think killing me will gain you anything."

Varas laughed softly. "Coming from you, one might consider that a compliment. As we have seen only too well, Thomas Marik has destroyed *your* plan. He will hunt you down as a rabid beast. I'm certain that killing you will buy me amnesty in his eyes."

Amaris laughed, a strange sound that might as easily have been a sob. "This plan was not mine alone, Varas. Your fingerprints are all over it. Kill me, and they will slay you as my proxy."

Varas was unmoved by the words. "A fine speech, but I'm afraid you must die nonetheless, Stefan Amaris. You're as insane as your namesake. Perhaps it is poetic justice that you meet your end like Amaris the First, at the hands of one who is your better." Varas aimed the pistol so that it pointed squarely between Amaris's eyes.

There was a shot, a blast of laser light. Amaris jumped slightly when he saw the burst. Then it was over.

Kemper Varas fell over dead.

No blood came from the laser hole that had penetrated out from the back of his head through to the front, all the blood vessels cauterized by the intense heat.

Then a figure dropped through the air vent, landing just before the clanging of the metallic cover. She stood there for a moment, holstering her pistol and staring at the lifeless form of her victim.

Dawn's arms and legs ached from the last few hours. She'd managed to eject from her 'Mech just before it exploded, and luckily had landed unhurt. Almost by some instinct, she'd run to the landing pad beyond the Cavern and discovered the *Leopard* Class DropShip preparing to take off. She'd sneaked aboard and waited the right moment to make her move. Varas had forced her hand in that matter.

Looking from Dawn to the fallen form of Varas, Stefan Amaris grinned broadly. "You have proven yourself a worthy member of my Republican Guards. You saved my life."

"He was a bandit in my eyes, unworthy of a Circle of Equals. Aiming a pistol at an unarmed man is not an action worthy of a warrior. It brings me no honor."

"Yes, but you stopped him, you prevented his treachery and that I will not soon forget. What is your name?" Amaris asked.

"I am Dawn," she returned, eyeing him calmly.

"No last name?"

"Neg. It is not the way of my people. I was once of the Clans, a Steel Viper."

"A Clansman, eh? I'm surprised you didn't try to kill me instead of save me."

Dawn stared into his eyes with cold fury. "Never fear, Stefan Amaris. Your death will be at my hands. If not for your attack on Cumbres, I might never have been driven from my Clan. Now you will pay."

"You cannot kill me, Dawn. Don't you see? Don't believe what the twisted historians have said of my namesake. See me for what I am—the chance to fulfill the dream of your people."

"Explain."

"Search your heart, you know it is true. The Clans are paralyzed with their own in-fighting and the Tukayyid truce.

The Inner Sphere is still caught in its petty internal bickering. I alone possess the vision and will to re-forge the Star League. Everything is right for this change. And you saved me."

Dawn could have laughed aloud, but she did not. She had saved him, but not for the reason he thought.

Amaris continued to ramble, trying to weave a web of words around her as he had so often with the Republican Guards. "I will make you a queen, no, the ilKhan. That is what your people call it, isn't it? Yes, you will sit at my side. Together, we will rule the new Star League. Together, we will make history. Think of it, Dawn, as military commander of my army you will be my Aleksandr Kerensky.

"You will go far beyond what any Clansman ever imagined. Power, wealth, acclaim, all can be yours. You will rule over worlds. Even the might of the Clans will blow before me and my armies under your command. No, you will not kill me, you can't. You stand at the very threshold of glory. Where the House Lords and the Khans only dream, you and I will dare to tread. I am Star Lord, and you will be the new Kerensky—Dawn of the Clans. Centuries from now they will sing songs to the empire that we will forge—together."

Dawn heard his words, but they only enraged her further. "You are a madman," she said, "and you will die by my hand. I claim the right to face you in single combat. I seek a different destiny with the Clans, and only your death can provide that."

Amaris's eyes darted from Dawn's face to the pistol in her holster and then to where Varas's pistol lay on the floor. It looked easy, all too easy. "Very well, Dawn. Let it begin now."

He leaped toward the floor, grabbing the pistol with both hands. Twisting onto his side, Amaris lifted the weapon to aim it, but Dawn's pistol flashed its laser before he ever got a bead on her.

She stood over his corpse, the pistol still held out before her. The combat had been fair, except that Amaris was not a true warrior. He never stood a chance against her speed and trained reflexes. But it was still true that she had shot him in a fair trial. *It is over now. The enemies of mankind*

*are destroyed, both dead at my hands. All that remains are
ripples in the water where once they were.*

From the lifeboat an hour later she saw the flash as the
DropShip disappeared from existence. Her last memory before surrendering to sleep was to make sure that she sent a
message to Duncan Kalma and the others. She wanted to let
them know the fate of the bastard offspring of the Amaris
line, as well as his henchman. Others might debate his true
end for years, but what Dawn carried in the small backpack
she had brought with her from the ill-fated DropShip could
end the mystery for everyone, once and for all.

34

Marik Palace
Atreus
Marik Commonwealth, Free Worlds League
16 August 3057

General Harrison Kalma stood in Thomas Marik's office, pondering the events of the last few months as he stood looking at a holotank map of the Inner Sphere. First the raids by the fake Knights, then the death of Sophina, followed by the discovery that Victor Steiner-Davion had substituted a double to keep the Captain-General from learning the truth that his young son had died in the Davion capitol. Just this morning Thomas had recorded a holovid message to Katrina Steiner, advising her that he planned to confront her brother Victor and demand reparations. The spectre of war loomed large; Kalma didn't see how they could avoid it. Duncan, Trane, and the others had done a great service in helping to contain another threat to the League. A part of him hoped that somehow Duncan's mother would know what her son had done. He felt an uncharacteristic moistness in his eyes.

"Father."

Kalma turned to see Duncan standing at the door being held open by one of the Knights who guarded the office. "Come in, son."

"The Captain-General sent a message asking to see me."

General Kalma nodded. "Where are your friends?"

"They're waiting outside. Marik has given Trane and his men a month's leave. We're hoping to spend some of it together."

"I understand that Lieutenant Bovos has accepted a commission with the Knights." Harrison Kalma refrained from expressing his disappointment that Duncan had declined a similar commission.

"You must be proud of this young man, Harrison."

General Kalma and his son turned to see Captain-General Thomas Marik enter the room by his private entrance. He'd aged visibly in the last months, but despite the weight of his sorrows he stood tall and erect as ever. And nothing in Marik's voice gave away the momentous plans that even now he had begun setting in motion.

"Very proud, Thomas." Harrison reached out and put a hand on Duncan's shoulder.

"I have something of a surprise for you as well, Harrison. Duncan has accepted a reserve commission in the Knights— the first such commission I have ever awarded, I might add."

Harrison Kalma felt his chest swell with pride. "Well done, son," he said, "well done."

Duncan bowed deeply to Thomas.

"Captain-General, Father, if my presence is no longer required . . ."

Thomas Marik smiled and returned Duncan's bow with a gracious nod. "Of course, Duncan. I know your comrades are waiting."

Then the elder and younger Kalma embraced quickly. "Godspeed, son," the General said. As he always did when they parted, he wondered sadly how long it would be before he would see his son again.

Trane looked toward the Marik Palace to see Duncan approaching with Hawkes and Bovos in tow. Karl Villiers and Jon Blix were behind them. The congenial group more or less surrounded him and Dawn on the tarmac that served as a parking area for the Captain-General's official residence.

Dawn had linked up with the team several days after her disappearance, and the tale she had to tell gave just the right ending to the story they'd all been part of. The grisly evidence she carried in her backpack had been the proof that the threat that had nearly engulfed the Inner Sphere had been stopped—permanently. She too had been offered a place among the Knights, but none of them had been surprised when she refused.

"Well, are you ready for some R & R, Rod?" Duncan said. "Oh, excuse me, I mean Force Captain Trane. Congratulations on your promotion."

"Thank you. And congratulations on becoming the first to receive a reserve commission in the Knights." Trane smiled to himself. Duncan no more wanted a reserve commission than a fatal disease, but one did not turn down such an offer from the Captain-General. "I can't tell you how pleased I am to be your superior officer."

"I'll bet. Look, Hawkes is going to take some time before returning to the Lancers, Bovos has got thirty days' leave the same as you, Villiers, and Blix, so why don't we all go somewhere and celebrate?"

"Sounds good, Duncan. But I think we're all a little short in the C-bill department right now," Trane said.

"Be of good cheer, fellow Demons. You may recall that we were somewhat successful in the games on Galatea. I am pleased to announce I made a few short-term investments with our winnings that have yielded some very nice dividends. In other words, we're stinking rich!"

Trane turned to Dawn. "What do you say, Dawn?" he asked. "Will you come with us?"

Dawn shook her head, but she couldn't help smiling at the antics of these freeborns who'd become her comrades. She would miss them.

"Neg," she said. "I will return to Jabuka. I believe I have found a way to reclaim my honor as a warrior."

Duncan threw an arm around her shoulders and gave her a hug. "So the next time we meet it might be on opposite sides of the truce line?"

"Who knows?" she said. "I might be back."

Epilogue

Council Hall, Steel Viper Garrison
Jabuka
Steel Viper Occupation Zone
30 August 3057

Head high, Dawn walked crisply down the long corridor leading to the Council Chamber, where she knew the Bloodnamed of Clan Steel Viper were gathered. In one hand she held the duffle bag she'd carried with her all the way from planet Marik. It was surprisingly heavy. In the other was her pistol.

Dawn had learned that a Grand Council of Khans had recently deposed Ulric Kerensky as ilKhan, charging him with genocide against *all* the Clans. She guessed that the Steel Vipers were now gathered to decide what role, if any, they would play in the Trial of Refusal Ulric had demanded.

That was all well and good. Dawn thought, but she had her own business with the Council of Warriors. Ahead of her were the massive doors to the chamber. She would pass through them boldly and freely, not like some bandit skulking through a side door, as she'd been made to do on the shameful day of her Judgment. Nobody tried to stop her from entering and no one seemed to notice her at first.

Dawn glanced around quickly as she came into the chamber. Unlike her last time here the Bloodnamed had not come in the formal dress and regalia of ceremony. Seated in the circular tiers that rose high around her, all wore a Clan warrior's preferred garb of combat jumpsuits and fatigues. Khan Perigard Zalman was standing on the revolving podium, apparently in the midst of addressing the gathering. Arthur Stoklas, Loremaster of the Steel Vipers, was also seated on the podium.

"Then we are agreed and may the way of the Clan prevail and guide us all," the Khan was saying.

"Seyla," the Bloodnamed said in deep unison, their chant like a sigh from the heart of the Steel Vipers. With that one word they became of one mind with all who had gone before and all who were yet to come.

Dawn paused, the same deep chord struck in her own being though she had no idea what had been in question or how it had been resolved. She gave herself a mental shake, rousing her own separate will to do what she had come to do. A few quick steps and then she leaped onto the rotating platform. The shock she saw on Khan's face bolstered her courage.

"Warriors of Clan Steel Viper!" she called out, throwing her pistol aside. "Hear me!"

Peigard Zalman had turned angrily toward her. "This is a Council of the Bloodnamed of Clan Steel Viper," he growled. "You were never that. And now you may not even claim to be a Clan warrior. You are worse than dead in our eyes, no more than a bandit. Nothing. You no longer exist in the eyes of the Steel Vipers. Have you not even pride enough to stay away from where you are no longer wanted? Do you crawl back like a pup, whipped but still begging to belong?"

While he spoke many of the Bloodnamed rose noisily and turned their backs on her as they had that day four months before. Dawn heard muttered curses of "freebirth" and "coward" and "bandit," but she felt no shame. She felt anger, the adrenaline pumping through her body as though she were entering mortal combat.

The last time she had stood before them they had stripped her of honor and position and place, then cast her out in a way that the Clans, who abhorred waste, rarely did.

Loremaster Stoklas spoke before Dawn could respond. "How dare you mock us by returning against the will of the Clan?"

"I do not mock the way of the Steel Vipers, Arthur Stoklas. But I come to tell you that this Council has condemned me falsely." Setting the bag down, she turned toward the tiers, holding up her arms and opening them wide.

"Bloodnamed of Clan Steel Viper, I call upon you to turn your eyes this way. I am Dawn, the warrior you banished and exiled. I have traveled near and far across the Inner Sphere and seen things you could not even dream, but now I have returned to take my rightful place among you."

The Khan pointed an accusing finger at her. "No more talk. You will leave now and return to whatever bandit existence you have scraped together since your trial."

Dawn shook her head. "Neg, my Khan. In my travels I faced a great foe. I killed him in fair combat, granting him the right to a Circle of Equals that he did not deserve."

Loremaster Stoklas had also risen by now. "You are mad, Dawn. You slay some Inner Sphere bandit and dare to come here claiming *that* restores your honor?"

"You condemned me as unworthy, banished me and exiled me, sent me to live like a wretch among the pitiful freebirths of the Inner Sphere. But I have returned with proof of my worth."

Dawn bent over and pulled open the duffle bag, freeing the distinctive vapor of carbon dioxide. Reaching inside she pulled out the severed head of a man. It was balding but the remaining long black hairs were a handle for her to hold. The head had been preserved and was still frozen in its death scream, a pale gray-blue in color, a gruesome sight. She brandished the head aloft like a trophy.

"Behold! This is the man I killed, spawn of the greatest enemy humanity has ever known."

Even the Khan drew back at the sight, but no one uttered a sound.

Again Dawn drew strength from his shock. She raised her voice and it rang clear and true in the cavernous Council Hall. "Everyone knows the Great Kerensky killed Stefan Amaris the First and all his kin, believing he had wiped out the blood of that evil line. But I, Dawn of the Steel Vipers, have finished the deed begun three hundred years ago.

"I bring you proof of the end of Amaris for all time. I bring you proof that the deed is finally done. The Usurper and his spawn are finally no more. I bring you the head of the last Amaris!"

Awesome

Atlas

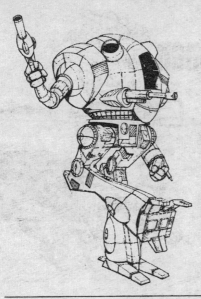

Caesar

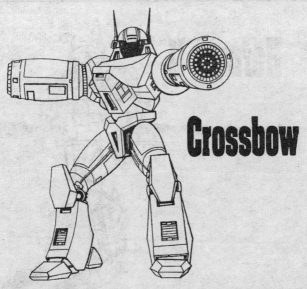

Crossbow

Hatchetman

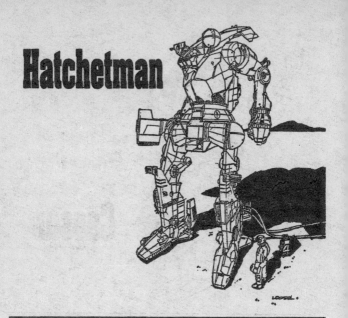

Hermes II

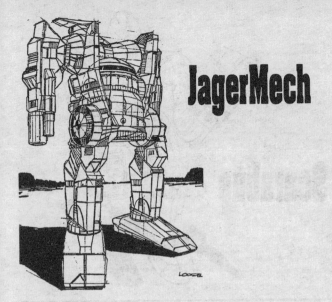

JagerMech

Orion

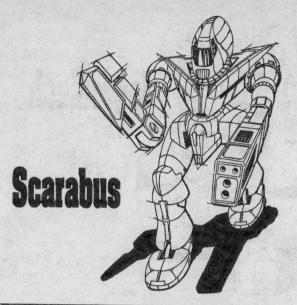

Scarabus

Valkyrie

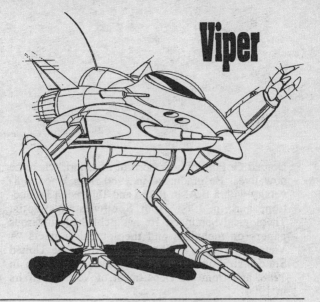

Viper

Whitworth

Donald G. Phillips was born in Missouri, where he now lives. He graduated in 1960 from Waco University with a B.A. in Radio and Television Production, and in 1963 from Southwestern Baptist Theological Seminary. He has published numerous papers on technical and theological subjects. A Vietnam veteran, Phillips retired from the United States Air Force after thirty years of service in 1988, and from the Department of Veteran Affairs in 1994.

Star Lord is Phillips's first novel.

Don't Miss
MALICIOUS INTENT,
a New Battletech Novel
by
Michael A. Stackpole,

Coming from ROC

Now *the Wolves belong to me.*

As he regained consciousness, this was the first thought that came to him. It worked its way past the fiery ache in his left forearm and the scattering of other stinging annoyances on his arms and legs. He clung to that thought and made it the core of his life and universe. *The rest are all dead, now the Wolves belong to me.*

Vlad of the Wards slowly turned his head, alert for any pain in his neck that might signal a spinal injury. It seemed unlikely what with his arms and legs faithfully relaying their discomfort to his brain, but with so much responsibility facing him he could take no chances. As he moved his head, dust and gravel rattled off the faceplate of his neurohelmet, pouring more grit down into the collar of his cooling vest.

Through the dust he thought he could see his left forearm, but it looked distorted and odd. He brushed the viewplate clean with his right hand and was able to correlate the bump on the top of his arm, and the bruise surrounding it, with the lightning-like shooters of pain emanating from that spot. Glancing up he saw the hole in the viewport of his *Timber Wolf* made when Wotan's Ministry of Budgets and Taxation building had been blow to smithereens. And buried Vlad in is smoking rubble.

One of those bricks must have struck his arm and broken

the bone that ran thumbside up the forearm. The bump meant the break was dislocated. Unset and unhealed, the injury rendered the arm all but useless. As a warrior beneath a building in an enemy zone, Vlad knew the crippling bonebreak could easily turn fatal.

For most warriors it would have been cause for panic.

Vlad smothered the first spark of fear rising in his breast. _I am a Wolf._ That simple thought was enough to forever tame his panic. Unlike the _freebirth_ warriors of the Inner Sphere, or even those of the Jade Falcon and other Clans, Vlad refused worry or anxiety. Such emotions were, to his mind, for those who abandoned all claim on the future—those who preferred to exist in a state of fear instead of pressing on to a point where fear was banished.

For him there was no fear because he knew this was but one more twist in the legend that was his life. His existence could not end so ignominiously, with him dying of exposure or starvation or suffocation in the cockpit of an entombed BattleMech. Vlad refused to let that possibility exist in his universe. _The Wolves belong to me._

That fact alone was vindication and confirmation of his destiny. Six centuries earlier BattleMechs—ten-meter-tall, humanoid engines of destruction—had been created and came to dominate the battlefield just so that he might one day pilot one. Three hundred years ago Stefan Amaris had attempted to take over the Inner Sphere and Aleksandr Kerensky had vanished into the Periphery with most of the Star League's great army precisely so Vlad would one day be born into the greatest of warrior traditions. The Clans had been created by Nicholas Kerensky to further his father's dream, and Vlad had been born a warrior among them expressly so he could guide the Clans to the ultimate realization of that dream.

Such thoughts allowed him to soar beyond the pain in his body. Vlad cared little how someone else might view this vision of himself as the end product of six hundred years of human history, for he saw no other way to interpret his life. He shied from the mysticism of the Nova Cat Clan and examined the events with cold logic. Occam's Razor sliced his conclusion from events cleanly—his reasoning, as extraordinary as it might seem, had to be true because it was the most simple explanation that wove everything together.

If his view were wrong, the Clans would have returned to the Inner Sphere a century before or after his lifetime. If it were not true, he would never have suffered humiliation at the hands of Phelan Kell—a humiliation that allowed Vlad to see the true evil the man represented while the ilKhan and Khan Natasha had not. The trauma of that defeat had left him immune to Phelan's charm and made Vlad the last true Wolf in the Clan.

Ulric knew that, which is why he entrusted the Wolves to me.

A cold chill sank into Vlad. He had come to Wotan with ilKhan Ulric Kerensky and had led him to a battlefield chosen by Vandervahn Chistu, Khan of the Jade Falcons. Ulric and Chistu were to fight a battle between them, a battle in which Ulric would have prevailed had Chistu not cheated. The last Vlad had seen of the Wolf leader was the firewreathed silhouette of a *Gargoyle* pressing one step closer to the enemy despite the withering firestorm engulfing him.

Lying on his back, Vlad glanced up at the dead instruments in his cockpit and smiled. Not only had he witnessed the Falcon Khan's treacherous murder of Ulric—he had recorded it. Chistu had to know the incriminating evidence existed in the cockpit recorder. Had it been Vlad, he would have recognized the threat immediately and poured fire into the midden that had swallowed Vlad until all that remained of him or his *Timber Wolf* or the building was a huge crater. That Chistu had not done so marked him as even more a fool than Vlad had thought.

This means they will be coming for me. Chistu would not order the destruction of the building now—*though he should.* Vlad decided Chistu would send people to look for the 'Mech and recover the recorder—under the pretense that the medical data recorded there would provide information on how Vlad of the Wolves had died. It would also allow Chistu to view for himself Ulric's destruction from another angle, and to see how handily his marksmanship had buried Vlad under the bricks and mortar of a huge building.

They will be coming and I must be ready.

With his right hand he unbuckled his belt and pulled it free from around his waist. Inserting the end back through the buckle, he then slipped the loop around his left wrist. He slid the buckle down until it snugged against his flesh. Pain shot up and down his arm, leaving him weak for a moment and nauseous.

Vlad waited for the nausea to subside before pushing on with his plan. He pulled his right knee up to his chest and hooked the heel of his boot to the edge of the command couch. He fumbled with the buckle at the top of his calf-high boot and undid it. He slipped the end of his belt through backward, stabbing the tongue through one of the holes at the very end. He thrust the tip of the boot-belt back over his other belt and fastened it in place. He tugged on the waist-belt until he was sure it would remain in place and would not pull free.

He lowered his leg again and his foot hit the pedal at the bottom of the command couch without using up all the slack in the belt. He took a deep breath, then gently pulled his leg up and hooked the heel of that boot over the belt. He eased his left forearm into his lap and let the intact bone rest on his thigh. With his right hand he took up all the slack in the re-straining straps that crossed his chest and lap to keep him in the command couch.

Sweat began to burn into his eyes. He pulled the medi-patch wires from the throat of his neurohelmet, then un-buckled it and tossed it off back over his head. He heard the helmet clatter against some debris, but he didn't care. He shook his head violently, spraying sweat into a vapor that drifted back down like cold fog over his face.

He knew what he had to do, and he knew it would hurt unbearably—worse than any physical pain he had endured till now. The wound that had torn open one side of his face and left a scar that ran from eyebrow to jaw must surely have been just as painful, but he'd been so dosed with painkillers that he wouldn't have felt a 'Mech tap dancing on him. Those same drugs all existed in the medkit located in one of the cockpit's storage areas, but if Vlad used them he'd never be able to set his arm.

Pain is the only true sign you are alive.

The light brush of his fingertips over the break felt as heavy as stone and started agony rippling out in waves that seemed to liquefy his body. His breath caught in his throat and a sinking sensation threatened to suck his guts down into his loins. Icy slush filled his intestines, and his scrotum shrank as his body recoiled from the pain.

Vlad smashed his right fist against the command couch's right arm. "I am _not_ a Jade Falcon. This pain means _nothing_!" His nostrils flared as he sucked in a lungful of chill air. "I am a Wolf. I will prevail."

He slowly straightened his left leg, his vision blurring as the belt tightened on his wrist. He tried to lean forward to give the belt slack, but the restraining straps held him in place. His left arm extended and the elbow locked. Shimmering bursts of pink and green exploded before his eyes, and blackness crept in at the edge of his vision.

He continued pushing and then dropped his right hand over the break. The fiery agonies consuming his left arm magnified what his right hand felt in incredibly fine detail. Millimeter by millimeter bone slid against bone as the belt tightened and the break began to slide into place. Each little bit of motion sent seismic tremors through Vlad's body, wrapping him in pain that seemed to have existed his entire life and promised to engulf his future. Yet, despite that, he knew from the sensations in his right hand that the ends of the bones were still kilometers apart and would never slide into place despite eons of torture.

The squeak of teeth grinding together echoed through his brain and almost drowned out the first faint click of bones beginning to slide into place. He almost let the tension on the belt go, convincing himself that everything was repaired and that what his right hand felt could not be right. A firestorm of pain flared up and through him. He felt his resolve begin to melt in its inferno.

Then he remembered the image of Ulric's 'Mech taking just one more step.

I will not surrender.

Screaming incoherently, Vlad straightened his left leg. Bone grated on bone, the lower half pulling even with the break, then slipping past it. The gulf between the ends of the break seemed to stretch on forever, but he knew that was an illusion. He clenched his right hand over the break, clamping it down. Bones snapped into place.

The argent lightning storm that played out from the break bowed his spine and jammed him hard against the couch's restraining straps. He hung there forever, his lungs afire with oxygen deprivation. He wanted to scream and his throat hurt as if he were, but he could only hear the wheezing hiss of the last of his breath being squeezed from his chest.

His muscles slackened and the restraining straps slammed him back down into the couch. He felt more pain, but his nervous system had not recovered from being overwhelmed and could only report faint echoes of it to his brain. He took a shallow breath, then another and another. Each one came deeper, and as his body learned that breathing would not hurt him, it allowed itself to return to normal functioning.

The break throbbed, but the bones had been slid back into place. Vlad knew he would find a splint in the command couch's medkit, but he didn't have the strength to get free from the restraining straps and go digging around for it. He let his head loll to one side and then the other to drain sweat from his eyes. It was not much, but along with breathing it was enough.

As strength gradually returned, Vlad wasted a bit of it in a smile. He had passed the first test in his ordeal, but he knew there would be many more. There would be enemies to be destroyed and allies to be used. The war—technically a Trial of Refusal—between the Jade Falcons and Wolves would have left both sides devastated. Vlad knew, based on the fact that he had not been rescued immediately, that the Jade Falcons had won. That meant he would have to appeal to the Falcons who shared his disgust with the Inner Sphere if he were to have any help from them. *Better I seek aid from the Ghost Bears, as they have long been allies to the Wolves.*

Vlad nodded slowly. *There are many considerations with which I will have to deal. I can use the time here, waiting in my cockpit, to consider them all. Those who come for me will believe themselves scavengers, only to find themselves rescuers. Little do they know they will be midwives to the future of the Clans.*

YOUR OPINION CAN MAKE A DIFFERENCE!

LET US KNOW WHAT *YOU* THINK.

Send this completed survey to us and enter a weekly drawing to win a special prize!

1.) Do you play any of the following role-playing games?
Shadowrun ———— Earthdawn ———— BattleTech ————

2.) Did you play any of the games before you read the novels?
Yes ———————— No ————————

3.) How many novels have you read in each of the following series?
Shadowrun ———— Earthdawn ———— BattleTech ————

4.) What other game novel lines do you read?
TSR ———— White Wolf ———— Other (Specify) ————

5.) Who is your favorite FASA author?

_____

6.) Which book did you take this survey from?

_____

7.) Where did you buy this book?
Bookstore ———— Game Store ———— Comic Store ————
FASA Mail Order ———————— Other (Specify) ————

8.) Your opinion of the book (please print)

_____

_____

_____

Name ———————————————— Age ———— Gender ————
Address ——————————————————————————————————
City ———————————— State ———— Country ———— Zip ————

Send this page or a photocopy of it to:
FASA Corporation
Editorial/Novels
1100 W. Cermak Suite B-305
Chicago, IL 60608